# THE

# SAINT'S

# MISTRESS

➤ · A NOVEL · ❧

# THE
# SAINT'S
# MISTRESS

⇒ · A NOVEL · ⇐

# KATHRYN BASHAAR

CamCat
Books

CamCat Publishing, LLC
Brentwood, Tennessee 37027
camcatpublishing.com

Hardcover ISBN 9780744301335
Paperback ISBN 9780744301069
Large-Print Paperback ISBN 9780744302684
eBook ISBN 9780744301076
Audiobook ISBN 9780744301649

Library of Congress Cataloguing-in-Publication
Control Number: 2020935482

Cover/book design by Maryann Appel

5    3    1    2    4

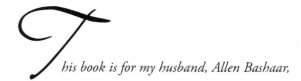his book is for my husband, Allen Bashaar,

who did extra work around the house so I could focus on the book,

who served as my photojournalist in Milan, and

who always encourages me to believe that I can do anything.

# AUTHOR'S NOTE

This is a work of fiction. History tells us almost nothing of Saint Augustine's longtime mistress, with whom he did indeed have a son. The facts of Augustine's life, on the other hand, are very well established, and I have used those facts as accurately as possible in my story. The basics of the opening scene in the pear orchard were described by Augustine himself in his *Confessiones*. He did teach in Carthage for a few years, and was converted to Christianity in Milan. He had friends who were very like Amicus, Quintus, Nebridius, and Urbanus, although I have changed some of their names. I had the pleasure of inventing Leona on my own. I hope my readers will enjoy her story.

CKNOWLEDGMENTS

I don't know how anyone writes a good book without the tough love of other writers. I offer my heartfelt thanks to my writer's groups at the Beechview and Pleasant Hills libraries here in Pittsburgh, and especially to Audrey Iacone, Claire Coyne, Kathy Hillen, and Genea Webb.

# PART ONE

## The Lover

# CHAPTER ONE

*Thagaste, North Africa*
*Anno Domini 371*

LATER, Aurelius was called a saint, but I first knew him as a thief.

My sister Numa and I walked barefoot the dusty couple of miles between the town of Thagaste and our family's hut in the shadow of the mountains. We knew a shortcut through Urbanus's orchards that avoided the foul-smelling suburbs. Dusk was falling, a time of release: the dirt path releasing the day's heat, the pear trees giving over their perfume to the evening breeze. My mouth watered as I inhaled, imagining the soft flesh of pear on my tongue, the bits of grit, the tough skin, the juice filling my mouth. I was hungry, looking forward to home and supper.

Numa and I always gossiped on the walk home from town, dissecting the little events of our day.

"Ariana will find herself pregnant soon if she doesn't watch out," Numa predicted. "During the noon rest, her and Tracchus, when they thought everyone was sleeping, right in the courtyard. Like dogs," she whispered, although nobody was near enough to hear.

"Dogs?"

"You know: her on her knees and him behind her." Numa motioned with her hands as if holding on to something in front of her and thrust her hips forward and back a few times. At sixteen, Numa was only a year older than I, but she paid more attention when she heard gossip, and always seemed to know more about secret things.

"Oh." I blushed and felt a tingling between my legs, pleasant and uncomfortable at once. I teased: "Maybe you want Tracchus for yourself."

Numa looked away from me toward the pear orchard, tilting her chin. "Not like that . . . not like his bitch."

I wrinkled my nose. "Tracchus has scars, and I don't like his teeth. I want someone handsome."

"You shouldn't be so particular, Leona," Numa scolded. Her smooth brown face folded into a frown.

"I don't see why I shouldn't be particular about the person I'll spend my whole life with . . . and have children with. I'm pretty. Men look at me."

Numa scowled at this. "I know they do, and you enjoy it too much."

I knew I was pretty, and I did enjoy knowing that men looked at me appreciatively. I was compact and muscular, with a narrow waist and small, high breasts. I had my Berber father's light skin and my Aitheope mother's full lips, broad nose and large eyes. I saw no reason why this shouldn't work to my advantage in a world where girls had few advantages of any kind.

"I don't want children who look like Tracchus," I said, drawing my lower lip below my top teeth to imitate Tracchus's overbite.

"Father will marry you off to whoever offers him the most anyway."

"I'll make myself look hideous and act like a shrew, so the ugly ones won't want me. I'm waiting for someone handsome and good-smelling and smart. And I want a man who really loves me, not just somebody who's looking for a drudge to cook his porridge and milk his goats."

Numa snorted. "Good luck."

She started to say more, but we both heard the noise at the same time: the slap of sandals in the orchard and the bark of laughter. Three boys burst out of the trees at us, bags slung over their shoulders. They wore the bordered tunics of aristocrats.

One of the boys crashed into Numa, knocking her to the ground and dropping his bag, scattering pears on the path. He kept running.

"You ignorant barbarians!" I yelled. "Watch where you're going!"

Another of the boys stopped and hesitated over Numa, shifting the bag on his shoulder. Finally, he let it drop and leaned over her. "Are you all right?" he asked. He looked like a young colt, all bulbous joints and round, dark eyes.

His friends stopped now too, several feet away. "Aurelius! Come on!" called the big one who had knocked Numa down. "Who cares about some pleb *lupa*?"

"Are you all right?" Aurelius extended a hand to help her up.

"No, she's not all right," I spat. "Your friend knocked her down, you stupid Gaul!"

Numa took his hand and rose to her feet. "I'm fine," she said, but she glared at Aurelius as she released his hand and brushed the dust off her tunic.

His friends came trailing back over. "Aurelius! Come on!" the big boy urged. His face was scarred. He sauntered closer to us and pinned me with his eyes. "Wait a minute, wait a minute," he drawled. "Maybe we've come across something more interesting than fruit." He dropped his bag and picked up a pear and held it in front of my face. His eyes were blue, a rare color in our part of the world. I was repelled and fascinated by those eyes, could not look away, could not move.

"Want a pear?" he offered, but his eyes were hooded and his smile was a leer.

I took a half step back, still trapped by those pale eyes.

He turned to Numa. "How about the blackie? You want a pear?" He stepped forward and Numa backed away from him.

"No, thanks," Numa said. She tried to step past him, but he veered left and blocked her path.

"Come on," the big boy argued. "Don't pleb girls like a little fun? Walk back to town, get us some wine and cheese and olives, and then who knows?" He shrugged one shoulder and smirked.

"No, thanks," Numa repeated and made another try at passing him.

The boy grabbed Numa's arm. "Not usually a good idea to refuse your betters. Maybe you need a lesson."

Numa made a face and tried to twist away from him.

I ran at him and slammed my fist into his ear.

"Ow! You she-wolf!" he snarled. He let go of Numa, grabbed my arm with one hand and slapped me with the other. My ears rang and I staggered for a moment, but the boy still had a painful grip on my upper arm.

The slap finally woke up one of his friends, a small, girlish-looking boy. "Marcus, come on. Leave them alone," he said.

"Stay out of it, Amicus. I intend to give this bitch a whipping," Marcus snarled. With satisfaction, I noticed a red trickle from his right ear.

Now Aurelius, the boy who had first stopped, spoke up. "Marcus, let's just go."

"Stay out of this, Aurelius," Marcus snarled. "Go home to your mommy, you teat-sucking baby."

Aurelius flushed, but it seemed he had found his courage. "Marcus . . ." He placed a hand on Marcus's shoulder and looked him in the eye, "remember our vow? We weren't going to touch women until we're eighteen, remember?"

Marcus frowned at me, as if his dilemma were entirely my fault. "I didn't take a vow not to kill any stupid peasant woman who pounded me in the ear," he complained.

"Leave it, Marcus," Aurelius urged. "Don't act like a peasant yourself. We're supposed to be better than that. She was just trying to defend the other one."

I tried to pull away from Marcus, but he tightened his grip on my arm and twisted it. "You're right, they've probably been had by half the plebs in town already in their little mud hut in the hills. I wouldn't dirty myself with them," he said, twisting my arm until I felt he would pull it out of its socket. "But I reserve the right to personally beat this one until she screams."

Amicus stepped forward. "You'll have to beat me first." He was pale and thin, much smaller than Marcus, but his gaze was as solid as the mountains.

Marcus looked from him to me, then thrust me to the ground. I landed in the dust on my bottom. "The hell with you, then," he said. "Stupid she-wolf!" he spat in parting. Marcus straightened his tunic and he and Amicus started across the next field. Aurelius offered his hand to help me to my feet. I shook my hand out of his grasp.

"You're all right?" he asked.

"No thanks to you," I replied.

His eyes widened and he opened his arms in plea. "But I did help you."

"No, you didn't. I looked to you for help and you just stood and stared. You didn't come to our defense until your friend spoke up."

"But I talked him out of it."

"Talk," I sneered. "Talk about some stupid vow when two women were getting beat up. Who offered to fight for us in the end? Not you. It was your friend, who's half the size of you and that ape dressed up like a gentleman. And look at these perfectly good pears you left lying in the road. You didn't need them. You stole them just for the fun of it."

Aurelius flushed again and hung his head. "Well, then. Good-bye." He turned to catch up with his friends, but looked back one final time and said, "I am sorry."

"Thank you," Numa called, as he disappeared into the now-dark field.

"*Thank* you?" I spat at her. "Why *thank* that pig?"

She shrugged, but she was shaking. Tears had left wavering tracks in the dust on her face. "He helped us."

I masked my own trembling with angry words. "Big help. Those boys are trash, making trouble for nothing. Look at this fruit they wasted. Rich boys with good names and nothing better to do than steal to prove they can do it. I hate them!"

Numa put her arm around my shoulder and said, "Come on. Father will be angry if we're late getting his supper."

We padded along on our bare feet again, making clouds of dust on the path, now cool against our soles. "No point mentioning this to Father," Numa said.

"What good would it do?" I replied.

"Yes, exactly."

"They get away with everything." Hate rose in my chest like a jagged stone.

"It's the way of the world, Leona."

My long life has since taught me that she was right.

# CHAPTER TWO

A TEARDROP of whey hesitated on the goatskin bag. I squeezed the bag and the last of the whey dripped into the clay bucket on the dirt floor of our two-room hut. I hefted the bag from its hook and emptied the cheese into a trough.

I had taken over the cheese making as soon as I could be trusted over a fire and was strong enough to lift the goatskin bag. Numa and I had shared the kitchen tasks since our mother died of a plague when I was eight and Numa was nine.

Numa stirred porridge with a wooden paddle. We were quiet this evening, each of us separately brooding about the attack on our way home.

I was kneading a little precious salt into the soft white cheese when Father and our older brothers, Maron and Tito, arrived home from their work in the fields.

"The number of Romans must be more than the stars in the sky then," Tito was complaining.

"The poor work and the rich eat. Always been that way and always will be," Father grunted. He hung his hat on a hook by the door without greeting me or Numa.

"Well, what's next? What are we supposed to eat?" Maron wanted to know.

"I hope Ammon feels like fucking Murzuk a lot this winter," was Father's reply. Father was a casual worshipper of the sun god Ammon and believed that sexual relations between the god and his consort Murzuk, the moon goddess, brought rain.

Father and our brothers sat down at the table and Father cut himself a slice of yesterday's cheese. Tito and Maron popped olives into their mouths, spitting the pits onto the floor. Our brothers were both tall, like Numa, with smooth, brown skin. They barely resembled our wiry, hawk-nosed father, with his weather-beaten tan face.

"Where's my supper, daughters?" Father called.

Numa hustled to the table with three bowls of porridge and a loaf of bread. I set a pitcher of whey on the table while Numa got bowls for the two of us.

Father, Maron, and Tito were already slurping porridge when Numa and I sat down.

"What's wrong, Father?" I asked.

"Grazing lands allowed to the plebs have been cut by half," he growled. "The lords have to plant more of their acres in grain to feed Rome."

Distant Rome was the hungriest city in the world, and western North Africa was its breadbasket. In every direction outside Thagaste, mile after mile of golden wheat shimmered in the hot breezes. The vast fields were sometimes owned by local lords like Urbanus, or more often by absentee Roman landlords who might never even see them and instead appointed local bailiffs to operate their acres.

Regardless of who owned them, the fields were worked by plebs like Father, landless peasants who were obligated to provide a certain number of days' labor to their lord every year. In exchange, they received the right to use small plots for crops of their own, and grazing rights on certain of the lord's pastures.

Father was prosperous for a pleb, with goats to graze on the public pastures, cheese to sell, two sons to work the fields with him, and two daughters to send into town to work for cash. If the pasturelands were reduced, he would have trouble keeping his goats alive.

"What will happen?" Numa asked.

Father took a long drink of water and it seemed he would not choose to answer. Finally he responded, "We can slaughter our goats if we have to, and dry the meat. It will last for a time."

"Why can't the Romans grow their own wheat and let us use our land for ourselves?" Maron growled.

Father grimaced. "Because they have the army. Or haven't you noticed?"

"There are more peasants than legionnaires," Maron muttered, frowning into his cup.

Tito stopped his spoon halfway to his mouth and glanced at Father, waiting for the explosion.

Father set down his cup. There was a short silence before he slammed his palm on the table and then jabbed a finger at Maron. "Now, you listen to me, boy. That kind of talk will get you nothing but crucified in the town square. It's those crazy hut people putting those ideas into your head. Yes, I know about it. I want you to stay away from them, do you hear?"

Maron pressed his lips together. I could see he was surprised Father knew about his associations. The hut people were a radical faction of the Donatist Christian sect, mostly young men, who stood up for the poor against the lords, and for the Donatists against other Christians. They sought martyrdom, believing that a martyr's death was rewarded with entrance into their Heaven. They were known to be violent, valuing Heaven so much that they saw death as a release from suffering.

"Bunch of nuts," Father muttered.

"At least they stand up for something, instead of always knuckling under to Rome," Maron argued.

"And get themselves killed. For what? So they can go straight to some made-up Heaven? Their god couldn't even save himself."

"Their god loves the poor."

"Their god *is* poor. Does he bring us rain? No. Does he have an army? No. Could he save himself from the Romans? No. Some god. The Romans crucified him, and that's what they'll do to you if you don't stop this foolishness."

"Brother Luke says their god will return and establish a rule of justice."

Father snorted. "Let him come back. They'll crucify him all over again." He rose and looked at me. "Did you bring the goats back?"

"Yes, Father."

"All right, then. I'm going out to do the milking." Before he went through the door, he turned around and drilled Maron with his small black eyes. "Rome is like those mountains out there, boy. They'll rule the world forever. You can either fight them and be crushed, or you can survive the best you can on their terms."

CHAPTER THREE

THE NEXT MORNING I hurried toward the cloth shop where I worked, after leaving Numa at the café where she spent her day serving goat meat, watered wine, and flatbread. My work took me into Thagaste six days a week. Miriam, the owner of the shop, was a Christian and did no business on Sunday, her Sabbath.

The empire had been Christian for forty years, but here on its fringes people honored that or not, just as they saw fit. Temples to the Roman gods still flourished, the cult of Mithraism had its adherents, and, like my father, many peasants still worshipped the old Berber gods. Scholars studied Platonism and Stoicism, and might never open the Christian Bible. And, if one did want to be a Christian, what kind of Christianity should they choose? Donatist? Manichean? Caecilian? Miriam was a Caecilian and never stopped trying to convert me.

Although I often teased her by parroting my father's arguments against her religion, I admired Miriam. Ten years older than I, she was a widow with two children, six-year-old Peter and Lucy, three. Her own family had died in the last plague and her late husband's family had agreed to pay for Peter's education but offered no further help, hoping to force her into another marriage and off their hands. Miriam was a talented weaver, owned her own loom, and made a living for herself and her children. She did well enough that she could pay me to tend the shop and the children while she sat in the back room working at her loom. Her shop and rooms were on the second floor of a narrow building on a side street, above where her brother-in-law, Xanthos, ran a grocery.

The jagged sun had already pierced me, making me squint and pricking my skin with sweat. I passed a public well where children stood in line, the lucky ones shaded by a few dusty trees. As I passed Urbanus's town house, I could hear the gurgle of his courtyard fountain, cooling and refreshing even in its sound. Now I reached the dense part of town, where the stone buildings squeezed shoulder to shoulder and provided some shade. By noon, the stones would have absorbed the sun's heat and would blast it back in my face, but at this hour when I walked into their shadow I felt a sudden cooling that brought out small pimples on my arms and made me shiver once.

I left four cheeses with Xanthos, who sold them in his grocery, and then I hurried up the stairs to Miriam's shop. There was no particular reason to hurry, except I was young then and hurried everywhere.

Miriam sat in the back room at her loom. Lucy crooned to a wax doll wrapped in a scrap of cloth, and Peter raced two clay horses around an imaginary circus oval. The stone rooms were cool and gray except for a knife of yellow morning light slicing through the narrow workroom window, falling directly onto Miriam and her loom. I stopped in the doorway for a second, gazing at my friend, her small hands tying weights to the bottoms of her warp threads. Her black hair was curly and unruly, escaping in spots from its bindings. Her skin and her enormous eyes were both the color of weak tea. She turned those eyes to me now and smiled her slow smile. I loved her more than anyone except Numa.

"Good morning," she said. "I want your opinion on something. Which do you think will be better as an accent thread: this yellow or the red?"

She already had green and blue warp threads hanging from her loom's heading band, in a random pattern completely unlike the strict geometric patterns of Roman cloth. Miriam's unique designs were becoming popular, and other weavers were beginning to copy her.

"The yellow," I replied immediately. "It will stand out more. Now that other weavers are copying you, you want to keep your customers' attention by creating things that draw attention."

She leaned back a little, as if trying to get a better head-to-toe look at me. "You're a businesswoman, Leona," she said.

"No, just a barefoot goat herder's daughter," I insisted, secretly pleased.

———

The shop was quiet for a short time, until our first customers appeared. In came the most beautiful middle-aged woman I had ever seen. Her hair, which must have been a rich brown in her youth, was faded and shot through with silver, and her skin was pale and unlined, as if she had always been protected from the fierce North African sun.

But her true beauty was in her bearing. Spine straight, shoulders squared, chin high, she moved with the authority of a man and the grace of a woman.

Behind her stood a young man who must have been her son. Although he was tall, towering over his mother, I at first barely noticed him, so impressed was I by his regal mother. I raised my eyes up to his face and, to my horror, I recognized him. It was Aurelius, the boy who had failed to defend me and Numa against his friend Marcus.

He recognized me in the same moment. Determined not to be the first to look away, I glared at him until he blushed and swiveled his head, as if looking for an escape route.

"How may I help you, my lady?" I asked his mother.

"My son needs a new cloak. He saw a cloak he liked on a man in town, and we found that the cloth had been bought here. The cloth was unusual: the pattern looked like it had leaves of many colors woven into it. My son would like something similar. He would not consent to my choosing it; he insists on making his own choice." She said this with a frank, wry smile, as if we already shared knowledge of her son's stubbornness. Aurelius blushed even more deeply.

"I know exactly the cloth you describe," I assured her. "We have many similar, and my mistress accepts custom orders too. Let me show you what we have first."

I had gotten used to spreading out bolts of materials for highborn customers. They usually liked me. I was pretty, and I knew how to be deferential and respectful, although I seethed inside at the inequality between us and envied the patrician women their lives of ease and their slaves and fine clothing. Wasn't I smart? Wasn't I as good as them?

It seemed to me outrageously unfair that some should have so much and others so little. It especially annoyed me now, to be forced to help select something beautiful for the back of this Aurelius, this careless hooligan who stole for the fun of it.

I turned to the storeroom and regained my composure. I was putting food into the mouths of Miriam's children and adding to my father's flock of goats. What did I care what this overgrown boy wore on his back? If his mother bought, I would take a sesterce of what Miriam paid me, and buy a bag of dates to share with Numa on the way home this evening. I smiled as my eyes lit on the perfect roll of cloth for young Aurelius.

"I think I have just the thing, ma'am," I announced, carrying the heavy roll in my arms. I laid it on the table and unrolled a bit. "Does the young master like pears, perhaps?" I asked, glancing at Aurelius out of the corners of my eyes. "Look at this gorgeous piece: brown, so it won't show the dust of the road, and look at how my mistress has woven in the design of this lovely green. The green comes from Persia, very rare, and such a beautiful color: bright as a ripe pear, don't you think?"

"Do you like this one, Aurelius Augustine?" his mother asked.

"No."

"You're not even looking at it. Come closer. The green is beautiful."

Aurelius shambled over to the table, close enough that I could smell him, a smell not like my father's or my brothers' at all, but a combination of sweat and olives and whatever sweet things must blossom in the cool courtyards where he lounged in front of fountains all day, reading books or whatever men of his social class did whenever they weren't stealing fruit and harassing peasant girls. I pressed my lips together and took shallow breaths, leaning away from him.

"You don't like this?" his mother insisted, and when he didn't reply, she nodded to me. "Bring us a few more, please."

I poked my head into the back room and whispered to Miriam before fetching more bolts of cloth. "A lady I've never seen before," I reported. "She seems important."

Miriam peeked into the sales room. "That's Monnica, widow of the deucile Patricius," she said. "No, she's not anyone that highly placed. She's a Christian," she added. "Do you need me?"

"No. I just thought she seemed important."

"Every sale is important. Call me if you need me. Try to sell the one with the red silk in it."

I scurried back out to the sales room, toting the bolt of dark blue patterned with red triangles.

Monnica gasped. "Oh, this one is lovely! Aurelius, look!"

I noticed his eyes light up. It was one of our nicest cloths, and one of our most expensive because of the silk.

"I had heard your mistress was a Christian," Monnica said, fixing me with a severe look, as if she could already tell I was not and the fact was not to my credit. "Look . . ." she pointed out to her son. "Triangles. Symbols of the Holy Trinity."

"Very nice," he agreed, finally gathering his courage and looking me in the eye. It angered me that his look seemed to cut right into me. I flushed.

"We can get Verturius to line it in red, to pick up the red in the cloth," his mother said. "This would make a beautiful cloak for you. This is the one you want?"

"Yes. Fine," he agreed, still looking at me and examining the cloth with his big-knuckled fingers. I itched to smack his hand away.

"Hold this for us," Monnica ordered. "Our tailor will pick it up when he's ready to make the cloak, and he'll pay you." She didn't even ask me the cost. I wondered what it would be like to have no need to know the price of the things you wanted. "Come, Aurelius, we have other errands," she continued. "Good day to you." She nodded at me without smiling.

I didn't suppress my smirk as Aurelius followed his mother out the door like her meek slave.

Despite myself, I rushed to the window to watch them climb into their sedan chair. Aurelius looked up and saw me at the window, and it was his turn to smirk, and to tap his forehead in a subtle salute.

---

I wasn't surprised when he was waiting for me after work, but I felt obligated to feign anger. "What are you waiting for?" I sneered.

"No, I was just hoping to walk a ways with you."

"I didn't think boys of your class walked anywhere. You had four slaves carrying you earlier today."

I noticed that he carried a rolled scroll, flimsy-looking in his large hands. I had always been curious about what was in the books fine people read, but I was too proud to ask him.

Instead I asked, "Why did you steal those pears? You're rich. You can eat pears any time you want."

"We're not so rich."

"You could have a pear any time you wanted."

He shrugged.

"So why?" I persisted.

"It was just something to do. My friends were doing it."

"So if your friend had gone ahead and raped me and my sister, you would have done that too?"

"No! I saved you."

"That was your friend."

"And me."

"Oh, maybe a little," I conceded.

We had turned off the dirt side street and the stones of the Cardo Maximus felt warm and rough under my feet. I easily matched his long-legged pace. I walked fast for a small woman. I knew he was looking at me too, and I enjoyed knowing he thought I was pretty, even this boy who I didn't like.

I decided to start another argument. "What does your holy-holy Christian mother think about you running around with a bunch of hooligans who molest helpless peasant girls?"

"I don't tell her everything."

"I'll bet you don't."

We passed the fountain in the town square, where a statue of a smiling maiden let water trickle from her pitcher. A mother fetched her filthy child from the fountain's bowl and gave him a hard slap.

"Are you a Christian?" Aurelius asked.

"No." I paused, but curiosity got the better of me. "Are you?"

"No," he said low, looking around him as though his mother could hear him even here in the square. "No, my mother has enrolled me as a catechumen, but I've never accepted baptism yet. I don't know. It's almost like believing in magic, isn't it?"

"I wouldn't know."

"I mean that a man could rise again after death. It sounds like a trick."

I felt compelled to disagree with him. "They don't think he's a man. They think he's God, and lots of gods rise from the dead. Are you saying gods can't rise from the dead?"

"I wonder sometimes if there are any gods at all. Maybe it's just us. Maybe we're in charge of our own fates." He fidgeted with the scroll in his hands, looking around again, as if afraid of being overheard.

I had often thought this myself, but I didn't feel like agreeing with him. "How can there be no gods?" I argued. "Who made the world then?"

"I don't know," he shrugged. "I'm hoping to find out by studying philosophy."

"Is there anything in your philosophy about stealing, or about attacking innocent peasant girls on their way home from work?" I asked.

He stopped walking and took me by the shoulders. I shook him off.

"I told you I'm sorry," he said. "I hope you can forgive me. We were wrong to steal the pears and wrong to assault you and your sister. And I've been thinking: you're right. I was wrong not to stand against my friends and defend you from the first. I was a coward and I am sorry."

He looked sorry, and my heart moved uneasily. "There's my sister," I said. "I have to go." And I ran.

## CHAPTER FOUR

"YOUR BOYFRIEND'S waiting for you," Miriam teased.

"He's not my boyfriend," I shot back on my way out the door.

Aurelius was indeed waiting in the alley and began walking with me, as naturally as if we were brother and sister, as he had for the last three days.

"My cloak is started," he said. He was carrying a bag of dates.

"I know. Your tailor came and picked up the cloth first thing this morning. It must be very nice to be able to afford something so beautiful."

"My family isn't rich, you know." He popped a date into his mouth and offered the bag to me. I shook my head, although I wanted one badly.

"Could have fooled me, with your slaves and your silk-threaded cloak."

"Really, we're not. My father was only a deucile, which involves a lot of responsibility, you know. They have to collect taxes, and they have to contribute to public projects from their own funds. New aqueduct or baths: he has to kick in money. More legionnaires to defend the border: he has to help support the legion. It's not the greatest job."

"And someday it will be yours."

He sighed. "If I became a priest, I'd be excused. But then my younger brother would have to do it; that is, if I don't take my land with me into the Church."

"Oh, the problems you rich people have. Anyway, I thought you didn't believe in any gods." Changing my mind, I reached over and plucked a date from his paper cone. He had plenty, after all.

"I wish we could be friends."

"You have other friends. Not such nice guys. They seem like your type."

"I'd rather have friends who would help me be good." We walked along without speaking for a few minutes, until he sighed again and said, "What I really want is to be a teacher. I was at school in Madaura for a time, but I had to come home when my father died, and now we don't have the money for more education. We're hoping Urbanus will finance me."

I stopped walking. "Urbanus? The same Urbanus whose orchard you robbed?"

"He was my father's patron." Aurelius shrugged, as though it should be obvious to me that Urbanus owed him assistance in spite of his behavior. All Romanized aristocrats patronized families below them in the empire's hierarchy, and were patronized by at least one man higher than they were. Your patron represented your interests to the government, and kept you out of trouble or provided financial help if you needed it. Nobody above the peasant class could survive without a patron. Even I knew this.

I shook my head, and we started walking again. "Nice way to pay him back."

Aurelius ignored me. "He'll probably pay for me to go to school in Carthage if I promise to come back and open a school in Thagaste. Urbanus has big plans for Thagaste. He wants us to be a center of learning and entertainment. We might even be getting a circus."

A circus would be exciting: chariot races and animal shows, a place to see and be seen.

"Can you read?" he asked me abruptly.

"Only a little," I admitted. I could sign my name, and read a little bit of Latin and Berber, enough to get by in the shop. I burned with curiosity about what was in the books rich people read. The books seemed to set them apart from my own people even more than the luxuries they owned. The silk cloaks and the carriages and the bags of dates were just things. The words in the books seemed to hold the secrets behind those fine things.

"How about if I teach you to read?"

"I can already read enough to do my job." I tossed my head, trying to ignore my jumping heart.

"You're smart for a woman. I can see that. You could read Cicero and Ovid."

I had been intrigued from the start, and now I was flattered too. Still, I felt obliged to keep arguing. "Why would you want to do that?"

"I told you. I want to be a teacher. I can practice on you. It's free."

"It had better be free. I don't have any money."

"You have a job."

I gave him a sour look. The boy knew nothing that wasn't written down in a book. "I hand my wages over to my father."

"Oh. Will you do it? Will you be my first pupil?"

I really didn't like this boy, I told myself, but this might be the only chance I would ever have to learn to read, and the idea began to take hold of me. "Oh, all right," I said.

And so it began.

———••———

I lied to Numa. I told her I was staying late in the shop, learning weaving from Miriam. It was the first lie ever between me and my sister. I knew she'd be enraged at the idea of my spending time with one of the boys from the pear orchard, and I suspected she would agree with Father that reading was a waste of time for a woman. Numa wanted nothing more than a husband and babies and a few goats of her own. She started walking home with a hunchbacked village girl whose family sent her into town to beg every day. After our reading lessons, Aurelius walked me as close to my village as we dared, and I ran by myself the rest of the way.

One evening, three weeks into our lessons, Aurelius and I sat in the courtyard of Urbanus's house, just off the forum. There was a bench under two orange trees that we used as our school, carved marble with acanthus leaves. I hadn't yet met Urbanus. He often had business in the ports of Carthage or Hippo. I wasn't in any hurry to meet the great man. It was enough for me to sit in his magnificent garden, with its orange and fig trees and its serenely flowing fountains. Everywhere in this garden, water flowed. Fish spewed it, mischievous cherubs poured it, a perfectly formed young man pissed it. I could hardly concentrate on the lesson the first time, so dazzled was I by the lavish use of water.

Aurelius had decided we would start with Cicero, his current idol. He couldn't stop talking about Cicero.

"Now try to read this to me," he urged me now. "Remember the sound each letter makes when you come to an unfamiliar word and try to sound it out."

"'Is . . .'"

"No, no, *are*. Go on."

"'Are the pleasures of the body to be sought, which . . .'"

"Plato. A great Greek philosopher."

"'Are the pleasures of the body to be sought, which Plato describes, in all seriousness, as 'snares and the source of all ills'? The promptings of sensuality are the most strong of all and the most hostile to . . . to . . .' I don't know this word."

"Philosophy. You're doing excellently."

I knew I was, and I was elated. I felt a sense of power in being both pretty and smart, and in sitting in the garden of the great landowner who held power even over my tyrannical father, hearing secret wisdom that my father had never heard. In my hidden heart, I was also glad to be pleasing to my teacher.

"Keep going," he prompted me.

The book was written on a scroll, the old-fashioned way, on vellum still creamy from the calf, feeling warm and almost alive in my hands. I rolled up a few more lines and continued, "'What man in the grip of this, the strongest of emotions, can bend his mind to thought, regain his reason, or, indeed . . .'"

"Concentrate."

"'Concentrate on anything?'"

"Excellent, Leona. Now read me the whole thing again, and remember to place emphasis on the important words." He leaned forward, close to me. His breath had a sweet, fruity wine scent.

"I don't know why you always say that. All of them are important."

He pointed to the scroll. "Look, for example, here Cicero is contrasting the pleasures of the body to the pleasures of the mind. You want to emphasize the words body and mind."

"Oh." I didn't really understand, but I knew I could read the whole passage now without hesitating. "'Are the pleasures of the body to be sought, which Plato describes, in all seriousness, as 'snares and the source of all ills'? The promptings of sensuality are the most strong of all, and so the most hostile to philosophy. What man in the grip of this, the strongest of emotions, can bend his mind to thought, regain his reason, or, indeed, concentrate on anything?'"

"Oh, well done," said Aurelius, applauding.

My face warmed with pleasure. I told myself I still hated him, that I was just using him to get something I had never dreamed of getting and that my father would deny me if he could. A part of me knew I was lying to myself. Now, I inhaled the clean, upper-class scent of him, and noticed the black hairs on his bronze arms, coarse and wiry like the hair of a wild boar. I had an impulse to run my hand lightly over those hairs and watch the pimples rise on his skin.

"Now," he continued, "stand up and try to recite it from memory, and put hand gestures into it." He stood and demonstrated, one arm held stiffly at his waist.

"Why?"

"Because that is what great orators do."

The spell of his scent and his springy black hairs was broken, and he just seemed silly to me. "I'll never be a great orator. I'm a woman," I reminded him.

"Then maybe I can make you a better scold."

I squinted at him, ready to be angry, until I saw a smile pulling at his full lips. I slapped his arm. "You're an idiot," I told him.

"Yes, but I hope not to be one forever."

"I have to go anyway. It's getting late."

He took Cicero from my hands and we walked to Urbanus's garden gate. Herbs grew by the gate, and the sharp scent of rosemary tingled in my nostrils.

We didn't notice Numa standing outside the gate until we almost bumped into her.

She stepped in front of us, arms crossed.

"Hello, Numa," I said casually.

"Hello. Care to introduce me to your friend? Oh, wait, I think I know him already. He's that pear thief and assaulter of innocent peasant women."

Aurelius bowed. "Guilty as charged," he admitted.

"Numa, I'm sorry I didn't tell you—" I began.

"Please at least tell me this wasn't already going on that day," she said.

"No, no, we never met before that day," I said. "After that, he came to Miriam's shop and we started talking and it's not what you think. He's teaching me to read Latin."

"Yes, I'll bet that's all he wants to teach you. Since we already know him to be a man of great virtue who would never harm a woman."

"Numa, really," I pleaded. "He did help us that day."

She snorted and rolled her eyes.

"Join us," Aurelius said suddenly.

"Join you?"

"Yes," he continued. "If you're worried about my intentions toward your sister, join us as her chaperone. And you could learn to read Latin too, if you like. I want to be a teacher, and a teacher needs more than one student to make a living."

I felt a stab of panic. At that moment I finally had to admit I wanted him to myself.

"I can't pay you anything," she said impatiently.

"No, of course not. It's free. I'm practicing."

Numa shook her head, her lower lip protruding, her arms still crossed. "What good will it do me to read Latin? What good will it do you, Leona? You'll work for Miriam until you find a husband, and then you'll be busy raising children and milking goats. Reading will only make you want things you can't have."

I couldn't find the words for what I wanted to say. I knew Numa was right. I also knew I could not give up my hours in the garden with Aurelius and Cicero.

"Don't worry," she continued. "I won't tell Father. But you mark my words." She narrowed her eyes and pointed to Aurelius. "He wants more than to just sit in a garden and read books with you. And when you find yourself carrying a bastard, don't expect me to help." She swung around dramatically and walked down the path away from us. I had to smile a little. Even in her righteous anger, Numa's gait was leisurely.

"I better follow her," I said to Aurelius.

"Will we still meet tomorrow?" he asked.

I nodded and ran after my sister.

# CHAPTER FIVE

THE NEXT MORNING, black clouds bore down from the direction of the distant sea. Miriam's shop and workroom were dark and close when I arrived at work.

"No!" I heard her say sharply to Peter. "You need to stay here in the shop where I can see you today. A big storm is coming. No running around the town today."

"Hello," I called. I entered her workroom to find Peter sitting at her feet, pouting.

"Well if it isn't Erebos, the god of darkness," I commented. He looked up and gave me an even darker pout.

"There's nothing to do here," he complained.

I gave Miriam a questioning look.

"The provincial governor and two bishops are coming into town today," she whispered.

"Why are we afraid of bishops?" I asked. I was unsure what a bishop was, some high official in the Christian Church, I thought, but I didn't think church officials were known to be dangerous.

"It isn't them we're afraid of," she said, rolling her eyes in exasperation.

"It's the rioters." She turned her attention back to her work, clicking her heddles forward and back, sending her shuttle flying between them.

"Rioters?"

"The governor is here to decide who will control the church in the center of town, near the well. It's always been Caecilian, but it's been infiltrated lately by Donatists." She paused and twisted her mouth. "Nice how they don't want to associate with us until it's time to try to take over our church." Miriam never took her eyes off her work as she spoke, now pausing to pack the weft thread with her shed stick.

I shook my head and prodded her to go on. "I still don't understand how this makes it unsafe for Peter to be on the street."

"The Donatist bishop petitioned for possession of the church and the governor has come to hear arguments from both sides. Each side will send their best speakers to present their argument, of course, but they'll also each try to have the biggest, loudest crowd on their side. And the Donatists will bring the hut people."

Now I understood. The Donatist leadership publicly disavowed the hut people but found them useful for intimidating both non-Christians and other Christian factions.

They carried staves that they called israels, and were known to beat rich landowners and tax collectors. The hut people never worried about punishment or reprisal because they believed that to be killed doing the Lord's work would earn them a martyr's crown in Heaven. Miriam's fear suddenly made sense.

"I guess we're in for a long day," I agreed.

———•••———

The day crawled by without even the slash of yellow sunlight to mark the hours. Miriam worked at her loom in the back room, while I tried to amuse the children with stories and waited on the occasional customer. But I was right: trade was slow, and as the heat built up like a physical presence without the relief of the threatened rainstorm, the children drifted off to sleep in the front room.

All day we had been hearing shouting from the forum. Peter kept peering out the window, trying to see what was going on. "Will they fight now?" he kept asking.

Now, with the curious boy finally asleep, I sat in the workroom with Miriam, watching her nimble hands and feet at the loom and chatting with her in quiet tones.

"How's your well-educated boyfriend?" she teased.

"He's not my boyfriend."

She was silent a moment, shifting her heddles and sending her shuttle flying through the shed. Without looking at me, she finally said, "You know he can't marry you."

"He's not my boyfriend," I repeated, "so I don't know why you think I care if he can marry me." I tossed my head and moved closer to where Miriam worked. I picked up the beater stick and gave her a questioning look. When she nodded, I used the stick to firmly comb upward Miriam's last several weft threads.

"By Roman law, their noble class can't marry a peasant," she continued. "He'd forfeit all of his property. He has to marry somebody of his own class."

"Doesn't that figure. The rich people get to keep the money all in the family that way. Not that I care," I added.

She smiled. "Leona, you sound like the hut people. You shouldn't hang around with them. Most women would run the other way from a big israel—and you a virgin," she teased. I liked the way Miriam joked with me about men, as if I were a grown woman like her.

"But seriously," she continued. "You're almost sixteen, and your father will be able to make a better marriage for you if you're still a virgin.

And you know there's always the chance of a bastard. Don't throw yourself away on this boy, Leona," she urged, looking me in the eye for the first time.

"I'm not throwing myself away," I insisted. "I'm learning to read Latin for free. That's all." I leaned over without looking at her and combed her threads up again.

"I doubt it will really be free, Leona," she replied. "Please be careful. You know I love you like a sister. I don't want to see your heart broken and your life ruined. You're a pretty girl. Use that and get yourself a nice husband who won't work you too hard."

I smiled, relieved to get off the subject of Aurelius.

"I will then. And I'll have three little girls and name them all Miriam."

She laughed.

"Where's Peter?" called a small voice.

We both turned to see Lucy in the doorway, rubbing her eyes.

"He's right in there with you," I assured her, "sleeping in the corner." I raced back into the sales room toward where I'd last seen Peter. Miriam was behind me.

I checked every corner of the room twice, unwilling to believe my eyes the first time. Surely he was there, curled up in a shadow somewhere. But Peter was nowhere in the room. My heart started pounding so hard I could hear the blood in my ears.

Miriam's face had gone pale. She knelt and took Lucy by the shoulders. "Where did he go? Did you see where he went?"

"I was sleeping." Sensing her mother's panic, Lucy started to cry. Miriam folded her daughter in her arms and looked ready to cry herself.

"I'm sorry," I said. "I was supposed to be watching him. I'll go look for him."

"I'll go," she said.

"No," I insisted, "You stay here with Lucy. He might come back," I pointed out. "It's my fault he got out. I'll find him."

——••——

The street outside our shop was deserted. I knew Peter would have gone straight for the excitement at the forum, so I ran in that direction.

I slipped through the narrow alleys and found myself in the fringe of a restless crowd.

"Have you seen a boy?" I asked the man nearest me. "A little boy, about six, by himself?"

He shook his head. I tried a woman next, expecting more sympathy. I tugged on her robe. "Excuse me. Have you seen a little boy by himself? About six?" I held my hand about four feet from the ground to indicate his height.

"No," she replied, and went back to craning her neck to see what was happening in front of the church.

I couldn't resist asking, "What's happened?"

"The arguments are finished. The governor hasn't made his decision yet."

"How will we know when he does?" I asked, stretching my own neck. We were far from the front of the church, and the space in between was packed solid with bodies.

She expelled a short, snorting laugh. "Oh, we'll know well enough. One faction or the other will be roaring in rage and itching to start some trouble. What do you think those legionnaires are for?"

I saw that the front of the church was guarded by a line of armored legionnaires with swords at their sides. And then I saw something even more ominous: a small crowd of men emerged from one of the small streets that fed into the forum, attracted to trouble like dogs to garbage. They were carrying the israels of the hut people: the same staves peasants used to beat the olives from the trees, but also punishing as weapons.

I squeezed through the crowd, yelling, "Peter! Peter!" The crowd was mostly men, stinking of sweat and urine and goat. My stomach and throat clenched. I couldn't get a deep breath. Then I felt a strong hand grip my forearm. I instinctively jerked away, but the grip held and I looked up to discover who the hand belonged to.

It was Maron, stick in hand. "What the hell are you doing here?" he hissed.

"I'm looking for Peter. He ran off."

"Well, get in somewhere and stay in. There's going to be trouble."

"Looks like you'll be the one causing it."

We both turned our heads toward a loud tramping, and saw another unit of legionnaires approach the crowd from the direction of the church. They cut through the swarm in two disciplined lines, and anyone who couldn't get out of their way fast enough was knocked to the ground.

Maron gripped my arm and shook me. "Just get in somewhere safe and stay there. Do you hear me?"

"No! I have to find Peter!" I twisted my arm out of his grasp and slipped away from him, into the crowd.

I slotted myself between milling bodies. My foot throbbed, and I realized it must have been tramped on at some point.

The swarm washed me toward the church. "What's the decision? What's the decision?" people kept asking.

Someone in front of us turned and shouted, "Paulonius's ordination stands! The church belongs to the Caecilians!"

Some nearby gave roars of victory, but I could hear a chant of "Injustice! Injustice!" which grew louder and louder as the news spread.

Some of the crowd started chanting, "Martyrs! Martyrs!" answered by cries of "Caecilian!"

Now that a decision had been announced, the crowd would turn ugly. It looked like everyone in town was now in the forum, but I couldn't catch sight of Maron or Peter.

If I were Peter, where would I be? I thought wildly. By now, he'd be frightened. Maybe he'd found some hiding place. As the press of bodies carried me closer to the church, I spied a pair of skinny legs that might have been Peter's and then lost sight of them. I pressed myself in the direction where I'd seen them and caught a glimpse again, just as the boy stumbled and was about to be trampled. I jabbed my elbows into the nearby legs and hauled him up by his arm.

"Peter!" My heart flooded with joy and relief, followed by anger. "Why did you go running off after your mother told you to stay in the shop? She's worried to death about you." I gave him a shake.

"I wanted to see what was happening."

I picked him up and he clung to my neck, his legs wrapped around my waist. I was slick with sweat, my hair separating into ringlets. I craned my neck, looking for an opening in the mass of people to lead back to the shop. It seemed impossible to make our way through that ocean, trying to move opposite to their surge. Exhausted and paralyzed, I looked around again. The street leading to Urbanus's house was only a few yards from us. It felt safe and familiar to me after my weeks of study there with Aurelius, but did I dare?

I made my decision and started pushing out of the crowd toward Urbanus's street. Going in that direction we were moving with the crowd, and the danger was that we'd be pushed along too fast and I would lose my footing. Using Peter as a wedge, I forced us between close-packed shoulders, trying to keep a little ahead of the heaving crowd.

"Watch it," a boy my age snarled, and shoved me back, hard. I felt my knee buckle and dropped Peter.

"Peter!" I bent, frantic to lift him before he was trampled. I gathered him up, scraping my knuckles and seeing his tunic rip under someone's spiked sandal. Still bent over, I lurched forward, trying to regain my balance. Finally, we were expelled into the side street like a pit popping from an olive. I fell onto all fours, dropping Peter again.

I paused to catch my breath and stood. "You can walk now," I told him. "We're going to see one of my friends." *I hope*, I added mentally.

We reached Urbanus's front door and I banged desperately. A door slave opened the door just a slit.

"I'm a friend of Aurelius Augustine. Please let us in," I pleaded.

The slave squinted at us and tilted his head. I could tell he was about to slam the door to the panicked peasant woman with her skinny little boy. "Please! Tell Urbanus that friends of Aurelius need protection!"

I could hear sandals pounding the street behind me, more rioters racing toward the trouble.

Then, to my joy, I saw Aurelius emerge behind the slave. "Leona? Let her in," he ordered the slave.

We were admitted, and the door was slammed and bolted.

"What are you doing here?" Aurelius demanded.

"Peter ran away from the shop to see what was going on, and I went to find him."

I was caked with sweat and dust, my head pounded, my knees and knuckles stung, and my throat was on fire. Blood trickled down Peter's knees, and the remains of his dusty tunic hung off his skinny body like the flag of a defeated army.

I had forgotten about my foot, but now I looked down and saw that it was bleeding, one toenail peeled off. As soon as I saw it, it started to sting and throb again.

"Your foot!" Aurelius gestured to the slave, and in a few minutes the slave boy returned with a basin of perfumed water. The slave boy knelt to wash my feet, but I gestured to Peter. "Please. Can you get him cleaned up and find him something decent to wear?"

Aurelius nodded to the boy, who led Peter away with surprising tenderness.

I sat and dipped my injured foot into the basin, wincing as I began to clean the damaged toe.

Aurelius knelt. "Here, let me."

I stared at him as if he were mad: a man of the aristocratic class offering to wash the feet of a peasant girl? But I was too tired to object. Now that I was safe, I was trembling from terror and exhaustion.

I watched mesmerized as he took my small foot in his hands and wiped it with the soft cloth. He was awkward but careful, gentle, and surprisingly thorough. He rubbed one spot at a time, in little circles, until my foot was warmed by a tingling feeling that began to travel up my leg.

"You know, in the Christian Bible, it says that Christ did this: washed his disciples' feet," he said, watching his own hands at work. Everything was a lesson with him, always.

I didn't respond. He was washing my ankle now, his strong hands circling it and moving up and down from my calf to my heel. I shivered, although the room was warm.

Gently, he set my injured foot on the mosaic floor, and lifted the other into the warm water. He pressed his thumb against my instep. I shivered again, and he looked up at me. His eyes burned with something that made my heart flutter, and I couldn't look away from him.

I pulled my foot away. "I have to get Peter home to Miriam," I said.

"Don't be foolish. You and Peter can spend the night here and go home tomorrow when it's safe." The spell of what I'd seen in his eyes was broken.

I shook my head. "Miriam will be frantic."

"We can send a slave to let her know Peter is safe. Please. Stay. You need something to eat and a good rest, and the streets will be safer tomorrow."

"How do you know it will be safer tomorrow?"

"The legionnaires will make sure."

I thought of my brother with a needle of worry.

"Please stay," he said again. "I promise we'll send someone to let Miriam know you're both safe."

I knew he was right, and I looked around myself in curiosity for the first time since we'd arrived. I would like to spend a night in this palace, I thought, and eat what food Urbanus ate. "All right," I agreed.

————••————

Peter was put to bed, a slave dispatched to Miriam, and Aurelius and I went in to dinner with Urbanus.

Until now, I had seen only his gardens, which were beautiful enough. To enter his dining salon was like seeing for the first time after a lifetime of blindness. The tabletop was a mosaic of small tiles set in a pattern depicting Sol Invictus, the Roman sun god, with his horses and his radiating diadem. The mosaic top rested on a set of immense bronze legs fashioned into thick vines, studded here and there with colorful jewels and ending in clawed lion's feet. Twenty could easily have been seated on the couches that surrounded this table.

The couches themselves, also ornately legged in bronze, were covered with thick silk cushions of various colors and patterns. A mural on one wall depicted a scene of satyrs and naked, full-hipped young women frolicking at the seashore. Three slaves stood silent around the table.

What left me even more speechless was the array and quantity of food on the table. I didn't know what some of it was, and began to worry that I would embarrass myself. Surely he was expecting more guests, to consume such a quantity. But who would come out on such a wild evening?

I hesitated before entering the room, taking it all in, and Aurelius had to nudge my back a little.

"It seems you made it just in time." Urbanus greeted us. "Storms of all kinds are about to break."

As if he had the power to cue the heavens, a clap of thunder broke the afternoon, and then came the drumming of rain on the roof. Urbanus grinned and pointed upward as if he had, indeed, cued the spectacle just for our entertainment. "Lie down and eat," he urged.

I was unused to lying on a couch to eat, although I knew this was the custom of the Roman nobility. My own family sat on wooden benches for our meals. I worried about dropping food on the silk cushions.

I lowered myself onto one of the couches and fidgeted into a reclining position. Aurelius lay beside me on the couch, completely at ease. I, on the other hand, felt as if my tongue had been cut out. I didn't know if it would be polite to start eating before the other guests arrived, I wasn't sure if there was some order in which we were supposed to eat the foods, or whether the host or the guests were supposed to eat first. For all my resentment of them, I was naïve about how the noble people lived. I realized suddenly that I knew nothing about these people, other than to envy from afar their carriages and gardens and fine clothes.

"Eat!" Urbanus repeated. "Is there something you'd like that isn't on the table?" he asked me. "I can have more fetched."

It was a wonder to me that the great man was being so solicitous to please us, and I found my voice. "No, nothing else." I couldn't imagine anything else. I looked pleadingly at Aurelius, and he seemed to awaken from some dream, beckoned to one of the slaves, and pointed to a plate of snails, glistening with oil and sprinkled with parsley. As each dish was served to him, he indicated that it should be offered next to me and I either accepted or declined each offering. By the time the slaves had finished serving us, a large goblet of wine stood in front of me and I had on my plate helpings of the snails, some spiced goat meat, asparagus and leeks covered in a yellow sauce, olives both ripe and unripe, stuffed and unstuffed, and some fish that looked like an enormous, many-legged bug from a child's nightmare. I accepted it only because Aurelius urged me to try it. It. I had no idea how I would manage to eat such a large quantity of food. At home, we ate bread and cheese and porridge at most meals, eggs and goat meat rarely, and whatever vegetables and fruits were in season.

While the slaves served us, Aurelius and Urbanus talked about the events of the day.

"Well, Aurelius Augustine, what do you think of the governor's decision?" Urbanus asked.

"It was the right one, sir," Aurelius replied confidently. "The Caecilians have held the church for many years. Even if the Donatists are right and the Caecilian priest's ordination is suspect, they should get another priest, not be forced to forfeit their property."

"Who's right in the larger situation, though? Say I'm a priest back at the time of the persecution. Was I right to obey the law and hand over sacred texts for destruction?"

"Yes," Aurelius answered immediately.

"Even if I had the only copy?" Urbanus prodded.

Aurelius shifted a little on the couch and hesitated. "Well, maybe not in that case."

"So I was wrong if I had the only copy. Why?"

"Well, because it's the only copy. Then that truth is lost to time forever."

"I see, I see." Urbanus rubbed his chin and smiled a little. It came to me that he was playing with Aurelius, and I wondered that Aurelius failed to see this and kept rising to his bait and answering impulsively. "So, right and wrong are situational, then? You can only tell what's right or wrong by knowing all the particulars of a situation."

He held up his cup and immediately one of the slaves refilled it with wine. Aurelius flushed. "No! I didn't mean that at all."

"Then . . . ?" Urbanus spread his hands, as if pleading for enlightenment.

"Then . . ." Aurelius hesitated, frowning. "Then, I would say that right is always right and wrong is always wrong, but human wisdom is perhaps insufficient to make the correct determination."

"Ah." This seemed to be the answer that Urbanus had been seeking. "Then," he concluded, "there's no point in my financing your further education in Carthage, is there? Since no amount of education could ever hope to ordain you with even so much wisdom as to determine whether you would be right to hand over your mother's Christian Bible to be burned."

It was Aurelius's turn to smile wickedly. I saw that he finally realized Urbanus was playing a game. "No, sir, your patronage wouldn't be wasted at all. I might still make wrong judgments, but, with an education, they would be less wrong and less frequent. And, I would learn the skills of rhetoric, grammar, and declamation that would allow me to defend any position, even my patron's, even if—not that this would ever happen, of course—he himself were wrong."

I had trouble following that, but Urbanus barked out a loud laugh and took a swallow of his wine. "Excellent answer. I'm sure my investment will not be wasted." He turned to me. "Your young teacher shows great promise. His family's finances will not allow him to continue his education in Carthage, but I have agreed to finance his studies and in return he will come back to Thagaste and teach, and to make arguments on my behalf in the courts when I need him."

Aurelius flushed and looked down at the mention of his family's finances. I realized he had been telling the truth when he insisted he wasn't as rich as I thought he was, and I saw that it embarrassed him. I was surprised too, that Urbanus knew about our reading lessons in his garden. I wondered whether he disapproved but was too shy to ask.

He saved me the trouble. Urbanus leaned toward me. "It interests me that you want to learn to read Latin."

"Yes," was all I could think of to say, but I held his eyes.

He nodded and took another sip of wine. "Tell me why."

I was having trouble continuing to hold his gaze. I looked down at my lap for a second, then lifted my head again. "Well, sir, I guess if I find an opportunity to have something the rich and noble have, I should take it."

He turned to one of his slaves and said, "Count the gold plate after she leaves, Saul." But he was smiling. He frowned again, toying with the stem of his wine goblet. "You're pretty. You have other ways of getting more than just book learning."

"Then I'd be just a whore, wouldn't I?" I responded. "I'd rather be a poor man's honest wife than a rich man's whore."

Urbanus raised his eyebrows at Aurelius. "Well. How refreshing. Some poor goat herder will be very lucky indeed to have a wife who is both beautiful and extraordinarily well-educated." He raised his goblet to us and took another drink.

Seeing he had no objection to the teaching arrangement, I began to relax. It had also become clear that no other guests were expected, that the whole array of food on the table was meant for the three of us. On the principle of taking good things when they were offered, I ate myself into a near stupor.

———◆◆◆———

When Aurelius found his way to my chamber after dark, while the crickets whistled and the fountain outside trickled under a silver moon, I was not surprised and not afraid. The terrors and alarms of the day had awakened my blood, and the heavy food and wine left me feeling languid and not myself. My determination not to be a rich man's whore seemed like words spoken by someone else, many years ago.

I was a virgin and had never even been kissed, except in play by village boys when I was a little flat-chested girl. Aurelius's eyes were hard and demanding, but his mouth was soft and tender. He leaned over and kissed me gently at first, questioningly, and when I responded, he gathered me up and kissed me harder. I was barely awake and determined to stay that way. If I could convince myself I was dreaming, I couldn't be blamed for not resisting. And so it was in complete silence that we first became lovers.

# CHAPTER SIX

BY THE NEXT DAY, order was restored in Thagaste, though rocks, sandals, and scraps of clothing littered the center of town, and here and there in the back alleys an unclaimed body remained for the constables to haul away.

I returned Peter to his mother in the shop that morning, and Miriam was so happy to see him, weeping with joy and scolding him at the same time, that she barely noticed me, and for that I was glad. I felt transformed, as if my whole body must glow with my new secret.

My sharp-eyed sister noticed that something was different about me. Numa walked into the shop at a pace quicker than her usual stroll, and her face sagged in relief when she saw me. But instantly, she frowned. "Well, you look bright for someone we thought was dead."

I wanted to hug her, but I looked down instead. "I'm sorry. Peter ran off and I had to find him. Then we got stuck and . . . a kind family offered us a place to stay the night."

She frowned again. I could tell she suspected there was more to the story. "Have you heard anything of Maron?" she asked. "He didn't come home either."

"I saw him yesterday in the middle of the riot," I admitted. I lowered my voice to a whisper. "He was carrying an israel."

.

Numa nodded. "That's what Father's afraid of. I have to get to work. I'm glad you're all right." Now, finally, she embraced me, but it felt awkward and she cast another puzzled frown over her shoulder as she left.

All day I saw the shop, and Miriam and the children and our customers, through a veil, my mind absorbed in the events of the previous evening: the tumult in the forum, the sumptuous dinner, and most of all, what had happened between me and Aurelius. My heart rapped against my chest all day, and I felt more than light-headed; I felt light all over, as if my mind had left my body, leaving my legs and arms with a simple drill to follow on their own: walk into the back room, reach for this roll of cloth, now open it for the customer, now smile pleasingly. Between my legs I still felt raw and moist. If I squeezed my legs together under my tunic, I could imagine I still felt his presence there.

My brain jangled with the question of whether to meet him in the square as usual for our reading lesson. I couldn't think of a reason not to, but I felt uncomfortable, as if our intimacy the night before had changed things in a way I didn't understand. I realized then how naïve and unknowing I was about such things, and wished I could ask someone how to conduct myself, but my usual confidantes were Miriam and Numa, the people from whom I most wanted to keep my secret.

I wished Aurelius would come to the shop and give me a signal that our daily meeting time remained unchanged, but as the afternoon sunlight puddled into the shop, I slowly put away the remaining rolls of cloth and sorted the day's coins into bags for Miriam, reluctant to make my way to the square, where I would either wait or keep going for my walk home.

"You're quiet today," Miriam observed.

It took me a few seconds to collect an answer. "I'm still upset about yesterday," I said. Not a lie, exactly.

She nodded, and rubbed my back. "Will you meet your friend for your reading lesson today?"

"I suppose." I shrugged, then squared my shoulders and took a breath. "I'd better be going or I'll be late. I'll see you tomorrow."

She gave my shoulders a squeeze, whispered, "Thanks again," and let me go.

I set off for the square purposefully, but my stride slowed as I approached, and once more I began to feel that everything had changed, that he might not be there waiting for me. I dragged my feet toward the town center, scanning for him so that if he wasn't there, I could keep moving instead of suffering the humiliation of waiting and waiting and finally giving up.

Who I saw was not Aurelius, but Numa. "Are you ready for a scene that will turn your stomach?" she asked me.

"What is it?"

She looked me in the eye and took my hands. "Maron is dead."

"Oh." The syllable was expelled from me by some force that knotted my stomach and numbed my face. "Oh," I said again, and Numa put her arms around me. Maron the man had been surly and angry and had treated us like his slaves. But now I remembered Maron the boy, the playmate who made the bigger children include his little sisters in their games of run-goat-run and Romans-and-Gauls, who twisted little dolls for us out of leftover wheat.

"I know," Numa said, reading my mind. "Do you want to see? It isn't pretty."

I shook my head and frowned at her, not understanding.

"His body and five others are hung outside the forum."

---

For once I was not impatient with Numa's slow pace. I wasn't sure I wanted this last look at our brother. Yet, another part of me buzzed with a mixture of dread, morbid curiosity, and impatience to get it over with.

We soon reached the gateway to the forum.

The six bodies hung from rough scaffolding in various states of ruin. Carrion birds swooped and cackled overhead. I was afraid to look up and identify Maron, hoping childishly that Numa had made a mistake. Slowly, though, I raised my eyes and scanned each body. It wasn't hard to spot Maron's, the darkest one.

His mouth hung open as innocent as a sleeping boy's, but the birds had already plucked his eyes and pecked at his smooth brown cheeks. His side showed a long sword gash and one of his arms hung from his shoulder by a few threads of muscle.

Numa burst into tears. A sour, burning liquid rose in my throat and I had to turn away from the sight.

I wrapped my arms around Numa. "Come on. We'll have to go home and break the news to Father."

---

Father already knew. We arrived at our hut to find it crowded with men we'd never seen before.

Father and Tito sat at our small table with a tall, sinewy man with a wild gray beard and the robes of a priest. Three younger men stood nearby.

Father glanced up when Numa and I came in but didn't greet us. "Burying dead bodies," he growled at his guest, "is a disgusting Hebrew custom. I won't have it even if it were possible. If I'm allowed the body, it will be burned the way my ancestors' bodies were burned. But you're wasting your time talking to me. The Romans won't allow a funeral of any kind."

"They might, with the right kind of persuasion."

Numa started stirring the porridge that had been simmering on the fire all day, gently, as if it might explode if she weren't careful. I took a lead from her and went to the larder and quietly unwrapped a cheese.

Father snorted. "You think because your Christ is the new official god they'll make exceptions for you? You're as naïve as your god." He jabbed a finger toward the bearded man. "The Romans understand one thing: power. Challenge their power and die. It's as simple as that. My boy's body will hang there until it rots, to get that message across."

"We can send a message of our own," the bearded man argued, tipping his head toward his silent companions.

Father stood. "The same kind of message you sent yesterday? My son was killed delivering your message, and now I have one less set of strong arms to help support this family in my old age. You used him. You used a stupid, headstrong boy to fight your little internal religious battles and now you want to use his body to make some kind of point to the empire. No. It's nothing to do with him, do you understand?"

I stole a glance at Numa as I started slicing cheese. She widened her eyes and shook her head.

"To the contrary," the priest answered. "Of the six dead, four are martyrs. Maron is one. He was a baptized Christian."

Father leapt from his seat. "What? No, he wasn't."

"He was. He was more Christian than many who claim the name. He was baptized by a legitimate priest, one ordained by a bishop of the martyr tradition."

I had seldom seen my father speechless. Numa and I stopped our work and turned toward the men, waiting to see what would happen next. Tito looked down, his folded hands nervously tapping on the tabletop.

Finally, Father leaned across the table toward the priest. "You and your martyrs. Now you have another, and I hope it satisfies you. But I will not consent to a burial. His body will hang and rot or it will burn. Leave my house now."

The priest rose. "May you and your family be led to peace," he said, and he left our hut with his still-silent companions following.

The next morning, when Numa and I came back into town for work, only two bodies still hung in front of the forum.

———••••———

Aurelius was at the fountain waiting for me the next afternoon. He sprang up and waved when he spotted me, the setting sun glowing orange behind him.

"Are you all right?" he asked me as we started our walk toward Urbanus's town house.

I nodded, embarrassed and awkward. I sensed in him the same awkwardness and tension I had felt for the past two days. All other days, we chatted about the previous day's lesson—Horace, Ovid, Cicero—Aurelius explaining to me in rapid Berber where I was deficient and how I could improve. That day, neither of us spoke at first.

"Where were you yesterday?" he asked finally. "I waited for you."

I took a deep breath. "My brother died in the riot."

He stopped walking and put his hands on my arms. "I'm sorry. Do you have to go right home?"

"I don't know."

"I mean, does your family have some ritual or . . . ?"

"I don't know."

"How can you not know?"

"Can we just go to the garden?"

We let ourselves into the garden and sat on our usual bench. Aurelius looked at me expectantly. I suddenly felt tired and irritable and I hardly knew where to begin. "Maron died in the riots the day before yesterday. I saw him, just for a minute, while I was looking for Peter, and he had a stick. We knew he was in with the hut people, but what we didn't know—well, at least the priest claims—was that he was a Christian. So, the Donatist priest and my father had a big argument about what should be done with the body. He was one of the ones hanging there outside the forum." I took a breath.

"I'm sorry," Aurelius said, and patted my shoulder awkwardly.

I went on. "So, the priest and my father had an argument about whether Maron should be burned, buried, or left to hang there and rot, and, I guess the priest won, because his body's not there anymore. I don't know if the Christians made a deal with the governor or if they just sent their thugs in to cut them down in the middle of the night or what, but there are four missing now. I guess they're going to bury him no matter what my father says. And I guess I should go home. I don't know how my father's going to react, and I shouldn't leave Numa and Tito to face him alone."

"Sure. Sure. I understand," Aurelius said, but he looked into my eyes and drew me to him and kissed me. My heart rose with joy, as if this was what I had been waiting for all day. The nervous rapping my heart had been doing for two days changed to a full-blooded pounding, and the space between my legs swelled and moistened and began to feel heavy. I forgot Maron, put Tito and Numa and my father from my mind.

After a few minutes of kissing, Aurelius rose, took my hand and led me to a corner of the garden that was screened by rosebushes. He lifted my tunic over my head and then removed his own, and stood for a moment looking at me. I loved the avid look in his eyes, loved the feeling of being worshipped. We lay down and kissed some more, and then he entered me, all in silence again. I was still too shy to look down and take a good look at his male parts, but it didn't hurt so much this time, and once again it was over quickly.

After, he lay on top of me, balanced on his elbows, and looked down at me, smiling slightly, saying nothing.

"What?" I asked. My blood felt thick, my limbs heavy.

"Well, I broke my vow for you."

"What vow?"

"To not know a woman until I was eighteen."

"Should I apologize?"

"No." He rolled over onto his back beside me and stared at the fading sky, eyes wide, smiling full now. "No. The Ascetics are all wrong. The love between a man and a woman is the best thing in the world." He rolled onto his side and propped himself on one elbow, looking down at me again. "I love you, Leona. Do you love me?"

"Yes," I answered, and at the time it was only because I didn't know what else to say.

"Can we keep meeting every day?"

"Yes."

"We'll still read too, of course."

"I'll insist on it."

He trailed his finger along the side of my breast and down my waist, over my belly, to the tuft of fur at the top of my legs. I shivered, he bent to kiss me, and we started all over again.

For the next month, I lived in a world suddenly brighter and fresher. Lovers sometimes say the moments drag until they are together again, but this was not so for me. I woke in the morning with joy in my heart because I would see Aurelius later, and the rest of the day was a golden road to our time together.

The white sun exploding over the purple-and-gold mountains in the distance, the soft dust beneath my feet as Numa and I walked to town in the morning, the tangy white cheese I ate with my bread and olives for lunch, all seemed suddenly more precious to me because they were part of a life that included him. I waited on customers in the shop with enthusiasm and good cheer. All of Miriam's cloth was beautiful, the colors brighter now, the weave smoother and softer.

Our daily time together was short. My father, surlier than ever since Maron's death and the kidnapping of his body by the Christians, believed I was learning weaving, and Numa kept my secret, but I was still expected to be home before dark. We met in the square every afternoon as before, and let ourselves into Urbanus's garden. Aurelius would sometimes have a treat for me: pears or dates or little spice cakes sweetened with honey.

I came to know his body as intimately as I knew my own: the black hair on his thighs, coarse and sparse like boar's bristles, the white scar on his forearm from his fall from a tree as a small boy, his ears large but so close to the head, unusual in a man, and his manhood, which I had first been afraid to look at, and now couldn't stop looking at and touching, with my hands, my mouth, and tongue—even once squeezing my small breasts together to make a home for it. We made love, lay in our hiding place whispering and caressing each other, and then made love again. I forgot that our original plan was for me to read Latin.

I could see in their eyes that both Miriam and Numa guessed my secret, but neither of them questioned me. Miriam was especially friendly and gentle, taking the time to teach me a little weaving when the shop was quiet and the children were occupied. She would let her hand linger on mine longer than needed, and smile at me, but with a sad tightness around her eyes.

Numa had become distant. We used to chatter the whole way to and from town, but now she looked down at her feet or off toward the mountains or the shops and wells in town, and answered briefly if I spoke to her.

"Are you angry with me for something?" I asked one morning on our way into town.

She stopped and looked at me, the corners of her lips turned down. "It all has to do with you, doesn't it, Leona? Nobody can have problems of their own. It all has to be about Leona."

I felt guilty and asked, "Numa, do you have a problem? I'm sorry. Tell me."

She waved a hand and started walking again, leaving me behind. "Never mind. What do you care?"

I shrugged. It wasn't my fault if she wasn't happy, was it? I had found happiness for myself; it would be just as easy for her; if she wouldn't do it, that wasn't my problem, was it?

And then came the night when I looked out my window at the full white moon and realized that a moon and a half had passed since my last bleeding.

No, that couldn't be right. I frantically tried to remember. The moon had been at half when I last bled, but was it the waning or waxing half? It was waxing, wasn't it? That would be only three weeks, not five. And then I remembered, with a plunging heart, that I had not bled in the whole month since Aurelius and I had been lovers.

A week late, I tried to convince myself, was not proof of anything, but in my heart I knew. I was never late, and I had not been hungry the past few mornings.

I got up and walked outside, dizzy with terror, needing a breath of fresh air. I paced the hard-baked dirt around our hut, meaning to think but instead just revisiting the horror.

I didn't sleep at all that night. Eventually, I stopped pacing our small yard and climbed back into bed beside Numa, but I lay there, rigid, staring straight up at the ceiling, while my blank horror slowly formed itself into well-defined fears: I would grow swollen and grotesque and Aurelius wouldn't want me anymore. I would never find a husband. My family would disown me. I would have to become a beggar or a prostitute. I squeezed my eyes against the tears that ran down my cheeks and into my ears. Finally, a solution began to present itself. There were ways of getting rid of babies, I had heard. But who could help me discover how to do it? My mind kept pushing aside the obvious answer, but by morning I was reconciled to confiding in Miriam, enduring her disappointment, and pleading for her help. She would know where I should go and what I should do, or she would know how to find out.

———••◦••———

I waited all morning for my opportunity and finally, while the children were downstairs fetching our lunch, said, "I have a friend who has a problem."

"Mmm," Miriam responded, not looking at me, frowning over the cloth that had slowly been growing on her loom.

"She's pregnant and not married and needs to know how to" —I hesitated and squirmed—"take care of it."

Miriam glanced at me sharply, then looked away and started turning the crank that scrolled her cloth around the beam. "And how far along does your friend think she is?"

"A month perhaps." I picked up a shuttle and starting winding purple thread on it so I wouldn't have to look at her.

"I see. And does she love the boy?"

"Yes."

"And does he know about the baby yet?"

"No."

"Then it seems to me she should confide in him and get his thoughts on what should be done."

"She's afraid—" I started and felt tears rising. I continued, "She's afraid he won't love her anymore." I lowered my face into my hands and let flow the tears I'd been too numb to shed through the long night.

Miriam left her loom and hugged me. "There, there," she consoled, rubbing my back. "You're not the first or the last girl this has happened to." She sighed, still rubbing my back, "Oh, Leona, I was afraid of this. I suppose your father doesn't know?"

I widened my eyes and shook my head. Was she crazy? My father would be the very last person I would tell.

"Nor Numa?"

"Numa doesn't like me anymore," I confessed through my tears and my fingers.

"And you want to get rid of the child if you can."

I nodded.

She tilted my chin so I was looking at her. "Listen to me. You must tell him first. There are ways to dispose of a child, but they don't always work and they aren't always safe. He may surprise you. Maybe he wants it, Leona. He can't marry you, but maybe he wants the child and will set you up a little household. His family's rich."

"Not as rich as you think. His mother can't afford to send him to school in Carthage. Urbanus is sending him."

"Still. That only proves he has a powerful patron, and that may help you. Tell him, Leona. Promise me this, and if he doesn't want the child, I'll help you get rid of it, may God forgive me."

I nodded.

———••————

Of all days, Aurelius was late to our meeting in the square that day. I stood in the late-afternoon sun, sweating and cranky, and as the hour grew later, a stone of panic began to lodge itself in my throat. Maybe he was already finished with me, child or not.

But finally, I saw him striding into the square from the direction of Urbanus's house. He raised a hand in greeting as he approached. I nearly fainted with relief.

"Wonderful news," he said. "I'm all set for school in Carthage. I leave in three weeks."

"Wonderful," I agreed faintly.

"What's wrong? I thought you'd be happy."

"The heat," I said. "It's just bothering me today."

"We'll get you some wine. Come on."

We walked the blocks to Urbanus's house in silence, and Aurelius had one of the slaves bring me a goblet of watered-down wine. As I sipped, I felt life flowing back into me and gained my courage. I might as well just come out with it.

"I'm with child," I blurted out.

"What? How could that have happened?"

I looked at him.

"I just mean that's terrible. I'm going to Carthage and—well, aren't there ways of stopping it?" He stood and walked a few steps, running a hand through his hair.

Although "stopping it" had been my first thought too, I was angry. "Yes, there are ways of stopping it. But Miriam thought you'd want to know first. She thought you might have another idea."

"Well, what else can we do? I don't see what else we can do." He stepped toward me now, with his hand still worrying his thick hair.

"Of course. You're right. I'm sorry I bothered you with it." I stood and set my wine goblet on the bench where we'd been sitting.

He tried to embrace me. "Come on, Leona, don't be this way. Surely you don't want a child either. And this doesn't have to change things between us, does it?" He put a hand to my cheek and tried to get me to look at him.

I shrugged him off and kept my eyes on the ground. "I'm not feeling well. I have to go now."

"Leona, I'm sorry. I'll pay, if there's a cost to getting rid of it."

I started walking toward the gate.

He kept pace beside me. "Do you want to have the baby? Just tell me. Leona, don't be this way."

I opened the garden gate, shrugged off his restraining arm, and passed through, back into the hot street, into my old, dusty world, not looking back.

---

I expected an evil-looking old crone and was surprised when Miriam's midwife was young and pretty, with three small children of her own playing in the room.

She asked about my last bleeding, gently felt my belly, examined my eyes and teeth, then leaned forward in her chair and said, "Are you sure you don't want this child?"

I nodded, lips pressed together.

"There are ways to abort a pregnancy that are almost certain to work, but they're dangerous. If you want to try one of them, find another midwife. What I'm going to give you won't hurt you, but it doesn't always work. You understand this?"

I nodded again, tempted to try the other midwife with the method that always worked but afraid to die.

"All right, then," she said, and took some pots off a shelf.

---

I spent another sleepless night, the air thick and still. I made a tisane of one bag of the midwife's herbs late in the afternoon and drank the bitter mixture. At night, while the rest of the house slept, I created another infusion by steeping the other bag of herbs in water. In this, I soaked a rag, which the midwife had instructed me to wring out and then wad into a pessary to place inside myself. I tiptoed outside to do this, but when I was finished, I turned and saw Numa standing in the doorway watching me, arms folded.

"So you got yourself in trouble, just like I said you would," she whispered, "and now you're trying to get rid of it."

"No, I just have cramps," I lied.

Numa rolled her eyes and curled her lip, expelling a disgusted breath. She was quiet a moment, then asked, "Need any help?"

I shook my head. Then I changed my mind. "I'm about done with this. Now I have to walk for an hour. You could walk with me."

I emptied the whey bucket I'd used to steep the rag, and we began to walk around the house.

"How long did you say you had to walk?" Numa asked me.

"An hour she said."

"Walk two hours."

"How do you know so much about this?"

Numa shrugged. "That Ariana at the shop. I told you she'd get herself into trouble. She took the medicine twice before it worked." Numa held two fingers in front of my face. "Almost killed her too. She bled so bad I swore she turned as white as a Roman." She grinned at me. Then she frowned. "Don't try this again. If it doesn't work, it wasn't meant to."

"It has to work," I insisted. "Talk to me about something else while we walk."

She looked down for a few seconds as we walked, and then she said, "Father's found me a husband."

I stopped and grasped her shoulder. "Numa! You didn't tell me!"

She shrugged again. "You've been a little preoccupied—and I was mad at you for carrying on with that boy, maybe a little jealous."

"Well, who is it? Is it anyone we know?"

"No, he lives in Hippo. His uncle is Corvinus, who owns the tavern."

"Have you seen him?"

She nodded. "I didn't like him at first. He's not beautiful to look at, Leona, not beautiful at all. He was burned by lye on the side of his face as a small child and he's wrinkled as a date on that side—brown as a date too," she added. "But I think he's kind. He makes me laugh, and he brought me a little gift when he came the second time: some flowers. Imagine, Leona, as if I were a lady."

"He's from Hippo? Will you have to go live there?"

Numa nodded. "He and his father work in the shipbuilding yards there. He says men with shipbuilding skills make a fine living in the sea towns, even if they are plebs and don't own property. Leona, I'll see the sea every day. I can't imagine what so much water must look like. He says the sea washes to the shore in great waves and then washes back out. I can't even picture it."

I remembered the mosaics in Urbanus's dining room. What a foolish girl I'd been, giving away my virtue for a few pompous words and a glimpse of a picture of the sea. Numa, no prettier than I was, had been wiser, and won the sight of the sea itself. I tried not to be jealous, but a hard lump of regret filled my throat. "I'm happy for you."

"I wasn't happy at first," she admitted. "I was afraid until I met him. And then the first time we met, I didn't like his looks at all. I wouldn't talk to him and I cried after he left. But I think he understood, and he tried hard to charm me on our second meeting. And I came to see his goodness. I think I'll be happy," she finished.

We kept walking. "Well, I'll be happy for you then," I repeated, but I was lying. As much as I loved Numa, I didn't want her to be happy while I was miserable, and I thought then about her leaving. I would be alone to face Father's wrath and to wait on him and Tito for the rest of my bleak life.

The night was pretty, with a little eyelash of moon and a smell of lilies. We walked carefully in the dark, the grass cool and damp under our feet.

"So," she asked, "your boy. . . he knows about the baby?"

"He knows."

"And what did he say?"

"He said get rid of it and that's what I'm doing." I lifted my chin and marched a little harder.

Numa nodded. "For the best, since he can't marry you. Now you're free to find a good man to marry—like I did," she added, her face lighting up. "Leona, you're prettier than I am, and look, I found a good man. Think how well you might do." She hesitated. "So, this boy? He's in the past for you?"

"Yes," I gritted through my teeth. I had gone to the midwife with Miriam after work that day instead of meeting Aurelius as usual, avoiding any thought about what might happen tomorrow and the next day and the next. But now, talking to Numa, I felt my decision was made. I would get rid of the baby and I would get on with my life: forget about Romanized men with their reading and their fine food and their ways of using common women, and find myself a good, plain husband with olive trees and a herd of goats. It occurred to me that Aurelius had gotten what his friend Marcus had been ready to take by force that first evening, and I had given it away for free. He'd just been more subtle than his friend about how he went about gaining it. I blushed to remember, and my heart stiffened with renewed fury and determination. "Yes," I repeated. "He is in the past."

We kept walking. We walked one hour, two, more than two, until the glowing ripe peach of the sun reddened the sky in the east. And still I didn't bleed. The child lived.

# CHAPTER SEVEN

HE WAS WAITING for me outside Miriam's shop when I turned into the alley the next morning. I ignored my heart's leap, and refused to make eye contact with him as I approached.

He was leaning on the building, looking this way and then that. "Where were you yesterday?" he asked without preamble when I reached the door to the shop.

I still refused to meet his eyes. "Trying to get rid of your baby, just as you asked," I hissed.

"Well?"

"Well, I'm sorry to tell you it didn't work—and, yes, I'm okay, thanks for asking."

"Are you okay?"

"I just said I was."

"You'll meet me today, right? In the square like always?"

I was still angry with him. I longed to tell him to go sell himself at a slave market, but I carried his child. I hated myself for it, but I also carried a small hope for something from him; I didn't know what. Still not looking at him, I agreed to meet him that afternoon at our usual place, and then I went upstairs.

He was waiting for me in the long shadow of the well, all concern. "How are you feeling?" he murmured.

Working hard to keep my heart from softening, I shrugged.

He cupped his hand under my elbow, steering me onto the road to Urbanus's town house. "I spoke with Urbanus this morning. He wants to talk to us together this afternoon. He may be willing to set up a household for me in Carthage."

I stopped walking and finally met his eyes. "What do you mean?"

"I mean a small house and a servant. So you and the baby could join me."

Against my will, hope began to blossom in my heart. What if it actually happened? I imagined myself and Aurelius, and our child in a house in the city of Carthage, with its markets and theaters far beyond anything we knew in Thagaste. I imagined having a servant put a meal in front of us every evening, dining at leisure in our cool, marble-tiled house, practicing our grammar and rhetoric while our child played.

Although the evening was cool, I was flushed and sweating by the time Urbanus's door slave let us in and led us to the sitting room, grateful for the watered-down wine that another slave poured for us.

Urbanus soon joined us, stretching himself out on the couch opposite us and motioning wordlessly for a goblet of wine.

"So you find yourself in a predicament," he said.

Surprised by his bluntness, I nodded, looking down.

"Have you considered getting rid of it?"

I looked up. "I already tried. It didn't work."

Urbanus nodded, frowning. "Well," he continued, "I have high hopes for your young man. I think you know that. At risk of swelling his head so it won't fit through the doorway and he'll be stuck in this room forever,

I will tell you that he is brilliant. I have extracted from him a promise to come back to Thagaste and teach, in return for my financing his further education in Carthage. I would like to see our town turn into a great center of learning and rhetoric. Not only that, but I need a rhetoritician to argue my cases with the government. And lastly"—he grinned—"I just enjoy the company of intelligent young men." He swung himself around to a sitting position and leaned toward me. "And here you sit: beautiful, intelligent for a woman from what I can see, and the daughter of a pleb and sister of an executed rebel. Yet, he is determined to have you, and I can't say I blame him. Further, there is a child. What to do?" He pretended to ponder, although I suspected he had already reached a decision. Finally, he sighed and rose to his feet. From my studies with Aurelius, I recognized in Urbanus something of the rhetoritician, his pauses and movements those of a professional who knew how to keep his audience's attention. "I can only see one solution," he said. "In order to protect the investment I've already made and guarantee the success of my plan, I see I must add to the pot. I am prepared, Aurelius Augustine, to finance a household for you and your beloved and child in Carthage."

Aurelius bowed his head. "Thank you, sir. I won't let you down."

"Thank you, sir," I murmured. "When shall we be married?"

"Married?" Urbanus's hand froze on its way to his lips with the wine goblet, and the word seemed to echo from every wall of the room, looking for a home. "Oh, no," he said, "you misunderstood. You must surely know it's impossible for young Aurelius to marry you."

I tingled with shame and could not look up at him, willing the tears to stay behind my cheeks.

Urbanus continued, "I thought you understood. You must think of his future, Leona. Not only would marriage to a pleb force him to forfeit his inheritance but it would also destroy his political prospects. Frankly, he'll advance only insofar as he's seen as eligible to eventually combine his fortunes with some other family's. And my investment is only good insofar as he advances. But, don't worry: he doesn't need to marry for years yet. In fact, he might do better by dangling the bait as long as he can. And a mistress and children are no impediment to that, believe me. This sort of thing happens all the time."

He shrugged and waved a hand and, with those gestures, effected an utter change in the way I saw my situation. How foolish I had been, to think the love that Aurelius and I shared was something uniquely beautiful. How foolish I had been, even in my fear and panic, when I found myself with child, as if this were a catastrophe unique to me. Urbanus was right: "this sort of thing" had been enacted on many, many stages before, with the stock characters of the randy nobleman looking for a little fun and the pretty peasant girl who is flattered by his attention and believes herself to be different from all the pretty peasant girls who had crossed the stage before her.

I looked down at my hands, two separate thoughts at war in my mind. *Welcome to the world of the Romans*, one of them sneered, *you're being offered not love, but a business proposition. And you're in no position to turn it down.* At the same time, I felt a tingle of victory. The door was opened to a way out: no more waiting on my father and Tito, no more terror of being married off to some brute with a scarred face, like Numa. I could go and live in a big city with Aurelius and our child and eventually, perhaps, figure out a way to convince him to marry me after all. I took a deep breath, inhaling the tears that had threatened.

Aurelius had said nothing throughout the conversation. I tossed my head as I raised it to look at him. "Do you agree to this?"

He stammered, "I—really, it's the best thing for us, Leona. I mean —it keeps us together, right? And what's marriage really? It's nothing. It's business. It's you I love."

I looked at Urbanus. "Thank you, sir," I repeated. "You're generous."

He narrowed his eyes and nodded. "Not generous. I expect a return from this young man. Now, come, let's seal the deal with a good dinner." He extended his arm, motioning us to precede him into the dining room.

I didn't think to ask, at the time, what would become of me when Aurelius did finally find a suitable wife. I didn't think to ask what would become of our child should he marry. And I didn't think, yet, to wonder how his family might react.

# CHAPTER EIGHT

I COULDN'T FACE my father. I made Numa promise that she'd explain after I was gone. With Miriam, I was distant, though it pained me. I longed to tell her my plans, but didn't want to tell my secret to yet another person I loved, forcing her to choose between loyalty to me and a duty to inform my father—because I knew she would want to know if one of her children was in any kind of trouble.

Over the next two weeks, I'd catch her gazing at me with her head tilted as if trying to figure out what I could be up to.

I deflected her questions by claiming I still didn't know what to do, and no, I hadn't told my father yet. To her offers of help, I said simply, "No, thanks," avoiding her eyes.

One day she took me by the shoulders, gazed into my eyes with her hazel ones, and said, "Leona, at least promise me this: that you will not go to a disreputable abortionist. Remember what Ruth said about the surer methods also bringing surer death. Promise me."

"I promise. I remember what she said. I don't want to die." That part, at least, was true. I had put out of my mind all of my worries over being the mother of a bastard, the mistress of a Romanized aristocrat, and was heedlessly in love all over again, eager to begin my life in Carthage with Aurelius. I felt sure I could eventually bind him to me permanently.

Life felt sweet again, and I felt sweet and full, as if honey flowed in my veins.

Little rain had fallen since the day of the governor's visit. One especially dusty afternoon, a slave plodded barefoot up the stairs to our shop and bowed to me. "Are you Leona?" he wanted to know.

"Yes."

"You're requested to come with me to attend to Monnica, widow of the deucile Patricius Augustinus. You're to come right away. A carriage waits for you downstairs."

Miriam, having overhead from the back room, drifted into the sales room. "You should go," she said gravely, "it's almost closing time anyway."

Heart pounding against my ribs, I followed the slave down to the street, where another slave guarded a sedan chair. The first slave helped me into it, and then the two of them picked it up and began running down the street with it, bare feet slapping up little clouds of dust. I had never before ridden in any kind of carriage. I felt off-balance in the swaying chair, and out of control behind its curtains, unable to see where we were going. But the ride had about it, too, a sly air of luxury, as if I were getting away with something. It occurred to me that I might be riding around in carriages a lot more in the future, and that it would be a lovely thing to get used to. Why settle for the Romans' reading only, when their wealth provided so many other good things?

When we arrived at Monnica's house, the slaves set the chair down gently and helped me out. The slave who had come into the shop led me to the lady's sitting room and showed me to a chair.

I looked around while waiting for Monnica. Her home was much less luxurious than Urbanus's. The floor tiles were large and made of simple red clay, rather than the ornate mosaic of Urbanus's dining room, and the walls were plain white plaster. But the chair I sat on had legs of bronze, in an ornate lion's-paw fashion, and a cushion of green embroidered with a pattern in white and gold. On one wall hung the cross that the Christians took as the symbol of their crucified god.

Monnica entered the room with such quiet grace that I didn't realize I was no longer alone until she spoke.

"Your ride here was comfortable?" she asked.

I nearly jumped out of my chair, I was so startled. I readjusted my tunic, composing myself a little before I had to look at her. "Yes, thank you."

"May I offer you some wine?"

Although I was parched, I felt uneasy accepting anything from her. "No, thank you." I finished my clothing adjustments, and slowly dared to glance at her as she settled herself on the couch across from me.

She picked up a piece of embroidery and started pricking it with a needle, frowning. She made a couple of quick stitches and then looked up at me. She compressed her lips slightly, as if sizing me up, and then she spoke. "My son tells me you are with child."

I flushed. I had assumed that, like me, Aurelius would keep our secret from his parent. "Yes, ma'am," I admitted.

"His child?" She gazed at me intently, as if her eyes could pierce my heart and read in it truth or falsehood.

"Yes, ma'am," I repeated, meeting her gaze. "It couldn't possibly be anyone else's."

She held my gaze a few more seconds and then nodded. "And Urbanus has offered you a household," she stated, and I sensed behind her carefully neutral phrasing the discipline it took to conceal her rage and frustration.

I nodded. Although I longed to rearrange my tunic again, I willed myself to stillness.

Monnica frowned down at her embroidery. I could see that she was stitching a scene of lambs and flowers. "Is that the life you dreamed of for yourself?" she asked me.

It was not the question I expected. "I'm not sure what you mean."

She set down her work and spread her hands. "Well, is this all you want out of life: a few months or years as concubine to a man above your station, and one or two children who you will have to hand over to him or to the Church when he tires of you?"

I felt the blood drain from my face, and knew I must look as startled as I felt. "What—what do you mean?"

"Aurelius Augustine is called to the Church," Monnica said firmly. "I've felt it since he was born. He doesn't see it yet, but he's young and" —she gestured toward my still-flat belly—"full of lust. He'll hear the call eventually, and if he hasn't tired of you before that, he will dismiss you then. Your child—or children? They, too, will be given to the Church, or to his brother and his wife to raise. This is what you want then?"

No response formed in my brain, only incoherent panic.

"There are other choices. You're a pretty girl; my family could help your father find a very suitable husband for you, who could raise your child as his own. We could quietly see to it that the child—and your whole family—never suffered any want, and we could use our influence to find a good match or a place in the Church for the child when he reached adulthood. He would have many of the same advantages he'd have as Aurelius's acknowledged bastard, with the advantage to you of keeping him by your side as he grows." Monnica picked up her embroidery again, smoothing it with her hand as if to soothe herself.

I was still speechless, trying to digest the possibility that I could be sent away without the child at some point. I had forgotten that I'd tried to abort it only two weeks ago. My child felt real to me now that I had imagined a future with him.

"Or perhaps you're not ready to be a mother at all?" Monnica continued. "You could enter the Church if you like. I know you're not a Christian, but there are communities that take any chaste woman as a catechumen. We could help you with that if you prefer." She paused. "We want to do what's right for you, of course, and the child, and for my son's future."

"I love him," I blurted out. I lowered my head and dug my fingernails into my palms, willing myself not to cry.

"Then you would surely want what's best for him," Monnica replied sharply.

I lifted my chin. "I think he should decide what's best for him."

She frowned, and waved a hand. "He doesn't know what's best for him. He's seventeen. He's blinded by lust. He is meant for the Church," she repeated, leaning forward, her eyes fierce.

"He's not even a Christian," I argued. "How can he be meant to serve a Church he doesn't even belong to?"

"He's been enrolled as a catechumen since birth. I pray on it every day. He's young yet. He's intoxicated now with the pagan philosophers, just as he's intoxicated with your body. But surely even you can see how brilliant he is. I refuse to believe that our Lord would have blessed him with such a mind unless it were for his own use."

"I love him," I repeated, hating how plaintive and childish I sounded, but having no better argument against the great lady and her God.

She stood and waved her hand again. "The kind of love you feel, that corrupt, physical kind of love? It fades very quickly, believe me. The love of the Lord endures forever. Consider joining a Christian community of chaste women. If you love my son, save his soul and your own." She approached me and spoke softly.

I saw that she sensed my vulnerability and hoped to take advantage of it, and that snapped my stubbornness back into place. I saw myself and Aurelius in a little house in Carthage, our baby playing at our feet, books and wine and olives on a table, honeyed evening sun flowing in through a window.

I saw the sea and felt its breezes. I would not give that up for something so abstract as a Christian's idea of a soul.

"I love him, and we want to make a life together in Carthage. I'll be a good mother to his child and a good"—I almost said *wife*—"a good partner. You are welcome in our home any time, lady, but I will not give him up unless he himself sends me away."

Monnica sighed and rubbed her forehead. "I already tried that. It seems our friend Urbanus has made an offer more attractive than our Lord's promise of eternal life." She sighed again and looked into my eyes. "He will tire of you, and you will lose your child. You must realize this."

I shrugged. I didn't believe her.

Monnica sighed one more time. "You have my word that the child will be well cared for regardless. Do one thing for me."

I remained silent, but raised my eyebrows and cocked my head to hear her request.

"If it is a boy, name him Tedeodonatus: 'given to God.'"

"We will consider that, lady," I replied, bowing my head to hide my little smile of triumph.

———•••———

I finally confessed my plans to Miriam the day before we were to go, and she and Numa both came to see me off on a cool fall morning with wisps of fog tangled in the olive trees outside town. I was leaving Thagaste with the clothes on my back, my single change of clothing, and the few coins from last week's pay that I had not turned over to our father.

Numa hugged me, and I felt her tears on my shoulder. "I'll never see you again," she mourned.

"I know." I felt a lump rise in my own throat. "Have a good life with your husband by the sea."

She peeled herself away from me reluctantly, and it was Miriam's turn to embrace me. "I got you this," she said, lifting a thong from around her neck and placing it around mine.

I lifted the amulet that hung from the leather thong. It was a Christian cross, but unusual in design, the arms of the cross carved to look like twisting grape vines.

"I got myself the same one," she explained, showing me. "You're my sister in Christ, even if you're not a believer yet, and I'll pray for you every day."

Now I started to cry, and I nodded and hugged her again. "Go with God," she whispered.

"Have a good life," my sister called to me, I headed through the forum to Urbanus's house, where horses waited to take us to Carthage.

# CHAPTER NINE

THAGASTE WAS more than a little goat town or trading post. We had a small garrison of legionnaires, brick grain warehouses, an amphitheater, temples to every known god, and, of course, local gentry in the form of Urbanus. But Thagaste was nothing compared to Carthage.

The city began well outside the pocked yellow walls. Here, dusty paths fanned away from the cobbled road, zigzagging between huts, tents, and small shops. Our horses and donkeys had to pick their way down the road, nearly tramping many times on wandering sheep, goats, pigs or their leavings, or on the thin brown children who darted around after them. Nobody did more than glance up at us, except for the ones who wanted to sell us spices or hair ribbons or jugs of water or sticks of garlic-smelling goat meat. The smell of the meat made me nauseous. I would have gladly paid all the coins I had for one of the sweating clay jugs of water, but our driver led us resolutely forward to the city gate.

We were delayed for a long, thirsty hour at the massive gate as each entrant paid their gate tax, and then we were in Carthage. My eyes took in the mellow shades of the setting sun reflected on the white stone: purple, pink, amber as rich as honey. Lined with palm trees, the Cardo Maximus ran wide and straight through the center of town, to a town square with a fountain, ten times the size of Urbanus's, surrounded by date palms.

Despite its width, the street was crowded. The people were more varied than the ones I knew in Thagaste. There were the Arabs and Berbers and the occasional Aeithiope as dark as a date, the same as home, but I had never before seen a person with yellow hair.

I turned and stared as two blond giants crossed the street in front of us, and Aurelius explained that they were probably Gauls or Saxons from the cold lands north of Rome, and many of them had yellow hair and white or ruddy skin—and often blue eyes as pale as the morning sky. To call someone a "stupid Gaul" was a commonplace insult in our part of the world, but I had never before seen one. I couldn't tell from their looks if they were really stupid, but they looked brutish and sinister to me, so large and pale.

The smells were different from home too. First, the smell of filth was stronger from the sheer volume of humans, animals, and their garbage. But rising above the odors of waste and cooking meat were sweeter and spicier aromas that I didn't recognize, smells I would later learn the names of and associate forever with Carthage: cinnamon and clove from the Indies, lavender from Gaul, lilies from Judea. And there was the fishy, salty odor I had yet to identify as the smell of the sea.

---

Our driver delivered Aurelius and me, and our small luggage, to the address Urbanus had given him, an apartment building owned by a distant cousin near the center of the city. We'd taken so many turns to get there that I couldn't imagine ever again finding our way to the university, the well, the city wall or anything else I'd seen. A slave girl with a mutilated face showed us to our apartment and brought us water for drinking and washing. Never had a sight been so welcome. I gulped water from the smaller jug and then happily washed from the larger.

As soon as we were clean, Aurelius wanted to go out and find something to eat and see more of the city.

"Give me a minute to rest," I replied irritably. At home, I was used to sleeping on a pallet stuffed with goat hair on the floor. Here, a bed of carved olive wood dominated the small bedchamber. I sat down on the pallet that covered the bed.

"This is so soft." I sighed and folded myself into a lying position. "What kind of goat gives fur so soft?"

Aurelius sat beside me and patted the bed with one hand. "It's not goat hair. It's probably sheep's wool." He bent to sniff. "And it stinks. We need a slave to find a place to air this."

I waved him away. "Not yet," I murmured and was instantly asleep.

———•••———

I must have slept only an hour or so, for when I woke it was still light, though barely. Pools of purple shadows spread in every corner of the apartment. I was starving. I sat up, shook my head, and got up to find Aurelius.

I found him in the front room, frowning over one of his books. He looked up when I wandered into the room. "Oh, there you are. I was about to give up on you and go out on my own to find us supper. But I thought you'd like to go with me and see some of the city."

Now that I'd rested, I once again felt excited to be in Carthage, and the idea of walking around the maze of the city seemed less daunting. "Let me just rinse my face," I replied.

The ugly slave girl had given Aurelius directions to a booth where we could get bread and meat and olives and fruit until after dark. Left, then left, then right, she'd said, but at the second left we hesitated. Did an alley count as the next left, or did she mean left at the next street?

As we stood trying to puzzle it out, two young men about our age approached. "Lost?" one of them asked politely.

"Well, yes, we are," Aurelius admitted, "we're looking for a booth where we can get something to eat. We were told—"

"Oh, you don't want to bother with a booth. You want someplace where you can sit down and have a little wine too. You new in town?"

Aurelius nodded and the two boys began walking, one on each side of us, as if we were old friends, steering us through zigzagging alleys. "I'm Quintus and this is Nebridius. You're welcome to come with us."

I would rather have just found the booth, but Aurelius didn't consult me before agreeing. "Sounds good. I'm Aurelius and this is my—this is Leona."

Quintus and Nebridius guided us into a tavern and we took an outdoor table. "So, where are you from?" Nebridius asked.

"Thagaste," Aurelius replied. "I've come to study rhetoric."

I thought I noticed an amused glance pass between Quintus and Nebridius. "Studying under Claudius and Titus, are you?" Nebridius wanted to know.

"Yes, I hope to."

"Well, us too!" Nebridius crowed, and he and Quintus clapped Aurelius on the back heartily, as if inducting him into some secret society. They seemed to me just a little too gleeful about this, as if they knew something he didn't, but they were scholars and wore embroidered tunics, and they were Carthaginians. I kept quiet.

Nebridius and Quintus ordered several plates of fish and shellfish and bread and olives for us to share, along with a flagon of wine and a bowl of fruit.

"So," Nebridius challenged, "favorite philosopher? Don't think. Just answer."

"Cicero, I suppose," Aurelius answered.

Quintus was already popping ripe olives into his mouth. "He's not a philosopher," he scoffed through a mouthful of olive. "Cicero was just a politician, and an old-school one at that. The Roman Republic is not only dead; it never really lived in the idealized way Cicero envisioned it. Come on, a real philosopher."

"I don't know. I suppose Zeno? I like the Stoics, but I really like the Ascetics best of all."

"Oh, absolutely, absolutely," Nebridius agreed. Watching him dig into the shellfish and olives, I mentally questioned any commitment to Asceticisim. Some of the foods were unfamiliar to me, even having eaten at Urbanus's table. There were hard, ear-shaped shells which I watched Nebridius and Quintus pick up with their hands. They then used picks to extract a pale, slime-covered scrap of meat, which they drowned in garum sauce and then swallowed without chewing. Our hosts consumed these one after another, tossing the empty shells to the ground. Although the sight of the nubs of meat made me nauseous, I longed to try it, just to see what it was like; and yet, I would have rather died than make a fool of myself by failing to extract the morsel or by choking on it. I stuck to the familiar fruit and olives and bread dipped in oil.

The three men continued their discussions of philosophy until well after dark, and I began to worry that we'd never find our way back to our apartment. We'd finished several flagons of wine by the time Quintus and Nebridius excused themselves to duck into the alley behind the tavern and relieve themselves.

"Can we go home soon?" I pleaded once they were gone. "I'm tired."

"Oh!" Aurelius replied, as if suddenly remembering I was there. "Oh, sure. As soon as they come back, we can settle up the bill."

"Do you remember how to get back to our apartment?"

"I think so." He hesitated. "Well, anyway, Quintus and Nebridius can direct us if we're not sure."

The tavern was lit with oil lamps, and only a few patrons remained. Aurelius and I sat in exhausted, sated silence for a while. Finally, I said, "Should you go look for them?"

"I guess I'd better," Aurelius agreed, and rose slowly, as if his body were a heavy weight he had to drag. He reeled a little when he stood. "Whoa," he whispered, and steadied himself.

Aurelius was gone for several minutes, and when he returned, I saw him in an animated conversation with the taverner. An uneasy feeling grew in my chest.

He steamed back over to me, flushed with too much wine. "I can't believe it. I can't believe they just left. And that guy says I have to pay for everything. Do you know what it comes to?"

I shook my head, too tired to care.

"Well"—he hesitated and then thought better of telling me the exact amount—"well, a lot." He stopped for a minute, frowning off into the distance, his hand fiddling in the purse attached to his waist, as if he were counting his coins by touch. "I guess we have to pay it."

"Let's just pay and go," I pleaded.

Aurelius settled with the tavern owner, for what looked to me like a sickening number of coins, and we walked back out into the night. It was not as black as a night in Thagaste, where any public shop closed at sunset. Here and there in this port city, shops were still open, with rush lights illuminating their entrances. Oil lamps glowed dimly from the windows of other houses and shops.

"Which way?" I asked.

Aurelius looked to both sides.

"Well, which way did we come from?"

"I don't remember. Don't you?"

"Not really."

"Well, how are we going to get home?" My voice rose.

I was so tired after the long trip, the wine, the heavy meal. I wanted to just sit down in the street and cry—or lie down and sleep right there, and wait until morning to find our home.

"This way," Aurelius said firmly, and we headed to the left. Soon the street headed steeply downhill and we could faintly hear the night sounds of the harbor: the creaking of ships and the slap of water against their hulls.

"No, this must not be right," he admitted. "All right, then, we know it must be the other way."

Near tears, I forced my legs to keep plodding on, back up the hill. "You should have kept track of where they were taking us," I said.

"You could have too, you know," he shot back.

"You're the one who wanted to go with them." We passed another tavern, smelling of wine and vomit. Someone was singing in a language I didn't recognize, not Berber or Latin.

"What do you mean? I didn't hear you objecting. I didn't hear you say anything all evening. You just sat there and pouted."

"I'm tired. I was riding a stinking horse for days and days. And I'm not some big scholar like you. I just wanted to get something to eat and go home and sleep."

"Well, you should have said something." We had reached another corner and he was frowning, looking both ways again.

I pointed. "There. I remember we passed that building with the bell tower. That way." I couldn't help adding, "I guess I'm good for something, even without reading Cicero and Zeno."

"What are you saying? Are you saying I'm not good for anything?"

"I'm not saying anything." I folded my arms.

"No, what are you trying to say?"

"Well, your book learning didn't keep you from being taken in by those boys, did it?"

I could see that my arrow had hit its mark. He flinched and didn't respond, marching doggedly ahead of me in the direction he thought would take us home.

"Do you even know the name of our building?" I called out from behind him.

To my satisfaction, he froze in his steps. I smiled and stood in the middle of the street with my arms folded. "Don't you think it's a good idea to know the name of the house we're looking for?" I called.

He turned. "I suppose you know?"

"So, an uneducated girl, who just sits around and pouts while scholars talk, is actually good for something."

"Leona, quit playing games."

"It's the House of Apollo. And, anyway, I know which way to go now. I can see our building from here." I pointed.

He followed my finger. "How can you tell?"

"I remember the sun carving at the peak of the roof."

"Come on," he said. "I'm sorry. Let's go home and get you to bed." He tried to put an arm around my waist but I shrugged him off and walked a little ahead of him the rest of the way home through the salt-smelling Carthaginian night.

# CHAPTER TEN

EVERYTHING FELT different after a night's sleep. A breeze tickled us awake in the early morning, and Aurelius went out and bought us breakfast: bread, dates and a fruit I'd never had before that he told me was an apple from Gaul. It had a thin, tough, rosy skin and a crunchy white inside, which was tart at first and then released sweet juices upon chewing. It pleased me so much and I felt so rested that when he fitted his hand around my swelling breast and teased at my ear with his tongue, I didn't resist and we made love in Carthage for the first time, lying afterward skimmed with sweat and filled with the sweetness. The previous night's quarrel and the miserable trip from Thagaste were forgotten. We decided to go and look for the seashore.

The sun-faded houses and shops along our street looked like steps descending the Byrsa hill as it wound its way down to the shore. We walked hand in hand in the morning sun, looking around us as Carthage wakened and began its bustle.

Aurelius pointed. "Look, there's the aqueduct."

From our vantage point near the top of the hill, we could see the aqueduct snaking through the city to provide water to the baths and public fountains. It looked like a high wall pierced with multiple arches.

"It's twenty-three miles long," Aurelius boasted, as if he'd built it himself. "It brings water all the way from the Atlas Mountains."

Slaves in short tunics hurried past us bearing burdens: baskets of fruit, bolts of cloth, a brace of complaining chickens. Carts clattered by carrying clay amphorae of wine and oil. Here and there, fishwives set up their stalls along the crowded street and called gossip to one another, while their barefoot children chased one another around their skirts.

I couldn't help staring at the matrons starting their morning shopping, slaves walking behind to carry their purchases. Nearly all of them wore red lip paste and elaborately twisted and coiled hairstyles. Their faces were coated so heavily with white paste that to me they looked like corpses. On the older women, the paste melted and sank into the folds of their skin. I nudged Aurelius and nodded to one of them. "What's wrong with them?" I whispered.

"Oh, that's the Roman fashion. All of the Roman women paint their faces so their skin looks younger and smoother."

We turned a corner and suddenly we saw the harbor, with its jutting piers of stone and graying wood, the ships rocking in their moorings, and men of all colors swarming over the ships and docks, loading and unloading treasures from every port in the Mediterranean. And beyond the bustle rolled the Middle Sea itself, dark blue, alive with rows of foam ruffling to shore one after another like a relentless army. We stood and stared for several minutes, both of us speechless. Sea met horizon in a crisp line dividing sapphire blue from the softer, cloud-strewn blue of the autumn sky. Gulls and pelicans soared and wheeled above the waves, warning each other in harsh tones.

"Let's see if we can get closer to it," Aurelius said. We zigzagged through more narrow streets and down a flight of stone steps and found a narrow beach, away from the harbor, strewn with gray boulders and the cracked and ground shells of sea creatures.

"The Middle Sea," Aurelius announced with a dramatic hand gesture.

I laughed. I thought I had never seen anything so magnificent. The waves roared softly when they approached the shore, and then hissed on retreat, leaving behind a sparkling mist that smelled of salt and fish and clean autumn air. Yellow shards of sunlight skipped on the dark blue surface.

I took off my sandals and ventured into the sea a little way, liking how the waves lapped and pulled at my ankles. I wished I knew how to swim, so I could throw myself into the waves and glide through them like a fish. Instead, I just raised my arms to the sky and laughed again. To entertain and outdo me, Aurelius ran into the sea up to his waist, and was instantly knocked down by a wave. When I laughed, he dragged me in, and we both emerged soaked and coated with salt. He drew me to him and we kissed with salt water running down our faces.

We played like this for almost an hour, running in and out of the water, chasing the waves and letting them chase us back, getting bolder and learning to let the breakers lift us, liking the weightless, bobbing feeling.

Finally, exhausted, we emerged and collapsed on the sand. I lay on my back, looking up at the sky, thinking I had never been so happy in my life.

Aurelius raised himself on one elbow to look down at me. "So, how do you like Carthage so far?" he asked, smiling.

"I love it!"

He lay back down and spread his arms. "This is the start of our real lives, Leona. I just feel that this is the right place for me." He stood again and raised his arms. "I love this!" he shouted.

I was content to be still. Aurelius started pacing in front of me. "I feel already like I belong here," he said. "This is the place where I will find truth; I feel it. Like, what makes these waves in the sea?"

"The wind, of course."

"But what makes the wind, see?"

"The gods, I guess." A prickle of annoyance disturbed my contentment. Why did he have to wonder about things that nobody could understand?

"The gods are superstitions," he said, waving a hand. "I want to know the real reason." He sat beside me again and sighed. "I feel today like it will all really happen. I'll discover things and be a great teacher who shares them with my students." He looked down at me. "And then come home to the prettiest girl in Carthage."

"Always?"

"Always," he agreed, and I believed that it might happen.

"And our baby."

He blinked. "And our baby, of course."

He bent to kiss me. His lips tasted of salt. I ran my hands through his wet curls and over his warm, drying shoulders. He took my face in his hands and I felt his long fingers press gently into my scalp. Then he picked me up and carried me behind a boulder, where we made love by the sea on our first day in Carthage.

# CHAPTER ELEVEN

TWO DAYS LATER, Aurelius began his classes. I was restless and lonely in our apartment all day, and as the afternoon advanced I started looking out the window every five minutes, watching for him. I went out to a stall and bought some peaches and roasted goat meat and a bread-and-cucumber salad for our supper, and still he didn't arrive. I was scrolling through one of his books when he finally came up the stairs and into our apartment. I leapt to my feet. "Well? How was it?"

"Everything I could have dreamed," he enthused. "I have so much to tell you, I hardly know where to begin."

I uncovered our supper, and he dove into both his meal and his story, talking with his mouth full as the words tumbled out. "This is the kind of place I've always wanted to be," he expounded, "with people who *think*. There's one fellow in my recitation who comes all the way from Hibernia, if you can imagine that, and yet speaks perfect Latin and orates like Cicero. I found Amicus."

Aurelius's friend Amicus, the same one who had spoken up for Numa and me that day in the pear orchard, had preceded us to Carthage by three weeks. He, too, was studying rhetoric and philosophy.

"Oh!" Aurelius added. "And I met up with our friends again!"

"What friends?" I didn't know we had any other friends in Carthage. I closed my eyes as I bit into my second peach, letting the juice run down my chin and between my fingers.

"You know. Nebridius and Quintus."

I could feel the blood rising to my face at the mention of their names. "Our friends? When did they become our friends?"

He waved his hand, then swallowed and wiped his mouth. "It was all in good fun."

"Did you get our money back?"

"No. Don't worry about it."

"They cheated us!"

"It's just something they do. You might not understand. I've already learned so much, just this first day. See, Cicero only talks about how people should interact with each other in the political arena, but real philosophers talk about why people are the way they are. Did you ever wonder about that?"

"The only thing I wonder is when we're getting our money back." I stood and started clearing the table.

"Think about God, Leona. See, if God is completely good he couldn't make anything evil, right?"

I was still thinking about this, but he went on. "Okay, so, where do our wrong actions come from then? They come from something separate, a separate substance if you will, which lives inside us, and over which we have no control. So, it isn't really Nebridius or Quintus—or Aurelius or Leona, for that matter—who cheats or fornicates or steals; it's the badness within."

"Then anybody can do anything and it's not their fault." I tossed the cheap clay takeout containers out the back window into the midden pile, and started stacking our own dishes for washing.

"I knew you wouldn't understand at first," he said. "I'll be able to explain it as I learn more about it. We're all going to a hearing tonight."

I shook my head. "A hearing?"

"See, the Christians have it wrong. The real Trinity isn't Father, Son, and Holy Spirit, the way my mother would have it. The Manichees have the Trinity as Father, Son, and Mani, and Mani speaks through their elect, and you can go and hear him."

"Uh-huh. And it costs how much to hear him?" I thought I was beginning to understand all too well.

"It isn't like that," he argued. "Hearers give what they can."

"Uh-huh," I repeated.

"Women can be hearers. It's very democratic. You can come if you want."

I didn't want to at all, but I was lonely, so if he was going, I was going.

———•••———

*I have known my soul and the body that lies upon it.*
*That they have been enemies since the creation of the worlds.*

The gaunt priest chanted a psalm as we entered the darkened room.

I had firmly avoided any conversation or eye contact with those devils, Quintus and Nebridius, on our way here, speaking only to Aurelius and Amicus.

The chamber we entered was a back room of someone's home, the shutters drawn closed so the room was veiled in shadow. Although seldom prosecuted, Manicheism was an illegal religion and had no temples. Well-to-do adherents offered their homes for worship. Already, several other hearers were seated in front of the priest, swathed in swirls of smoke from the incense burners to either side of him. Bread, cheese, and fruit lay in front of him, and we added our own offerings to the pile before sitting on the floor with the others.

"I call the spirit of light out of the darkness of matter. I call the spirit of the Christ out of the darkness of matter. I call the soul out of the darkness of matter," the priest intoned.

"Tell us a story," one of the hearers urged.

The priest slowly opened his eyes and gazed around the room. "A parable," he began. "Once a shepherd saw a lion stalking his flock. What should he do?" He gazed around the room, but he clearly expected no answer, so he went on, holding up three fingers. "The shepherd worried about this for three days, and on the third day he made a plan. He dug a pit and placed in it a new young lamb to tempt the lion. But he tied a rope around the lamb and left the long end in his own hand. Having already secreted the rest of his flock on the hill behind, he waited for the lion. And the lion came and leapt into the pit to devour the lamb. But the shepherd quickly drew the lamb up by the rope before it could be eaten. So the lamb was safe, but the lion was trapped in the pit and perished." He paused. "Who can tell me what this means?"

Quintus ventured: "The shepherd is the spirit and the lion is matter. The lamb is a human soul. The story tells how good and evil battle for the fate of our souls."

"Just so," the priest agreed. I glanced at Aurelius, knowing he was accustomed to being the brightest student in every class and wondering how he reacted to being outthought for once. I saw a little twitch in his cheek, and it amused me in a mean way. For myself, I wondered, What if the shepherd hadn't been quick enough? What if the lamb had been devoured before the shepherd could manage to pull it out of the pit? What if the rope had broken? What if the lion had attacked the flock on the hillside instead, while the shepherd was digging the pit? But not being a scholar, I kept these thoughts to myself.

The priest turned to another topic. "We will speak today of so-called miracles." He paused. "What is a miracle? It is whatever the poor human mind, imprisoned in matter, cannot explain. And so they believe that these phenomena they can't explain are caused by invisible spirits, either good or evil. But Mani tells us it is knowledge that will save us. It is knowledge that will free our inner light from the dark matter wherein it is imprisoned. It is for knowledge that we must strive. Mani was the perfect student. Through study and self-denial he found wisdom, and explained for us the composition of the universe, how it was made, of what it was made, who made it and its inevitable future. These are not stories, such as the pagans told. This is science. Would you like to know what causes the moon to wax and wane?"

We all leaned forward slightly.

The priest went on, "It's simply caused by the influx and outflow of light particles from the world. No miracle. No spirits. Light, freed from matter and light trapped by matter again. That's all."

"How do we come to understand these things?" he went on. "How do we purify ourselves so the light particles within us can absorb Mani's wisdom? Through self-denial. Who can tell me our only two duties?"

"Prayer and fasting," Quintus called out.

"Prayer and fasting," the priest agreed. "Exactly right. Through self-denial, we free the particles of light within. When all the particles of light are finally gathered together, then the messenger will appear. Soon may he come."

"Soon may he come," repeated the hearers, lifting their hands to the heavens.

The priest blessed the bread and shared it with us, and then the service was over. But the priest beckoned to Quintus as the rest of us filed out. Amicus whispered to us, "He's been chosen to prepare the priest's supper. It's an honor." As we emerged into the amber light of evening, he went on, explaining to me and Aurelius, "This is one of the privileges of being a hearer. We serve the bodily needs of the elect so they are free to concentrate on the world of the spirit."

"How is that any different from the same old class system everywhere in the empire? With some serving others?" I blurted out.

The men stared at me blankly for a second, and then they all started to argue at once. "It's not the same at all," Aurelius said.

"No, not the same at all," Nebridius agreed.

"What do you mean?" Amicus asked. His brown eyes settled patiently on me.

I felt myself flush. "Nothing. I don't know why I said that. Of course it isn't the same."

"No, definitely not," Aurelius went on, "because, after all, we give willingly to the elect, and their focus is on the spirit, not on matter. They're Ascetics."

Nebridius nodded, and he and Aurelius started into a conversation about the moral value of Asceticism. Amicus smiled at me and patted my shoulder, and I felt a little less stupid. We emerged into the rush-lit Carthaginian night, and started toward home, the cobbled street under our feet still holding some of the day's warmth.

"I'd like to be able to ignore the needs of the flesh," Aurelius was boasting, "but not yet. I'm not ready yet. But someday."

Nebridius and Amicus murmured assent. Perhaps not right now, they all agreed, but yes, definitely, the ideal eventually was to give up all of the pleasures of the flesh. I was smart enough, this time, not to voice my thoughts, but I wondered, if Aurelius ever found the willpower to do that, where that would leave me.

# CHAPTER TWELVE

I DREAMED of the sea and woke in a puddle, feeling like my swollen belly was a boulder twisting against my spine. I didn't know at first what was happening. Still half asleep, I reached down to confirm that I was lying in a puddle of sticky fluid. Then the rock twisted harder against my back, as if pressed down by a giant vise, and I knew.

I nudged Aurelius. "Run for the midwife."

He kept snoring and barely stirred, frowning in his sleep.

I nudged him harder and shook him. "Aurelius. Aurelius. The baby's coming. Go for Aleia."

His eyes flipped open and he stared at me as if trying to figure out who I was.

"The baby," I reminded him, and then gripped his hand and went silent as the vise bore down again.

He was sitting on the edge of our bed strapping on his sandals, babbling something about how I shouldn't worry, that Amicus—or someone else with no reason to know—had assured him that first babies always took a long time, but he'd be back in just a few minutes, which was the only part I cared about.

———••———

The time while I waited for him to return with Aleia felt endless, and I was beginning to feel sorry I'd sent him, when he finally came slapping back up the stairs well ahead of the woman who delivered babies in our neighborhood. Although not old, she labored up the stairs on legs of uneven lengths. Her face, too, was uneven, one eye cocked permanently shut, one side of her face hanging lower than the other.

She took a second to pant at the top of the stairs and then approached. "Well, let's see what we've got," she said, and her ugly face looked kind, the one visible eye brown and gently compassionate. Her hands, too, were small and gentle, as she examined with one hand on my belly and one inside, her brown eye turned to the ceiling modestly.

She frowned when she withdrew her hand. "The labor is well along but the baby is turned sideways."

This didn't sound like good news. "What does that mean?" I asked.

"He may turn yet," she replied. "If not, we'll have to try to force him."

"What happens if it doesn't work?" Why had I not listened when the village women gossiped about childbirth? It had seemed at the time not to concern me at all, a topic for old women with sagging breasts and slack bellies.

Her compassionate eye met mine and she patted my hand. "Let's not talk about that right now. Let's give him a little time and see what happens."

I knew then she meant the baby and I would likely die if he failed to turn. My blood turned to iron and I felt my eyes widen, and still she held my gaze.

Aurelius, though, demanded to know, "But you're a midwife. Surely you must know how to make the baby turn. How is it done?"

She turned to him slowly, as if he were an annoying child who shouldn't be in the room. "There are no woman relatives who can come?" she asked.

He shook his head.

"Then," the midwife continued, "you will be my assistant. We will press on the baby from the outside, just as I show you, and we will try to persuade him that his head should be born first." She shrugged. "Don't worry. It usually works."

"And if it doesn't?" he demanded.

She stared at him for a few seconds, and finally he understood too, and was silent.

---

The rest of the night passed, marked not by hours but by waves of pain, increasing in intensity and increasingly close together. Each time, it felt again like my womb was a boulder, as large as the world, being twisted and pressed by a giant hand against my spine. I felt the pain of both my own back and of the rock being pressed against it, and it was relentless, twist, twist, twist, until finally it abated for a few moments and I drifted out of consciousness, only to be wakened . . . moments? hours? days? . . . later by another wave of pain.

With gray-and-yellow dawn leaking through the small windows of our apartment, I faded after an intense contraction, to find Aleia's crooked face close to mine, her lips to my ear.

"Leona," she whispered, "your baby will not turn and is soon to be born. Your man and I must try to turn him for you. Do you understand?"

I thought I nodded. I must have, for she continued, "I want to warn you it will be painful, but you must be brave. Your labor is nearly behind you, dear. Your child will be born very soon after we turn him. Don't be afraid." She placed a small, soft hand on my forehead, and I felt tears of gratitude prickling behind my cheeks.

The next wave of agony was the worst yet, and I dimly felt Aleia's hands inside me again as, her voice suddenly harsh, she commanded Aurelius to press down on my belly. "There! No, there, where I showed you the last time! Harder! Harder!"

I felt like I was in a dark hallway where a giant was crushing me with an iron hand while a sword twisted deep within me. For the first time, I let out a shriek.

"Don't stop pushing or she'll die! Push! Push! Harder! If you love her, don't be afraid to hurt her!"

Suddenly something released within me. The pain was lessened, but a great force bore down on my pelvis and I felt an irresistible compulsion to expel something.

"He's turned!" I heard Aleia announce. "That's it, dear, push down, push with all your strength. Your baby's on his way now."

I grunted and squeezed my eyes shut and bore down with a might I hadn't known I had. I felt my arms and my spread legs shaking, and then I shrieked again and the compulsion abated, like waves ebbing from the shore.

I collapsed onto my back, panting, noticing now that I was covered with sweat.

Aleia pushed my hair back from my forehead and cooed at me, "You're a very brave girl, and your child will be born soon. The next time you feel the urge to bear down, do exactly what you did this time: push with all your might."

I barely had time to nod before another wave rolled over me. I gripped the sides of the bed, shrieked like a lunatic and pressed down with all the strength I had in me. There was nothing in the universe except the force crushing my torso and the irresistible urge to bear down, and Aleia exhorting me, "Push, push, push, push, harder, harder, harder." And then I felt a great sense of release, as if all the pain and all the urgency in the world had been swept away by the hand of some great god, and something large and slippery slid out of me. I lay back, exhausted, until I heard a weak mewing.

I lifted my shoulders with a jerk. "Is that my baby? Is that my baby?"

"Yes, it's your baby." Aleia was busy doing something to it.

I thought of Aurelius for the first time in an eternity and spun my head to find him. He was sitting in the corner with his head in his hands. "Our baby, Aurelius, our baby. Is it a girl?" I finally thought to ask. I knew Aurelius hoped for a son, but in my own heart I had imagined the baby to be a chubby, pink little girl.

"It's a boy, a fine boy for all he's been through," Aleia assured me.

And then Aurelius looked up and went over to my feet where Aleia held our son. "Hand me that knife," she ordered, without looking at him, and he did it without taking his eyes from our son. She laid the baby in the warm bath that had been prepared for him ahead of time and cut the cord that had held him to the inside of my womb for so long. I started to cry, thinking how I had tried to destroy him, who was already so precious to me.

"When can I hold him?" I pleaded.

"In a minute, when I get him washed. Here, tie this string around the cord," she ordered Aurelius. "Tight, tight, as tight as you can," as if he were an incompetent child who would surely make a mistake if not directed in every movement. And he did look incompetent to me then, fumbling the string with those big hands of his.

Finally, Aleia handed my child to me, and I was lifted by a wave of joy the like of which I had never experienced before and have never experienced since, not in the arms of a man nor even in communion with my Lord. Nothing else before or since has compared with the bliss of first laying eyes on the face of my son, my beloved, he who was given by God.

"What shall we name him?" Aurelius whispered, brushing a tentative hand over our child's scalp, furred with dark hair already.

I thought of Monnica's request, felt filled with the power to grant or subvert any desire, and smiled to myself. "Adeodonatus," I said. "Given by God."

# PART TWO

# The Beloved

# CHAPTER THIRTEEN

*Carthage*
*Anno Domini 373*

ADEODONATUS. The center of my world. As small and as brown as a nut he was, and he nursed greedily and grew into a chubby little creature with a halo of straight black hair surrounding his head like a nimbus. His arms and legs were in constant motion, and his cheeks grew so plump that when he laughed his eyes shrank to tiny black seeds. I loved to tickle his little drum of a belly and see those fat cheeks rise up to his eyes and hear his deep-throated chortle. Soon he was crawling on the stone floor of our apartment, getting dark calluses on his dimpled little knees.

I took him with me to the baths every afternoon during the women's hour, when the pools were crowded with other mothers and their noisy young children. I oiled our naked bodies and then removed the oil and the day's dirt with a scraper. Then we progressed through the hot, warm, and cool pools. I loved the cool pool the best, the frigidarium with its bright sea-themed mosaics: Neptune driving his chariot, nymphs with wild, flowing hair like seaweed, and writhing fish in bright colors. Adeo loved the fish, with their glittering glass tiles that made them appear to swim when water flowed over them. This was my favorite time of day. The toddlers sat in the shallows, crowing and flapping at the mosaic fish with their chubby arms, raising little sprays of water, and I had other mothers to talk to. I learned a great deal from my new friends that I desperately needed to know about babies: what soft foods to give him first, little rhymes to sing to amuse him or send him to sleep, what herbs to use for fevers or vomiting or loose bowels.

I emerged from the baths on a windy spring afternoon when Adeo was not quite two years old. I still carried him strapped to my back, but he was heavy and my back was already complaining.

I was turning into a tavern to pick up some fish and fruit for our supper when I saw Aurelius and Amicus striding toward me with their cloaks whirling and flapping in the breeze.

"Don't worry about stopping for food. We have to get home right away," Aurelius said. Taking me by the elbow, he nudged me toward home, and I picked up his rapid pace.

"What's the big hurry?" I asked.

"A magistrate will be coming to our apartment. You need to tell him Nebridius and Quintus were with us last night."

"I'm not lying for them." After two years, I had still not forgiven Quintus and Nebridius for tricking us on our first night in Carthage. They kept Aurelius out late many nights, and he often came home reeling and slurring his words. I knew they still cheated the simple and the new to town. They had gathered around them a group of younger students who were their accomplices. They called their gang the *eversores*—"overturners"—and they got their amusement from making fools of people, as they had Aurelius and me that first night.

Amicus and Aurelius swore that they had nothing to do with any of that, but still they sat up with Quintus and Nebridius late into the night, tavern philosophers fueled by cheap, watered-down wine. Aside from Amicus, Aurelius always seemed to choose the worst of companions, and we had had many bitter, late-night arguments about it.

"I know you don't like them," Aurelius said now, "but Leona, they're in big trouble. We have to help them."

"They're in big trouble, are they? Good. It's about time. I hope it's really, really big trouble. I hope it's the kind of trouble that gets them sent out of town."

"It is really, really big trouble."

I still had no intention of lying for them, but now I was curious. I looked at Aurelius and raised my eyebrows.

"A Greek merchant was found murdered in an alley by the docks. A taverner identified Nebridius and Quintus as being in his tavern with him that night."

"So maybe they killed him."

"You know they wouldn't do that."

I had to admit that was probably true. Quintus and Nebridius were self-centered hooligans, and laughable hypocrites with their talk about Asceticism and their pious worship of the Manichean elect, but I doubted they were killers.

"They could be sent into exile," Amicus said.

"Oh, what a shame. They might be sent away. If they were plebs, they'd be crucified or sent to the tin mines for less. My brother was put to death for carrying an israel."

"But you couldn't save him," Aurelius pointed out. "You could save our friends. Don't you feel a little bit responsible for their fates?"

"Me? Me, responsible? How about them? I'd say they're responsible. And oh, then there's the little penalty for lying to a magistrate. I could only be scourged, that's all. And anyway, they're not my friends; they're yours. Forget it. I'm not doing it."

"No, of course you're not responsible," Aurelius agreed. "Absolutely right. But you could save them. Look at it as saving two lives. Leona, you know they didn't do it."

"They might as well have. I bet they were the ones who directed him to some dark alley where he was bound to be robbed. They've done it before." We turned the corner past the thick-walled Christian church of St. Felicity, with its permanent population of filthy beggars on the steps.

"You might even help them to reform by saving them," Amicus pointed out.

I snorted. "Why don't you lie for them?"

"I was at a hearing last night. Many people saw me. You were at home with Adeo. You can easily say that our friends were with you. We'd have to say you were my wife, of course," Aurelius went on. "As a pleb and an unmarried woman, your statement would carry no weight."

"So, I have to tell two lies." But, it would not be hard to just leave the impression that Aurelius and I were wed, and that I was therefore of the class of women whose word would be taken as evidence in some cases. Since Adeo's birth, I had begun wearing the stola of a Roman matron, and even my friends at the baths assumed that I was of noble birth and Aurelius's wife. Strictly speaking, it was illegal for me to wear a stola, but almost no one here in Carthage knew that I wasn't a legal wife and the sartorial laws were seldom enforced in this corner of the empire anyway.

"It's not so much of a lie. We're married in our hearts," Aurelius said. This was an argument that he had made to me before, but I knew what a vast difference there was between our situation and a legal marriage, and this worry was my only companion many nights when he was out late with his friends. He could cast me aside at any time, leaving me to fend for myself and Adeo, or he could cast me aside and keep my son from me. I thought for a second and then stopped in the middle of the street and looked at Aurelius.

"I won't swear that I'm your wife, but if you will swear it, then I will say that Quintus and Nebridius were with us last night."

Joy rose in his face like the sun. "I knew you'd do it." He wrapped me in his big arms. "Oh, Leona, thank you. I love you. You'll see: Amicus is right. Those two rascals will reform after this."

---

The magistrate came to our apartment at suppertime to question us.

"You are the wife of Aurelius Augustine?" he asked me.

I lowered my eyes, trying to look shy and cloistered.

"She is my wife, sir," Aurelius confirmed.

He questioned us some more about whether our friends had been at our home the previous evening, what hour they had arrived and departed, what we had done. In the end, the case came down to the word of a taverner against the word of a young citizen and his wife, and the magistrates in Carthage didn't care much about a stranger from Greece. Quintus and Nebridius were released, and came right to our apartment to shower us with their thanks. They swore that they had learned a lesson, and would immediately cease being slaves to their evil material natures. They would become Ascetics, starting tomorrow, they said, as they drained the third of the four flagons of watered-down wine they had brought with them.

Late in the evening, as they prepared to stagger home, Quintus leaned in, breathing wine vapor into my face, and took my hands. "I owe you my life. I am forever in your debt," he declared.

It meant nothing to me at the time. I still hated him, with his long, droopy face and his hair already thinning at twenty, and his breath smelling of fish and wine. But I felt a sense of victory that night. Aurelius had sworn in front of a magistrate that I was his wife. Surely this was the first coin in a treasure that could be used to tie him to me and Adeo. I just had to figure out how to add to it.

# CHAPTER FOURTEEN

A FEW EVENINGS LATER, Amicus stopped by on his way to a hearing, hoping to take Aurelius with him.

"Out drinking with Quintus and Nebridius," I told him. "You know, the two who were going to reform and never drink again."

Amicus smiled. "Their intentions are good."

I snorted.

"Here, I brought a little sweet for Adeo," he said, lifting our little boy onto his lap and handing him a date-and-honey cake. Adeo leaned on Amicus's chest, nibbling on the cake. Aurelius's other friends ignored Adeo, as if he were a small piece of furniture, but Amicus was as tender as a woman, always bringing a sweet for our child or ready to sing him a song or tell a story.

"I don't understand why you bother with those two devils," I said.

Amicus shrugged. "If we could only love people who were completely worthy, we wouldn't love at all, would we?"

"Some are more worthy than others."

"True," he laughed. "True. I don't know. I guess it's their minds, truthfully. I know they seem like apes to you, but you don't see them at school. Quintus is a really brilliant man, Leona. Nebridius, maybe not so much, but he's got a way with words and he really is good-natured at heart. They're young."

"So are you. So is Aurelius."

"They need some responsibilities and a good woman. They'll be all right."

Adeo finished his cake and started fidgeting. Amicus drew a ball of wax out of his pouch for Adeo to play with.

"Talking of a good woman . . ." I began.

Amicus cocked his head and frowned.

I went on. "I was wondering about marriage among the Manichees."

"Ask Sextus. He'll know all about it."

I worked a few hours a week as a scribe for Sextus, the Manichean priest, hoping to ingratiate myself with him.

"I already tried that. I got a theoretical lecture about matter and light particles. What I really want to know is . . . well, is there such a thing? Can two hearers be married by a Manichean priest?"

Amicus looked at me warily. "Shouldn't you be asking this question of the other potential party to such a marriage?"

"I'm asking you." I rose to clear our wooden plates from the table and briskly scraped the leavings into my scrap bucket.

He sighed. "Yes, there is a marriage rite. The Manichees completely ignore the empire's laws and don't even recognize civil marriage. But I have to warn you, the Roman authorities don't recognize the Manichean rite either. Such a marriage would be meaningless, Leona. From a legal standpoint, it would be no different from what you have now."

"Who can perform the rite?" I insisted.

"Any of the elect."

"Sextus?" I returned to my seat at the table and gazed intently into Amicus's eyes.

"Sextus would probably do it, on the theory that it is better for two souls to be united by light than by matter, but Leona, truly, I think you should leave well enough alone. He loves you. I'm an independent witness and I'll swear to it."

"I need to bind him to me. The marriage might not mean anything to the law, but it would mean something to him. I have a child, Amicus. I will do whatever I can to make sure that I am never separated from him."

"How can you imagine that Aurelius would for a minute consider separating you from Adeo?"

"But he *could*, Amicus, that's the point. I don't think he would either, but he could."

"Come here." Amicus had one arm around Adeo, now dozing on his lap, and held his other arm out to me. I rose and went to him.

He put his arm around my waist and pulled me to him. "You have my word," he said, "that, should Aurelius become someone other than who I know him to be, should he turn away from you and try to keep you from your child, I will defend you. I will make sure that you are taken care of and have access to Adeo. You have my word on this. Do you believe me?"

"Yes."

"Good."

"But I'm still going to persuade him to marry me." I had added another coin to my store of treasure, and I had plans to make another deposit as soon as I could.

———•••———

One night, a few weeks later, I was rocking Adeo forward and back in my arms. His eyes had flickered shut and his pulls on my breast had slowed. Soon it would be time to wean him and I would miss the intimacy. I swayed for a few moments longer, making sure, then inched my index finger between his rosebud lip and my brown nipple to break the suction. Adeo's heavy head fell back and his mouth fell open, breathing the waxy scent of my milk. I smiled down at him, comparing his sack-of-grain heaviness now to his whirl of activity throughout the day: careening across the floor on his sausage legs at the sight of his father coming in the door, stretching for the table to reach for a knife and screeching with rage to find it out of his reach, then instantly forgetting his frustration to intently stack the wooden blocks that Amicus had made for him as playthings.

He was something new every morning, and he exhausted and delighted me, but tonight I was glad to lay him down on his pallet in our bedroom. I had other plans for the evening.

Reaching into my bag, I drew out the red paste that I had bought at the baths that afternoon and applied some to my cheeks and lips. Then I withdrew another alabaster flask and opened the cork stopper. I sniffed and felt pleased. I had never worn scent before, and this perfume had cost more than all of the others, but the woman in the booth had assured me that it worked like a love potion: one drop behind each ear, and then seduce your man just as usual, and he would do whatever you wanted. I'd had to present the seller with a few strands of Aurelius's hair, but this presented no difficulty, as his hair was so luxuriant that he constantly shed all over our apartment and still had a mane like a black lion. I had then whispered my intention in her ear while she cut the hair into tiny shreds and sprinkled them into the flask. Then I had paid her a whole denarius, saved over the weeks by bargaining sharply at the markets. Surely something so costly must work as planned.

My stomach fluttered a little, and I composed myself by smoothing my best tunic over my thighs. I took a deep breath and walked into our sitting room.

Aurelius sat at our dining table, frowning over a book by the light of an oil lamp.

"You'll ruin your eyes," I said.

"You're right," he admitted, "and this is so hard to read. I've gotten used to reading your beautiful hand." It was true that my writing was fine and clear. I took all of Aurelius's dictation for him, and even occasionally attended a class with him and recorded his masters' speeches. Even the taciturn Sextus complimented my work. Sometimes I forgot that three years before, I had been illiterate.

"I have a better idea anyway," I said, and slinked over to him and sat on his lap. I ran my hands through his hair and drew his face toward mine.

To my shock, Aurelius sprang up, nearly throwing me to the floor. "Don't do that!"

I regained my balance and stared at him.

He walked to the other side of the room, hand to his head, and stood staring back at me, his eyes huge, as if witnessing some horror. "I . . . I was looking for the right time to tell you."

"Tell me what?"

"I've decided to become one of the elect. I've chosen to become an Ascetic."

"You *what*?" I felt like I'd been clubbed in the stomach by some fanatic's israel.

He held up his hands. "Listen. Listen. Just listen to me, Leona. It's all right. I checked it out. We can still live together and we can raise Adeo together and you can write my books for me and everything. We just have to be celibate, is all."

"That's all? That's all?" Then I laughed. "You won't last a week. You can't do this any more than Nebridius can stop drowning a pound of spiced goat in garum."

"Well, that's it, see. We're all doing it: me, Amicus, Nebridius, Quintus. We've been talking about it and talking about it, and we finally decided to do it. You know, that arrest gave them a real scare. I don't know if you've noticed, but they've reformed. Quintus doesn't even go to watch the gladiators anymore. He's really trying, Leona, and when he decided to go celibate, Amicus and Nebridius and I decided it was time for us too."

*Quintus, that* diabolus, I thought bitterly, *will he ever stop being a thorn in my foot?*

"You know," Aurelius said, "Cicero said, 'If the souls which we have are eternal and divine, we must conclude that the less they are caught up in the vices and errors of mankind, the easier it will be for them to ascend and return to Heaven.'" He placed one hand across his waist and raised the other as he declaimed, like some senator in the curia, and I felt such a thunderclap of fury that I could have murdered him in that moment.

Instead, I threw his book at him, grunting with rage and frustration. I was grimly elated to see the corner of the binding strike his eyebrow, and he winced and clapped a hand to his eye.

"You won't last a week," I repeated over my shoulder, as I marched into our bedroom and threw myself onto our bed.

# CHAPTER FIFTEEN

SUNLIGHT BORE DOWN on us, heavy as an anvil, and the crowd roared as the charioteers made their seventh and final lap around the circuit. Standing next to me, Quintus jerked his torso back and forth spastically as if he were the one driving the chariot. "Drive, you bastards! Come on, you *diaboli*, you sons of dogs! Drive! Drive! Send those red bastards straight to hell! Oh! Yes! Yes! That's it! Hurt that *cevor*!" He and Nebridius hugged each other as their blue driver lashed a red charioteer in the face with a whip. Amicus and Aurelius flung their fists into the air in approval. The four great Ascetics, I thought sourly. They had even painted themselves blue for this event, and had not failed throughout the race to shout encouragement to their beloved blues to visit every form of pain on the rival red, green, and white charioteers. It was still only the first race, and all four of them were already hoarse.

Just to spite them, I had tied a green ribbon in my hair. Like many Carthaginian women, I favored Justin the Saxon, a handsome yellow-haired charioteer of the green team.

"Go, Justin!" I screamed now, just as a matter of form. That day, my hero had fallen far behind the reds and the blues.

I glanced toward the stairway nearest us, where Adeo was playing with some other small children. The bigger boys skipped and galloped around in circles, pretending to be chariot drivers, and Adeo and the other littler boys toddled behind them, laughing. I smiled to see how easily our little boy mixed with the other children, his raisin eyes sparkling.

As soon as Aurelius and his friends had made the decision to become ascetic, they had given up going to the gladiatorial games at the arena. I was glad for that. The blood sports of the arena sickened me, and Adeo and I had to stand in the upper stands with the other women, children, and slaves, while Aurelius and his friends sat in the mid stands, where the students and common men sat. At the circus, men and women, citizens, freemen, and slaves all mixed, and though the sport could be cruel and violent, death was not the point as it was at the arena. Adeo enjoyed the animal spectacles that were performed between races, and I liked watching Justin the Saxon's arm muscles ripple as he controlled his reins and lashed at his horse and the other drivers.

The Carthage circus was not as massive as Rome's, which was famous for seating 250,000, but it was large and magnificent enough to my small-town eyes. Row upon row of seating rose around the oval racetrack. In the middle of the oval one of seven dolphin fountains spit sprays of water as each of the seven circuits of the race was completed. Between races, other entertainments were offered: animal shows, comic battling dwarves, female gladiators fighting with wooden swords that never drew blood. The crowds were always noisy and excited, constantly placing bets before and during each race.

The seventh circuit was almost complete. Quintus's blue charioteer lashed his whip at the red driver again, and the red driver let go of his reins. The red chariot careened into the stands and splintered wood flew into the air. I craned my neck. The oppressive heat had kept that day's audience small and we had been able to sneak into good seats close to the track, but this limited our view of what happened closest to the stands.

"He's been thrown!" Nebridius shouted. Everyone on our side of the stands crowded close to the rail and leaned forward. The red driver was lying on the ground behind his chariot, and the trailing greens and whites barely missed running him over.

The blues had won. Aurelius, Amicus, Quintus, and Nebridius clapped one another on the back as if they had been driving the blue chariots themselves. "Too bad I quit drinking!" Nebridius declared. "With what I won on that race, we would have had quite the evening tonight, my friends."

Aurelius and his friends had maintained their ascetic resolve for thirty days now, which was twenty-nine days longer than I would have predicted. Nebridius still ate like a pig, but the drinking had stopped, the *eversores* had disbanded, and my own bed had been cold.

I fixed Aurelius's meals, we laughed over Adeo together, and I patiently transcribed his class notes and speeches onto precious parchment folios. But every night it felt as if a rope had been strung taut between us, and we set it humming every time we came close to each other. I longed for the feel of his sweating, muscular body pressed to mine, and I knew he felt the same. He held himself stiff, seldom made eye contact with me, and never, ever touched me. I knew that celibacy was a heroic effort for him, and I thought at first that it would not take much to break his resolve, but I was wrong. He averted his eyes if I undressed in the same room with him, and the one time that I had disrobed and then tried to press myself seductively against him, he had pushed me away as if I were on fire. "Never do that!" he commanded in a voice that frightened me, and then he left our home for the rest of that evening. I slept little, tortured by my own desires and by a sense of unmoored panic at losing what little power I had had over Aurelius.

I was especially cranky that day, with the sun assaulting my brow, Justin the Saxon in eighth place, and that *diabolus* Quintus, who was already rich, flush with gambling winnings.

"I'm going to place a bet for the next race," Aurelius said. His friends were already headed for the betting stalls.

"Fine."

"What's wrong?" he teased. "Upset that Justin the Saxon made such a poor showing? Must have been up too late last night with one of his lady admirers. Although I heard it's not the ladies he likes best."

"Shut up, Aurelius."

"What's wrong with you?"

"Gee, I don't know. The sun's as hot as a blacksmith's anvil, my bed's as cold as the top of Mount Zaghouan, and we never have enough money, but you seem to have enough to keep up with your friends' betting habits." As we spoke, we were jostled by winning bettors crowding past us to collect their payout.

"I won."

"This time."

"I have to have a little fun sometimes. We're getting by."

"Only since I started taking on extra scribe work. That was supposed to be so that we could set something aside." I didn't admit to Aurelius that I had been able to put aside a few coins a week from what I earned copying news from the forum. The price of everything kept going up, but I had learned to bargain hard in the markets and managed to save some of my earnings against the day when Aurelius and I might be able to marry and become independent of his family and patron—or against the day when, despite Amicus's assurances, he might cast me out. That day seemed closer all the time since he had taken his vow of celibacy.

"It's not my fault bread got more expensive," he complained. "I don't know what you want me to do about it. Take Adeo and go home if you're not having fun."

"Maybe I'm tired of always being the one responsible for Adeo too. Maybe you could be in charge of him every once in a while, instead of burying your nose in a book while I wear myself out running after a two-year old."

"Fine. I'll keep him here with me. Where is he?"

"You don't even know where he is. I'm sure he'd be fine if I left him here with you."

"I thought you were watching him. Where is he?"

"He's right—" I looked over to where Adeo had been running in circles with the other boys only a few minutes ago. The group of children was gone.

I felt more annoyed than panicked. They couldn't have gone far, but now I would have to wedge myself through this crowd in the merciless heat, looking for him. "He was right there." I pointed. "I'll find him."

The animal show was starting. A gang of slaves hauled a wheeled cage containing three snarling wolves through a yawning archway on one short end of the oval racetrack. Behind them, another gang drove a small young elephant.

The first time I had seen an elephant, I had been fascinated and terrified. Who could imagine that such enormous, sail-eared creatures existed outside of children's tales? Now, after two years in Carthage, I had seen many elephant shows at both the arena and the circus.

I had seen elephants scratching letters into the dirt of the racetrack with their trunks in answer to trainers' questions. I had seen them trample to death prisoners armed only with a whip and a knife. I had seen them dance and balance balls on their trunks at the command of their painted and bejeweled keepers. Elephants were as common to me now as dogs, and Adeo adored them. We had a small slate at home on which I would sometimes draw pictures to amuse him, and he almost always insisted that I draw an elephant.

I squeezed myself between more sweating bodies and found a space by a railing where I could breathe and scan for Adeo.

Normally, animal fights took place in an enclosed pen in the middle of the oval, but the circus masters must have wanted to give the crowd a special thrill that day and released the animals right onto the racetrack. A slave unlocked and opened the door to the wolves' cage and then the slaves scurried away.

The elephant shuffled its feet and shook its massive head, looking bewildered. The wolves crouched in their cage for a few seconds, eyes narrowed, ears back. The oily, earthy smell of their matted gray fur reached my nose on the hot breeze. The outcome of this was inevitable, and I turned my head to one side and then the other, searching for my baby and frowning against the blasting sun.

And then I saw him, about twenty feet from me, leaning over a lower railing to get a better view of the elephant.

He seemed to fall in slow motion, leaning forward, forward, and then toppling headfirst, tumbling over as light as a falling leaf and landing on his back.

My heart stopped and then burst into wild hammering. I elbowed people aside in a panic to get to a stairway. "My baby!" I choked. It was a fall of only about six feet, but he lay motionless at the edge of the oval, where he could be trampled to death or torn to pieces at any second.

Now others in the audience noticed the child down on the oval and a murmur rose. It wasn't hard for those near me to tell that the panicked, thrashing woman was the child's mother, and they began to make way for me, as I fought my way closer to Adeo, never taking my eyes off him. The harsh noises of the crowd subsided into a background hiss, like ocean waves, and the stifling day seemed to slow to a crawl: me swimming through the sea of people, Adeo lying in the shade on the race track, the shuffling elephant lit by glassy white sunlight, the wolves now circling in their cage, snarling and assessing the elephant from the corners of their yellow eyes.

I could find no stairway that led to the oval and was preparing to leap over the railing to rescue him, when the wolves shot from their cage as one.

They crouched in front of the elephant in a staggered row. The elephant now sensed danger and let out a trumpeting cry. I choked out a cry of panic.

But then I saw Aurelius leap the railing and run for our baby. Hope exploded in me, but time seemed to slow even more; all sound and scent disappeared and the world was reduced to the sight of the running man, the limp baby, and the circling animals.

Two of the wolves split off to either side of the elephant, and the beast swung its head to one side and then the other. The calculated cunning in the eyes of the wolves looked almost human. Then the third wolf struck, leaping for the elephant's neck and taking one snarling bite. The elephant swung its head wildly now, trying to shake off the attacking wolf.

Aurelius picked up Adeo and ran to the railing with him, lifting him toward me. I leaned forward, sobbing, and took my baby's limp body in my arms. His eyes were closed and his moist mouth hung limp, but he was breathing, and when I placed my ear to his chest, I heard the tapping of his little heart. I hugged him to me, sobbing and wailing, and suddenly Aurelius and Amicus were at my side.

"Is he all right? Is he all right?" Aurelius demanded, prodding at my arms, trying to get a look at our son.

"Let's get him home," Amicus suggested. "Quintus and Nebridius will find us later."

Aurelius wrapped his arms around me and Adeo, and Amicus cut a way through the crowd in front of us. The sea of people parted as we passed through, but our contribution to the day's drama was already forgotten.

By the time we made our way to an exit, the carcasses of one crushed wolf and one torn, bloody elephant had been carted away, the surviving wolves had been whipped back into a cage, and slaves were circling the track flinging perfumed water to mask the animal smell of the blood before the next race.

───•••───

Adeo briefly regained consciousness once, vomited, and then slipped back into limp unconsciousness. I sat in our apartment clutching him on my lap, rocking back and forth and crying, not caring about the sour-milk-smelling vomit dripping down my legs. Aurelius tried once to pry him from me, and I rebuffed him with a swinging arm and an animal cry. After that, he receded into the background, pacing the room and checking the window every few seconds for Amicus and the doctor.

In desperation I fingered the cross that Miriam had placed around my neck before I came to Carthage. I sent a prayer to her god: *I'll believe in you if you let him be all right, just let him be all right, just let him be all right.*

"Here they come," Aurelius said finally.

I heard feet taking the steps two at a time, and Amicus burst in, flushed and panting. "The doctor's right behind me," he announced. "How is he?" He bent over my limp child.

Amicus could calm and persuade me when even Aurelius could not. I sniffed back my tears and held Adeo so that Amicus could have a look at him. "He vomited once and then went right back to sleep." Then I bent over my little boy and started to sob again.

"Here's the doctor," Amicus said soothingly.

The doctor inspired no confidence. He was not much older than Aurelius and Amicus and had let his beard grow. I noticed this because it was a very uncommon thing. All men except the Hebrews had their facial hair shaved each day at the baths in the Roman fashion.

"I need to examine the child," the young doctor said, bending over me.

Amicus took Adeo from me and handed him to the doctor.

We crowded around him as he laid Adeo on our dining table and spread his eyelids to examine his eyes. Aurelius placed an arm around my waist and I didn't shake him off.

"Did the child vomit?" the doctor asked.

"Yes, once," I answered. "Will he be all right?"

The doctor ignored me, put his ear to Adeo's chest, and felt his cheeks and forehead, then squeezed each of his limbs and probed his round little belly. Finally, he very gingerly prodded the swelling at the back of Adeo's head. Adeo frowned and stirred, and then went still again.

"Will he live?" Aurelius demanded.

The doctor smiled for the first time. "He will live." He slapped Adeo's face gently and our baby's eyes fluttered open. The doctor pried open each eyelid again and peered intently at Adeo's black eyes. "Try to keep him conscious for the next few hours," he said.

"But he'll live?" I pleaded.

"No bones are broken and he doesn't seem to be bleeding inside. He just had a bad bump on the head and had the wind knocked out of him when he fell. He'll live. Keep him still for a few days, until the swelling on the back of his head goes away—and keep him away from the circus. It's not a place for children." He shook his head as if wondering what could have possessed us, and a knife of guilt sliced at my heart as I remembered that Aurelius and I had been arguing about who had to tend to our little boy when he wandered off and fell. I made a quick, fervent promise to any gods who might be listening to never, never neglect him again, even for a second.

---

In the days that followed, Adeo slowly recovered. The severe young doctor had offered no instructions on how to enforce stillness on a two-year-old boy who, by the next day, felt ready to gallop around the apartment like a pony and fold himself in half trying to do a somersault. My only desire was to hold his sweet flesh to mine and kiss his face and the top of his head over and over, but he twisted out of my lap and pointed to the door, demanding, "Outside!"

I left our apartment not at all for those few days, and Aurelius left only to bring food to us. We amused Adeo with his wooden blocks and with endless drawing on the little slate.

Aurelius watched intently as Adeo once again began to build a tower with the little wooden blocks. "Look at how he learns, Leona. He tries different things, more often than not they fail, and then he tries something else. He learns by doing the same thing over and over, each time a different way, until he has it right. He hardly ever makes the same mistake twice."

"I think that's how all children learn." I spoke with some authority, having watched the other children at the baths and in our neighborhood.

"But how do they know what to try first? And how do they know to try a different way when the first way fails?" That was Aurelius, still: always wondering about things that just were, that people had no business wondering about, always wanting to know the "why" of everything.

"I don't know," I admitted.

"Look at the joy he takes in learning." He smiled when he said this, but then his forehead creased and he seemed to turn his gaze inward. "What changes a child into a reluctant scholar?" he mused. "Why does this small child learn so easily and with so much joy, while a bigger boy puts in his hours grudgingly?" He sighed. "I have to conclude that it's fear of punishment. Adeo knows that we won't beat him if he confuses a square with a circle, whereas the ten-year-old scholar knows that he will face a beating if he fails in his arithmetic or grammar, and that fear makes him hate his lessons."

I could see him already preparing for our return to Thagaste and his teaching post there, but I had also seen in these days a new tenderness for our little boy, whom we could have lost. Aurelius had hardly known what to do with Adeo when he was an infant, but now as a child he had become more interesting to his father, and the days of his recovery had strengthened the bonds of our little family. I had completely forgotten my promise to Miriam's god that I would become a believer if only our little boy would recover.

Finally, the swelling subsided and the bruising faded, and Adeo looked like himself again—except for a slight crescent-shaped indentation at the back of his head. The bearded young doctor visited again, and frowned and prodded the dent very gently. "His skull was cracked," he said. "In such a young child, it will probably heal completely. He'll always have this dent."

"Probably heal completely? Why do you say probably?" Aurelius argued. "He's as healthy and energetic as a young colt."

"Later in life, a shard of bone perhaps, a brain fever . . ." The doctor shrugged. "Probably not. Anyway, there's no way to tell, and nothing to be done for it. Call him healed and thank God for it."

Aurelius and I both stood over Adeo's bed that night long after he had fallen asleep. Aurelius put his arm around my waist. I snuggled into his shoulder and now, for the first time since the day of the accident, I let myself cry. He wrapped his other arm around me and rested his cheek on the top of my head.

"I should have been watching him every second," I sobbed.

"I should have too. I'm always having a good time with my friends and assuming that you're watching him, as if he were only your child. I've thought a lot these days: I was only starting to get to know him. I didn't know what to do with him when he was a baby, but now . . . He's a whole separate and interesting small person and my son, and I almost lost my chance to know him. I'm going to change, Leona. I'm almost finished with school and I'll be going back to Thagaste to teach. I'll be a man and I want to start acting more like a man and a father."

I clung to him and wept harder, and he tightened his arms around me. "Shhh," he crooned. "It's all right now. He's all right."

I raised my wet face to him. His full lips and large brown eyes were soft as he took my face in his hands, but then his gaze grew sharp and he bent to kiss me hard on the lips. Wild with the relief and joy of our child's survival, I threw my arms around Aurelius's neck and kissed him back. His beard, unshaven these many days, was rough against my cheek, and his muscular thighs were pressed hard against mine. He placed his hands on my buttocks and lifted me, and I wrapped my legs around his waist, still kissing him as he carried me to our bed. Urgently, wordlessly, without removing our tunics, we became lovers again.

Afterward, he laid gazing at me and stroking my cheek. "If only we could be married." He sighed.

I smiled. "We can," I said.

## CHAPTER SIXTEEN

FACED WITH the prospect of confronting Monnica in just a few minutes, my courage wavered. My stomach fluttered and my hand on Aurelius's arm felt cold and sweaty.

We had arrived back in Thagaste that morning and were in the entrance hall of Aurelius's childhood home, waiting for his mother to return from a trip into town. Adeo had been laid down for a nap in Aurelius's old room.

"Slave market today," the servant who greeted us explained. "Your mother goes when she has a few extra denarii and buys girls who would be sold and frees them. Then she finds a place for them with the Christians. Your mother's a very great lady."

The home in which Aurelius had grown up was as small and simple as I remembered it. The furniture was luxurious but sparse and the only ornaments were the large bronze cross on one wall and the sunlight and birdsong that streamed in the windows.

The minutes dragged. Dust motes swirled in the buttery morning sunlight. Aurelius patted my hand, but I could tell that he was nervous too, because he was uncharacteristically quiet. And then there she was.

Monnica's face broke with joy at the sight of Aurelius, and she opened her arms.

He rose to embrace her, but I could see how stiff and awkward he felt. "Mother," he said.

She leaned away from him and assessed the changes in him. "I didn't think you could grow any taller," she remarked. Monnica was a small woman, only an inch or so taller than me, and her son towered over her. "Safe trip?" she asked.

He nodded, and shifted his feet on the floor. Then his mother cast a sharp glance at me, but returned her gaze immediately to her son. "Where's the child?"

"Sleeping," Aurelius told her.

She pressed her lips together and frowned, glancing at me again. "I hoped that we might speak alone."

Aurelius squared his shoulders. "Leona can be a party to anything that we have to say to each other. She is my wife."

Monnica's face paled as she looked me in the eye for the first time. Then her eyes narrowed, and she said, "It surely can't be a legal marriage."

"It's legal enough for us," Aurelius said, not meeting her eyes. I twisted the carnelian ring on the third finger of my right hand.

"And who married you, if I might know?"

Aurelius squared himself again, as if preparing for a blow. "A priest in the Manichean rite."

"A Manichean priest," his mother repeated slowly, pouring herself a cup of water from a sweating clay jug. "Not a marriage in law. And you're not even a Manichean. This can easily be nullified when you come to your senses, Aurelius." She glanced at me as if I were a mouse that had crept into her pantry and must be swept out. "You may think you've tied him to you, but you haven't. This is completely meaningless."

"In fact, I am a Manichean, mother."

Monnica's face turned pale again, and I could see her muscles tense. "Surely not," she said slowly.

Aurelius nodded, looking straight ahead, stiff as if waiting for a blow to fall. "Yes, mother."

Monnica glanced at me again, as if considering placing the blame on me and then thinking the better of it. She set down her cup and paced closer to her son. "Look me in the eye," she said.

Aurelius inhaled sharply and met his mother's eyes.

"The Manichees"—she spat the word as if it were poison—"are worse than heretics. They claim association with the Church to win the gullible, but they deny the Holy Spirit, they deny the Holy Trinity, they make Satan equal to the Lord in power, and they create fantastic stories about how the world came to be. You know that this heresy is illegal?"

Aurelius stood before her, chin out. "The truth is no less the truth whether it's legal or not."

"The truth! You're still a boy. You don't know truth."

Aurelius's face softened, and he met his mother's eyes again. "Christianity is a religion of magic and miracles, Mother, no less than the old Roman religion or the cults of Ammon or Mithra." He was going into patient-teacher mode now. "The state can outlaw our way, but the truth can never be outlawed. Our way is scientific. We can explain everything."

Monnica was silent for a second. I saw sorrow in her face and for a moment felt sorry for her. "Aurelius, speak with my priest, Father Bartholomew. I think he'll very quickly demonstrate to you the errors in your so-called explanations of everything."

"I doubt it." Aurelius folded his arms, then let them drop to his sides as if not sure what to do with them.

Monnica closed her eyes and stood for a moment with her hands folded. When she opened her eyes, she said, "You can inherit nothing as long as you declare yourself Manichean. Heretics cannot inherit by law.

And you will have nothing from me as long as you cling to this evil. You will not live under my roof and you will receive no stipend from me. I will pray every day for your soul to be saved. Now fetch me my grandchild so that I can see him before you leave this house."

———•••———

We went looking for Miriam next, but when I tried the door of her workshop, it was locked. I ran back down the dusty stairway and into her brother-in-law's grocery. "Xanthos, it's Leona. Do you remember me? I used to work for Miriam."

"The cheese girl." He nodded, unsmiling.

"What happened to Miriam?"

"Found a new husband," Xanthos said. "Gone to live in the borderlands with him." To the south of Thagaste, nearer the mountains, lay the undefined border with the Aitheopian lands, where trade in ivory and exotic skins took place and where the Roman governors placed small forts at intervals to defend against raids by Aitheopian war parties looking for slaves or gold.

"I see. Thank you," I said. I felt a stab of disappointment not only because I had looked forward to seeing my friend but also because I had hoped that she would have news of Numa. Now I would have to face my father if I wanted to hear about my sister.

Aurelius sat in the forum, where Urbanus and the other town fathers had recently donated a small outdoor bath. Adeo, naked, ran through the pool with another small child, in one of those pointless toddler games where it's hard to know who's chasing whom. Everywhere he went, he immediately made a new friend. Glistening beads of water scattered from his wet head, and his face shined with delight as he glanced back to make sure that his new friend was still running after him.

"Any luck?" Aurelius asked me.

I shook my head. "I have to decide if I want to know about Numa badly enough to face my father. He might not even speak to us. Or he might want to know how many goats you've brought him to pay him back for stealing his daughter."

Aurelius barked a short laugh. "Well, we know the answer to that now that I'm disinherited. You've married a poorer man than he could have chosen for you after all."

"There's still Urbanus."

Aurelius nodded. Then he shook his head once, sighed, and looked at me. "Well, what are we doing?"

"Oh, my father's had almost three years to calm down, so I don't think he'll actually kill us. Let's go."

——•••——

As we approached the hut where I had grown up, I could see that the years of my absence had not been kind to my family. Father had always carefully maintained our poor little home, replacing the thatch roof yearly and rebuilding the mud walls every few years. Now, the thatch was dried out and crumbling, and holes scarred the mud walls, exposing the twig frame.

Two figures sat in front of the hut, playing a game of nuts.

"Hello, Tito," I said.

My brother looked up and frowned for a second, and then his face bloomed into a smile. "Leona!" He rose and wrapped his arms around me, then presented me to his companion. "Pala, this is my sister, Leona. My wife," he explained to me, beaming.

Tito's wife rose from the dirt. She was my size, barely more than a girl, and heavily pregnant. "Welcome," she whispered.

"And this is your man and, oh! Two men!" Tito enthused, bending solemnly to Adeo. "How do you do, young sir? I'm your Uncle Tito."

Adeo giggled and slipped behind his father's leg, peering out and giggling again.

"Where's Father?" I asked, determined to get it over with.

Tito's smile faded. "Oh, sister," he said. "Oh, I'm so sorry. Our father died last harvest."

I forced myself to feel a small stab of grief. "How?"

Tito shrugged. "One morning I woke up and he didn't."

"I'm sorry," I said, as if I were comforting a stranger and not my own brother on the death of our father.

"I'm sorry too," Tito said. "But, you're here and you'll have dinner with us. Pala, go fix us a meal," he ordered, waving her inside. *Like father, like son*, I thought. The girl lumbered into the hut, a melon on a stick.

"Numa," I said. "What do you hear of her?"

"Oh, Numa," he replied, as if he had forgotten all about her until this very moment. "I heard of her one time, right after our father died. She was well then, the mother of two boys. Twins, can you imagine! Bad luck, the Romans say, like their Romulus and Remus, but who knows?"

Our meal was poor, just thin porridge and cheese. I noticed that Pala had a gaunt, unhealthy look and wondered if she and the child would survive. Tito explained that the workday had been expanded to eight hours, and the number of days owed to the landlords by the plebs had steadily grown.

The old public grazing lands had all been turned to wheat, so Father's goats had long ago been slaughtered. Tito and Pala lived on what they grew on the small plot left to them, and whatever the lords saw fit to share. But they seemed not unhappy. Tito had never been dark and dour like our father or angry like Maron. He had always been content with whatever came to him.

I noticed a twig cross hanging on one wall of the hut. "Tito? Are you and Pala Christians now?"

"Sure, we're following the Way. Pala brought me over. You join the right church, you get a little alms sometimes too. Even if you have work, the priests sometimes help you out if you help them."

"What help could a priest need from you?" I spooned up a little porridge, but it was tasteless to me. I'd become used to finer food in Carthage.

"Oh, you know, sometimes they need some big guys in the crowd when they get in an argument with some other church. You know how that goes."

I certainly did. "Tito, that's how our brother died."

"Don't worry, sister. I'm baptized now. I'll go to Heaven and be with Jesus when I die, plenty to eat, no work. You ought to come over. Jesus is coming back anytime, real soon. You want to be on the right side when he comes."

We parted with hugs, and I was surprised to find myself feeling real affection for this brother, whom I had hardly missed and almost forgotten. I had associated Tito with angry Maron and our dark, bitter father, and had forgotten his carefree warmth.

"It was good to see him," I said to Aurelius as we walked the dusty path back to town. Adeo rode on Aurelius's shoulders, his head resting on his father's black curls.

"They're certainly in a bad way," Aurelius answered.

"They can't help it! The lords keep demanding more and giving less!" I tried not to remember that one of those demanding ever more was Aurelius's own patron, who was our next stop.

"Don't get mad at me. I wasn't criticizing your brother. I know it's the demands of the empire that put the plebs in that state. That's what I'm saying: how much farther can it go?"

I snorted. "As far as they want it to."

"But isn't there some limit? Amicus thinks the empire's in trouble. How can they continue to feed their city and their army if there's some kind of famine or rebellion? Their borders stretch across Europa in the north. Rome's already been sacked from that direction. And look at the southern border.

The Aitheopes raid pretty much at will now. The only reason they don't cause more trouble is because there aren't as many of them as the Saxons."

I thought of Miriam, living now in that wild borderland. I found myself echoing my father. "They're the Romans, Aurelius. They don't get in trouble. They're everyone else's trouble."

———•••———

The contrast between my brother's mud hut and Urbanus's palace was disorienting, like first waking and wondering which world was the dream and which real.

A slave brought us wine and a dish of honeyed nuts for dessert. Adeo stuffed his cheeks with the nuts until Aurelius scolded him, at which time he retreated to a couch and fell instantly asleep, sticky flecks of nut skin clinging to his round cheeks.

Urbanus heard our story of our marriage and Monnica's reaction without comment. When we finished, he frowned and toyed with his wineglass, rings glinting on his broad hands.

"The Manichean marriage is a minor problem," he said finally. "No one has to know about it."

I had grown bolder in my years in Carthage. "You don't understand us, sir," I said. "Since Aurelius is disinherited anyway, we would like to be legally married as well."

Urbanus looked at Aurelius and raised his eyebrows.

Aurelius held his eyes, but I noticed his hands fidgeting in his lap. "Yes, sir, that's true. If . . . if possible . . ."

Urbanus stood suddenly and paced to the wall, his back to us. Then he spun around to face us. "I sent you to Carthage to become educated," he said to Aurelius, "and you return still a foolish child."

Aurelius's mouth fell open and his face turned pale.

Urbanus continued, "Do you think that because I'm fond of you I will continue to fund you no matter what you do? Let me explain something that I thought you already knew." He swept his arm around the room. "Everything we have is dependent on the empire. Let the empire fail and all of our pleasures and comforts would desert us soon after, even assuming that we survived. And the empire is dependent on two things." He held two fingers close to Aurelius's face.

*The empire is dependent on many thousands of things,* I thought: *the peasants who grow its wheat and olives, and its vast army of legionnaires, conscripted in these days from every corner of the empire except the Roman elite.* But, of course, I kept this thought to myself.

"Those two things," Urbanus went on, "are discipline and patronage. The army runs on discipline and maintains order from Britannia to Palestine. What makes you think that no self-discipline is required of you? We don't marry whoever takes our fancy, like peasants. We marry to maintain and advance our own fortunes and that of the empire. We marry someone who can advance our interests and the interests of our patrons. In your case, that would be me."

Aurelius and I sat before him like two statues.

"Your mother will come around," Urbanus said, with a wave of his hand. "Christians are all fanatics, but her love for you and her own self-interest will win out in the end. The marriage is meaningless, and you can still inherit as long as you worship your Mani in secret. But, you are only half as useful to me if you are unavailable as bait to some wealthy young virgin's influential family. Do we understand each other now?"

Aurelius nodded. "Yes, sir."

Urbanus looked at me for the first time. "You're as clever as you are pretty. But, you surely see that you can't be allowed to ruin your young man's prospects."

My heart was pounding, but I had to ask, "But what about our son's prospects, as a bastard?"

"Knowing his parents as I do, I don't doubt that your boy is extremely bright. Intelligent bastards often do very well in the Church or the civil service, *if* they have the right patronage. Without a patron . . ." He shrugged. "Are we all in agreement now?"

We both nodded.

"Good. Now, we need to talk about how you can best be of use to me." Urbanus sat across from us, forearms on his knees, swirling wine in the goblet dangling from one hand. "I've postponed some of the plans I had for Thagaste. The empire is spread thin. It seems dangerous to invest in a town so close to a border that may not be defensible any longer. I'm expanding my interest in Carthage. I have a factotum there, but I need a rhetorician, someone to argue my cases before the courts when I have a need."

"But I wanted to teach," Aurelius objected.

"Open your school. Go ahead. I'll send you a monthly stipend. As long as my interests come first. You will go in front of the judges or governors whenever I need you and I expect you to make useful contacts for me. Am I understood?"

It was rhetorical question. Urbanus had already made clear that Aurelius would do what was most useful to him, regardless of how we felt. But I felt my heart lift. I had dreaded settling into Thagaste under Monnica's disapproving eye, and with both Miriam and Numa gone, there was nothing drawing me here.

And so we would return to Carthage, where Aurelius would represent Urbanus's business interests in the provincial courts, make influential contacts—and be dangled as marriage bait before every prominent family in the province.

# CHAPTER SEVENTEEN

A WHIRLIGIG of flying arms and legs in a cloud of dust burst through the gate. "Mama! Mama! Look what we caught!" Adeo shouted as he skidded to a halt in front of the chair where I was taking the sun on this pleasantly cool winter afternoon.

Eight now, Adeo was tall for his age and wiry, all arms and legs and enormous brown eyes. He was the leader of a pack of energetic boys, most of them a year or two older than he. Two of these trailed along behind him now.

Adeo held a basket in front of my eyes. "Guess what's in here."

"I can't imagine. Will I like it?"

"No!" he announced proudly. "You'll hate it! Are you ready?"

I nodded, and Adeo backed away from me a little, peeled the lid halfway off his basket and peeked into it. Then he held the basket in front of my face, still holding the lid partly closed.

I lowered my face to peer into the basket. A bright-green lizard darted toward me. I gasped and Adeo slammed the lid back down.

"Did you see it? It's a lizard! We caught it in the wadi." The winter was yet young and the rains were late. All the little streambeds outside the city were still dried into wadis, some muddy, some as dry as ancient bones.

But water still reached Carthage through the mighty aqueducts that snaked into the city from the Atlas Mountains, a distance of over one hundred miles.

"Can we have another basket? We're going to put this one away and take the basket and try to catch more."

"Go up and see what you can find. Not my good willow one!" I called as he sped off toward our second-floor apartment, taking the steps two at a time, his minions still trailing behind.

"Do you know those children?"

I turned, startled. It was Aurelius, home from school. I shrugged. "Just local kids."

"He's getting older," Aurelius pointed out, frowning. When I failed to respond, he continued, "We'll need to start being more careful about his companions. He isn't too young to start meeting the kinds of boys who can introduce him to patrons, as opposed to the kind who introduce him to lizards."

"He'll certainly need every advantage he can get in life," I agreed drily. Aurelius and I had long since reached a bitter truce on the topic of legitimizing Adeo. He claimed to want to marry me and legitimize our son, but was constrained by his family's and his patron's continued opposition. He still received no funds from his mother and only a small stipend from Urbanus for representing him in Carthage. We were dependent for a living on the tuition from the school that he ran, and the parents paid only sporadically.

We made do without a servant and still lived in the same two-room second-floor apartment that we had moved into when we first arrived in Carthage almost a decade ago. I had taken on more scribe work to supplement our income.

When Aurelius failed to rise to my bait about the advantages that he had failed to provide for our son, I asked, "How was school?"

"Terrible!" he spat, and started pacing in front of me and running his hands through his thick, wavy hair. He had only grown more handsome now that he was fully a man, heavier and more muscular, even his face and his large hands firm with manly muscle, his beard so thick and black that he needed to be shaved at the baths twice in one day.

"How can I expect them to treat me with respect when their parents don't even respect me enough to pay me on time?" he said.

I began to answer, and then realized that answers weren't what he was looking for, as he kept pacing and went on, enumerating sins on his long fingers. "Theo's parents: Haven't paid in three months. The Lupins: wanted to know if they could give me one of their slaves in payment. Oh, but by the way, the slave's my mother's age and looks one hundred. How clever of them to think of a way to make the dumb schoolteacher care for her in her old age and at the same time skate out from paying the teacher! They're geniuses! I don't know why they have to pay me to teach their brats when they're so brilliant themselves! And are you ready for what those boys did today? Are you ready?"

I nodded, since it seemed this was the only possible response.

"They slipped senna into the water jug! All of us were running back and forth to the outhouse all day! I almost didn't make it once. Oh, wouldn't they have loved that!"

Once, when I had reminded him that these sorts of pranks were exactly the kind that he had played as a teenager in Thagaste, and that his friends had often done far worse as young university students here in Carthage, he hadn't spoken to me for the rest of the evening. So, having learned my lesson about that, I chose to soothe him now. "They're just boys. They're probably looking for a firm hand."

"I know what kind of firm hand I'd like to give them. But, then their parents would accuse me of brutality and pull them out and send them to a cheaper, gentler teacher, from whom they will learn nothing." He sat and sighed. "Oh, who am I fooling? They're learning nothing from me. Theo's a bright boy. I see so much potential in him, but I can't seem to bring it out. I'm constantly distracted by keeping the other boys from either killing each other or making a complete fool out of me." He looked up at me. "Maybe I'm not cut out to be a teacher."

I was so startled that I stared at him without replying.

"Amicus is coming back. He's got a position in the civil service and his betrothed is a Christian with contacts in the Church. He might make some contacts for me."

Finally, I found my voice. "All you ever wanted to do was teach."

"I don't know what I want. I'm not making enough money, I'm not finding new patrons, I'm not effective with my boys." Twice in the five years since we had returned to Carthage, Aurelius had managed to avoid betrothal to young women whose families could have advanced his career, and my insides began to twist with the usually suppressed fear that the next time a rich young virgin was dangled in front of him he would not be so ready to resist the bait.

And so, even though I also worried about our limited funds and inability, so far, to secure any kind of future for Adeo, I soothed Aurelius. "You've just had a bad day. Here, sit. I'll run out and get us a nice fish for supper, and some fruit."

I decided that the next day I would go to the forum and work harder to earn more clients for my scribing service.

# CHAPTER EIGHTEEN

THE SKY SLOWLY darkened to indigo, and I shivered and wrapped my cloak closer against the spring evening. Parents from all over the city fidgeted in the seats of the outdoor theater, each waiting for their own child's turn in the annual declamation contest at the open-air Mariners' Theater. Seats rose in arc-shaped tiers surrounding the stage below. Stone masks formed the backdrop for the stage, and, beyond that, a colonnade of cypress trees led to a small forum bequeathed by the same marine traders who had endowed the theater. Around the forum, they kept offices where they traded goods, accepted payments, and booked passage for people and commodities.

Slave children clambered up and down the tiers selling fruit, nuts, and clay cups of watered wine.

"Will it never be Adeo's turn?" Aurelius muttered, as we listened to a painful recitation of Terence by a ten-year-old.

"The youngest go last, and the order is chosen by lottery," I reminded him. "Adeo must have been unlucky in the lottery."

Finally, the torture of Terence was finished and now our own Adeo marched onto the stage, wearing his first off-white toga and bulla, a pouch on a neck chain that contained good-luck amulets. Aurelius believed the amulets were nonsense, and I suspected he was right, but an upper-class young citizen should have a bulla for special occasions, and so I had used some of my savings to purchase the toga and bulla. The money I earned copying the news gave me a feeling of fullness and comfort. Every night, I reminded myself of my growing pile of coins in the vault of Piso the money changer and wriggled with contentment before falling asleep. I knew to the copper the exact amount that Piso held for me, but seeing Adeo look like such a little man tonight, I was not a bit sorry to have drawn it down by several denarii. It was an honor for a boy so young to be included in the competition.

Aurelius tensed as Adeo stopped in the middle of the stage and took his first pose. I felt twittering in my stomach too, and took Aurelius's hand. Adeo had only to recite a few short lines from Cicero. I knew he had them memorized. We had practiced and practiced in the weeks leading up to the contest. But would he freeze and forget once he stood on a stage? Would he stumble on his words? I wished that I had a god that I believed in. I fingered the cross that Miriam had placed around my neck so long ago for good luck.

Adeo raised his right arm, and his toga draped impressively. He surveyed his audience and began: "Cicero on wisdom." He paused again, as his father had taught him. *Good so far, good, good*, I thought, leaning forward and biting the inside of my lip.

He went on, his forehead wrinkled appropriately in a thoughtful frown. He spoke slowly and clearly, his boyish soprano audible in the highest tiers. "'If the souls which we have are eternal and divine, we must conclude that, the more we let them have their head in natural activity, that is, in reasoning and in the quest for knowledge, and the less they are caught up in the vices and errors of mankind, the easier it will be for them to ascend and return to Heaven.'" He lowered his arm so that his elbow bent at waist level, again showing a smooth toga drape, and bowed his head slightly.

"Bravo!" Aurelius burst out, and began clapping wildly. I noticed his eyes filled with tears and felt a lump in my throat myself. I clapped until my hands hurt and blew my little boy a kiss, which he did not see. He strode from the stage with the folds of the unfamiliar toga swirling around his skinny legs. How I loved him at that moment, with his glossy cap of curly hair like his father's, and his square chin and full lips, which suddenly reminded me of my brother Tito.

"He'll win," Aurelius assured me, still clapping. "He should definitely win. Oh, he did excellently, excellently," and he folded me into a hug.

A restless murmur ran up the tiers as anxious parents and friends awaited the announcement of the awards. Aurelius grabbed my hand and we tensed and leaned farther and farther forward as the awards were announced for the bigger boys.

"Finally," the moderator announced, "in the eight-to-ten-year-old category, this year's declamation prize goes to Adeodonatus Augustinus, for his fine delivery of Cicero."

Aurelius leaped to his feet and banged his massive hands together over and over, stomping his feet, and finally whistling through his teeth. His face radiated joy and pride as he looked over at me. "I knew he would do it! Oh, Leona, he'll outshine me in every way! Our boy's star will rise higher than I could ever dream for myself."

———•••———

Most of the crowd had already streamed out of the theater by the time we found Adeo and collected him to head out.

His father wrapped him in a fierce hug first, lifting him off the ground. "You did better than I could have dreamed of at your age!" He put Adeo down and held him by the shoulders at arm's length. "Have I ever told you how proud I am of you?" he asked.

"Thank you, Father," Adeo replied formally, as if the donning of the toga had stripped him of his North African warmth and transformed him into a different person, more formal and dignified.

"We're proud of you," I said softly and gave my newly dignified son a quick hug.

"Get that blasted blanket off now," Aurelius ordered, "and let's go out and celebrate. Is the Goat's Head still your favorite tavern?"

Adeo's eyes lit up. "Yes."

"Fried squid?" his father asked knowingly.

"Yes!" Adeo began to flail at the folds of the toga, in his hurry to shed the heavy woolen garment. "I'm roasting in this," he admitted. I helped him unwrap it and folded the voluminous material over my arm as best I could.

"This thing weighs a ton," I complained. "Can't we drop it off at home before we go to the Goat's Head?"

"Yes," Aurelius replied. "Actually, I wanted to stop to visit Amicus anyway. Quintus let me know he's sick."

"Amicus is sick? What's wrong?"

Aurelius shrugged. "Probably some foul bug he picked up in Rome or at sea."

Amicus, Nebridius, and Quintus had just returned from a trip to Rome. Amicus and Quintus had received imperial commissions through their patrons, and Nebridius had tagged along just for fun. I knew that Aurelius had mixed emotions: he would have loved to see Rome and he envied his friends their powerful patrons and imperial commissions, but he had a dread of the sea.

I doubted he would ever set foot on a boat. It was irrelevant anyway: we lacked the funds to finance the trips ourselves, and in the absence of any work that Aurelius could do for him in Rome, it was not even worth asking

Urbanus to finance the trip. We had not seen our friends since their return to Carthage.

"All right, home, then say hi to Amicus, then Goat's Head!" Aurelius said, clapping Adeo on the back.

Amicus's sister and widowed mother had come to Carthage to stay with him now that he had an imperial commission. The commission provided enough income for a house and servants, and we were shown to Amicus's tiled sitting room by a quiet teenage girl with the brand of a runaway on her forehead. I wondered that Amicus would consent to have a slave who had previously tried to run away.

Our friend lay on a bronze-legged couch covered with an embroidered cushion. Quintus reclined on a similar couch nearby, a cup of wine in his hand.

"Adeo won the declamation prize for his age group!" Aurelius announced before we were even halfway across the floor.

"Prizes already at such a young age!" Amicus exclaimed. "What did you recite?"

"Cicero," Adeo told him, smiling.

"Let's hear it then."

Adeo recited his piece, minus the heavy toga, but with the arm gestures and pauses at all the right places again.

"Bravo!" Amicus cheered.

"You'll soon outshine your father," Quintus said.

Aurelius beamed. "That's exactly what I said." He turned to Amicus with concern. "Quintus said you were sick."

"I haven't felt well since we set sail from Ostia," Amicus admitted. "I feel weak and my chest hurts when I breathe. The doctor says to rest and breathe vapors of rosemary. That's what you smell." I did notice the astringent scent of rosemary slicing the air of the room.

"And is it helping?"

"Not yet." Amicus coughed, and I could see by the folds of pain in his face that his chest was hurting him very badly. "Aurelius, sit," he said. "We have other news for you. Good news, but news that I don't think you'll like hearing at first."

Quintus glanced at Amicus out of the corners of his eyes, then his gaze skittered toward Aurelius.

Aurelius frowned and gestured for his friend to continue.

"We've become Christians, all of us: Quintus, Nebridius, and I."

"You can't be serious."

"I am. We are to be baptized Good Friday next, all three of us together."

Aurelius flushed. "But, we always agreed that Christianity was just a bunch of hocus-pocus. It's Mani that offers a scientific explanation of the world."

Quintus gestured with his cup and the slave girl poured him some more wine. "Aurelius," he said, "stop and think for a second: how is the story of the Five descending to the realm of darkness to rescue the First Man any less fabulous than Christ's resurrection?"

"It's completely different! Amicus, Quintus, you know what these Christians are: they're women and slaves who believe that relics of the true cross can heal leprosy and the bones of their saints can bring sight to the blind."

"Anything is possible with the power of God," Quintus replied.

"But can you explain how that happens?"

"Can you explain how the particles of light are entrapped and then released?" Quintus shot back.

"No, but Faustus can." Faustus was a renowned scholar and speaker, the most famous of Manichean priests. "He'll be in Carthage later this summer to debate Christians and conduct seminars," Aurelius went on. "He'll explain the origin of the universe and the path to goodness scientifically, not all wrapped up in magic like your Jesus."

Quintus took a long sip of wine and smacked his lips. "Aurelius, you had better open your eyes. The empire has become Christian. Anyone who wants to get ahead should do the same."

"I thought we were scholars. I thought we were seekers of truth before we were seekers of power. Didn't we agree to that one night, or was I so drunk that I'm remembering wrong?" Aurelius's voice was rising.

"Aurelius is right," Amicus said to Quintus. "He shouldn't pretend to accept the Lord just because it would help his career. It would be a grave sin to convert just to gain political advantage." He paused to cough, and then continued, "No, Aurelius, you're right. You should follow your conscience. God will know if you try to deceive him or use him to advance your career. We'll pray every day for you to see the light."

"I'll pray too," Aurelius answered. "But I'll also come back to you with answers once I've spoken with Faustus. Then we'll see who converts—or de-converts."

"We will," Amicus agreed.

The serving girl refilled Quintus's wine cup again. I whispered to Amicus, "Why did you buy a runaway?"

"To free her," Amicus answered. "She had run away not once but twice, and the penalty this second time was to be amputation of a foot. I bought her from her master to save her from that fate and she now works for me for a small wage."

"Aren't you afraid she'll run away on you too?"

"Not really. She's grateful and I treat her well. But if she should want to leave, then she's free to do that. Christ came to bring a new age, when the last shall be first," he added, with a nod toward Aurelius. "He leaves us no room to mistreat others. He was clear: do unto others as you would have them do unto you."

"Cicero says almost exactly the same," Aurelius grumbled, "and he says it without all the mystery and magic—oh, not to mention virgin birth."

"No more unlikely than the half-fish, half-bird Prince of Darkness," Amicus replied.

Adeo sat silently, his wide eyes shifting from one speaker to the other.

Clearly, he was the night's only winner; neither Mani nor Christ would win a convert this night.

———•••———

Aurelius railed the whole way home that night about his friends' conversions. Poor Adeo's triumph was nearly forgotten in the complaints about mysteries and suspicious healings, about cynical conversions and proliferating splinters of Christ's cross. "That thing would have to be one hundred feet high to account for all the pieces of it that have been miraculously 'discovered' and put in gold boxes on altars," Aurelius complained. "Adeo, you spoke well tonight, but be sure that you always speak truth. Don't be taken in by claims that can't be proven. The other word for *miracle* is *lie*."

Later that night, though, after lovemaking had drained his tense peevishness, I lay with my head nestled in his shoulder and he stroked my back lightly. "Did you think Amicus looked bad?" he asked me.

"It looked like it hurt him pretty bad when he coughed."

"His color was bad and he was thin."

"It's probably nothing," I said. "A chill he caught in Italy or at sea. After a few more days' rest, he'll be fine."

Aurelius shook his head. "I think I'll go see him again tomorrow."

———•••———

Amicus was worse when Aurelius looked in on him the next day: blue lipped, coughing almost constantly, too weak to sit up on his couch. Aurelius began stopping in every day after school, and every day Amicus was bluer and weaker. I went one afternoon about a week after the declamation contest.

My nemesis, Quintus, met me at the door with the branded servant girl. "He's taken a turn for the worse," Quintus told me. "We've sent for a priest."

"Will the priest be able to cure him?" I shared Aurelius's doubts about amulets and miracles but thought that, since the Christians were growing so powerful, perhaps their priests had special magic.

"With God all things are possible, but we shouldn't get our hopes too high for this life. The priest is coming to baptize him."

Amicus had taken to his bed in the past few days, and we crossed the courtyard to the sleeping wing of his large house, the branded servant girl following us like a shadow.

I felt shaken when I saw him. His face was grayish, and he lay on his bed gasping for air like a fish out of water. From across the room, I could hear the wet rasping of his breath. I went to the bed and took his hand. "Amicus?"

He opened his eyes and smiled at me, too weak to speak. I squeezed his hand and he squeezed back, faintly, then exploded into helpless coughing.

I felt tears coming to my eyes. It was clear that he would be dead before nightfall. "Quintus, could we send someone to fetch Aurelius?"

Quintus snapped his fingers at the servant girl and gave her directions to Aurelius's school. She scurried out.

"Where is that priest?" Quintus fretted.

"I thought he had to be immersed in the font to be baptized," I said.

"Illness near death is an emergency. He can be baptized in his bed with a small amount of water and oil," Quintus told me. "Our God is merciful," he added piously, "to those who truly seek him."

He was just starting to pace the room, when a young priest in a long black tunic came in. He was so comically ugly that even Quintus was handsome beside him: bulbous nose, bulging fishlike eyes of a muddy hazel shade, and a row of teeth that looked meant for some much larger mouth.

"Brother, thank you for coming," Quintus said.

The priest quickly embraced Quintus and then lost no time in hurrying to Amicus's bedside and removing vials of oil and water from a pouch at his waist. "Can you confess your sins?" he whispered to the sick man.

Amicus raised his head from his couch and opened his mouth to speak, but only gasped and was overcome by a fit of coughing.

The priest waited for the coughing to subside, and then took Amicus's hand. "Never mind then, brother, don't speak. Only confess your sins to your Father in your mind, and squeeze my hand when you've finished your confession."

Amicus lay back and closed his eyes. I felt tears stinging my own again. *Oh, Amicus, of all our friends, your confession would be the shortest,* I thought. I recalled that he alone had stood against Quintus and Nebridius and their *eversore* pranks, when even Aurelius had one foot in their cruel and petty way of life.

I remembered his courage on the day when I first met him and Aurelius, and his reassuring presence on the awful day when Adeo had his fall, and I began to sob aloud.

Now the priest began his baptismal rite. "Do you believe in God the Almighty Father?" he whispered. "Only squeeze my hand for yes, friend."

"Do you believe in the Messiah Jesus?"

Quintus intoned, "I believed in the Messiah Jesus, His only begotten Son, Who is ruler over us, Who was born of the Holy Spirit and of Mary, the virgin, who was crucified under Pontius Pilate and was buried, and on the third day rose from the dead, Who ascended into the realms of Heaven and sits at the right hand of the Father, from where He will come to judge the living and the dead."

"Do you believe in the Spirit?"

"I believe in the Spirit, who is holy, one holy Church, forgiveness of sins, and the resurrection of the flesh," Quintus said.

The priest shook one of the vials, sprinkling water first on Amicus's forehead and then down the length of his body. "I baptize you in the name of the Father, the Son, and the Spirit," he said. He dipped his thumb into the vial of oil and made a sign of the cross on Amicus's forehead.

I saw Amicus turn grateful eyes to the priest, and hoped that the Christians were right, that we would see him again with the Messiah in some far-off Heaven. The room was silent for a moment except for the scraping rasp of Amicus's breath and the smaller sound of my own weeping. I saw Quintus's shoulders shaking soundlessly.

"I see that you're a Christian," the priest said to me, nodding to the cross that Miriam had given me almost ten years ago.

I felt embarrassed. "No, I . . . This was just a gift from a friend."

"Oh," he said. "I was hoping we could all pray together." He nodded to Quintus. "Let's you and I pray as Christ taught us."

The cross had never left my neck since Miriam had placed it there, and I occasionally fingered it when I had some kind of trouble in case it had of special power, and only rarely did I guiltily remember my promise to become a believer if only the Christian god would heal Adeo from his fall.

Now I felt sorry that I didn't know the Christian prayer to offer for Amicus, who had always been my friend. I stood sobbing as Quintus and the priest said their prayer.

*Our Father, Thou who are in the Heavens*
*Thy Name be honored;*
*They kingdom come,*
*Thy will be done,*
*As in Heaven so on earth;*
*Give us this day our daily bread,*
*And forgive us our debts,*
*As we also forgive our debtors,*
*And do not lead us into temptation,*
*But deliver us from the evil one,*
*For to Thee belong the power and the glory into the ages.*

As they ended their prayer, I moved closer to Amicus's bedside and began to bathe his face with cool water. He opened his eyes and his face flickered into a blue-lipped smile.

His eyes urged me to come closer, and I leaned toward him.

"Tell Aurelius," he rasped, and then paused to gather his strength for the rest. "Seek the one true God," he finished, and collapsed into a weak, rattling cough.

Time seemed to stop in the room now. At some unnoticed point Nebridius had arrived, and I don't know how long the four of us stood vigil listening to the soft rasp of Amicus's breathing. Every third or fourth breath, he would labor to take a deeper inhale, and his chest would jerk slightly and then collapse. His breath slowed and softened until finally he took one of his jerky inhales and then we no longer heard his hoarse breath.

We stood for a minute, no one wanting to be the first to admit that he was gone. It was the priest who finally approached the bedside, felt for a pulse and announced, "He's gone from us."

Nebridius and Quintus embraced and sobbed like little boys. I sat on a couch and held my face in my hands. Now, finally, Aurelius swept into the room. When he saw us crying, he stopped and the question appeared in his face.

I nodded.

Aurelius hurried to Amicus's bed and lifted one of his arms. Then he held Amicus's shoulders and gazed at him intently as if to verify that the corpse was really his friend's. And finally, he knelt with his face on his friend's shoulder and cried with the rest of us.

# CHAPTER NINETEEN

BEFORE FAUSTUS could deliver his lecture, he had to break out of prison.

The ban on non-Christian religious gatherings was enforced erratically, depending on which generals and imperial officials were currently in residence in the city, whom they owed favors to, and what level or target of persecution might serve their own political ends. Within Christianity itself, one sect or another might find themselves persecuted one year and favored the next. Arians, Donatists, Caecilians, and Gnostics found their fortunes changing depending on who was in power.

Faustus had the misfortune to arrive in Carthage while the intolerant Bishop Parmenianus still held power, but he was fortunate in that the bishop was also in need of money to build a new basilica, and many of Carthage's Manichees were wealthy merchants with the means to pay several substantial bribes—which ultimately persuaded a guard to look the other way while Faustus left his cell with some followers who had arrived to bring him a light meal of almonds and melon.

The agreement with the bishop included a stipulation that Faustus would leave Carthage immediately, without delivering any lectures or holding audiences with any of his followers—but within hours of his jailbreak, word went out to the most prominent Manichees in the city that the great man would deliver one lecture, with an audience afterward, before his escape from the city. Aurelius was one of those who received an invitation.

He put on his new cloak for his meeting with Faustus: saffron-colored, trimmed with dark-red lozenges around the border. I had ordered one made exactly the same for Adeo, and I had been delighted to see them walk together wearing their matching cloaks, two dark heads, two determined strides, Adeo's legs pumping faster to keep up with his father's long ones.

He fastened the cloak at his shoulder with a carnelian brooch made to look like a bunch of grapes.

"How do I look?" he asked me.

"Like you should be the emperor," I answered, and it was no exaggeration. To me, still, he looked like he should rule the world, with his firm gaze, his prominent nose, and his commanding height.

He laughed and kissed me, running his hands lightly down my hips and making me shiver. "The truth means more to me than empires. This will be a great day for me—and for my students. I can feel it, Leona. I'll have answers. I wish I could have persuaded Nebridius and Quintus to come with me. Even more, how I wish Amicus . . ." He shook his head and stopped.

"Nebridius and Quintus are new converts. They don't want to hear anything that might feed them new doubts."

"The truth should never be feared."

I shrugged. I had been surprised by how the Christian priest had handled Amicus's lifeless body; every priest of every religion I had ever heard of considered it a defilement to touch a corpse, but the ugly young Christian brother had treated Amicus's body with reverence and a kind of tenderness, tending to it himself instead of leaving the task to a slave. I had been astonished too, that rich and poor alike were buried in the Christian burial grounds, regardless of ability to pay. True, the poor were simply wrapped in a shroud and put in the ground with a wooden marker, whereas Amicus lay in a brick sarcophagus, but I had never known the corpses of the poor to be treated in any way except to be burned or to tossed into a dump far out of town, where they were subject to rot and raptors along with the animal carcasses and other garbage. Yet Aurelius responded to any favorable remark about Christian practices with the same disparagement about mysteries and miracles. His response to any questioning of his own beliefs was also always the same: that Faustus could explain everything scientifically. I was excited too, about his meeting that day with the great man. It was an honor and signified the respect that the Manichean elect of Carthage must have for Aurelius as one of their most eloquent apologists.

He kissed me again, quickly. "All right then, I'm off. Don't expect me until late."

From our window I watched him march down the street, always confident and purposeful, always in a hurry.

———•••———

It was very late when he returned. Adeo had pleaded to be allowed to stay awake until his father got home, but had long since fallen asleep sitting at our table over a book. He was too big now for me to carry him. I had to lift under his shoulders to get him to his feet and then drag him along to his bed. He was almost as tall as me now, lean and muscular like his father.

My eyelids felt gritty and heavy and I was just getting ready to give up myself and go to bed, when I heard Aurelius's tread on the stairs, slower and heavier than usual.

I stood when he entered the room, eager to hear about his meeting, but something stopped me from asking. He shuffled into the room, head down, shoulders hunched, and he closed the door quietly, as if the room held a sick person who might be disturbed by the noise of a door against a jamb.

I sat back down at the table. Aurelius sat across from me, hands folded on the table, head down at first. Finally, he raised his eyes to me.

"How did it go?" I asked.

He didn't answer for a few seconds, only stared into space with wounded brown eyes. "Not as I expected."

I waited for him to continue. He looked at me again and went on. "At first, I let myself be convinced that Faustus was all that I had been led to believe. When he began repeating the same stories that I already knew, I told myself that he was just setting the background. And then, finally, later in his lecture, he got to the part that interested me: the scientific explanations— and at first I tried to convince myself that it sounded implausible because I didn't have the mental powers to understand."

He paused. "But, then . . . Cicero has a better explanation of eclipses than Faustus. And I knew that Faustus's explanation made no sense, and I thought, well, it's just that, anybody can be wrong about one thing, but it made me listen more carefully. And I saw then that he wasn't really proving anything. He was just telling the same stories, only he was telling them more beautifully." Aurelius paused again and smiled wryly. "I don't know much, but I know good oratory when I hear it. He's a master of that, but . . . well, I still wanted to believe that he was all that he claimed and so I took advantage of the opportunity to question him after the lecture. I asked him how some of his claims were proven. I asked specifically about the eclipses, and cited Cicero. And do you know what he said?"

I shook my head.

"He said we just had to take it on faith!" He leaned back in his chair and spread his hands. "Well, that's exactly what my mother says about Christ's resurrection and the miraculous healings. That's not science!" He snorted a bitter laugh. "Anyway, he was impressed with me. He told me my questions were good, and flattered me with all he'd heard about my skills as a teacher and a speaker, and spent a long time with me, explaining his views further."

"Well, that's flattering." I poured him a glass of watered wine.

He scowled at me, and pushed the cup away. "It means nothing. The man is a fraud. I'm interested in the truth, Leona, a truth that can be demonstrated logically and understood by any honest man with a good mind. I'm starting to think that there is no such thing." His shoulders sagged. "I'm almost thirty. I've dedicated my whole life to the search for truth and ended up wasting ten years on a belief that turns out to be just another form of magic. My school is failing. Your news writing contributes almost as much to the household as my teaching—more, if I'm having a bad month and more than one student decides not to pay. I can't provide any kind of future for our son. My best friend is dead and my other friends abandon truth for mystery and a chance at power. My life is a failure."

I had no encouragement to provide, because everything he had said was true. "Come to bed," I said finally. "It will look better in the morning."

He shook his head. "You go ahead. I can't sleep yet."

I left him bent over the table, deep in thought. Many hours later, when the earliest light began to crack the eastern horizon, I dimly woke when he finally joined me in our bed, but he did not caress me into wakefulness and lovemaking as he usually would. As I drifted back to sleep I felt his stiff back facing me and knew that he would not sleep at all that night.

# CHAPTER TWENTY

ADEO AND THE LITTLE HEBREW BOY ran at each other with their sticks and then stopped a few feet apart.

"You'll pay the reckoning in full for all the pain my men have borne who met death by your spear," Adeo declaimed. Now they began to parry and thrust at each other with the sticks.

All summer, Adeo had been directing the neighborhood children in an enactment of Homer's *Iliad*, and on this calends of September, they had reached the climactic battle between Hektor and Akhilleus, with Adeo playing the role of Akhilleus. Our neighborhood was poor, and most of the children Adeo's age did not attend school. Adeo, the only literate child in our apartment block and a passionate fan of Homer, had begun entertaining his friends with war stories from *The Iliad*, and the stories had morphed into a play that had boys and girls playing, at various times, gods and goddesses, kings and warriors, in the pidgin of Berber and Latin that passed for language in the poor sections of Carthage.

When they felt that they had a particularly good scene to portray, they pleaded with parents and neighbors to watch in the small courtyard of the apartment block.

"War for the Trojans would be eased if you were blotted out, bane that you are," the little Hebrew Hektor cried, and he thrust at Adeo.

My mind was only half on the play that meant so much to Adeo. Since his failed meeting with Faustus, Aurelius had been like a man recovering from a serious illness. He came home after school and laid his books carefully on the table, instead of slamming them down and ranting about his pupils as he had virtually every single day since our return to Carthage. He was quiet during meals, responding mildly if Adeo spoke to him and usually pushing his plate away before he had eaten half of what was on it. After supper, he retired to our bedchamber with a pile of books—Plato, the Christian Bible, his old friend Cicero—and read himself to sleep. For that whole month, we did not make love a single time, and I had reached a state of barely suppressed panic.

What hold did I have on him if he no longer desired me? Finally, his mother's words came back to me in full force. I could be abandoned at any time. The tenuous hold of the Manichean marriage ceremony was irrelevant now that he had abandoned that sect. Legally, he owned Adeo and could forbid me to see him. If our physical passion disappeared, then I had only friendly affection and our son's attachment to me in my favor. I suddenly felt very vulnerable, and the money that I had slowly saved was little comfort.

Adeo and the Hebrew boy thrust and parried with their sticks and their words until Hektor lay in dramatically feigned death throes at Akhilleus's feet, and Adeo declaimed, "Die; make an end. I shall accept my own whenever Zeus and the other gods desire."

The scene ended with the wailing of Hektor's father and wife, and the enthusiastic applause of the small audience of parents and neighbors.

Adeo ran off with his friends, and Aurelius and I trudged up the stairs to our apartment. The evening was hot and dry, and I poured us some watered-down wine.

"I had a letter today," he said, "delivered to the school."

"From Thagaste?"

He nodded. "From my mother."

Most of the news we received from Thagaste came from Urbanus, when he occasionally wrote to direct Aurelius to conduct some business in Carthage on his behalf. We heard rarely from the still disapproving Monnica. "What's the news?" I asked.

"She and Urbanus are both coming to Carthage."

Unease squirmed in my belly. I sat down. "When? Do they say?"

"They say at calends, so they should be here any day. She says Urbanus has business here. And she says they want to talk to me about my future."

Unease turned to panic. "They have a bride in mind for you again."

He held up his hands in a calming gesture. "Maybe not. Maybe Urbanus knows of a better position for me." But I could tell that he wasn't convincing himself either.

"They can't take Adeo away from me. I'll run away with him." My heart churned with a dark combination of mother love and wild panic.

"Leona, nobody is going to separate you from Adeo. I promise. I will not let that happen."

I mentally calculated how much money I had saved. There was enough hidden to last me and Adeo a few months if I ran away with him. After that, I could surely find some kind of work, but where would I go? Why hadn't I thought about any of this before?

"I will, Aurelius. You see if I don't. I will go as far as I need to go to prevent them from finding us. I will not be separated from my son."

Aurelius's eyes softened sadly. "Leona, do you think so little of me and of my feelings for you? And for our son? I know it would break his heart to be separated from you. And as for you . . . you're the queen of my heart. Do you think I could bear to be apart from you? Why do you think I've turned down the other noble young 'virgins' they've dangled in front of me? Because I would rather be with you and Adeo in these two rooms, teaching in my shabby little school. I care about only three things: knowledge, our son, and you. That is all to me. I thought you knew that."

I started to cry, and he pulled me to sit on his lap. "I'd kill myself," I sobbed. "Really. It would be like ripping out my heart to be without him."

Aurelius patted and shushed me as if I were his child. "I know. I know. That will not happen. You have my word on it."

———

In the years since we had last seen her, Monnica seemed to have faded more than aged. Her face was still only lightly lined and her brown hair had bleached to tan. She had grown paler, thinner, more luminous, as if she would not die but was instead slowly being transformed into a spirit.

Urbanus, by contrast, had gained weight and did not look well. His hair and fierce eyebrows were frosted mostly silver now, and his skin hung coarse and loose like damaged leather.

There was no question of their staying in our two rooms. Urbanus and his knob-kneed teenage son, Licentius, had taken a vacant apartment in a building that he owned, and Monnica had a cell in a nunnery nearby.

Monnica's eyes filled with tears upon meeting her grandson for the first time in six years. She held him by the shoulders at arm's length. "A gift from God indeed," she admitted, "so like your father. I understand you're a scholar of Homer and a winner of prizes for your oratory. Tell me."

And in the easy way that he had with almost everyone, Adeo sat down with his grandmother, who five minutes ago had been a stranger to him, and described to her the oratory contest and the summer's performance of *The Iliad*. I felt, all at the same time, jealous, threatened, tender, and proud.

I ordered a light lunch and some wine to be brought in, and we spent the afternoon catching up on Adeo's development and events in Thagaste, Carthage, and the empire. An observer who didn't know any better might have thought that I was Aurelius's legal wife, Licentius his awkward younger brother, and Monnica and Urbanus both doting grandparents to Adeo.

But when evening came, Monnica and Urbanus took Aurelius and Licentius to Jupiter's Palace for dinner, leaving me and Adeo. The look that Aurelius gave me as he left our apartment was meant to be reassuring, but seemed pleading and helpless to me.

———•••———

He returned very late, closing the door quietly and tiptoeing past Adeo's pallet to our bed.

"I'm awake," I said as he crept into bed. "How could you think that I could sleep?"

He took off his cloak and sat on the bed to remove his sandals.

I sat up. "Well?"

"As we expected, they have found another likely wife."

"And?"

"And . . ." He pressed his lips together and looked away from me. "And a minor position with the imperial civil service . . . back in Thagaste."

"You've told them no before."

"They haven't threatened to cut off all my funds before."

"You mean Urbanus will no longer fund you either?"

"Will no longer help fund my school. Will no longer give me commissions for arguing his cases in Carthage. That's right. Cut off."

My heart started to pound and a storm whirled in my brain. "We can get by without his money. I can take on more clients."

"Leona, my school is barely profitable now. Without the backing from Urbanus, it will lose money. You'd be supporting us."

"I'll do that. You can find something else."

He was silent.

I rose from the bed and stood. "You can't be considering this."

Aurelius still failed to answer, staring toward the window, one sandal in his hand.

"You can't take Adeo! I told you I wouldn't let you take him from me! I'll run away with him. Do you hear me? You will not take my son!" I bent to look him in the eye.

"Leona, please calm down. You'll wake him. Listen to me. Nobody is trying to separate you from Adeo." He paused. "They've found you a husband."

"What?" The storm in my head gathered violence.

"In Thagaste, so you could be nearby and see Adeo regularly."

My eyes widened. "You cannot possibly be serious."

"According to Urbanus, the man remembers you from when you lived in Thagaste and is interested enough in your charms and in the dowry that Urbanus is willing to put up for you that he will allow you a continued relationship with Adeo."

"Allow me," I said quietly, then more loudly, "Allow me? And for how long? And for how long will you and your mother and your patron continue to 'allow' me? Do you think I'm stupid?" I leaned toward him again, so that my face was right in front of his. "Listen to me. I will never agree to this. Never. I will not be married off to some ancient pig that your mother chose for me."

Aurelius continued to stare down at the sandal in his hand and didn't answer me.

I started pacing. "Oh, and how are you feeling about this? You seem perfectly fine to me. Looks to me like it's okay with you if I'm gotten out of the way by being married off to some filthy old goat that your mother picked for me, while you get the rich young virgin with the honeyed thighs. Is that it? Maybe you're tired of me and this is just a good excuse to get rid of me." I started to cry. "Your mother said this would happen."

"There is another way," he said.

I raised my face, waiting.

Aurelius stood and finally looked me in the eye. "I had a letter a couple of weeks ago from some friends of Faustus, offering me a chair at a small university if I want it." He shrugged and one side of his mouth folded into a wry smile. "Faustus himself recommended me. Apparently, he liked me more than I liked him."

I looked at him without answering and he went on. "I would not have considered it, and was ready to send a reply turning down the position, but now . . . I feel false accepting help from the Manichees, and I suppose they expect that I will teach their philosophy in addition to rhetoric and oratory, but I guess I can't afford my principles now." He ran one of his big hands over his weary face. "And too . . . the position is in Rome." He lowered his voice to a whisper. "Leona, I've always been afraid of travel by sea."

It felt to me that the storm inside me had ended suddenly, but left devastation in its wake. I stared at him. "Rome." The word was lead.

Aurelius sat on our bed again and put his face in his hands. "I don't know if I can do it, get on a ship and trust my life to the sea. It's one thing to look on it, to splash around in it a little, but to set sail and see nothing but blue waves for days . . . I'm afraid that I will be unmanly and lose my mind."

My heart, too, was heavy with terror. Slowly, I lowered myself to the bed beside him.

"It's a way out, though," he continued, "and I don't see any other way. You're wrong in saying that I'm tired of you. I don't know how you can think that. The thought of you in bed with someone that my mother chose for you . . . that's torture to me. That's so awful to me that I would face the sea instead." He turned his head to look at me, and I saw the pain in his eyes and knew that he was telling the truth. "But there's the issue of the fee for passage," he said.

Now I smiled. "I have over one hundred denarii saved with Piso the money changer."

Aurelius's mouth fell open. He knew that I had money of my own saved, but I had never told him how much. I smiled wider at his astonishment and said, "I'll brave the sea if you will."

Aurelius was Romanized and seldom allowed himself tears as a Berber would have, but now I saw water rise in his eyes. "We're agreed then?"

I nodded, terror and joy rising in my heart in equal columns.

He started ticking off plans on his fingers. "I'll respond to the letter by tomorrow's mail ship then, and go down to the docks to arrange our passage. My mother and Urbanus will be staying for another week. We'll have to keep this from them. I must tell my students though, to give their parents time to enroll them elsewhere. I can leave the impression that I'm going back to Thagaste." He stood now and smiled for the first time. "This might turn out to be the best thing that ever happened to us."

---

We left most of our possessions behind for the family who took our apartment. Two weeks later we sailed, taking only our son, our clothing, Aurelius's books and what was left of my savings after paying for our passage.

# CHAPTER TWENTY-ONE

ADEO SQUIRMED as I tied the white scarf around his mouth and nose.

"Do I have to wear this mother?" he protested. "Please! None of the other boys wear one."

"None of the other boys are my son. I don't care if any of the other boys die. I care if you die." I tied the scarf at the back of his head, and lifted a garlic necklace over his head.

"Mother! No! Please! I won't go to school if I have to smell like garlic. Everybody laughs at me already."

I shook my finger in his face. "You listen to me. Do not come home without the mask on your face and the garlic around your neck. I don't care what the other boys do, and I don't care if they laugh. I will keep you from getting sick or I will die trying."

"You too," I said to Aurelius as he approached the door on his way to walk with Adeo to school. "And make sure he keeps his on," I added to their retreating backs. I glared out the window at them as they reached the street, to make sure that they didn't rip off the masks the minute they were outside. Aurelius looked up at the window, saw me, pointed to his face mask and saluted me. He gestured to Adeo to do the same, and I had to smile then at their dark heads and square shoulders, our son the smaller version of his father, even to the matching ocher tunics that I had bought them in Carthage.

Our time in Italy had not started well. The voyage across the Middle Sea was stormy. Aurelius was uncharacteristically quiet, and his mouth and eyes were tight with the effort to hide his fear from Adeo. As we tossed and pitched, I once again found myself fingering Miriam's cross and promising devotion to her God if only he would deliver us safely to dry land.

Deliver us he did, and Aurelius started his new job at the university. The Manichees at least paid on time, but they didn't pay well and we lived no better than we had in Carthage, taking an apartment in Rome's Subura district, a hive of windowless tenement buildings and poor immigrants from every corner of the empire. The imperial government had abandoned Rome for the relative safety of Milan, and the old capital had grown tattered. The students in Rome were every bit as unruly as those in Carthage, and Aurelius once again despaired at turning any of them into philosophers or orators. Worse, his principles chafed at teaching Mani's tenets when his eyes had been opened to the emptiness of the Manichean claims. In private, he read Plato and had joined a Platonic discussion club.

Then he was finally the recipient of some good luck. In Carthage, he had once been introduced by Nebridius to a visiting Roman senator named Symmachus. Symmachus was a lover of classic literature, and he and Aurelius had become passionate friends during the senator's short stay in Carthage. At the time, Aurelius had hoped that this friendship might become a patronage relationship and advance his career, but Symmachus returned to Milan and it seemed that he forgot Aurelius. It was I who reminded Aurelius of Symmachus after we had been in Rome for six months, and Aurelius wrote to him in Milan. Within weeks, he had an enthusiastic response and not long after that was offered the position of professor of rhetoric in the new capital.

In Milan, we had a small house of our own with a courtyard and apple and cherry trees and two servants. Aurelius was so busy that I could no longer keep up with all of his writing and correspondence, and he hired an additional scribe. Adeo attended lessons with a famous grammarian. Had I been able to convince Aurelius to marry me, my happiness would have been complete, but he took up Urbanus's argument that his career advancement depended on his marital availability.

We had been in Milan for two years when plague seeped into the city, first only a few rumored cases in the slums outside the city walls and then steadily increasing as winter advanced. Aurelius had always been opposed to charms and amulets, but as the plague worsened he didn't protest when I hung a string of garlic and a fisheye amulet on our front door. Nobody knew what caused plague. The pagans accused the Christians of bringing a curse on the city by offending the old gods. The Christian priests attributed the sickness to the wrath of their own god on those who refused to accept him. But it looked to me like the wracking cough and black swellings and vomited blood were no respecter of any religion.

I tried every preventive strategy that I heard of at the baths, the taverns, and the markets: the garlic, the fisheye, the face scarf. I kept in the house no leftover food that might attract flies. So far, my measures had worked. All three of us were healthy. I wasn't satisfied though, and sought additional insurance. That was when I remembered my many broken promises to Miriam's god and started praying in the Christian church.

---

I stepped carefully around the beggars who littered the steps in front of San Lorenzo, waiting for the daily alms distributed by the priests and the occasional copper quadrans that might be put in their hand by worshippers. I felt special compassion for the staring, hollow-eyed mothers with children draped across their laps and leaning on their shoulders, and sometimes brought with me a quadrans or piece of flatbread to give.

I arrived early to get a place toward the front of the courtyard that led into the western apse of the basilica. Only baptized Christians could enter the basilica itself during worship. Catechumens and casual worshippers like me were restricted to the courtyard, lined by the same rough gray stone columns that marched through the nave of the basilica.

Only a few other worshippers drifted around the courtyard when I arrived, chatting quietly with one another and selecting spots close enough to the three plain wooden doors to hear the service, but soon the court swarmed with activity. Women and children gathered around the central fountain to wash hands, face, and feet before entering the church. The small children squirmed and twisted, trying to escape their mothers' scrubbing hands. Slaves in their short tunics slid into spots toward the back of the courtyard, and a few noblemen in bright cloaks and embroidered tunics strode past the entrance columns and claimed places in the courtyard or continued through the doors. The men congregated on the right side of the courtyard and the women on the left, just as the baptized worshippers inside sat on separate sides of the church. Many worshippers wore face masks similar to the ones that I had improvised for my family. Pale sunlight swam on the water of the fountain on this late winter day. Even in the press of warm bodies, I felt chilled and longed for the hard, bright sun of our African home.

A child jostled me and his mother apologized as I stretched my neck, looking for my friend Cornelia. At last I spotted her entering the courtyard and waved her toward the spot I'd saved for us.

She shouldered her way through the growing crowd to join me, and folded me into an embrace. "Everyone wants to hear Ambrose," she remarked, nodding at the crowd. "How is everyone at your house?"

"Still well. And yours?"

"Well, thanks be to God," she said, her response muffled behind her face mask. "I heard a rumor."

"About the plague?" I was almost afraid to know.

"Yes, but it's good. I heard that Bishop Ambrose will announce today that one of the churches will be designated as a plague hospital. Any baptized Christian, rich or poor, can come and get care. And those who die will be buried on consecrated ground. He's asking for volunteers to staff the hospital."

"You're not thinking of signing up?"

"No, of course not. I have my family to think of, but Leona, think of it. They'll be doing just as Christ instructed: I was sick and in prison and you comforted me."

No church I knew of had ever done such a thing. I'd felt pulled toward the Christians in Milan for this reason. The Church in North Africa, riven by the Donatist schism and subject to both ecstatic frenzies and rigid legalism, had never held any appeal to me. But, Milan's Christians, under the leadership of Bishop Ambrose, exerted a pull by living the command of their Christ to feed the poor, visit the sick and imprisoned, comfort the afflicted.

From our place in front of the door, we could see the bishop under his canopy in the far apse: small and pale, with a halo of thinning hair and a forehead so large and prominent that he looked as if he might at any moment tip over from the weight of his thoughts. His dark eyes seemed as large and round as plums, and when he preached he leaned forward and turned his head slowly to fix those eyes on every person in the crowd, great or low, seeking out their sin, inviting them to redemption. Yet he was so small that he looked more like a prematurely aged child than the man who had discovered the remains of Saints Gervasius and Protasius, was rumored to be able to reach into a beehive bare-armed without being stung, and packed the baptized and the nonbaptized alike into any Christian church in Milan, where he spoke in a voice so full and commanding that it seemed impossible that it could come from his frail chest.

He had introduced singing into western churches, chants of such hypnotic beauty that I often felt tears as I hummed along. I longed to believe, but I had never received instruction and Aurelius had planted in me too much skepticism.

I listened to Ambrose's golden words, more beautiful by far than his embroidered robes or the ornate gold cross behind him, but still, they were only words to me.

The humming and jostling of the crowd stilled as he spoke for half an hour on the subject of everyone's worries: the plague. He quoted the Hebrew scripture that the Christians had adopted into their own sacred book: "You shall worship the Lord your God and I will . . . take sickness away from among you." The crowd sighed at these words and leaned forward in a wave. A few women began to weep. The bishop went on to explain that these words were meant not literally, for our own world, but referred instead to the life that baptized believers would know in Christ after death, a life without hunger or sickness or sin. "What is the body, after all," he went on, "but a tattered garment that we wear? It is that which we cannot touch or see that is most real about us and about which our Lord is most concerned. It is the soul that is the real man. The body, maimed or ugly or starving, poor or ill clad, wracked by disease or by sinful desire, will be cast off, leaving naked and visible our true essence, that which is already known to God."

I heard in this echoes of Plato, who was currently much admired by Aurelius and his circle of mostly-pagan academics, and I wished again that I could persuade him to come and hear the bishop, but Aurelius scoffed at the miracles of resurrection and redemption, and reserved special scorn for Ambrose's convenient discovery of the remains of Gervasius and Protasius, just at the time when he needed relics for his new cathedral.

As the sermon ended and Cornelia and I shuffled out of the courtyard shoulder to shoulder with the other worshippers, she gave me another tip. "I heard don't eat any meat," she advised, "just fish and fruits and vegetables and bread. I heard that the animals breathe in the plague ether and you catch it when you eat them." She shrugged then, as if to admit that it might be just a silly rumor. "Anything's worth trying, right?"

I shrugged back and nodded. She squeezed my hand and we parted at the courtyard exit.

---

"You should come and just hear Ambrose sometime," I told Aurelius again that night. "He's such a compelling speaker."

"That's exactly what makes him dangerous," Aurelius replied. "His listeners are mesmerized by his oratory and don't hear that half of what he says is hocus-pocus nonsense."

"He sounds a lot like Plato to me."

"Plato never conveniently 'discovered' the bones of dead martyrs just at the exact moment when he happened to need relics for his cathedral. Plato never claimed that anyone came back to life again after death. Read their Bible sometime, Leona, instead of just credulously soaking up whatever this great bishop concocts. It's full of contradictions."

"Only if you read every word of it literally."

"People should say what they mean," he shot back, frowning over a letter from a professor in Saxony. Since rising to his important position in the capital, he was often impatient with me, and the addition of a hired scribe had made me less useful to him. I often felt lonely and idle. Church, and my friendship with Cornelia, were my solace.

My thoughts about my own problems were interrupted when Adeo wandered into our study. "Mom? I don't feel good."

My head jerked up and I rushed toward him. His eyes were glassy and his skin was pale and sweaty. I put a hand on his forehead: burning. My heart started to pound and my head felt light, but I kept my voice even. "Come, let's lay you down on your bed and have Calla bring you some theriac." As I led him back to his bedroom, I glanced back at Aurelius and saw in his face the same panic that I felt washing over me.

———••———

I had Calla, our boy slave, bring a pallet to Adeo's room and I lay there all night, alternately praying, drifting into a restless sleep, and waking to pierce every inch of his body with my terrified eyes, willing the signs of plague not to appear.

By morning, he was covered with pink splotches and when I fearfully felt for the telltale swellings, I found one starting in his armpit, already darkening with poison. The blood drained from my head so quickly that I nearly fainted.

Anyone who had a country home was fleeing Milan, and many of the doctors went with them, but Aurelius sent Calla out to search for a doctor anyway and joined me in my vigil at our son's bedside.

I sat in a chair beside Adeo, bathing him with cool water and drinking in the sight of him, spotted and fevered as he was. Beneath the pink splotches, his face was the gray of pale stone, and yet his skin was almost too hot for me to touch. He drifted just below consciousness, tossing occasionally or clawing at some unknown attacker and then settling back with a moan. Sometimes his eyes opened and he stared into space as if wondering where he was; other times he turned his gaze to me and whispered "Mother?" reassuring himself of my presence and then fading back. The day advanced. Milan's frail late-winter sunlight splashed into the room, and my tears spilled onto my lap. Aurelius stayed with me, now still and as silent as a statue, now restlessly moving to the window and swearing under his breath at Calla, now pacing and running his hands through his wavy black hair.

Finally Calla appeared, flushed and sweating. His eyes were large as he hesitated in the doorway. "I couldn't find a doctor, sir. I did look everywhere you told me, I swear. They've all either left the city or were out on other calls. One doctor's servant said he might be able to come tomorrow."

"Tomorrow!" I cried. I raised my hand to slap him, but Aurelius gripped my arm in time to stop me.

"It's not the boy's fault," he said gently.

Calla cringed, glancing at me over his shoulder.

I pressed my lips together against the tears and frantically gathered my thoughts. "Go to my friend Cornelia Juliana. She lives on Dolphin Street, right outside the Christian quarter. Tell her to send a priest here. Don't come back without speaking to her, do you hear me? Now, repeat back to me where you're going and who you're looking for."

"Dolphin Street. Cornelia Juliana."

"Don't come back without that priest."

Aurelius looked at me sternly after Calla left.

"What?" I said. "I can tell you're thinking something."

"What do you think a Christian priest is going to do?"

"Try to make our son better."

"How?"

"I don't know how. That's for them to know. But I know that, while most of this city's doctors are running off to the country like rats, the Christians are staying and taking care of their sick. Do you have a better idea?"

"No," he admitted. "But, you know they don't have any special magic, any more than anyone else. If they're surviving in higher numbers than others, it's because they're giving each other better care."

"I'll take that," I snapped. In my heart, though, I was hoping for magic. I would have offered my soul to Christ, Moloch, or any other god who would spare my child's life.

---

Calla returned, out of breath, assuring me that he'd spoken to Cornelia and that she was sending us a priest. Very shortly, the priest, Brother Mark, appeared, a tall young man, handsome beneath the rings of fatigue around his eyes. He hurried to Adeo's bedside and examined him while Aurelius and I hovered.

He lifted Adeo's armpit, and our son moaned softly. The black swelling was the size of a small melon now. It hurt even to look at it.

"That swelling . . ." I fretted.

"It's a good sign," Brother Mark explained. "The ones with a swelling sometimes survive. We think the poison concentrates there instead of infecting the whole body. The best thing to do is to lance it. If he survives that, he has a chance to recover. Will you consent to this?"

I looked at Aurelius, who nodded, and sent Calla for towels.

Brother Mark gently lifted Adeo's shoulder and placed the towels under him. "This will be painful, but it may save his life," he said. He nodded first at Aurelius, and then at me. "You hold his chest and you hold his arm above his head to keep him still."

I bent to our son and whispered in his ear, "Adeo? The priest is going to cut open the swelling. It will hurt, but it will make you better." His eyelids didn't even flicker. I brushed my hand over his forehead.

We took our positions, and Brother Mark extracted a knife from the bag at his waist. He probed at the ugly tumor and Adeo flinched. I turned my head.

Adeo's body strained and I heard him gasp. Then he began to struggle against our grip. "Hold him still a minute more," Brother Mark commanded, but it was unnecessary. Adeo's struggles were so weak that it was no job at all to keep him still. I dared a glance back at him, and my stomach turned at the sight of dark blood and brownish pus staining the towels beneath his armpit.

Brother Mark held the towels against Adeo's armpit for several minutes, all the while bathing our boy in his intense gaze. I stared too, leaning toward Adeo, willing him to stop bleeding, to open his eyes and smile.

Finally, the priest straightened and stood. "With God's help, he may live," he said. He extracted a small vial from his pouch and rubbed a little oil on Adeo's forehead with his thumb. Then he placed both hands on our boy's head and prayed silently.

Brother Mark looked up at us at the end of his prayer and smiled. "His fever's already down. Feel."

I placed my hand on Adeo's forehead. It felt cooler. I looked up at Aurelius and a smile broke across his face as he saw the relief in mine.

"I'll come back tomorrow or the next day, if I can," Brother Mark promised. "It's in God's hands, of course, but I think your son is one of the lucky ones. I think he will survive."

<hr/>

Adeo flickered in and out of consciousness for the rest of the day, twisting and murmuring in dreams for a time and then blinking and fixing me with a vague frown. A few times he moved his lips as if to speak, but no sound emerged.

Once he tried to lift his hand to me but winced at the pain in his armpit and let his hand flop back down on the bed. I sent Calla away and nursed my boy myself, dosing him every few hours with theriac, wringing drops of water from a rag into his parched mouth, and bathing him with rose-scented water.

Aurelius sat in the room with me, Plato unread on his lap. "Remember how he used to pretend to read?" he said.

I smiled, picturing Adeo at three or so, unrolling a scroll and "reading" aloud in his high-pitched baby voice, as Aurelius read beside him. "'A big elephant comed and eated the fishes. And then a big whale comed and eated the elephant. And then a boat comed and all the men on the boat eated the whale.'" I quoted Adeo's first made-up story.

"Always the elephants, with him," Aurelius remembered. "How about the story where the little boy finds a ring and sells it for one hundred denarii and buys his mother a house? And the father's only allowed to visit them at the house?"

"Before he ever even heard of Oedipus," I added, and then we both fell silent again for a moment.

"I've never thanked you for him," Aurelius said.

"It never occurred to me that you should."

His eyes began to fill and his voice was wet. "He'll be brilliant someday. All his teachers say so. And winning that declamation prize back in Carthage when he was only eight . . ." He wiped the tears from his cheeks and quoted Cicero. "'Of all men, he is the only one that I would hope would surpass me.' And he will, Leona. Thank God." He put his face in his big hands and began to sob. "I thought he would die," he choked. "I didn't say it to you this morning, but I thought he would die before sunset today."

I went to him and stood beside his chair, and he wrapped his arms around me and clung to me. Sitting, he was only a few inches shorter than I was standing, and he buried his head in my breast and wept. I held his head and let my own tears of relief wet his black hair.

———•••———

I didn't expect Brother Mark to return, but the next morning Calla showed him into Adeo's room, where Aurelius and I still sat at our boy's bedside. Adeo was conscious but weak as a newborn, speaking little, his arms lying limp at his sides. I spooned thin porridge between his lips, and saw that it was an effort for him even to open his mouth and swallow. But he lived.

Not trusting a servant, I was hardening myself to change the dressing on his armpit as soon as I thought he'd eaten enough, when Brother Mark arrived.

He smiled gently. "I see our little lamb made it through the night."

"I can't thank you enough," I replied. "Look, Adeo, here's the priest who saved your life."

"Not I, the power of God," the Brother corrected. "Can I have a look at him?"

I would not move an inch from my child, but Aurelius stepped aside to allow the priest access. He laid a hand on Adeo's forehead while scanning him with his eyes. "Did he pass a good night?"

"He slept restlessly, but the fever seems to be broken."

Brother Mark gently lifted Adeo's arm and cut away the binding on the dressing. As he peeled away the dressing, Adeo winced and flinched, and I couldn't help doing the same. The priest moistened the dressing where it had stuck to Adeo's skin and eased it off so that he could examine the wound where he had lanced the swelling the day before. "The danger now is infection," he said. "Do you have any rosemary?"

"Yes."

"Boil rosemary leaves in water, a cup of rosemary to four cups of water, and use this water to bathe the wound once it cools. Bathe the wound every morning and every night, and dry it thoroughly before replacing the dressing. The dressing must be clean. Have your servant boil the rags and dry them in the sunlight."

I nodded. "Thank you for coming. We didn't really expect you back."

Brother Mark lifted his weary face into a wan smile. "It was a little selfish. I thought that your boy would live, and I needed a shot of hope. So few survive."

"Is the plague getting worse?"

He nodded. "Saint Hilary's is full. But fewer came yesterday than the day before, so perhaps . . ." He shrugged wearily. "It's in the hands of God."

"Not completely," Aurelius pointed out. "Our son would be dead if you hadn't lanced his swelling."

"But it was God who sent me to you," the priest pointed out. "And remember what your friend Plato said," he added, nodding toward Aurelius's book, "'The greatest mistake in the treatment of diseases is that there are physicians for the body and physicians for the soul, although the two cannot be separated.'"

Aurelius blinked. "You know Plato?"

"I studied Plato for many years, along with Cicero, Homer, and Aristotle. I'm still an admirer of the wisdom of the ancients, but wisdom is nothing beside the Word."

"Then you were an educated man?"

"Yes, I had a classical education, and houses in town, and estates in Tuscany, but my sister was converted by Bishop Ambrose and took me to him, and when our parents died, we were both baptized and gave all of our estate to the Church and dedicated our lives to serving the Lord. He has said that whatever we do to the least, we do to him, so in the face of every sick and dying person I see my God, and that helps me to do my work."

His words spoke to a stillness in me so that I momentarily forget even my sick child. Even Aurelius was speechless.

Brother Mark squared his shoulders now, as if heading for some battle. "Now, the two of you should rest. Nobody knows what causes this plague, but it can't do you any good to be exhausted and run-down. Your child will live, by the grace of God, and he will need his parents. Have your servant throw away everything that the boy touched before and during his illness, and open the windows to the sun. Nobody knows why, but these things seem to help."

I nodded, still under the spell of his words about his God. He said a last prayer over Adeo and was gone.

"Ambrose is the one I told you about," I said to Aurelius. "The one who he said converted his sister? That's the bishop that I told you about, that I go to hear."

Aurelius grunted.

"He's a great speaker. You should want to hear him just for the sake of that."

"Maybe sometime."

"His god healed our child."

"That priest healed our child, and Adeo was fortunate to have a strong body to start with. Ask yourself why not all who pray to the Christian God are healed."

I had no good answer for that, so I fell silent. But, in the days that followed, as Adeo regained his strength and good spirits, I felt myself in the presence of a miracle worked by the suffering God who admonished his followers to care for the poor and heal the sick.

# CHAPTER TWENTY-TWO

ONCE ADEO HAD regained his strength and it was clear that Aurelius and I had been spared, I thought to look for Brother Mark to thank him and offer a donation. The plague loosened its grip on Milan with the coming of spring. Fewer were falling ill, and the church bells tolling the count of the dead had fallen almost silent.

I knew Aurelius would try to talk me out of going to St. Hilary's to look for Brother Mark. Why risk illness now, with the plague almost defeated? I could hear him asking. But I felt compelled to seek out the handsome young priest who had saved our son's life.

I entered the foul-smelling dimness of St. Hilary's on a day of sunshine and fresh spring breeze. Motes of dust and little bugs floated and spun in the shafts of dirty yellow light near the windows. Many sick still lay on pallets and on the cold stone floor of the simple church. The stench of illness, sweat, and human waste was so stomach-turning that I drew the end of my headdress over my mouth and nose, and still my stomach roiled. The weak moans of the suffering and the rustle of the woolen robes of the nurses combined in the echoing stone church into a general swishing sound that was almost soothing.

I picked my way down an aisle, fearful of stepping on some poor soul, living or dead. I squinted into the dimness, seeking Brother Mark, and finally disturbed a nurse in a brown robe and foul spattered apron. "Is Brother Mark here?" I asked.

Without slowing her steps, she pointed to a corner of the apse near the altar.

As I approached, he was closing the eyelids of a gaunt man in a slave's tunic. It was hard to tell whether the dead man was young or old. He skin was gray and mottled, his cheeks sunken. I shuddered. How easily it could have been Adeo!

I could see the gleam of tears on Brother Mark's cheeks, and he buried his face in one hand, shoulders shaking. I stood awkwardly for a moment, trying to decide whether to speak or to leave him alone with his grief for a moment. Finally, I placed my hand on his shoulder and asked, "Someone you knew, Brother?"

"No, I—oh, it's you. The mother of the young man whose father reads Plato. How does your son fare? He still lives, I hope."

"Yes, yes, he's fine, thanks to you. But this man—was he a friend?"

"No," the priest replied, rising wearily, and gazing at the dead man with regret. "No, he was left here two days ago by another slave. The family they served were in a hurry to get out of town, and left them here. I thought he might live, but . . ." He rubbed his face with one hand.

"You seemed so upset, I just thought . . ."

"No, I never even got his name. He reminded me of our Lord. He was a Jew like our Lord. I knew by his facial hair and his . . . they have a distinctive ritual having to do with the male organ, you see. And, of course, he was of a lowly caste, like our Lord Jesus." He looked softly at the dead man. "It was especially for the ones like him that our Lord came among us."

"He . . . your God was born a slave?"

Brother Mark looked at me with something like amusement in his weary eyes. "Not a slave, no, but of humble parents. You didn't know that, I see."

"I knew that many of the poor follow your God. My brother . . ." I started, then finished: "No, I didn't know. I thought he was powerful, like other gods who rise from the dead."

"He is like no other god you've heard of. He gave up that power to be among us, to be like us, even the lowest of us, like this poor slave."

I felt light-headed, maybe from the stench in the church, and my heart was hammering too, as if I were in the presence of Brother Mark's strange god, the god whose symbol I had carried around my neck for years with no real understanding at all.

"You're surprised," Brother Mark said.

"I . . . yes."

The priest fixed on me the same tender gaze that had rested on the dead slave. "He loves you too, child. Go and sit with Him awhile." He gestured at the crucifix hanging behind the altar and, patting my shoulder, walked away.

I did as he said. I knelt in front of that image of the dying god for what might have been a few minutes or a few hours. Aurelius had taught me to be so clever with words, but I had no smart words during that time in the plague-infested church. Only *One of us! One of us!* my heart kept singing.

I had worn his symbol for years out of loyalty to Miriam, and had made careless promises to him in times of trouble, which I promptly broke. I had listened to Ambrose's sermons and found him to be as subtle and logical as Aurelius's beloved Plato—and far more comforting. I had been drawn to the Christian church, as so many were in these hard days, by their care for the poor and the sick.

But never had I known the astounding fact that this Christ was one of us, one of the poor and lowly.

I felt like a gong that had been hammered and made to sing some sweet music. As I knelt, my soul was slowly and willingly given over to this greatest and humblest of gods. After a while, I noticed that I was still clutching the gold coins that I had meant to offer to Brother Mark. I opened my fist and left them before the altar. Then I walked back home, feeling insubstantial, as if my body were made of light.

———••———

"You must do as you think best, of course," Aurelius said stiffly.

"And Adeo."

"Adeo must decide for himself when he is old enough. Do as you wish, take him to your Masses if you must, but don't fill his head with miracles and fairy tales when he's too young to tell the difference between truth and magic."

"I want the three of us to be together in Heaven," I pleaded.

"In Heaven. And where exactly is this Heaven?"

"I don't know."

"And yet you do know that if we're all baptized we will be joined there." I made no answer.

"Well, go ahead. I'm not stopping you. But you know what I think."

I hesitated over the words that I had to say next. "You know that we can't continue to live in a sinful relationship."

"Leona, don't be ridiculous. Priests live with women not their wives all over Italy and the empire."

"They live in sin then."

Aurelius flushed and didn't respond.

"We can marry now. You said so yourself before we left Africa."

"We can't marry now," he argued impatiently. "Leona, my position at the university depends partly on my availability as a mate to important men's daughters. They favor me as a potential son-in-law. Married to you, I'm far less valuable and therefore vulnerable."

I had half expected it, but still my body went heavy with disappointment. I knew better than to argue, but I couldn't help it. "There's always some reason. I've been a wife to you in everything but name. I'm the mother to your child. Think of him."

"I do think of him. Why do you think I'm so worried about my position?"

"Haven't I been as good as a wife to you?"

"Yes, yes, of course," he assured me, reaching to pull me to him. "Oh, Leona, you know I love you."

His touch was so warm, his hands so large and strong. I melted into his familiar body with the old ease, inhaling the sweaty, manly scent of him, his smell of olives and salt. My cheek brushed the coarse, springy hairs of his broad chest.

He cradled my face in his two big hands and lifted it to look into his eyes. "Listen to me. You are the only woman I have ever loved or ever will love. Nothing can change that. I admit that I'm ambitious, but that can't come between us, and your Bishop Ambrose can never come between us."

My heart sprung toward him, but I knew that I had to resist. Tears rose behind my cheeks. "It isn't Ambrose that comes between us, but the one that he speaks for."

"I speak a wholly different language," he teased, bending to kiss me, his full lips covering mine, his firm tongue probing behind my teeth. One of those hands that I so loved cradled the back of my head and the other gripped my bottom and pulled me tighter against him, so that I felt his swollen penis pressing against my belly. I melted farther into him, dizzy with lust—*oh, one last time, only once more and then I will be chaste.* He broke away from me and smiled, then lifted me and carried me to his bed. He laid me down, then lay on top of me without undressing, kissing me again, hard, my lips, my neck, my shoulders, biting lightly with his teeth sometimes, in the way he knew I liked. I clung to him and squirmed beneath him and he entered me and first his movements were slow, smooth, and taunting as he gazed down at me. Then his eyes closed and he lowered himself to me and moved faster and I moved with him, until pleasure came like a suddenly blooming flower, and he shuddered and groaned on top of me.

The familiar honey filled my veins. I couldn't move. I felt disappointed that my resolve had failed so easily and so completely, but I wasn't sorry. At the same time, I knew that this was the last time, that I would make my confession tomorrow and sin no more.

He knew that he was heavy on me and rolled quickly to his side, drawing me onto my side to face him. We lay like that in silence for several minutes, the sweat drying on our bodies, our breath slowing.

Finally, I broke from his embrace and stood, reordering my robe and smoothing my hair. He smiled up at me. "Leaving me so soon?" he teased.

"I make my confession tomorrow," I reminded him. "After that . . ." I looked down. "After that, I can't do this anymore unless we're married. I hope that out of love for me and your son, you'll allow me to live on here. I hope that I may continue as your friend. But, I can't sin with you anymore." It was the speech that I had intended to make earlier.

"You can't be serious!"

"Of course I can be serious! Weren't you serious every time you and your friends took a notion to dabble in Asceticism and you avoided my bed for weeks at a time?"

"That was different." He sat up.

"Different? Yes, I suppose it was. With you, it was the philosophy of the week. Oh, what am I today? An Epicure, a Cynic, or an Ascetic? Or shall I be a Stoic? Or a Platonist or a Manichean?"

He flushed and didn't respond.

"So, yes, I guess it is different," I went on. "You change your philosophy as often as you change robes. I waited until I found the truth."

"Are you so sure? So sure that you would willingly give me up? And your son?" He stood and took me by the shoulders, looking at me through narrowed eyes, testing me, but I finally understood him now and I knew that he would never be so cruel as to separate me from Adeo.

I shook off his hands and backed away from him. "If I had to, yes. I don't think I have to."

"We'll see. Clearly, you've made your choice. Don't expect me to bother you anymore," he snapped, and he rose and left the room. A few minutes later, I heard the front door slam, as if to add a close to his oration.

———

Robed in white, I filed toward the baptismal font, third in line behind Cornelia, with my fellow catechumens. The interior of the cathedral was lit by dim yellow candles belching wisps of gray smoke that burned my eyes.

"Do you believe in God?" Bishop Ambrose demanded of us in that startlingly powerful voice.

We responded: *"I believe in One God,*
*The Father Almighty*
*And in His only Begotten Son*
*Jesus Christ, our Lord,*
*And in the Holy Spirit,*
*Giver of new life,*
*And in the resurrection of the flesh,*
*And in one only, apostolic, holy Church everywhere,*
*Which is His Church."*

Nobody made a mistake. We had been memorizing the creed and the Lord's Prayer throughout our Lenten instruction. None of us had bathed since starting instruction, and we had fasted since dawn the previous day, Good Friday.

When my turn came, I handed my robe to an acolyte and stepped into the eight-sided font, in water to my knees. Ambrose quietly asked my name and then dipped the pitcher into the font and poured cold water over my head. It ran down my face, dripped onto my shoulders, made icy streams down my torso.

"Leona, die to sin and be reborn. By sharing in Christ's death, share in his Resurrection. I baptize you in the name of the Father and of the Son and of the Holy Spirit." Another rain of frigid water drenched my head and drew rivulets in the coating of sweat and body oil that caked my skin. Ambrose's thumb was firm as he traced the sign of the cross on my forehead.

The rising moon spilled watery light through the cross-shaped window above the altar. I had been light-headed all day, and now I suddenly felt lighthearted too, as if sin and cares that had been weights were lifted. Peace came over me, and ecstasy, a sense that I could lift my arms to the heavens and be borne up to hover over the dim cathedral, bathed in light and impervious to the choking smoke and the smell of sweat. I felt myself sway and the acolyte righted me and wrapped me in my robe again, guiding me out of the font.

Thus it was that on Easter Eve of the year 382, my life was made new.

# CHAPTER TWENTY-THREE

AURELIUS LOOKED up from his scroll and noticed my hungry gaze. He met my eyes, nodding and snorting, "God give you strength. If your eyes could undress me, I'd be shivering now."

"I still love you," I admitted.

"And your God more," he finished for me.

"Yes." Since my baptism, Aurelius was polite to me if Adeo was with us, cool and distant otherwise. Sometimes I looked at him across the table and remembered the touch of his firm lips on mine, the feel of his hands owning my breasts and hips, and I felt weak with desire for him. My confessor had warned me that my baptism would not drown that fire, only give me the means to keep it banked. I spent many hours praying for strength.

He tossed aside his scroll and stood. "I'm still a normal man with normal desires, you know, Leona, and I'm barely thirty."

"God provides a remedy for that. It's called marriage."

"We've already discussed that. You know why it isn't possible."

I said nothing, and looked down to at the scroll I had been reading, to avoid further betraying my body's longing. As he paced in his short robe, the muscles of his brown thighs and chiseled calves writhed, and the vigor of his movements put me in mind of another kind of vigor. How well I knew about his normal desires and his youth. My chest tightened so that I could barely breathe.

The air between us seemed alive with our desire, as if it were a physical presence like the elusive substance of evil he used to try to puzzle out. He paced over to me and stood over me. "You're torturing me. You know?"

I nodded and looked down, unable to meet his eyes.

"And you know," he continued, "that I could put you out at any time? You have no rights, either to your son or to any shelter of any kind from me. You have a home and contact with Adeo only because I'm good-hearted. I could change my mind anytime." He snapped his powerful fingers.

Now I looked up at him. His dark eyes were hard, but when they met mine, he crumpled to his knees in front of me, laying his head in my lap. "Leona," he whispered, "can't it be like before? What God could judge real love between a man and a woman? A man and a woman who have a son together? I swear I'll never abandon you. You know that."

He kneaded my bottom with his strong hands and raised his head to gaze at me pleadingly. I couldn't help it. I raked my fingers through his wavy black hair and lowered my face to kiss him, and he began to sweep me away again, when Calla appeared in the doorway and cleared his throat.

We turned our heads.

Calla cleared his throat again. "Beg pardon, sir. Guests."

"Who is it?" Aurelius snapped. It was very late. Adeo had been in bed for hours.

"The lady says she's your mother, master."

———•••———

Calla and Lavinia laid the table with bread and olives and fruit left over from supper. Monnica's servants were bedded on makeshift pallets on the covered porch off our kitchen. After the flurry of arrangements, Aurelius and I settled down in the dining room to hear the reason for his mother's visit.

As soon as she was seated and had a glass of watered-down wine in her hand, she sighed and visibly relaxed. She closed her eyes for a moment as if gathering her strength and then said, "I dreamed about you."

Small muscles around Aurelius's mouth twitched. I could see him struggling not to roll his eyes, instead holding them on her patiently.

"In my dream, I wept for your immortal soul, and a voice came to me and said, 'Where you are, he will be.' I spoke to my priest the very next morning and he promised me that my tears weren't wasted, and that the dream meant what I thought: that you will one day be baptized into the Church."

"It could mean instead that you will someday leave it."

"No. It said, 'where you are he will be,' not 'where he is you will be.'" She picked at a piece of fruit and continued, "I was angry when you sneaked out of Carthage. Urbanus and I had to make excuses to the girl's family. It was wrong of you. Your brother Navigus is married to the girl now. She came with land in Thagaste and connections in Carthage. They are expecting a child finally. She would have been a good match for you." She paused, but Aurelius reacted to all of this with the same patient face.

"Your brother's wife likes to do things her own way," Monnica went on, and I suspected that she was leaving out a lot. "I felt strongly that the dream was instructing me to come to you. I pray every day for you to accept the Church."

"Then the heavens are beset with prayer," Aurelius replied wryly. He gestured at me. "Leona has been recently baptized, and also prays daily for my salvation."

Monica looked at me for the first time, the obvious question evident in her eyes. I lowered mine, fearful that they would reveal more of my very recent lust than of my newfound chastity.

"Well," she said, "your brother has taken over your father's land and obligations, as well as what his wife brought. And it seems that you've found a good position here, so perhaps it was all for the best." She looked around. "We'll need to find larger quarters, though."

"You'll be staying then?"

"I plan on it, yes. Navigus is capable of running the family's affairs and his wife seems capable of managing the household."

My stomach wrung into a knot.

Monnica sighed again and stood. "I'm so very tired. Could your servant show me to my chamber?"

"You can use mine for tonight, mother," Aurelius said, "until we can make better arrangements for you. Calla," he ordered, "please show my mother to my room. I'll bunk in with Adeo for tonight."

———••••———

I was just finishing my prayers when I heard a tap on my door and I rose from my knees to answer. I knew that it could only be Aurelius, and I offered one last silent prayer for chastity before cracking the door open.

"For the love of your God, let me in, Leona," he hissed. "I won't rape you. I only want to talk to you."

I pulled the door open the rest of the way and pulled a shawl over my tunic. When I ended our physical relationship, I'd insisted that he keep the bedroom that we had shared, with its bronze-footed bed and cushioned chairs. The little chamber that I called my own now was furnished only with a wooden bedstead, a wooden table and chair beneath a small mirror, and a few hooks for my clothing. Aurelius folded his powerful body onto the edge of my bed. I remained standing in the corner, arms wrapped around my shawl.

"Sit down," he said. "You're making me nervous standing there like a terrified hart."

I lowered myself onto my chair, my eyes not leaving his, waiting to see what he would say.

"It seems we're stuck with my mother for at least a time," he began. "We'll have to look for a bigger house—unless you're willing to share my bed again."

"No."

He raised his eyes and his arms to the heavens. "Why? Why must I be tortured by women?" Now he looked at me. "Do you know what I wish? I wish with all my heart that I didn't feel any desire at all for you, or for any woman. No man can be a true philosopher while he's the prisoner of desire on one hand and of his mother's manipulations on the other." He rose and started pacing the room. "She won't leave me alone! She just goes on and on with her dreams and her prayers and her tears and her threats of eternal damnation. And now that she knows that the bond between us is broken, it will only get worse."

"I told you what the remedy for that was."

"Didn't we just have this conversation a couple of hours ago? You know that's impossible, and you also know that I will never desert you. I haven't yet, though you've refused to sleep with me for months now. Isn't that proof enough of my love?" He approached me, and gently pushed aside my shawl. "Leona," he murmured, "I will always, always love you. Love me back again." He ran his hand lightly down my back and sent shivers through me, even through the light wool of my tunic. With one hand, he cupped my head, and with the other he reached under my tunic, between my legs, where I was already wet and swollen.

My heart banged against my chest as his fingers began to move. I raised my face to his, closed my eyes, and prepared to surrender, and then I found my strength. I twisted away from him, and took hold of his wrist, to pull his hand away from my thighs.

He stiffened his arm. "You can't tell me you don't want me as badly as I want you," he said, and pulled me toward him again.

I twisted my face away from his. "Stop. You said you wouldn't do this. Stop it, please, Aurelius."

His hand went still and he examined my face. Not liking what he found there, he frowned and let go of me. "Fine," he said. He walked toward the door, but then turned. "You're not helping me against my mother at all, you know. She wants to run our lives and she wants to run Adeo's, and you're not helping me stand against her."

I felt a dart of panic. "What did she say about Adeo?"

"She's been here only a few hours and hasn't even laid eyes on him yet and she's already got ideas about his education. She's got some notion about a school in Rome run by Christian priests."

"You can't let her take him from me!" My legs had suddenly turned weak, and I sank down on my chair.

"I don't want him to go either. I'm an educator. Wouldn't I know what's best for my son? But you're not helping me, Leona. Between you and my mother, you both seem determined to make my life a living hell." His face was flushed and his eyebrows bore down on his dark eyes.

"You're threatening me."

"What on earth are you talking about? Don't be ridiculous."

"You are. You're threatening me. Unless I give in and return to your bed, you claim that you're helpless to stop your mother from sending Adeo away."

"I haven't said that at all. I only said you make it hard. Can't you show any sympathy at all for my position?"

"Get out!" I screamed. I whirled, looking for something to throw at him, and my eyes lit on an alabaster jar of perfume. I flung it, and it flew within inches of his temple and shattered against the wall, spilling its musky scent through the room. "Get out of here!"

"No man should have to endure this much misery," Aurelius muttered, right before he slammed the door behind him.

I prayed until it was no longer night, but my snarled feelings of panic, rage, and lust would not leave me.

# CHAPTER TWENTY-FOUR

THE NOVEMBER WIND blew through fish alley like a broom, sweeping before it the dried leaves and bits of bone and broken amphorae that littered the corners and carrying a decaying, salty smell that reminded me of Carthage.

The last time I had sent Calla into town to shop for food for the household, he spent every coin that I sent him with and still came back almost empty-handed. He whined that the shops were nearly empty and prices had gone up on what little was available, but Monnica implied that I allowed the servants to take advantage of me, and goaded me into coming to market to see for myself.

In the weeks since Monnica's arrival in Milan, we had reached a tense peace. She was warily pleased by my acceptance of Christ, and we attended church together on Wednesdays and Sundays, but she was constantly interfering in my management of the household, and Aurelius spent as much time as possible away from the house, so that he and I seldom even spoke to each other.

Nothing more had been said about Adeo's education. The subject lurked at the back of my mind, dark and heavy. I had done no better at the market that day than Calla had done. Only salted fish was to be had, or tough mutton, and at prices that amounted to robbery. At every shop, the muddy-eyed Milanese clerks shrugged and blamed the shortages on the barbarians camped one hundred miles north of Milan at the foot of the Alpine Mountains. They had arrived during the harvest, just in time to drive up the price of bread and firewood and everything else, by carting off what they could steal and burning what they couldn't. And they had skulked there ever since, like a cloud hovering over the city, threatening deluge.

I drew my cloak around me and put my head down into the wind. Never would I get used to the Italian winter. I thought longingly of the cool, damp African winter. The winter months in Milan felt as hard and dry as iron, all the moisture sucked into the snowcapped mountains. The cold settled like a weight or sent blades of wind that cut through the dark, winding alleys, whipping faces and slashing at legs.

I was grateful to see my front door, and delivered my meager harvest to the kitchen without comment, then went to the sitting room. Aurelius sat on a couch, chewing his lip over a scroll, and glanced up when I entered the room.

"Come and sit by me," he said.

I hesitated, and he said, "You don't need to be afraid of me. You're not that irresistible."

I sat next to him.

"Leona," he began, "we need to talk about Adeo's future. We're thinking of sending him to Rome to school."

I leapt from the couch. "By 'we,' you mean your mother, of course. I knew it! There's no reason for him to go to Rome. Milan is the capital now, and he already has good teachers right here! And he has you!"

He spread his hands. "Leona, you and I both know that I'm not a good teacher for Adeo. I love him too much. I become emotionally involved and press him too hard when patience is needed, or I pity him too much when

I should press him. I can never get it right. It will do him good to leave the womb of his family. You and my mother both indulge him too much. He'll grow soft."

"And speaking of your mother . . ." I spat.

"She and I have talked about this, yes."

"Oh, what a surprise." I rubbed my hands together. The northern chill easily permeated the stone walls of our house and our slaves had laid only a small fire, to conserve wood.

"Leona, she loves him too."

"And she hates me. She'd do anything to separate us. Sending her grandson away to a strange city must not seem too high a price to her."

"You're not being fair. My mother is a thorn in my foot too, but she loves Adeo, and she's had only this little bit of time with him. If she wanted to be selfish, she'd keep him here, just as you would. But he is at the age when he should be educated away from home. I was sent to school in Madaura when I was his age. And my mother doesn't hate you."

I snorted and walked to the fire to warm my hands.

"Think of what's best for our son," he urged.

"He's only eleven."

"That's not too young to start making the right connections. Bishop Ambrose knows influential people in Rome. He can open doors for him. He's already spoken with the master of one of the best schools in the city, and Adeo can have a place."

"So, it's already been decided, and all wrapped up like an eel from the fishmonger and tied with twine. Why even consult me? Why not just send him away in the middle of the night?" It was especially bitter to me that Monnica had swept into town, befriended the very bishop who had baptized me, and conspired with him to remove my son.

"Because you are his mother. I watched you bring him into the world, remember? I watched you nurse him through the plague. I know he's all the world to you. I wouldn't let him leave without giving you your chance to say good-bye. You know this is right for him, though. Look into your heart." He stood and joined me by the fire.

I glanced into my heart and didn't like what I saw, so I quickly slammed it shut again. "So, it's all decided?"

"He leaves as soon as the roads are safe."

I knew what he meant: when the barbarians retreated back behind the Alpine Mountains. As long as they lurked in the surrounding countryside, it was too dangerous for anyone to travel. I began to cry into my hands, and Aurelius wrapped his arms around me, kissed the top of my head, let me weep into his shoulder.

⸰•⸰

Milan waited and waited, like a host dreading a demanding dinner guest, but the barbarians never came. They melted back over the jagged mountains that separated sunny, civilized Italy from their own cold, wet, savage lands. Nobody expected that they would fail to return. They would spend the winter wrapped in their filthy animal skins huddled around the open fires in their damp, miserable huts, eating our grain and olives and plotting how they would steal from us as soon as the weather improved again. They were hardened to suffering, where the Italians were softened by luxury. The Roman legions were drafted now almost exclusively from the lower classes and the conquered lands.

With the roads safe, Aurelius determined that the time had come for Adeo to be sent to school in Rome.

The trees still held a few golden leaves, wrapped in cold, translucent cloaks of fog on the morning when I bid my boy good-bye.

Monnica rose early too, to see her grandson off, wrapped in a woolen cloak and still shivering.

"How does anything survive in Italy?" she complained. "This horrible cold! It seeps into your bones."

"This isn't even cold yet," I warned her. "It's only November. January and February are the worst."

She widened her sleepy eyes for second, then turned away, waving a cloak-shrouded hand as if I must surely be joking.

Adeo was to travel with a group of priests on their way to Rome. Four bodyguards traveled with them. The trip to Rome would take five days, over stone-paved, relatively safe roads. Still, I wouldn't sleep until I knew that he had arrived safely.

How handsome he looked on that misty morning, already taller than I, still slender at eleven but showing every indication of becoming a large, physically powerful man like his father. He had Aurelius's long-fingered hands, too big right now for his slender adolescent body, so that they looked like paws and constantly bumped into things. I had been impatient sometimes with his clumsiness and coltish energy. Now tears came to my eyes at being parted from him. His dark eyes stared eagerly ahead under his heavy black brows. He wanted to be off.

Monnica tucked something wrapped in cloth into his saddlebag. "A treat for you for on the way," she said, patting it. "I can't believe I found one in the market. I saved it for you." She reached her arms up to receive his good-bye, and he hugged her and pecked her forehead. I hung back, waiting my turn, suddenly shy with my own son.

He stepped away from his horse through the mist, arms open to me, smiling patiently as if he were already a man. I flung myself into his arms, my tears soaking the front of his robe. I inhaled his smell of apples and woodsmoke and clean young skin. My fingers dug into the muscles of his back.

He patted my back. "Mother, don't cry," he pleaded. "I'll be back. And I'll write you letters."

I nodded, unable to speak through my tears.

"Mother, I have to go."

I pulled myself away from him and tossed my head to shake away the tears. Holding him at arm's length, lips compressed against my sobs, I drank in my last sight of him for I knew not how long. "I love you," I said, quavering.

"I love you, Mother. I'll be back," he said firmly, as if to a child.

He turned to his father and they kissed ceremonially, one cheek and then the other, gripping each other's shoulders. How alike they looked, one just a larger and more powerful version of the other. "Safe trip," Aurelius said, clapping Adeo on the shoulder.

Adeo stepped up on the block and swung his leg over his horse's back as if he'd been born to it. "Good-bye," he called to us, and he turned with his party and they began to clop down the road south out of Milan. The fog muted the sound of the horses' hooves on the cobblestones. Aurelius, Monnica and I stood and watched them, waving, until the mist closed around them.

# CHAPTER TWENTY-FIVE

MONNICA SETTLED with a deep sigh in front of the sitting-room fire. "No wonder these people took over the world," she remarked. "It gave them the chance to live elsewhere than in this godforsaken place. I can't remember the last time I saw the sun. When does it come back?"

"We'll start seeing it a little in a few weeks, but it will be April before it's sunny every day again," I told her.

We had taken a house on a hill, which had seemed a good idea in the summer, when the sun was a bronze shield and even the buzzing of the bees was lazy. Now, in February, we had come to regret our location. July's gentle breeze was January's icy blade, slicing through every crack and cranny of our stone villa.

Monnica suffered the most. Nearly fifty, she retained much of her pale beauty. Her brown hair was frosted here and there with strands of gray, but her lips were still full, her teeth still whole. Her ivory skin was only faintly lined and freckled, where many women her age were as brown and wrinkled as raisins.

She was thin, though, from fasting, and her bones ached from the cold. She spent mornings in her bedchamber, praying for an hour and then calling her personal servant to bring her a breakfast of bread, milk, and, when it was available, fruit. It was near noon most days before she ventured into the family rooms, feet buried in sheepskin slippers, a wool cloak wrapped around her shoulders.

She sighed again, and patted the couch beside her. "Sit down."

I sat warily.

Monnica gazed into the fire, not at me, as she spoke. "I have a proposition, and I don't want you to answer right away. I want you to think first, and I want you to know before I say my piece that I love you as a fellow Christian and the mother of my grandson." She sighed a third time and now she looked at me. "I have found Aurelius a wife. Now, don't say anything, just listen. This is a marriage that can be extremely advantageous to him. The young lady's family are very large property owners in the north of Italy. Aurelius has nothing. I maintain some acres of my own that I can leave for Aurelius if he ever accepts the Church, but his brother has inherited their father's land in Thagaste, and Aurelius is completely dependent upon his own labors for a living. He's in favor right now with the current powers, but these Romans . . . someone else could be in power overnight. He needs land, he needs some independent means of support, and Adeo will need the same in his turn. I thought he was meant for the Church. I still think so, and I pray for it every day, but . . . he's not practical. He claims to be so stubborn about the truth, when the truth has been staring him in the face all his life. But my point here is the wife. I'm asking you to free him to make this marriage. I know that he will not agree to set you aside without your consent. Therefore you must consent."

I listened in silence, my face turned to ice.

Monnica went on, twisting the fringe on her cloak. "I know that since you accepted the Church, you have no sexual relations with him. Nevertheless, this girl's family will not tolerate your remaining, and if you're honest with yourself, you wouldn't tolerate it either. I have found a place for you too, back in Thagaste."

I found my voice. "Thagaste! I'd be across the sea from Adeo! You can't possibly think that I'd agree to this!"

"He's almost a man, Leona. Your work is done."

"My love isn't done. He's still my son. He'll be my son until I die."

Monnica held her hands up. "Just hear me out. There's a community of chaste women in Thagaste. They live to serve our Lord. I could purchase you a place there. You would want for nothing. Adeo could visit you anytime he wanted."

"Anytime he wanted to make the journey across the sea! Which could be never! I will not agree to this! I will not!" I stood, vibrating with rage. "I don't need to think about my answer. The answer is no. I won't be separated from Adeo by an ocean. I can't believe you would even suggest this to me."

Her fading brown eyes pleaded with me. "Please think it over. The girl is won't be legally able to marry for two more years, but I want the commitment now, before someone else snatches her up, and her family won't consent to even an engagement unless the mistress is out of the picture."

"Too young to be married? How young is she?"

"Ten," Monnica admitted. She burrowed farther down into her cloak and gazed at the fire.

"Ten! You want to marry him off to a girl younger than Adeo!"

"She comes with ten thousand acres. Her family's wealth and connections could secure not only Aurelius's future, but Adeo's as well. Think of your son."

"I am thinking of my son. This conversation is over."

I whirled and left the room, my feet beating against the carpeted stone floor. When I reached my own chamber, I sat, breathing hard, listening to the blood pounding in my ears. The nerve of her! The nerve! Making plans to send me away without any regard for my own feelings or Aurelius's. I stood again and paced the small room, picking things up and throwing them to the floor in impotent rage: a hairbrush, a wooden cup, a book. My eyes rested finally on a small icon of Mary, the mother of Jesus, which I kept on my table. I picked it up and peered into her sad, inscrutable eyes. "What shall I do?" I whispered.

She remained lost in the heartbreak of her own loss, too grief stricken to respond to my smaller sorrow.

I knelt then and prayed until my knees were raw.

———••———

That evening, Aurelius knocked on my bedchamber door for the first time in a very long while.

"You've spoken with my mother?" he said.

I raised my eyebrows and nodded.

"For my part, you're welcome to stay under my roof forever. You're my son's mother."

I avoided his eyes and started brushing my hair. "And what about the ten-year-old bride and her family?"

He rubbed his face. "I'd just as soon never marry. And a child! But you see how it is. It's a good match. It secures my future and Adeo's."

"Then I'm not welcome under your roof. Because—or so I'm told—her family will not permit it."

"Let me work on that. We'll work out something." His face had the hard look of a man who wants to appear more resolved than he is.

"Fine," I said. I put the brush down and turned my back to him, busying myself with rubbing lotion on my sore knees.

"Leona . . ." His callused fingertips brushed the small hairs of my arm, raising gooseflesh and sending a shivering pang through me.

I turned and I knew my desire was in my face, because I saw it reflected in his. He tightened his grip on my arm and drew me closer to him, staring fiercely into my eyes. I was held by his gaze, unable to look away and compose myself.

He placed a hand on each of my cheeks and bent his lips toward mine. His lips were barely moist. He kissed me gently at first and then harder, his thumbs pressing on the delicate blades of my jawbones. Then my arms clung to his back and I pressed against him, our bodies warm and wildly alive against each other.

"Leona," he rasped, grazing his lips over my cheek, my ear, down my neck, branding each spot with his warmth.

He lifted me, carried me to my bed, and laid me there, his eyes never leaving mine. He laid beside me and drew me to him again, pressing firmly against me. And then he rolled on top of me and entered me, both of us still in our robes. My desire, like a spoiled child, slammed the door on my resolve and I gave myself over to the sweet music of joining with him.

Afterward, though, my joy ebbed and remorse spread in my heart like a stain. My stomach heaved with shame. Aurelius was lying with his eyes closed, a relaxed smile on his full lips, gently stroking my belly. I recoiled from him, and his eyes sprang open.

I covered my face with my hands. "I can't believe what I just did," I moaned.

"But we can't help ourselves," he replied, as if that explained and excused everything.

"We can help ourselves! We should help ourselves! You're still a Manichean at heart, Aurelius. You think that anything you do wrong is out of your control." I leapt from the bed and rearranged my disheveled robe, as if to hide myself from him.

He raised himself on one elbow and his voice hardened. "You underestimate me, Leona. Or maybe you overestimate me; I don't know. You're wrong if you think I don't try to resist you. If you recall, I've believed in celibacy longer than you have. I just can't do it. I fail every time. So it clearly is out of my control, isn't it?"

I crossed my arms over my chest. "Here's the difference between me and you, Aurelius. You think it's just a philosophical thing, with no consequences anywhere except in this life. I know that the fate of my immortal soul hangs on it."

"You know? Really? And you know this how?"

"I hate when you take that Socratic tone with me! Have I ever told you that? I hate it! Your eternal fate is at stake here and you don't even know it! So you're not as smart as you think. No, no, wait, it isn't that." I put my face in my hands for a second, trying to gather my thoughts. When I looked up, I felt calmer. "Here's what it is: you thought you could save yourself with your own willpower. And you've found that you can't. You're right about that, but you think that's the end of it, and that's where you're wrong."

He sat up and leaned toward me. "Oh, really? And what is the end of it, since you're suddenly such a scholar?"

"You have an option other than your own will."

"I'm waiting, Leona, to hear what that is."

"You can surrender to Christ and place your hope of salvation in the cross instead of in your own will. You can take your sins to him and let him heal you."

"Well. I see how well that's worked for you."

The urge to slap him flared and then subsided into the stinging pressure of tears. "It worked until today," I whispered. He was still sitting on my bed with his robe open, his flaccid penis leaning off to one side atop his powerful thigh, as if temporarily cast aside. He was still so beautiful to me that I could barely breathe in his presence.

"I can hardly be near you without wanting you," I confessed. "I pray every day for strength."

This silenced him. His face softened for a moment and he seemed ready to say one thing, but he set his jaw and said instead, "Well, let me be the first to wish you success."

He lifted himself from the bed. "Decide as you wish about the community. Stay if you like; as Adeo's mother, you always have a home under my roof, and the ten-year-old virgin and her family can be damned. Don't worry about me. I'll be glad to support your Messiah's efforts by not bothering you anymore."

I reached out an arm to him. "Aurelius.."

"Good night, Leona." He left the room, closing the door quietly behind him.

I spent the rest of the night on my suffering knees, and in the morning I knew what to do.

# PART THREE

## The Love

# CHAPTER TWENTY-SIX

*Thagaste*
*Anno Domini 389*

I HURRIED to the bishop's house, the dust of the path soft and warm under my callused bare feet. Our previous bishop had died suddenly eight weeks ago, and all the chaste women of our community were eager to meet the new bishop of Thagaste, but I couldn't imagine why he had summoned me alone, first.

The bishop lived in a house that I remembered from my childhood, on the opposite side of the forum from Urbanus's palace, spacious and comfortable but not as grand as Urbanus's. Aurelius's former patron conducted his business back and forth between Rome and Carthage these days, leaving his fields and orchards near Thagaste to be managed by business agents. I had not seen him a single time since my return to my old hometown six years before.

My heart beat fast from my brisk walk in the heat and from nervous curiosity as I lifted the heavy door knocker. An Aitheope servant opened the door and showed me into the bishop's sitting room. I gazed down at the mosaic floor, which showed a scene of Neptune and several naked water nymphs. Neptune's oversized penis plowed ahead of him like the prow of a ship.

"Mind you don't have cause to pluck out your eye, Sister. I've already ordered carpets to cover that and several others."

I jerked my head up at the sound of the voice, and my astonishment stopped my heart for a second. "Quintus?"

The new Bishop of Thagaste sat on a red-fringed stool across the room, sweeping his robe over his knees and crossing his legs. "I anticipated that you would be surprised. This was one of the reasons why I did you the courtesy of calling for you alone."

"You're the new bishop." I blinked, still not quite taking it in.

"You should be pleased. We're old friends."

I wouldn't quite have put it that way, but I said, "Of course. I'm only surprised."

"I thought, too, that you could tell me something of how the women's house is currently managed."

A servant brought Quintus a tray bearing a decanter of wine and one cup, and set it on the table near his stool. Quintus poured himself a cup of wine without offering any to me.

The cup was a jeweled glass one that I had never seen before, one of Quintus's own, I imagined. Well, I thought, he was a rich man before he was a bishop.

"What did you want to know?" I asked.

Quintus sipped his wine, closed his eyes blissfully for a second, and then waved his hand at me. "Everything you can tell. Who manages the work and spiritual life of the women? What work do they do? Who manages the finances? Is the community growing? Is it self-supporting with the endowments that the women bring?"

"God, of course, is our ultimate lord," I said carefully, "and we obey our bishop, his representative here on earth."

Quintus pursed his lips and gazed at me over the rim of his cup, eyebrows raised.

"In recent years," I continued, "I've managed the women—under the supervision of the bishop, of course."

"Go on," he urged.

I hesitated.

Quintus waved an impatient hand again. "Leona, you always seem to consider me your enemy, when I am, in fact, your friend. You can be frank with me."

I went on. "The community is growing. In the past year alone, three widows have joined us, bringing with them substantial estates and, in one case, several thousand denarii. So, the Church is enriched by their generosity, and we are able to take in some young women on charity."

I glanced at Quintus to gauge his reaction to this, but he just nodded distractedly and motioned for me to continue.

"The strong young women work in your fields," I told him. "The older women who have less strength do the work inside the women's house and the monastery, preparing meals or sweeping floors and so on. We also grow herbs and make cheese. We have a small flock of goats and I learned to make cheese as a young girl. We are self-supporting, even without endowments."

"And any profits that you earn?" He stood and poured himself another cup of wine.

"We earn no profit, Bishop. Any little extra above our own needs and our tithe of labor to the bishopric we dedicate to the poor of Thagaste. Many of the people in this town are desperate, Father. We distribute our excess weekly, whenever we have any, and there are always more people in need than food to feed them."

Quintus frowned at this, and I added, "We're following the instructions of our own Lord Jesus, Bishop. 'I was hungry and ye gave me to eat.'"

My new bishop's frown softened, but he stared into the distance as if contemplating something. "Go on," he urged.

I took a deep breath. "And I take a few hours on the Lord's day to teach some of the women to read and write. Most are illiterate, of course, even some of the wealthy widows."

Quintus looked down at his cup, swirling the remaining wine. "And the benefit of this to the Lord is what exactly?"

"Most of your priests and monks are illiterate too, Bishop. Educated converts like yourself who are interested in the priesthood are still as rare and valuable as purple dye. Having women to help them with copying the scriptures is a help—and the bishop's sermons too, of course."

"The women attend Mass daily?" Quintus asked.

"Yes, Bishop."

"Have there been any instances of concupiscence?" His eyes bored into me.

"Two, bishop. One last year between two of the young women. I thought it best not to make much of it. We sent one of the women to another community. The other instance was between one of the women and a monk. The woman . . . a child was born."

"What was done?"

"The baby is being cared for by my brother Tito and his family, who live nearby. The woman was whipped and sent to another community." My heart twisted at the memory of Hanna's suffering under the whip and worse agony at her separation from her child. "The monk she named was a highborn bishop. He confessed his sin and got a penance of self-flagellation and ten days of bread and water."

Quintus shuddered and shook his head at the mention of the whip. "There will be no whippings while I'm in charge," he told me. "We're not barbarians." He sat and swallowed the last of his wine. "I'll meet your women next week. I'll come to your house myself, unannounced. Oh," he added, setting down his cup, "there was another reason why I called for you alone."

I waited.

"I wondered if you had news of Adeodonatus and his father," he said.

*How like Quintus to make me wait for that, while answering all of his questions first*, I thought. I answered, "My son writes to me occasionally. I know that Aurelius has finally accepted the one true God, and that they live a life of retirement and contemplation at a villa outside Carthage. I heard that Aurelius's mother had died."

Quintus nodded. "Just wanted to share it with you if you didn't already know. I'm trying to persuade Aurelius to take a more active role in the Church. He was not made for the life of a hermit. There is also the matter of some land that his mother left to the bishopric that requires his signature. I think I have persuaded him—and your Adeo—to come to Thagaste and pay me a visit. So, you see, I am your friend whether you know it or not."

Tears pressed at the back of my eyes at the thought of seeing Adeo again. "Yes, Father," I whispered.

"You may leave me now. I'll visit with you and your women next week, and if I am satisfied with what I see, you don't need to worry that I'll interfere with you."

"Yes, Father," I repeated, and left with my head down to hide the emotion in my face.

To see Adeo again! His face was before me the whole walk home, like a melody that wouldn't leave my head. In my first years back in Thagaste, the separation had been torture, as if my heart was ripped out of my chest anew every morning. In the course of hard work and much prayer, the raw pain had receded to a dull ache, and I came to see the pain of separation as the penance that I paid for the sin that had given him life. I devoted myself to serving God, and slowly came to feel that life was endurable as long as I knew that Adeo still lived. Once or twice a year, I received a letter from him, full of the love of God, and I treasured these, bringing them out every Sunday evening to reread.

I hardly ever thought of Aurelius. In the early years, lustful feelings had still occasionally tortured me, but I had done many severe penances and had not had more than a fleeting sinful thought in a long time now. I was confident that, by the grace of God, I was freed of that.

# CHAPTER TWENTY-SEVEN

MONTHS PASSED and, true to his word, Quintus interfered little in my management of the women's house. I met with him weekly to report on our activities and turn over any excess produce and coin, and he was satisfied. This week as I walked the dusty path into town, the roads were unusually crowded, and I knew why.

I stepped aside to let a train of wagons pass me. It was the longest train I had seen yet, twenty wagons by my estimation, clattering on the cobblestone road to Carthage, the same road I had taken with Aurelius when I was a girl, pregnant with Adeo.

I stood watching them pass, the wagons loaded with carpets; bronze tables; silver plates; hams wrapped in moist cloth; amphorae of wheat, oil, and wine. Scarred, muscular men marched or rode alongside, narrow eyed, stern mouthed, and armed with swords. Yet another caravan of the wealthy who could afford to abandon Thagaste ahead of a rumored attack by the Aitheopes.

The withdrawal of the legions from smaller cities in North Africa had made towns like Thagaste the new frontier, and it had been only a matter of time before the savages on the borders of the empire would take advantage of that. Rumor in town was that bands of Aitheope warriors were massing to our south and that occasional raids were about to gather themselves into a full-scale attack on the city. The rich escaped if they could. Any poor who had not already accepted Christianity lined up for baptism.

After the caravan passed, I continued my walk to Quintus's office. I carried with me a basket of cloth-wrapped cheese and fresh-picked vegetables for the bishop and his household. Normally, I would have had bread for him as well, but flour was hardly to be had anywhere near Thagaste.

It was bitterly ironic to me that, in the breadbasket of the empire, bread could not be found to feed any but the wealthiest. Almost all went to Rome in the form of taxes or as a cash crop, and the little that was left on the continent immediately filled the tear-shaped clay amphorae of the rich, heading to Carthage in their wagons.

I sighed. As I passed Urbanus's town house, I heard my name.

"Leona! Sister!" It was my brother, Tito. He beckoned me from the door of the town house.

"Tito? What are you doing here?"

He waved me into the house and slammed the heavy door behind us. "The agent headed out of town. Pala worked for them, washing their clothes, so he left me and Pala to guard the house. You want anything from this house for the holy women?"

I frowned. "Do I want anything? Tito, what do you—? You aren't giving away Urbanus's property?"

"They don't need all these things. Nobody needs all these things. I'm doing like Jesus said. I'm sharing." Tito was still a fairly young man, only three years older than I, but his years of hard work and semi-starvation had left their mark. His skin was grayish and wrinkled and he was missing most of his teeth, but he grinned that old grin at me now, and I couldn't help smiling at his literal interpretation of Christ's admonitions and his carefree notion that property laws were mere suggestions. And the fact was, that if the Aitheopes did sweep into Thagaste, this property would only make it into their hands anyway. Toward Urbanus, the owner of that property, I no longer had any feelings either way.

He had been my patron in a way, as well as Aurelius's, but had never failed to act in his own best interests. On the other hand, our Lord also admonished us not to steal or covet.

"They left lots of good stuff," Tito continued wonderingly. "Look at this jewelry Pala's wearing."

Pala, sitting in the corner of the reception room sorting through a trunk of robes, was laden with necklaces, bracelets, anklets, and rings, and wore a tiara. I could see that it was cheap stuff, tin and carnelian. Surely whatever gold, silver, and precious gems Urbanus had left behind, his agent had taken along in his escape from town. Suddenly, it angered me that my brother and his family could see as precious these trifles that a rich landowner cared so little about that he would leave it behind in a threatened city. Why, I wondered for the thousandth time, should some have so much and others so little?

"Be careful you aren't robbed yourselves, Tito," I warned.

"Nobody needs to rob us. Some other poor person wants some, they can have it. Anyway, I already told her she can't keep it all," he added. "Some is for sharing, some little bit she can keep, and some we'll sell for food money. This rich man, he hardly left behind any food."

"That's because there's hardly any to leave, and it's worth more than all that jewelry Pala's wearing. I don't think you're going to find anyone right now who will trade you food for tin jewelry."

Tito's face fell for a moment, but then it brightened. "Yes, but later."

"True. Later," I agreed, adding mentally, *if we're all still alive and not enslaved somewhere in Aitheopia.*

"Where are the kids?" I asked.

"Playing in the courtyard," Tito said. "That man has orange trees right in his own courtyard," he added, shaking his head. "And flowers! The children are outside eating oranges and playing with the flowers."

"I'll just go out and give them a hug," I said. "Then I have to be going."

Pala had endured half a dozen pregnancies and had only two living children: their first, Juliana, and their youngest, a boy named Marcus. It was Marcus who Pala had been nursing when I gave her Hanna's baby to wet-nurse, and two-year-old Marcus and Hanna's Paul sat in Urbanus's courtyard now with orange juice running down their chins, while Juliana picked herself a bouquet.

I thought how lovely Juliana was, how like Numa she looked with her long neck and smooth, dark skin. At fourteen, her breasts and hips had begun to bloom under her plain tunic. I hoped to save her from the hard life of a peasant's wife by bringing her into our community, but Tito and Pala kept putting me off, hoping for grandchildren someday.

"Auntie!" she cried when she saw me. "Look at these flowers!"

"They're beautiful," I agreed.

"When I find a man," she said, "I hope he'll have a house with flowers."

"You shouldn't hope for too much," I scolded. "You're a peasant girl, and I haven't given up hope that you will commit your life to God."

"Yes, Auntie, but before that I'd like to have one boyfriend who will bring me flowers and will kiss me and say that I'm pretty."

Hearing her say those words, so like my own at her age, was like a splash of cold water in my face, especially hearing them in this place, where my own sin had begun.

I took my niece's face in my hands. "You don't need a man to tell you that you're pretty. You are very pretty, but our Lord cares more about your soul. Just be sure that your insides are beautiful. And listen to me: if the Aithiopes really come, run to the church. You may be safer there."

"Yes, Auntie," Juliana smiled, and went back to plucking flowers.

I sighed, gave the two little boys quick, sticky hugs, and let myself out. On my way, I left half of what had been meant for my bishop's household for Tito and his family.

———•••———

"This city is ready to panic," I observed to Quintus when I arrived to deliver his reduced food supply. I handed my basket to a servant to be taken to the kitchen. "I wasn't able to bring you much, and no bread at all. Urbanus's agent has skipped town, along with anyone else with the means."

"God uses all things to his purposes," Quintus replied with a smirk.

"What do you mean?"

"We've had more people ask for baptismal instruction in the past two weeks than you've had in the past two years, if I read the records right. Of course, the Donatists have more," he frowned, "but I have the answer to that now."

"How's that?"

Quintus smiled again and drew from his desk drawer an alabaster vial. He held it in front of my face. "The milk of Saint Perpetua," he whispered, caressing the vial with his eyes.

"Saint who?"

"Perpetua. I preached a sermon on her not three weeks ago, Leona. Don't you pay attention? She was put to death while still a nursing mother for refusing to renounce her Christian faith during the Severan persecution. Precious drops of her milk were preserved in this vial."

"Two-hundred-year-old milk."

"Miraculously preserved." He wrapped the vial in a piece of wine-colored velvet and tucked it back into the drawer.

"How did you come by it?"

Quintus glanced at me sharply and slammed the desk drawer. "Why should that matter? Are you doubting the relic?"

"Certainly not, Bishop, or not so much doubting as wanting to help you be certain."

"I'm already certain, and when the vial is presented at Mass this Sunday, it will be obvious which is the true faith and those who want baptism will come here and not to Saint Cyprian's."

"I see." Weary from my walk to town, I sank down on one of his chairs without being invited.

He ignored my breach of etiquette, just shaking a finger at me. "Think what you like; this will be good for those peasants you love so much too. You're not the only one who sees how terrified they are. I'm only trying to bring them some comfort."

"We're going to have to bring them more than comfort, Bishop. They'll be starving soon. Nearly the whole wheat crop went to Rome this year, and what little is left is being hoarded or has been carried off by people leaving town. Anything left over at all will just be scooped up by the Aitheopes if they come."

"Well, what do you expect me to do?"

"Butcher our own stock. The Aitheopes will just carry them off anyway. It will provide meat for you and free up feed to grind into bread for the peasants."

"And what will they eat next year when the same thing happens? You know, Rome will raise taxes if they have to defend us against the Aitheopes."

"Defend us? They've abandoned us."

He shrugged and popped an olive into his mouth.

The idea didn't come to me until just that moment. "Plant the acres that Monnica left and dedicate them to feeding the poor."

"We'll see. For now, the milk will give them hope," Quintus insisted.

He spit the olive pit onto the floor and poured himself a goblet of red wine. "You are excused, Sister," he told me.

# CHAPTER TWENTY-EIGHT

QUINTUS PRESENTED his vial at Mass the following Sunday, and, as he had predicted, our number of converts that week did exceed the Donatists'. There were also two murders in the town that week. Har, a Saxon slave, was killed trying to steal a chicken from a peasant's yard, and a shopkeeper was killed by a mob when he claimed—accurately, as it turned out—that his storeroom was empty and he had nothing to sell. People were half starving and on edge, and nobody believed the rumor that the Aitheope army had disbanded.

I arrived on Wednesday for my weekly visit with Quintus to find him in a panic.

He slammed his office door behind us, and turned to me with a face like a storm about to break at sea. "They've stolen it!"

"Stolen what?" But as soon as I asked it, I knew the answer to my own question. "Your relic? Who?"

"Who would have reason to steal it, Leona? You're the most intelligent woman I've ever known, perhaps the *only* intelligent woman I've ever known. Use your head."

"The Donatists. Are you sure?"

Quintus flopped onto his velvet-upholstered couch. "They're using it already. They're claiming that it has special protective powers." He rolled his eyes, and I refrained from reminding him that he had strongly implied the very same thing himself, when the vial was in his possession.

"How in the world did they get hold of it?"

"I suspect that stupid Banco went to them with it. I haven't seen him since it disappeared. So now I need a new servant too." He rubbed his forehead, and gestured for me to bring him his wine decanter. "We have to get it back."

I poured him half a cup and he motioned for more. "Bishop, how much does it really matter? You surely can't think that God's love for us is any more or less depending on whether or not we have an ancient vial of dried-up saint's milk?"

"No, of course not, but *they* do. The people. They're simple. They need signs and miracles."

"Maybe they're simple because we keep them simple, Bishop. Maybe they need signs because that's what we offer them."

He gave me a sour look that let me understand that he thought my idea utter nonsense. "We have to get it back," he repeated. "Our enemies are getting most of the converts again now."

"Our enemies? Father, if I may, that's a pretty strong word for fellow Christians. I thought Satan was our enemy."

Quintus waved an impatient hand and took a quick, deep swig of his wine.

"Aurelius has much to answer for, for ever teaching you that you had a brain. A brain is a powerful tool; women don't have the capacity to use it correctly. But do try. Think, Sister. Look around you. Do you see legions in Thagaste anymore? Are the roads as safe as they were when you went back and forth freely to Carthage in your youth? The empire is dying. What can take its place? Shall we leave it to barbarians? Will they keep the roads safe and the seas open to trade? Will they keep the people working and fed? No. The Church must take over where the empire fails."

I set the wine decanter back on its table in the corner. "Won't we have a better chance of success if we work together?"

"We'll have a better chance of success if we are united around one truth. Heresies must be stamped out. You took vows. It is your duty to help." He pointed a finger at me.

"What would you have me do, Bishop?"

"Your brother Tito is one of them, and, I believe, close to their bishop."

"I don't know that I'd say he's close."

Quintus ignored this. "I also happen to know that he and his wife stole certain items from the home of an old friend of yours not too long ago."

The trend of his thinking hit me like a slap. "Go on."

"The legions may be gone, but we still have magistrates and they are still bound to uphold the law. The mildest penalty for such a theft is loss of a hand."

I folded my arms. "And you want me to ask him to commit another theft."

"It isn't a theft to restore something precious to its rightful owner."

"I want protection for him."

"God will protect and reward him."

"I want *you* to protect and reward him." I approached closer to Quintus and leaned over to look him in the eye. "I want him and his family sent away from Thagaste. Find him a spot somewhere else, on Church lands."

"Yes, yes, all right."

"Your word as a Christian."

Quintus looked up at me sadly. "Why is it that you never trust me? Yes, you have my word as a Christian. I will find your brother and his family a place outside Thagaste."

"A good place. Not the tin mines or something."

"A good place. My word as a Christian."

I nodded. "I think I can persuade him."

———•••———

Night still chilled the air when Tito and his family crept into Quintus's courtyard, where Quintus and I waited for them.

Tito reached into a fold of his tunic and withdrew the vial. "I hope I did right," he said. "Father, tell me, will I go to hell if I die on the road today?"

"No, no, of course not, son," Quintus replied, snatching the vial. "You will go straight to Heaven and see Jesus."

"I hope that's right," Tito repeated. I had never seen carefree Tito so worried, and felt sorry that my bishop's dispute with the Donatists had caught my brother in such a dilemma. Quintus had found them work on Church lands near Hippo Regius on the Numidian coast.

I hugged my brother and his wife and the children and gave them some cheese to eat on the journey. "God go with you," I said. "If you can find a messenger coming back this way, send us word that you're all right."

"And with you, my sister. Pray for us."

Tito and his family walked out into the cool black night then, to meet with the carter that I had demanded that Quintus pay to transport them, Tito carrying on his back their few possessions, Pala and Julia each carrying a baby. I offered a silent prayer for their safety.

"You have your relic back," I said to Quintus.

"Yes, and I'll take better care of it now. It will remain in a locked box, in a location that nobody knows but me. Who could have imagined that a servant could be so dishonest as to take it to my enemies?" He shook his head.

I realized that he was oblivious to the irony of his complaint, and held my tongue.

We walked back toward Quintus's palace, breathing the cold dawn air. "Well," he continued, "I have news that I think will interest you. Aurelius and Adeodonatus will be here any day. I myself wouldn't travel under current circumstances, but I had a letter from Aurelius yesterday. It was dated ides of last month and he said that they would be underway in ten days, so we should see them here anytime."

Joy leapt in my heart like a fish. "That is good news to me, Bishop," I replied.

"You shall have as much time with your son as you wish," Quintus assured me. "They're coming to settle the matter of the inheritance. When Aurelius's mother left this life, she left a few acres of the family's land to the Church. We have his brother's seal on the transaction, but not Aurelius's yet." Quintus sighed. "It will be good to see him. I miss the company of other educated men, and I always felt that he surpassed all the rest of us in brilliance."

I could see that he was sincere. "It will be good for you to be reunited with him for a time."

"Of course, we were all sinful during our time together in Carthage. So sinful, and yet happy, weren't we? That's how we are so easily tempted to sin, because, from a distance the flames of perdition feel like the warm glow of a hearth fire. Still, I miss our old friends." He gazed off into the distance for a second, and then recovered himself. "Well, a good morning's work already, Sister, and I thank you again and will keep your brother and his family in my prayers. I'll send for you when your son arrives."

"Yes, Bishop."

He slopped a sign of the cross before me, and I walked into the gray early morning, humming with joy at the prospect of reunion with Adeo.

# CHAPTER TWENTY-NINE

I PACED Quintus's anteroom, my heart buzzing in my chest. Every few minutes I glanced into the front hall to see if anyone approached, then slumped back into the chair, sat for a few minutes, rose and glanced back into the hall and started the whole cycle over again. Quintus had sent word this morning that Aurelius and Adeo had arrived the previous night, but by the time I reached town, they were away from the bishop's house and I had to wait.

This time when I ventured into the hall and looked through the open portal, my heart stopped. Was it? I squinted. It was surely Aurelius, but where was Adeo? A young man walked beside him, but I couldn't see my son.

As they approached, my heart restarted wildly, and I ran out the portal and down the short lane toward them. The man—no longer a boy, of course, after six years—walking on Aurelius's left was our own Adeo, nearly as tall as his father.

When he saw me coming, he opened his arms and smiled, and I slammed into him, laughing and crying at the same time. Quickly, though, I leaned back to get a good look at him, my hands on either side of his face. How like his father he looked, with his thick, curling black hair and his straight, white teeth, and his heavy brow, his eyes as round and as brown as a horse's, with thick, dark lashes. His jaw was squarer than Aurelius's, the bridge of his nose flatter like my own. I took in every detail of him, my hands on his warm, smooth cheeks, my tears choking any words I might have spoken. My boy, the only child of my body. I hugged him again, my cheek to his chest and cried unabashedly.

"I'm happy to see you, Mother," he said, patting my back, and I knew that I was embarrassing him, so I flicked away my tears and tossed my head.

"You've grown tall," I said.

"I may pass Father yet," he replied, although, at seventeen, he was still an inch or so shy of Aurelius's six feet.

I looked at Aurelius for the first time, composing myself. "Aurelius," I said, nodding slightly.

Eyes focused away from me, he also gave a brief nod. "It's good to see you looking well, Leona," he said. A few strands of gray had appeared in his black hair, I saw, and the skin around his eyes was creased from long hours in the sun.

"I was sorry to hear of your mother's passing."

Aurelius's voice was harsh and authoritative. "She'll be raised again to eternal life when our Lord comes again."

"Of course," I agreed. "Did she—she must have been pleased that you accepted the true faith? I'm glad she had that comfort before she died."

"Yes. "

"And you traveled safely?"

"Completely. I brought news for your bishop on that score. The Aitheope army has returned to their own lands. They did some damage on the borders, but the threat to travelers and to small cities like Thagaste has passed."

"Thanks be to God," I said, thinking of my brother and his family, probably still on the road.

"We'll want to wash before supper," Aurelius said. "We'll see you later in the bishop's dining room." We had reached the house. I kissed Adeo one more time, and reluctantly allowed him to follow his father to their chambers inside the house.

———••———

"And that's why we need a scholar priest in Hippo," Quintus explained over supper. "We need someone who has a solid education and who knows the Manichees' arguments. Their strength is in their claims of scientific reason. We need someone here who can fight them on their own terms."

"I'm not yet ordained," Aurelius pointed out. "And Hippo already has a bishop."

Quintus waved his hand. "He wants you too. You have a reputation."

"Why not yourself?"

Quintus sighed, sipped his wine, and then leaned toward Aurelius. "You have something that I have always lacked, Aurelius. What shall I call it? Charisma? You're big. You're handsome. And I'm"—he grimaced and gestured at his pale, thin body with its bubble of a stomach. "And you're a powerful speaker. The Donatists still plague us. The Manichean heresy is stamped out almost everywhere in the empire. Right here, in our own backyard, is the last place where it is still strong. We need to wipe it out here." He swung a veiny fist across his front to emphasize his point. "You're the man to do it," he concluded. "And you can bring Adeo along as a scribe. If he's anything like his father, he'll have a good future in the Church as well."

"If you think I'm equal to it, then, of course, I must consider it," Aurelius replied.

I frowned. It was unlike him to show self-doubt. His vice always been in the other direction, along the lines of self-importance and overconfidence.

"Yes, you must," Quintus agreed cheerfully, and set down his wineglass. "But the bishop will convince you when you meet him, I am sure of it, and we have the land to discuss too."

"Certainly. You may have my seal tomorrow."

"Your mother was a good woman. Acreage is vital to the Church. Rome speaks only the language of power, and they have an urban peasantry to feed. The church with the acres to help them do that can secure its position."

I sat straighter in my chair. "You're planning to use the acres to produce more grain to sell to Rome?"

"Of course. What else would we do with it?" Quintus speared a slice of spiced goat with his knife and folded it whole into his mouth.

"I thought it would feed our own people."

"It can be better used in trade."

I felt my face flush. "What are our own peasants supposed to eat? Most of the land they work now is fully earmarked for the state or the Church."

"You forget yourself, Sister," Quintus snapped. "Don't try to interfere in things that you don't understand."

Aurelius was silent, and Adeo looked down at his plate. I thought that I must be embarrassing my son, so I compressed my lips. "Of course, Bishop," I murmured.

"Well," Quintus said, "you and I can talk some more tomorrow, Aurelius. My work here alone tires me and so now I will retire to my chamber and leave you and your son to catch up with his mother."

Work alone? As if the rest of us did nothing. My anger flared, as it so often did around Quintus, and I had to say a silent prayer of contrition.

Already, Quintus's servants were silently clearing the table of the remains of our supper of bread and cheese and goat meat, fruit and wine. Quintus stood and made the sign of the cross before us. "God keep you overnight," he said and swept out of the room, his small legs rippling the surface of his robe.

———••———

Silence smothered the room when Quintus was gone, as if, after the first flush of our joyful reunion, Aurelius, Adeo, and I had nothing to say to each other. Adeo's face looked pale to me, his eyes shrunk in shadow. I opened my mouth to ask Adeo if he was tired and would like to rest, when Aurelius finally spoke.

"So you keep well?" he asked me.

"I have plenty to do. I proofread copy for the priests and do some of my own copy work. I have you to thank for my work." I smiled at him, but his face remained politely impersonal. "And my health is still good, thanks be to God. Were you sorry to leave Milan?"

He shrugged. "I go now where God calls."

The words burst from me without forethought. "Aurelius, don't let Quintus dedicate that land to Rome."

"My mother left it to the Church. He can do as he likes with it." Aurelius poured himself another cup of water. I noticed that he had taken no wine during our meal.

"Not so. He needs your mark for the transfer to be complete. He said so himself. You can put conditions on it."

"Leona, your bishop is correct. This is none of your affair."

"It is my affair! The people here are half starving, and I have to watch it happen every day: mothers who are too weak to survive childbirth, babies too weak to survive infancy. My brother is your age and has lost almost all of his teeth. This in the richest empire the world has ever seen! It isn't right, Aurelius. These are your people. You grew up among them." *Let me convince him, Lord*, I prayed silently, and then added, *if it's your will.*

Aurelius looked away from me and rubbed his forehead. "Leona, you tire me. My mother's few acres can't solve the problems of the empire."

"Father, Mother is right."

We both looked at Adeo.

He continued, "Our Lord Jesus said, 'I was hungry and ye gave me to eat.' He himself was one of the poor when he lived among us."

Joy and pride swelled my heart. I could have died happy at that moment, no matter what happened to Monnica's acres.

Aurelius was silent, frowning and staring out the window at the darkening sky.

"The psalmist said it too," Adeo went on. "'Happy is he . . . who gives food to the hungry.' And in the second chapter of the Book of James, verse five . . ."

Aurelius held up a hand. "Yes, yes, Adeo, yes." He turned to me. "You see I've done a good job of educating our son as a Christian."

"Yes, you have, and he's right."

"Remember how Grandmother was always buying slaves and freeing them?" Adeo said. "She used her money to help the poor. I think she would have wanted her acres to help them."

With a pang, I suddenly missed Monnica, who had always felt like an enemy to me.

Aurelius nodded, and placed his fingers to his forehead again, eyes closed, forehead creased. I understood that he was praying. Finally, he looked up at me. "And I suppose you have thoughts on how this could be effected?"

"Yes, I do."

Aurelius rolled his eyes and nodded. "I thought so. Let's hear it."

"Sign over the acres to the women's house instead of the bishop."

"Peasant women can't own property, Leona. You of all people know that."

"But our community includes a woman of the citizen class. Leave it to the women's house in her name."

Aurelius toyed with his water cup, avoiding my eyes. "Quintus will never agree to it."

"Quintus owes me, Aurelius. I got his ridiculous relic back for him. And, if memory serves, I once saved him from prison. Let me see if I remember his words at that time. I believe he said he'd do anything for me. He will do this if you are determined."

Aurelius thought for a few seconds again and finally broke into a reluctant smile. "My wife and my son. Gifts from God to keep me righteous. All right, then. I'll do as you ask."

Adeo and I smiled at each other. I wondered if Adeo had been as startled by the word *wife* as I had, but he had seemed not to notice, and I, too, forgot it for the moment, in the joy of gazing into the eyes of my son and knowing that he had grown to be a good man. I noticed again that there were shadows under his eyes, and his head seemed to slump toward one shoulder.

"You look tired, Adeo," I said.

"I'm sorry, Mother," he replied, "I am. Would you mind if I just went up to bed? We can talk some more tomorrow."

"Let me walk up to your chamber with you," I said.

"No need, Mother."

"Please let me. I long to be your mother again. Let me tuck you into your bed and kiss your forehead like I did when you were little."

"All right, then."

Adeo's bedchamber was small, and his father waited outside while I went in to put our boy to bed. His face held an inward, pinched look while he removed his outer clothing, and he moved slowly, as if he had to consciously remember exactly how to do it. He had his father's muscular build. I fleetingly thought it a shame that he seemed destined for the Church. What a prize he would have been for some pretty girl, and what beautiful grandchildren they could have made for me. Then I said a quick, mental prayer of contrition. He was God's, as are we all.

He lay down on his bed, clad only in his tunic, and managed a faint smile. "Will you sing to me too, Mother?" he teased.

"If you like."

I sat on the edge of his bed, just as I had when he was a small boy, and smoothed his hair away from his face, humming softly. Still stroking his face, I sang the song he had liked to hear at bedtime back in Carthage.

*My baby is as small and as plump as an olive in the tree*
*Sheltered by the side of a hill.*
*My baby is as fair and gay as young lambs on the lea*
*Leaping in the sun as they will.*
*Sleep little baby.*
*Fisheye protect you.*
*Sleep like a lamb in his cote.*
*Sleep little baby*
*Safe from fox and lion*
*In the shade of my cool olive grove.*

"I remember that," he said sleepily.

"I didn't get to hear much about your life," I complained. "Your father and the bishop did most of the talking during dinner."

"Father tends to do that," he admitted, smiling a little again.

"We can catch up tomorrow."

"Mmm-hmm." His eyes were closing already. I sat at his bedside for a few more minutes, until I was sure that he was asleep. With his full lips relaxed in sleep, and his thick eyelashes sweeping down over his high cheekbones, he looked to me like an angel or a young pagan god. I knew it was sinful to be vain of my child's beauty, but I gave myself over to it for this brief interval, drinking him in like nectar, until his breath deepened and I kissed his warm forehead and tiptoed from the room.

Aurelius waited outside his door.

"He's so handsome," I whispered.

"Physical beauty is fleeting and vain. Don't encourage him to think of himself that way."

"No, of course. Is he—? He was always so smart. I trust he's a good help to you?" We came to the end of the hallway and walked out into Quintus's courtyard.

Aurelius warmed to the topic of Adeo's intellect. "He puts me to shame, Leona. He's the best scribe I've ever had, and a brilliant rhetoritician. I set him the task of drafting an answer to the Manichean heresy for me, and he thought of points that I'd never even considered. I'll include them in my first sermon in Hippo. He will go much, much farther than I ever will. He's more worthy to be a bishop than I am."

I smiled inwardly at his tacit admission that he would go to Hippo and preach as Quintus had urged him. "Your mother would be proud," I said.

Aurelius looked away from me. "I regret the pain that I caused my mother over the years."

The moon cast a bluish light on him and darkened the creases in his face. I waited for what he would say next.

"I don't blame you," he assured me. "I sinned of my own volition with you. You were a young girl and I seduced you, and then we were captive to our sinful desires. It was you, after all, who finally forced me to chastity. It had been my lifelong goal, but I could never achieve it until God saw fit to grant you that grace first."

"There's been no one since?"

"No one."

I had to ask, "And what about the disappointed ten-year-old?"

He scowled. "Don't you think it's beneath you to ask that?"

"Yes. But I'd still like to know what happened."

"When I finally accepted the one true God, I knew that I could only live a life of chastity and poverty. Her family found her another fiancé very quickly."

We came to a stone bench, sheltered by a small grape arbor, and we sat quietly for a moment, looking down at the stones of the courtyard. "You called me your wife tonight," I said finally.

"Did I?"

"Yes, right before Adeo went to bed. You said 'My wife and my son. God's gifts to keep me righteous.'"

"I guess I did. Why are you surprised? I always thought of you as my wife. You were too insecure, Leona. You never believed me. You were always the wife of my heart, and you always will be. But God had other plans for both of us."

"How were you finally won, Aurelius? You resisted for so long."

He stood now and gazed up at the watery moon. At first I thought he wouldn't answer.

"It was Ambrose," Aurelius finally replied. "I finally gave in to my mother's pleadings and became acquainted with him. I couldn't just shut off my mind, Leona. There was too much in the Christian Bible that didn't stand up to reason. But that was only because I was reading it literally! Ambrose taught me to read it as a story that God tells us in terms that we can understand. He didn't create the earth and the heavens in six days. You and I understand that that's nonsense on its face. It's an allegory that simple people can understand. Once I understood that, I was prepared. And then one day I went out into the country to read and contemplate. I sat under a tree half asleep, with my Bible in my lap—because, by that time, I had a Bible with me always. I was ready, standing in front of the door to faith, ready to place my hand on the latch. And I heard the words *tolle, lege*— take up and read—as if God were calling me. I took this to mean that I should pick up the Bible and read whatever my eyes first rested on. My eyes fell on Saint Paul's letter to the Romans, chapter thirteen: 'Arm yourselves with the Lord Jesus Christ; spend no more thought on nature and nature's appetites.' I read this and I was like a blind man seeing for the first time, or like someone struck by lightning. Finally, I *knew*. I broke off the ridiculous engagement, and decided to found a community of chastity, poverty, and study at a country estate that one of my friends offered to us. But when I returned to Milan for my baptism, Ambrose had other plans for me. He sent us back to Africa. It was the time of the war between Theodosius and Magnus Maximus, and the seas were unsafe then. We had to wait some months at Ostia. It was there that my mother took a fever and died." His voice broke. "Leona, my mother was a saint and I caused her grief and now she's gone. I'm never free of sorrow."

"Of course. If it's any comfort to you, your mother died knowing that your soul was saved." I stood to embrace him. It felt so natural, even after our years apart.

He wrapped his arms around me and I felt the muscles of his chest and even the coarse, springy hairs there, between the thin wool of our tunics. I inhaled his scent, clean and musky at once, as familiar to me as if we had never been apart. My skin suddenly felt warm and I felt the spasm of desire in the pit of my stomach. Without thinking I ran my hands down his back and moved against him, rubbing against the hardness of his thighs.

He sprung away from me as if I were on fire. "I can't trust myself around women yet," he said, "and you least of all. I still burn with lust, the same as always."

I flushed, still burning with feelings that I had thought long tamed: warm skin, racing heart, moist swelling between my legs. Well past thirty now, an age when my own brother was already an old man, Aurelius still glowed with muscular virility. I was stunned by how quickly my lust had returned, the second our bodies touched. I turned my head away from the sight of him pacing away from me.

He walked back toward me, but stopped short. "Will I ever be free of these temptations? I pray for it every day, and yet memories of our time together dance in my head like devils."

I still couldn't look at him. "I don't know. I thought I was free of these feelings forever and now . . ."

His eyes were wild and tortured, and his voice raspy. "I'll leave you now, before my devils get the better of me."

He crossed the courtyard, his powerful body filling the space with its vigor. I knelt at the bench and prayed the Pater Noster over and over until repetition and exhaustion tamed my own renewed desires.

# CHAPTER THIRTY

ADEO WAS NOT WELL when he woke the next day. I had been allowed to stay the night in the servant's quarters of the bishop's house, and in the morning Quintus's new slave came to me and let me know that my son was asking for me.

I arrived at his bedside to find him more feverish than the night before. The paleness of the previous night had given way to a splash of livid red across his face. When I felt his forehead, it was more than warm; it was almost too hot to touch.

"I'm sorry, Mother," he whispered. "I hoped to have some time with you today."

"We can still have time together. I'll sit with you. I'll read to you or just watch you sleep. It will be enough."

I sent the slave away with orders for theriac and I held Adeo's head up to sip it hourly for the rest of the day. He wanted nothing to eat, his head thudding back to his pillow in exhaustion after the effort of lifting to sip the medicine.

I read to him from the Beatitudes in the Book of Matthew, those plain and comforting admonitions to simple goodness. He seemed not to hear, except once when he corrected some phrasing in the Latin translation from Greek. I smiled to find how much his father's son he was.

Aurelius looked in on him late in the afternoon, when his business with the bishop was finished. He entered the room silently, nodded at me, felt Adeo's head and frowned. "What medicine did you order for him?"

"Just theriac."

Aurelius nodded. Still scowling, he examined Adeo more closely. "It's not the same fever that took my mother," he said, "or, if it is, it is manifesting itself differently in him. I'm concerned, though. I'll ask the bishop to recommend a physician."

I had kept fear at bay all day, concentrating on reading to Adeo, and the joy of just soaking in his presence. Now worry began to tickle the back of my mind. "What do you think it is?"

"I don't know, Leona. That's why I want a doctor."

———•••———

Adeo was no better the next day, nor the next. Quintus's physician speculated a brain fever of some kind and asked if Adeo had ever had a head injury. Aurelius and I looked at each other for a moment, remembering the long-ago day at the circus, and finally Aurelius said, yes, he had a bad fall and hit his head when he was very small.

The doctor nodded and had Adeo bled. The morning after the bleeding, he was whiter and weaker, but still just as hot. His skin had a clammy feel to it that I didn't like at all. I had not left his side for days, sleeping on a pallet on the floor of his room, rising every few hours to coax some liquid between his lips. My bones ached, my eyes burned, and my head felt stuffed with wool.

"You'll be sick yourself if you don't rest," Aurelius scolded. "Let me sit with him awhile."

I nodded, too weary even to speak, and pulled the weight of my body out of the chair. But instead of going to my own room, I dragged myself to Quintus's chapel, where I collapsed onto my knees, dropped my head onto my folded hands and began an exhausted, incoherent silent prayer. *Just let him get well even if I never see him again after this, just let him get well, just let him get well, just let him get well, just let him get well, I'll never ask for anything else again, just let him get well . . .*

I must have fallen asleep there. I was jarred awake by Aurelius shaking my shoulder. "Leona! Leona, come quickly!"

I was afraid to ask why. Shaking off my sleep, I followed him back to Adeo's room. Quintus was standing over him, performing last rites.

"No!" I screamed. I dashed to Adeo's bed and threw my body over his, as if to protect him from death's hand.

Aurelius sat on the bed beside me and covered both of us with his large body. In Adeo's last moments, the three of us were once again a little family.

I lay over my boy, weeping wildly, until he drew his last breath. And when I knew that he was gone, I heard a wail, as from someone being torn limb from limb, and was only remotely aware that it was coming from me.

———•——

I spoke not at all for the next three days. I sat in silence through my son's burial, and through every meal, at which I took only water and bread. Aurelius was quiet too, his handsome face painted with gray shadows that I'd never seen before, his muscles so tense that he looked carved of wood. He tried once to talk to me about God's inscrutable but reliably loving will, and about joining Adeo again at the Second Coming, but his arguments were muted and my eyes on his were a wall. Aurelius, always so sure of himself, even in heresy and error, seemed diminished by our son's death, in both body and mind.

I never cried. I knelt in the chapel and willed myself to pray, but no prayer would come. I knelt perfectly straight and rigid, as if to soften or bend would be to melt into a puddle of nothing but yielding sorrow.

Why was Adeo taken from us? When I left Milan, I accepted that I might never again see his face, but I learned to be happy as long as I knew that he lived somewhere in the world. Aurelius and I had both renounced our old sinfulness and devoted ourselves to chastity and poverty. And still God took our only son. A little voice kept trying to remind me that this was the same God who had sacrificed his own only son for the world, but I hated that voice.

———••••———

The day after the interment, Aurelius and I sat silently in the graveyard. The family mausoleum was modest, rising from the ground only about five feet, of mortared red brick, with a diamond pattern of red-and-black bricks laid on end over the entrance. Nearby were larger, more ostentatious buildings with pillared marble fronts, and a few individual marble sarcophagi, but most of the graves were simple mounds of brick. In the Christian era, as burial had overtaken burning as the treatment of the body after death, this graveyard, stretching over several acres now among the live oaks and pines not far from where I had first laid eyes on Aurelius, had grown rapidly.

Aurelius quoted Cicero: "'Of all people you are the only one I would wish to surpass me in everything.' He would have too."

Grief filled me, black and cold. I didn't think that I would ever feel anything else again, and was not sure that I would be able to speak, but after a short while I answered, "It was our fault."

Aurelius didn't reply.

"It was our fault," I repeated. "The doctor said brain fever from his fall. We should have been watching him that day at the circus in Carthage."

"He *guessed* brain fever, *perhaps* from a fall. There's no way of knowing for sure." Aurelius picked up a pine cone from the ground and turned it over and over in his hand.

"God took him from us to punish us."

"God doesn't work that way, Leona."

"God is punishing me for wanting too much. My desire for you was rekindled the minute I was alone with you. And I wanted your mother's land. And I wanted to see Adeo again, when I should have been content to just know that he lived. I wanted, I wanted, I wanted. I wasn't content to just do his will. And so I am punished."

Aurelius had no reply. The breeze that hissed through the oaks felt cool to me, and I shivered.

"I don't want the acres," I said.

"Don't be ridiculous. You're right. You'll make better use of the land than Quintus would. And it was Adeo's last wish that you should have it."

"I don't want it. I don't want anything in this world. I only want to spend the rest of my life in prayer and hope to die soon and be reunited with my son."

"Well, it's probably good not to be focused on things of this world, but I'll still see to it that you get the land." He was quiet for a minute and then said, "How I will miss him."

"At least you got to watch him grow into a man. You and your mother saw to it that I was deprived of that privilege."

"You're not being fair."

"Fair? You're a good one to talk about that. I missed the second half of my child's short life." I stood and walked away from him.

"I'm sorry," he called after me. "Is that what you want to hear? All right then, I'm sorry that was how it went. Did I have foreknowledge that this would happen? Am I God?"

I turned to face him. "You and your mother acted like you were, arranging everybody else's life without consulting them."

"Leona, you are a woman of God. These childish emotions are unworthy of you."

My grief and rage were like molten iron, rising in my throat. "Childish emotions? My son just died, and I had only hours with him before he took ill."

"My son just died too!" Aurelius roared. His cloak swirled around his legs as he sprang up and loomed over me. He jabbed his chest with his finger. "I grieve too, and yet you feel the need to torture me further with these accusations about things that happened long ago. I'd give anything to have him back, do you understand me? Anything. I would endure the fires of hell for all eternity for one more minute with him."

I noticed that tears ran down his cheeks and that his brown eyes seemed sunken in their sockets, but I was locked in my own grief and was unmoved by his. I stared at him coldly.

"I'll leave you to enjoy your bitter memories," he said, and walked away.

————•••————

Quintus was furious about the disposition of Monnica's acres.

"I won't lie to you," he said. "I did everything I could to talk him out of this, but he was insistent that they be left to the women's house, not to me, his friend. It seems you still have a certain power over him."

Quintus always had the ability to inspire opposition in me, regardless of what else I was feeling. Even though I cared nothing about the land anymore, I was glad he didn't have it, and in my grief I was beyond caring about any vows of humility and obedience to my bishop. "I have no power over Aurelius. He saw what was right."

"How can it possibly be right to leave productive acres in the care of women? I would have used it to advance our Church. You think you'll use it to feed your peasant population, but you don't know how to manage it. I can't imagine how you persuaded him."

"Partly by reminding him of your debts to me."

"Yes, yes, he reminded me too." Quintus waved this off as if it were irrelevant. "How many of them can you feed on a few acres anyway? This is foolishness, Leona. They shouldn't be concerned with their comforts in this world anyway." He popped an olive in his mouth and reached for the goblet of wine beside him.

"And what about you? Shouldn't you be unconcerned with your own comforts?" I said.

Quintus's hand stopped halfway to his mouth. "I'm doing God's work, and I'm used to living a different way," he said after a pause. Then he completed his sip of wine and scowled at me. "Anyway, I'm your bishop. I'm not answerable to you for what passes my lips. Sometimes you go too far, Sister."

I shrugged. It didn't really matter to me what Quintus ate or drank, didn't matter whether I was insubordinate to my bishop, didn't matter what happened to Monnica's acres. Buried in the dark weight of grief, I felt myself already in hell.

"You lost your son," Quintus said. "You're not yourself, and so I excuse you." He paused and then continued, "Aurelius has gone on to Hippo as Ambrose and I had both urged him to do. I believe he will find God's work for him there and be comforted in his sorrow. I pray the same for you."

He made the sign of the cross before me and dismissed me.

# CHAPTER THIRTY-ONE

PUNISHING HEAT beat down on Thagaste for the next several days, adding to my sense that I was living in hell. The sun was a white explosion as soon as it cleared the horizon, blasting skin and piercing eyes. North Africans are used to intense heat, but those days were like standing inside a bread oven.

I instructed the sisters to rest during the heat wave and do only such work as was necessary for survival: fetching water, milking the goats, plucking fruit and olives for our meals.

But I myself could not be still. Whether lying on my bed or seated outside in the shade, stillness brought me to the black wall of my grief, a wall that stretched forever in all directions, so that I could see nothing but darkness and stone. So, instead, I worked, and remembered, and argued with God.

The bishop had made a small scriptorium for the monks who worked as scribes in the town. My women had no such luxury. We worked by the light that streamed into our dining hall, and I worked there now, putting a binding on a Hebrew scripture that I had spent many months copying from a crumbling scroll.

With a clean old cloth spread on the table to protect my pages from any oil or stain, I pierced the folds of each quire with an awl, carefully measuring so that the holes were spaced exactly the same on each sheaf of pages. Next I picked up a larger awl and pierced the faces of each quire in five places to prepare them for the thongs that would bind them to the book's cover. Then I threaded my needle with linen thread and began binding each individual quire by sewing along the folds.

The work with the awls had been very exacting, taking all of my concentration and making sweat prick my face and trickle down my sides. The sewing was more mindless and my thoughts began to scurry around the wall of my grief, looking for an explanation for my loss.

Why? Why had Adeo been taken from me? I had left him in Italy and come back to North Africa specifically so that I would no longer be tempted to sin with his father. I had devoted my life to my community, eating little, resting little, copying the word of God, and when necessary laboring in the African sun beside the younger women whose care and spiritual welfare had been entrusted to me. Should I not have been rewarded for this?

Unbidden, words from a recent sermon of Quintus's came to me. He had been quoting the Hebrew scripture: "I the Lord your God am a jealous god, punishing children for the iniquity of the parents, to the third and fourth generation."

I thought again of my years of sin with Aurelius, and of the greed I had felt before we lost Adeo: greed for Monnica's land, greed to lay eyes on my son again, and then my surprising renewed greed for Aurelius's body. A fist of guilt squeezed my heart as I remembered the horrible day of Adeo's head injury, how angry and petulant I had been that day over being left to mind him while Aurelius enjoyed the circus with his friends.

But then I started to argue with God. Adeo was full of goodness and would have been a gift to your Church. Yet You took him from us because of our past sins. Why? Why would You look only at our sin? Wouldn't all lives come to nothing but sorrow if You looked only at our sin?

I could almost hear God's response in my head: *Most lives do come to nothing but sorrow.*

Not rich people, I thought bitterly. Not people like Quintus, who always find themselves power and comfort, whether in an empire or a church. What about him and his sins? What about all the innocent people he and Nebridius harassed back in Carthage? Even now, what good does he do for anyone except himself and his own ambitions?

*Even the rich die.*

Then how can you be good? You told us to treat the poor and the suffering as we would treat you, and then look at how you treat us. If you are all powerful and all good, then why did you make a world filled with nothing but sin and misery and death? What's the point? If life is all sorrow, why even live?

No answer. No comfort. Just that black wall, and the feeling that I was dying from the inside out.

———••———

Later that afternoon, a sweating boy arrived with the message that Quintus summoned me right away, but I waited until evening to walk into town, and still arrived light-headed and prickly with sweat.

I met with him in his dining room while he ate his supper.

"I expected you earlier," he complained.

"It was too hot earlier."

He ignored this and plowed on. "A situation has arisen: refugees from the borderlands, driven north by the Aitheopian skirmishes. Their village, it seems, was completely destroyed, nearly everyone killed or carried away as slaves. A small handful survived and somehow managed to make it to towns north. Two of them have landed here on our doorstep."

I waited for him to go on, too sunk in my own sorrow to spare any thought for what these refugees might have endured.

He speared a boiled quail's egg into his mouth and continued, "The older woman claims to have grown up here and hopes she might still find family. She begs the protection of the church while she and her daughter resettle themselves here. I naturally thought of you. With your compassion for the poor and suffering, it seemed to me that the women's house would be willing to take them for a time. And, of course, they should be among other women."

"Of course," I agreed, out of habit more than compassion.

"I was hoping that you would take them back with you this very day."

"Of course."

Quintus gestured for his new slave, the one who had replaced the disloyal Banco, to fetch the women. The slave returned with two dusty wraiths, one old and one young. The older woman was small and sinewy, with large, sad eyes. The feeling that I had seen her before tickled me, and then I noticed the unusual cross around her neck, the exact match of the one I still wore. My heart began to pound.

"Miriam?" I said.

The older woman frowned at me at first, then her eyes widened. "Leona?" she whispered.

I stepped toward her falteringly, still thinking I might be mistaken or dreaming, and then I folded her in an embrace, and joy and wonder rose in me like a dawn.

"Leona," my old friend repeated, and collapsed into rasping sobs in my arms.

———•••———

I took Miriam and Lucy back to the women's house with me that night, and into my own bed, dusty and bad smelling as they were. They were too exhausted to say much that night, but in the morning I questioned Miriam over a breakfast of cheese and grapes, while Lucy still slept.

"Can you talk about it?" I asked her. "Did anyone else from your village survive?"

"Survive, I think yes, but carried off for slaves," she told me. "I think we're the only ones who lived and escaped."

"How did you manage to escape?"

"When they came, Lucy and I were away from the village, hunting for herbs. We heard the noise: men yelling and women screaming and horses. So I knew what must be happening. We hid in an olive grove all day. Lucy kept crying for her baby and I told her it would be all right, they don't hurt babies, but we both knew I was lying."

"She had a child?"

Miriam closed her eyes and nodded. "A beautiful, healthy little boy, not yet twelve moons old. She left him with her sister-in law while we went out for our herbs. Olivia had a baby too, and she and Lucy used to care for each other's babies, each just like her own, even shared their milk at times. Those two little cousins were like brothers to each other."

"Oh, Miriam." I reached out and squeezed her shoulder.

Miriam pressed her fingers to her forehead and shook her head. "He was my grandbaby, Leona, and I knew what was happening in that town. If there was any way I could have given my own life to save that baby, I would have done it, but the only way I could save my Lucy was to make her stay in those trees. It was a long, long day, listening to the screaming coming from our village, and then the Aitheope army passed on the road behind us, with their stinking horses. It took them almost an hour to get past us, and I had to hold Lucy down and clap my hand over her mouth to keep her from crying out. Even after they were past, we waited a long time to creep back into the village. My heart was in my throat the whole time, wondering if maybe they left someone behind to guard, but . . . well, they didn't need to, because they didn't leave behind anything alive. Took all the food, took everything. Left not one person alive."

She paused to take a ragged breath, and I waited.

Miriam stared into the distance, as if the horror were still before her. She went on, "We found the babies, both dead, their necks broken, and Olivia . . ." Miriam put her face in her hands and rocked back and forth. "Oh, Leona, that poor, sweet girl. I don't know how many of those men must have violated her, but there was more blood on her legs than on her throat that they cut when they were done with her. My poor Lucy, she about went crazy when she saw that, the babies dead, her friend dead like that. I had to wait until she slept to pry that baby out of her arms. I washed all three of them myself, and then I tried to sleep, but all that death around me and still feeling like those soldiers might come back anytime . . . We didn't find Lucy's or Olivia's husbands' bodies. Probably they were taken away for slaves—strong, young men like that."

"Oh, Miriam," I said again. My own breath was ragged, my heart writhing, as if her loss were my own.

Miriam shook her head. "Two women, dry soil, there was not any way we could dig a grave for Olivia and the babies. We put the babies in her arms and covered them with rubble to keep the birds off them, but we left the rest. We needed to get someplace before we starved and the only place I could think of was here, back home." Miriam shuddered, sighed, and continued her story. "I scrounged through the village for whatever was left of our food, to take on the road with us, and we set out. We walked by night and found places to hide in the day, and so we kept safe. We ran out of food the last day and were lucky that someone passed on the road with a cart and gave us a ride the rest of the way here. I don't know if we would have been able to walk the last miles, as hungry and weak as we were. Lucy never talked the whole way, never said a word and never cried one tear. I don't know, maybe she's lost her mind." Miriam put her face in her hands again and wept. I drew her into my arms and let her tears soak my shoulder.

———•••———

A rainstorm had broken overnight, bringing relief from the brutal heat of the past several days, and after Lucy woke and picked at breakfast, I thought it a good idea to take Miriam and Lucy to town to allow them to bathe thoroughly after their long journey.

"Our Thagaste baths are nothing like Carthage," I apologized.

Miriam snorted and her mouth twisted into a half smile. "Oh, Leona, what a rich city girl you've become. When do you think was the last time I even saw a bath? It will seem like Nero's palace to me, I promise you, and Lucy—well, she's hasn't seen a bathhouse since she was four years old."

We undressed in the apodyterium, and Miriam and I rubbed each other with oil, but Lucy cowered in a corner, hugging her arms across her chest, and we decided to leave her alone for the time being.

As I rubbed Miriam with oil, I felt a swelling at the side of her left breast. "Miriam, does this hurt?"

She winced when I touched it, but said, "Oh, only a little every now and then. It's nothing. I'm old now; we get these aches and pains."

"We have a sister who makes poultices. I'll have her make you one when we get back," I said.

When we finished oiling and scraping ourselves, we headed into the tepidarium.

Miriam sat back in the pool and closed her eyes in bliss.

"May I wash your hair, Lucy?" I asked.

Lucy neither answered nor looked at me, still hunched and hugging herself, so I gently guided her by the elbow into the hot pool.

Lucy's long hair had clumped into bad-smelling snakelike strands that writhed down her neck to her shoulders. Chaste we may be, and vanity is surely a sin, but it seemed to me that I would be performing a kindness for Lucy, and for everyone who had to be near her, to clean her stinking hair.

I had brought olive oil, a lemon, and a small scrap of soap, and borrowed one of the cracked pitchers lined up near the pool.

"Lean back," I instructed, gently pressing on her forehead, and I began to pour the water from the pitcher over her hair. It took many passes with the pitcher before her greasy hair was drenched enough that I could begin working in the soap. I worked slowly, taking pleasure in the feel of the creamy soap in my hands as I worked up lather in the girl's hair. With the work-hardened balls of my fingertips, I scrubbed at her scalp, the feeling of her skin shifting over her skull somehow pleasing, like scratching an itch. I scratched at her scalp more vigorously with my nails, and the soap foam bubbled like a stew.

"Feel good?" I asked, but Lucy didn't respond.

Humming, I rinsed her hair with the pitcher until no soap remained and then repeated the lathering process and rinsed again. When the last of the soap was rinsed out, Lucy's dull, greasy snakes of hair were transformed into a tangle of wet, glistening strands. I squeezed the lemon over her hair and massaged the juice into the strands with my palms to counteract the alkalinity of the soap. Her hair would be beautiful, now that it was clean: thick and coarse and wavy, like my own Adeo's. Clean now, the strands were like tangled skeins of linen.

I rubbed a little of the olive oil into my palms, and then rubbed that into Lucy's hair. I had to repeat this process twice to coat every strand, which would make the tangles easier to comb out.

"You have beautiful hair," I told her. "I'm just going to comb out the snarls now. I promise to be gentle."

I picked up a bone comb that I had brought with me from my old life of luxury with Aurelius and started at the bottom, combing gently. Lucy's hair exuded the combined tart and oily smells of lemons and olives. As I worked, I hummed a tune from a play that Aurelius and I had seen many years ago in Carthage.

Thirty minutes of combing and humming, and finally Lucy's hair was combed smooth and glossy.

Miriam joined us, fresh from her own bathing in the hot and then the tepid pool. Thagaste had no multichambered bath complex with elaborate mosaics, like what I had known in Carthage and Italy, just this one room with two pools, and yet Miriam sighed with delight. "I had forgotten the pleasures of the baths," she said. "Oh, Lucy, how beautiful your hair looks, honey."

"I knew your hair would be beautiful once we got it clean and combed," I added. "Doesn't this feel a whole lot better?" I stretched my neck to look at the girl's face. It was then that I saw tears running down her cheeks.

I straightened and resumed my combing, following each stroke of the comb with a smoothing with my palm, and returned to my humming, a softer tune this time, the one I used to sing to Adeo at bedtime long ago. I kept combing, while Lucy's shoulders heaved, and after a while her dark hair was as smooth and gleaming as a nighttime pool and she spoke the first words I had heard from her. "Thank you, Auntie," she said softly.

"No, thank you," I replied. "You and your mother coming has brought light back to me." I hadn't known it was true until I said it. I still felt myself in a dark cave of sorrow, but a faint light now wavered in the gloom.

# CHAPTER THIRTY-TWO

I THOUGHT to teach Lucy the art of bookbinding. She was illiterate, of course, a girl who grew up in the savage borderlands, but I thought there was no reason why she couldn't learn to bind vellum between leather.

Lucy herself had other ideas. She was tall and sturdy and seemed meant for the outdoor life that she had known as a girl. She lasted only a few days fumbling with an awl and linen thread before pleading to be allowed to work in the fields with the other strong, young women. She swung her scythe through the dusty golden fields with almost the strength of a man and raised her alto voice in the work songs that the girls sang as they harvested. She could carry on one shoulder a bundle of harvested wheat that would have been heavy to two of the other girls. Lucy took joy in physical labor, as if it were a gift from God and not at all a punishment for our ancestors' sin in the garden, and gradually the fearful, haunted look left her eyes. I smiled to see her white teeth gleaming against her bronze skin as she teased the other girls about their weakness. They were a pretty sight, I thought, in their light tunics and bare, tanned legs, their hair bound in scarves, swinging their scythes and singing in the dusty sunshine.

I turned to Miriam. "The sisters like Lucy. She's a hard worker, and her jokes and teasing keep them laughing during their work."

"She was always that way," Miriam said. "Made friends with everyone. Those days that we walked, and our first days here, when she never spoke and her eyes looked so dead, I thought my happy girl was lost to me. It's a miracle that we found you and you brought her back to life."

"A miracle for me too."

Miriam looked out the window and shook her head. "I can't believe you do this all yourselves, a bunch of women."

"This is just our own little field, and, between the fields and the goats and the vegetable garden, we can feed ourselves and still spare labor for the Church's lands," I told her. "Now that we have the acres from my son's grandmother, we'll be able to feed more of the poor after our first harvest." Since Miriam's and Lucy's coming, the dark weight on my heart had lightened some, and I took new interest in my work, but I felt distant from it, as if all that happened in the women's house were something happening to someone else, and the only thing that had ever happened to me was to mother and then lose Adeo. My prayers, too, had become rote and perfunctory.

"As soon as I'm feeling better, I want to help," Miriam said.

"Just rest and get better," I replied.

Miriam was not well. The swelling in her breast had grown sorer and redder each day, and she could no longer lift her right arm. She had trouble keeping food down and the lack of nourishment weakened her. I kept her in the dining hall and gave her easy work to do when she felt up to it.

We had caught up on many things in the weeks since she and Lucy had been restored to me. Miriam had known great sorrow since our parting. Her first husband's family had left Thagaste long ago with her son Peter, and she had no knowledge of where he was or how he fared. She had borne three children to her second husband, but they and her husband all had died in a fever that swept through their border village. Her balm for these losses had come from her daughter, her loom, and her Christian faith. I described my sinful life with Aurelius, my travels to Italy, my acceptance of the one true God in Milan, and finally of the death of my only child.

I worked in silence for a while, threading my needle with linen thread to start binding a book. I looked up when I felt Miriam's eyes on me.

She looked at me thoughtfully. "I think of my little grandbaby, Lucy's baby, all the time," she said.

"Of course you do." My heart softened to her sorrow.

"I think of little things that he did. Even as little as he was, he already had ways of his own. You know? If he thought we weren't paying enough attention to him, he'd call out to us, some little nonsense sound. And then when we looked over at him, he would laugh at how clever he was at getting our attention. I like to remember how his fat little belly shook when he laughed, and his eyes scrunched up like little raisins." She glanced at me, then turned back to the bowl of dried peas that she was shelling.

I felt tears sting my eyes. "I know. Adeo did the same thing. I remember exactly how he looked. I know exactly what you mean."

"I wish I could have known him. What was he like as a child?"

"Oh, Miriam, he was so smart. We were vain about him, Aurelius and I, and eager to see what he would accomplish as a man. But when I think of him now, I think of little moments like the one you described about your grandson. I think about the things that he loved, how he was obsessed with elephants as a little boy, how much he worshipped his father, how he loved books." I smiled. "He was like his father. He could never be still. He'd sit reading a book and his fingers would be drumming on the table, or his foot would be tapping up and down. I think about those little things, how he looked and how he smelled. I make myself remember what his voice sounded like. I'm afraid I'll forget."

"You were blessed to have him."

I made no reply at first, intent on pressing my needle through the awl holes in the vellum folios. But I found that my hands were unsteady and needle dull. Finally, I slammed the folio on the table before me and cried, "But why was he taken from me then? I compound sin upon sin, because I can't accept God's will on this. I'm so full of rage and bitterness." I lowered my voice. "I curse God sometimes. He said he punishes the children for the sins of the parents, to the third and fourth generation, but I want to know why. I want to know how a good God could do that."

Miriam looked at me steadily.

I went on. "I missed his last years. I left him in Italy and came back to Africa because I couldn't trust myself not to sin with Aurelius, and because his father and grandmother convinced me that his prospects were better without me. And *then* God punished me—not when I was sinning, but when I tried to do right! And I want to know why. And I want to know why it was Adeo who was punished, not me. Why wasn't it my life that was taken?"

Miriam shook her head. "I don't know."

"He was so good. His heart was so big. Everyone who met him loved him. You think this is just his mother talking, but it was true. One of the last things he did . . ." I felt tears welling and swallowed before I could go on. "The night before he took sick, I argued with his father about the land that his grandmother left to the Church. I wanted it used to help feed the poor in our own community, and I knew Quintus would just use it to add to the Church's wealth and his own power. Aurelius saw both sides of the argument, as usual. It was Adeo, eighteen years old—eighteen years old!—who convinced him to do what was right."

"I thought you didn't care so much about the land." Miriam rose and emptied the bowl of pea husks out the window for our goats to chew on.

"I don't care about anything anymore."

My friend sat back down next to me, the bowl of shelled peas in her lap, leaning toward me. "But it seems like these acres were your son's last gift to you."

"Miriam, I know what you're doing, and stop it. You're trying to give me a reason to go on. It's not that simple." I picked up the folio and began jabbing my needle through it again.

"No, of course not," Miriam agreed.

"I'm sorry. I don't mean to scold. You've suffered far more than I."

"And our God brought us back together to comfort each other."

"Well . . . yes, I guess He did." But, grateful as I was to be reunited with my friend, I was sure that there was no comfort possible for me.

———•••———

Miriam lasted four more months, through the cool, rainy winter, until almost the time when we would harvest our first crop of winter wheat on Monnica's land.

The day we buried her, the sun shone, lending shimmer to the ripening wheat. Sprouts of spinach and lettuce and beans emerged from the vegetable garden beside the burial ground.

Lucy dug the hole herself, grunting through her tears.

Quintus prayed over the grave and returned to his house in town, and the other sisters went back to their work after offering their own prayers and condolences.

Once we were alone, Lucy put her face in her hands and sank to her knees on the damp ground, sobbing.

I squatted beside her, placing my arms around her. *Help me,* I prayed, *I don't know how to comfort her.*

For long minutes, I held Lucy, rocking her gently in my arms while she sobbed.

Finally she turned her wet face to me. "Why did God take away from me all of the people I loved, Auntie? My husband, my baby, my mother, all gone. How can God be good when He does this?"

"I don't know," I admitted.

"I try to pray. I try to be good. But, I don't understand this one thing. I don't understand it."

"We'll all be together again someday with Jesus," I told her. "We'll understand then. And in the meantime, I love you and you have friends here now. I'll take care of you just as your mother would have." The words sounded hollow to me even as I said them. The questions that tortured Lucy were the same ones tearing at my own heart.

In my dream the sky was the color of iron. I kept thinking that God was capricious and cruel, and every time I thought it, lightning bolted from the sky and struck near me. Yet I kept thinking it as I walked toward a walled garden, lightning stabbing and burning the earth all around me.

I reached the garden and went through the gate. The sky was still dark, but the garden seemed protected from the lightning. Aurelius sat in the garden, reading St. Paul's letter to the Romans. "Take and read," he urged me, but when I tried to take the book that he offered, I found that my arms were paralyzed.

I woke in a panic, thinking my arms wouldn't move, and for a moment, until the dream faded into waking, they wouldn't. Fully awake, I sat up and looked around the moonlit dormitory at the sleeping women around me. "Take and read," Aurelius had said. I rose quietly and padded to the closet where we kept our small store of books: carefully rolled scrolls in boxes and the bound books in a small, plain trunk.

Aurelius had been reading a bound book in my dream, so I opened the trunk and selected the volume that lay on top and opened it at random.

It was a volume of Hebrew lamentations translated into Latin, and I could remember no reason why it should have been on top of the pile in the trunk, but the words pierced me.

*My soul is bereft of peace;*
*I have forgotten what happiness is;*
*So I say, "Gone is my glory,*
*And all that I had hoped for from the Lord."*
*The thought of my affliction and my homelessness*
*Is wormwood and gall!*
*My soul continually thinks of it*
*And is bowed down within me.*

My throat closed and tears gathered in my eyes as I read. Yes, I thought, and bowed my head and let the sobs come for a moment.

I sniffed and wiped my eyes and read on.

*But this I call to mind,*
*And therefore I have hope:*
*The steadfast love of the Lord never ceases,*
*His mercies never come to an end;*
*They are new every morning;*
*Great is your faithfulness.*
*"The Lord is my portion," says my soul,*
*"therefore I will hope in him."*

My sobs stopped and I sat very still. How could both be true at the same time? How could unendurable sorrow exist beside God's steadfast love?

And the answer came to me: how could they *not* be true at the same time? At every point in my life when darkness has threatened to overwhelm me, some gift of love and hope had been given to me. I sinned with Aurelius and found myself pregnant while still a young girl, and I despaired. But Adeo was a gift to me and to all who knew him in his short life. Adeo was lost to me, but his last act was to leave me the means to help the humble people among whom I was born and who were now so desperate in their poverty. My friend, so long lost, had been returned to me, and when she, in turn, was taken, I had her daughter as a comfort.

I closed the book and laid it back in the trunk. Adeo's death was still unendurable. That had not changed and I knew that it would never change. I also knew now that I had been given what was needed to bear the unbearable. I thought of the words again: *The steadfast love of the Lord never ceases.* To prove it, he gives us each other to care for.

# CHAPTER THIRTY-THREE

*Thagaste*
*Anno Domini 430*

ONE OF THE LOCAL PEASANTS, Rufus, tightened the harness around the borrowed mule's belly, then stood back and gave his rump a slap. I held my breath and then let out a sigh as the mule jerked forward and we heard the stones of our little mill scrape against each other. The milling of our winter wheat had officially started.

"Mother, I hope you won't tell the bishop on me: I buried a fish under the floor for good luck," Rufus whispered. "I know we should trust in the Lord, but the folks still like the old ways a bit too."

"It's God that brought us such a good harvest, and your hard work that repaired the mill," I scolded. "The buried fish is just one less fish on someone's table. But it can be our secret."

I looked out the mill window, through a golden haze of wheat dust, at the surrounding fields, where my young women moved as busily and purposefully as bees, some carrying a few last sheaves, others pacing the fields with bags on their shoulders, collecting the gleanings, and yet others threshing the grain from the chaff by tossing it in the air on thin wool sheets. The youngest, strongest girls then slung the grain-filled sheets over their shoulders and carried them up to the third floor of the mill, where Lucy directed the feeding of the harvested wheat into the mill shaft. Everyone except the ill and the very old was busy from sunup until sundown during the harvest.

"You okay up there?" I called to Lucy.

"Just tell them to keep it coming," she yelled back. "Thanks be to God that we got it going. Lydia! Too fast! You'll clog it! Slow down!" I smiled and shook my head at her shouting at the young novice assisting her. At more than fifty, my faithful, tireless Lucy was as straight-backed and strong as ever, but her hearing was failing and she shouted at everyone.

"What would we do without you?" I said to Rufus.

"Mother, what would we do without the mill? If it couldn't be repaired, half the town would starve this year. My Stephen is a big, strong boy and can do enough work on Licentius's land for two of us today. The repair wasn't hard."

"Nobody but you could do it," I reminded him, and regretted again that most of Rufus's time was owed to the fields of his lord, Licentius, Urbanus's son. Urbanus had died years ago, and Licentius spent all his time in Rome and Carthage, but the agent who represented him never failed to enforce the labor due him.

Rufus's son Stephen—along with all other male peasants in the Thagaste countryside—was in Licentius's fields from dawn until after dusk these spring weeks, bringing in his harvest. I wished Rufus could have been spared to work with us for more than just this day. His mechanical talents were a gift from God. When still a young man, he had built our mill from a drawing in a book in Quintus's library, quadrupling the speed at which we could process our grain using hand mills.

"Let me help you down the stairs, Mother," he said now, taking my arm.

I hadn't kept track of my age, but knew that I must be over seventy. My eyesight and hearing were still sharp, but I tired easily, my bones often ached, and I knew that I wasn't steady enough to take stairs without help. It was a wonder to me that I still lived and worked, my hands still steady for copying, and my mind still clear for the endless verbal duels with Quintus, who never ceased trying to gain control of the acres that Monnica had left and the mill that we had erected on the land.

But we had managed to hang on to our land and remain independent of the bishop for our material needs. We paid the bishopric a tithe of our harvest each year, and the rest was ours to use or distribute as we saw fit. Our little community prospered. We raised wheat, vegetables, sheep, and goats, and were able to feed our own community of one hundred women, plus provide food in the lean months for the poorest people of Thagaste and its surrounding countryside. I had a few literate girls to help me copy scripture, Quintus's sermons, and other books that occasionally came our way. Many a Christian missionary had been sent to the borderlands with a small, leather-bound Gospel copied by me or one of my young women.

As we made our way back to the kitchen complex, Rufus squinted down the road. "Mother, it looks like travelers." He pointed.

Already, the ground was dry, and the approaching travelers kicked up a big enough cloud of dust that I could see that there were many of them.

"What should we do?" Rufus asked. He was right to be fearful. Legionnaires had not been seen in North Africa outside the biggest cities in many years, and travel of any distance was increasingly precarious, with bandits of all kinds roaming the roads. Most people stayed where they were, eating what they could grow nearby and communicating little with the outside world. And so it had become unusual to see a large party approaching.

But our Lord commanded us to welcome strangers, and when I looked around at the nearly one hundred women busy at work, I knew that we could never get them all gathered inside before the travelers reached us anyway. What's more, Rufus was the only man in the vicinity right now, and our buildings were designed for living, not defending. "There's nothing to do except wait for them and see what they want," I said.

It seemed to take an eternity for the party to reach us. Rufus and I stood silently, but my heart drummed rapidly against my ribs. For myself, I was old and ready to die, but I was responsible for the welfare of the other women, most of them young with lives yet to be lived.

Finally, we could see that the travelers were not bandits but an unarmed party of about twenty-five men, women, and children, dusty and shambling. My heart slowed and I turned to Rufus. "They look harmless. Come out with me to meet them."

Rufus and I arrived in the small orchard outside the dormitory at the same time as the ragged party of travelers. A hollow-eyed, slump-shouldered man led the party.

"We need food and rest," he announced without preamble. "Please. Whatever you can offer. We've been walking for three days from Liberium."

"Of course," I said. "Please come in."

—•••—

We seated the travelers in our kitchen and brought them a meal of bread, dried fruit, cheese, and olives, and had water brought from the well.

"You should abandon this place as soon as you can," their leader, Julian, told me as soon as he had washed his hands and wet his mouth. "The Vandals will surely reach here within days."

Rumors had reached us for months of the army of Vandals that had already thundered across central Europe to Spain and from there had crossed the Middle Sea to land on North Africa's northwestern shore.

"How far are they?"

He shrugged. "We didn't wait to find out after Deborah barely escaped with her life." He nodded his head toward a woman sitting near him, a small child on her lap. "She came from a town just north of Liberium, on the coast, and she and her child were the only people to survive the Vandals from their city. The city surrendered in hope of mercy and were slaughtered anyway."

Deborah's eyes were sunk deep in their sockets and seemed to look inward rather than outward as she told her story. Most of the men of her town had been put to the sword immediately. Then the Vandal general, Genseric, had gathered the children and threatened to kill them one by one if the women didn't reveal where they might have hidden food or treasure. The women gave up what little they had, but Genseric had two children put to the sword anyway, to prove that he was serious, and gave them one day to produce more.

Finally, when he was sure there was nothing more to take, Genseric's men forced the remaining women and children into a wooden warehouse and set fire to it. They left Deborah and her baby alive to warn other towns of their coming and tell what happened to anyone who held anything back from them.

"We held back nothing, and still they put the whole town to death. Then they put me and my baby on the road with only a skin of water. We nearly died too. You should flee with us to Hippo," Deborah warned.

Hippo was the only walled city within hundreds of miles, and the only possible protection against the Vandal horde. I knew also who was bishop there, and it passed through my mind to wonder how he had fared all these years and whether I would get a look at him.

"They call themselves Christians!" Deborah spat.

"Christians?" I blinked. Surely she was mistaken.

"They all wore crosses painted on their leather armor, and wooden crosses around their necks."

I turned to Rufus. "Take charge here. I'm going to town. I should talk to Quintus and Marius right away."

———•••———

"We should evacuate to Hippo immediately, of course," said Marius, Quintus's assistant.

Quintus laid claim to seventy-five years, and even I believed that he probably spoke the truth. He was completely bald now, and his freckled skin hung like feedbags from his jaws. He was as thin and bent as an olive tree, and his brown eyes had gone muddy. Marius did most of the preaching and most of the management of the priests and monks and the acres owned by the Church in Thagaste.

Quintus nodded slowly. "We should leave," he agreed.

"And take as much of the town with us as wants to go," I added.

"Of course, of course," Quintus agreed, waving a feeble hand.

"Bishop?" I said.

Quintus's eyes were closed and he seemed to have nodded off. "Hmmmm?"

"The woman who escaped said something that surprised me. She said the Vandals were Christians."

"They're Arians," Quintus told me. "Heretics. They deny that the Father and the Son are co-eternal. The empire and the Church must put them down."

So it was true. I sighed. Would there never be an end to the claims of heresy?

Marius had been busy pouring himself a goblet of wine, but now he spoke. "It's a shame you'll have to leave your harvest behind."

Regret pricked me at the thought of the stacks of newly harvested wheat that we would be leaving to the Vandals. "The timing couldn't be worse," I agreed. "If only we had a few more days."

"A shame for the Church also," he went on, "since without a harvest you won't be able to pay your tithe." He watered down some wine for Quintus and the bishop accepted it with a trembling hand.

"We'll make it up next year."

"Who's to say what might happen next year? There could be a drought or another invasion."

"Or Christ could finally come again," I snapped. "Why are you talking nonsense at a time like this?" But with a sudden stab of rage and horror, I realized exactly what he was getting at.

"If you can't pay your tithe, we could discuss turning over some of the women's acreage to the bishop," Marius continued, and could not keep a tight smile from his lips as he sipped his wine.

Now Quintus's soggy eyes lit with understanding as well. I longed to slap him.

At that moment, I hated Marius and Quintus far more than I hated the heretical Vandals. I ground my folded hands together in my lap and offered an incoherent silent prayer before I replied. "I'll stay then."

"By yourself?" Marius snorted.

"Lucy will stay with me, and Rufus, and perhaps a few others." I prayed that this was true. "We'll bring in a harvest and pay you a tenth of what we yield, just we are obligated to do."

Marius flushed. "Don't be foolish," he argued. "You said you had no idea where the barbarians were. They could be here tonight for all we know. And, even if you bring in your harvest, how will you protect it from them?"

"We'll bring it with us to Hippo. We have two wagons."

"You're out of your mind!"

I stood. "Marius, listen to me," I said, but I was looking at Quintus, my old adversary. "You will never get my acres. Do you hear me? Never. They came from my son's grandmother, and it was his last wish that they be used to feed the needy people of this community, and that is what I intend to do until I drop dead. And if I drop dead under a Vandal sword, so be it. I'm almost as old as the bishop and I'm ready to meet my Lord."

Quintus looked away from me.

"Fine," Marius snarled. "Meet him then. We're leaving tomorrow and taking the church's valuables with us. Follow us when you're ready with your little bags of grain—if you live."

"And my relic," Quintus quavered.

"What?" Marius replied.

"My relic. Saint Perpetua's milk. It must go too."

"Of course, of course," Marius said. He curled his lip and shook his head at me. "Let us know if you change your mind. If you don't, I doubt that I'll ever see you again."

## CHAPTER THIRTY-FOUR

PARCHED AND SWEATING, we approached the city walls of Hippo one week after my argument with Quintus and Marius, our exhausted mules pulling two wagons filled with bags of milled wheat.

Lucy had remained, as well as Rufus and his sons Stephen and Leo, along with Julian and six young sisters. The twelve of us had worked from the time the sun first appeared between the eastern hills of Thagaste until its remains lit the hillsides with red. After two days, we had filled our two wagons with as much bagged grain as we dared try the mules to carry, and stored the rest of the unmilled wheat in the barn, in the small hope that it would be safe there from the Vandals.

Thagaste was empty when we set out at dawn on the third day, and the countryside that we passed through on our sixty-mile journey to Hippo was equally deserted. We made good time on the cobblestoned Roman roads, through a landscape as lovely and orderly as any other North African spring: ripe yellow winter wheat ruffled by the breeze, tulips and daffodils and yellow pea flowers blooming on the side of the road, small shoots of vegetables raising their green heads in household plots. The sun was warm by afternoon, in blue, cloudless skies.

But we met no one on the road or in any of the villages we passed, and we saw tools abandoned in their fields, and laundry left on tree branches, and here and there, cows bellowing sadly in their pastures, as if all the population of Numidia had been gathered up in God's hand. The sisters kept looking over their shoulders, as if the Vandals might at any moment appear on the road behind us.

The first human beings we saw were the remains of a legion, marching toward Hippo from the west as we approached from the southern road.

"Look! The legion!" Stephen cried when he spotted them, and the young sisters cheered.

"Thanks be to God," Lucy whispered to me.

But we were disappointed when we came closer to the soldiers and got a good look at them. Most of their horses were dragging litters or wagons carrying wounded, and many of those still marching were filthy and bleeding. For all their wounds and their empty eyes, they marched at a quick pace, already flowing through the city gates ahead of us.

"This looks like a defeated army to me," Rufus said.

<hr />

Hippo was a more ancient city than Thagaste, and its winding streets were clogged with people and their animals, stinking of *merda* and sweat. It seemed that all of North Africa had been harvested by the approaching Vandals and deposited in this one town. Colorless, exhausted forms, like giant snails, were curled up on blankets in the first town square we passed, and the water of the fountain was already gray with their filth. It took us an hour to get directions to the basilica and then climb the hill to the old Christian quarter where it was located.

"Wait out here with the rest," I instructed Lucy. "I'll go inside and see if anyone knows where our bishop is and where we might stay."

As I passed into the cool darkness I was once again overpowered by a nauseating stench. The interior of the basilica was as littered with bodies as the town squares that we had passed. Some were asleep on thin pallets on the stone floor. Some sat talking quietly in corners. I paused, looking around in blank discouragement for the second time that day.

A young priest with a sharp nose and thinning hair approached me. "Sister, do you need assistance?"

"I've brought a party of refugees from Thagaste. We're looking for our bishop, Quintus, and wondering if there is any place we can stay."

"You can stay here in the basilica. Bishop Augustine has given instructions that no religious are to be turned away, but it's getting harder and harder to feed everyone and find places for them to sleep. As you see," he added, gesturing toward the crowd in the cathedral. "You might be able to ask Bishop Augustine about your bishop. He's right over there." He nodded toward another corner of the nave. "He walks through every evening," he added worshipfully. "It gives everyone so much hope."

I gazed on Aurelius now for the first time more than thirty years. He was still large even in his old age, dressed simply in a black tunic. His hair was white and he had let his beard grow to his chest. He walked with a stately pace that contrasted with the impatient hurry of his youth. But the biggest change was in his eyes. The fading orange light illuminated his ancient, lined face and I could see that his dark eyes had faded to tan. The skin of his cheeks sagged toward his neck and the sockets of his eyes were hollow and dark, so that his eyes looked enormous. But now they burned, not with the old sharp brilliance, but with the glow of some constant inner flame.

Others saw it too, and they crowded around him, on their feet or their knees, pleading for his blessing, touching his plain robe, kissing his staff. Slowly and patiently, he worked his way through the crowd, making the sign of the cross on each forehead.

I stared at him as one might stare at God himself. It was the setting sun from the windows, of course, but he seemed to have about him an aura of light. It felt impossible that this was the same dark, virile young man I had known, and at the same time I knew in my heart that this was what he had wanted during those restless years: to be a leader and a teacher, someone the great mass of people could look up to and trust. Finally God was using him as he was meant to be used. I felt the urge to fall to my knees and bow, and then he was before me.

He made the sign of the cross on my forehead, his large-jointed thumb still firm. "Bless you, Sister," he murmured.

"Bishop, don't you know me?" I asked.

His thumb stopped, still pressing into my forehead, his fingers pressing lightly on the side of my head. Slowly, he repositioned his hand so that it cupped my chin. His ancient eyes burned into me, puzzled at first and then fierce. He raised his other hand to the back of my head and solemnly kissed my forehead. "You still live," he said, smiling slightly.

"And you."

He turned to the astonished priest. "Eraclius, this sister is an old friend of mine. Can you please take her to the bishop's guest house?"

"I came with a party of eleven more and two wagons of milled grain," I told him.

"Two wagons of grain," he repeated. "God bless you. We can make room for your party in the guest house. Can you please see to it, Eraclius?"

The guest house was already crowded and there was no place for us except the floor of the kitchen, but it at least held the smells of lemons and rosemary instead of the stench of unwashed bodies. I took time to wash myself with cold water from the well in the small, walled courtyard.

Bishop Augustine soon sent for me.

His chamber was even plainer than what we had known in our poorest student days in Carthage. Four plaster walls. Two chairs and a desk holding a popping, flickering candle. For a bed, a stone shelf covered by a thin pallet. A wooden cross on one wall.

He sat in one of the chairs, Bible on his lap, and when I entered the room, he smiled and indicated that I should take the other chair.

"Quintus is safe," he said first. "He and Marius are staying here in my own house."

"I'm glad to hear it," I said.

"I wondered about you many times," he confessed. "You've spent all these years in Thagaste, then?"

I felt a flash of irritation that Quintus wouldn't have kept him informed of this, or that he wouldn't have asked; and then I recalled that I hadn't asked about him either, out of a kind of spiritual pride in considering that door closed.

"Since we last parted," I answered, and the faint echo of that old agony flickered, the pain of losing our son.

Reading my thoughts, he said, "I think of him every day, and pray for his soul. We loved him too much."

"Loved him too much?" It seemed a nonsensical statement to me. He was our child.

"The Lord demands that our love be all for him, Leona, and that we love each other as an expression of that, unselfishly. I loved Adeo egotistically. I was proud of him."

"And you think that's why God took him from us? To punish us for that?" This same notion that had so tortured me in the first months after Adeo's death now sounded childish and simplistic, and I observed dimly that Aurelius could still manage to annoy me with his theorizing, even at our advanced age.

Auurelius's long face creased into a gentle smile. "No. To be merciful to us. To remove the one obstacle to our loving him first and foremost."

And how could he still do that to me as well, after so many years: confuse me with a completely unexpected statement that I would have to ponder for days to even begin to understand?

He sighed. "How strange that we have all lived this long, you and I and Quintus, when all my longing is for Heaven and my body is shriveled and broken."

"Mine too."

He shook his head. "When I look at you, I see you as you are today, shrunken and dark and wrinkled. We're raisins, Leona, and soon we'll be dust. But I also see you as the beautiful young girl you were, and I think that is how our Lord can see us, now that I think about it. He sees our sinful selves and at the same time he can see us as He meant us to be: beautiful not in our bodies but in holiness. I think you've just inspired next week's sermon. Always my muse." He smiled faintly, but then turned serious again. "Leona, I'm glad to see you this last time before we both leave this earth. I pray every day for God's forgiveness for leading you to sin when you were a girl. My life's work is to save souls, and I led yours into sin and I am as grievously sorry as it is possible to be."

I couldn't find it in myself to claim to be sorry, although I knew I should be. I said nothing.

"Well, as you can see," he said, "I'm no danger to you now, nor to anyone in that regard. Old age has finally done for me what all my good intentions could never do: I am completely chaste, both in body and in mind. And so you and your party are welcome to stay here as long as needed, and your virtue will be in no danger." His ancient eyes sparkled with amusement at his own infirmity. "May I ask you to do me a favor?" he asked.

"Certainly."

"I must meet now with your bishop and with General Boniface, who is responsible for the defense of the city. Will you come with me and make notes of the meeting discussion? In all these years, I've never met anyone whose notes are better or whose hand is clearer. You got me through university, remember?"

"I think you're remembering wrong, but I'll be glad to help you. My eyes are still clear and my hand is still steady."

As we walked down the narrow hallway I felt relaxed and at ease, until we entered the bishop's office and I saw Quintus and Marius sitting at the meeting table, looking clean and well fed. Beside them sat the priest Eraclius and a square-shouldered, scar-faced man, with his long hair caught back in a tail in the fashion of the barbarians. I thought this must be the Roman General Boniface.

Quintus reached for my hand and squeezed it. "You've arrived," he said fervently. "Thank God."

I was startled by his concern. "Yes. We made it in just behind the army."

"Yes, yes." He grasped my hand harder and looked into my eyes. "Did you bring the relic?"

"The what?"

"The relic. Saint Perpetua's milk. You brought it?"

"No. I thought you took it when you left."

"You were to bring it," Marius argued.

"I?" I lowered myself into the chair beside Quintus.

"Yes, you," Marius replied. "When we were in the bishop's office and you were so insistent on staying behind, you said you would bring the relic."

"Why would I bring it? You were the ones who took the other treasures from the church. The bishop was the one who cared about it so much. Why leave it behind?" I suspected that Marius had just forgotten it and then convinced Quintus that I had agreed to be in charge of the vial.

Quintus's face crumpled. "The people believe the relic will save us."

"What people?" I asked.

"Every church in Hippo is packed with refugees," Marius replied. "The bishop and I have traveled around the city and brought comfort to them. The bishop has shared with many the hope of Saint Perpetua." He looked away from me.

I felt myself flush. "These people don't need two-hundred-year-old dried-up breast milk. They need food and some kind of work to do to keep their minds off their terror."

"Are you questioning that the relic can work miracles?" Marius snapped.

"I'm saying that it is irrelevant, since we don't have it here with us."

Marius rolled his eyes. "Thanks to you."

We all looked at Bishop Augustine. His eyes rested on me with amused pride, and I felt like his young pupil again. "We should think," he said, "about what will bring the lambs to the shepherd."

We waited while he paused to gather his thoughts. "Our goal should be the eternal salvation of the souls under our care," he went on. "We must do everything we can to keep Hippo from falling under the control of the heretics. And so I think we had better hear from the general on the topic of the defense of the city."

"Pardon me, Bishop," Eraclius put in, "but should the woman be here while we discuss these matters?"

"Sister Leona is my scribe from many years back and I asked her to join us to take the notes of the meeting," Bishop Augustine explained.

Eraclius flushed as if he'd been slapped.

"You'll be useful in other ways," his bishop assured him, and turned to Boniface. "Tell us what we must do to defend our city, my old friend."

Boniface still wore his dusty, blood-stained battle tunic. He stood to speak. "The horde is over eighty thousand, but not all of them are fighting men and not all of them will besiege Hippo. We went up against about twenty thousand, and I estimate that that is the number they will send to besiege us. They can last a long time. The winter wheat is ripening in the fields, and in the fall they will have our fruit and our olives. We have the port, but they can still be resupplied by sea if needed."

"And we can as well, no?" Bishop Augustine pointed out.

"As long as we continue to control the port—*and* if we can get word to Rome or Carthage, *and* if they choose to help us. We shouldn't count on that. Food should be rationed immediately. Hoarding should be punishable by death."

Bishop Augustine looked around the room. "Agreed?" When no one objected, he said to Boniface, "Make it so right away. What else must we do?"

"During our retreat, we burned as many fields as we could, and I'm sending out details today to burn what's closest to the city walls," Boniface continued.

"But why not bring it in for food for the city?" I cried.

The general glanced at me, but then spoke to the men. "Because there isn't time, and burning is a quick way to deny it to our enemies. What's more, it clears some of the area so that we can watch their movements. I'll schedule continuous watches on the city walls, day and night. When they try to build their siege works, they'll have to be out in the open and then we can start picking some of them off. I've brought catapults. We can bathe them in fire if they try to attack. If we have enough food we can probably hold out for quite some time unless . . . How much water is in the cisterns?"

"As much as usual after the winter rains," Eraclius replied. "Enough to last the summer if the aqueduct keeps flowing."

Boniface rubbed his chin. "And how long if not?"

Nobody responded. Eraclius blanched and looked down at his hands.

Boniface strode to the window, where the aqueduct was barely visible in the distance. "Our greatest danger will come when Genseric severs our aqueduct—as he surely will. We'll be completely dependent on the cisterns then until next winter's rain."

"Then water must be rationed also," Bishop Augustine said.

"Yes," Boniface agreed. "The baths should be closed right away. I'll put my engineers to work diverting as much water as possible from the aqueduct directly to the cisterns, so that they're filled to capacity."

"How much time do we have?" Augustine asked.

"We were two days' march from here when they routed my army and we marched hard to get here. Their vanguard can't be more than a day behind us."

# CHAPTER THIRTY-FIVE

THE FIRST THING that the Vandals did was torture their captives. Some of the soldiers that Boniface had sent to burn the fields, along with a few farmers and their families, had been caught outside the city walls and taken captive, and were made examples of what might befall all of us if we failed to immediately surrender the city. These people were staked out in the fields directly outside the city walls and left to die of starvation and exposure in full view of anyone who dared to climb to one of the parapets.

The bodies were returned to us, in pieces, via catapult. Lucy and I were witnesses to one such horror, one day early in the siege as we walked uphill toward the forum to take a little precious bread and cheese to Rufus and his sons for lunch. I caught it first out of the corner of my eyes: a dark object hurtling through the sky overhead, plummeting to the ground at the feet of a woman and her small child, landing with a heavy squish like a ripe melon.

The woman screamed and her child started to cry. At their feet lay the rotting head of one of the tortured captives, darkened by exposure and decay, tattered from the attentions of the birds and now flattened and oozing from its sudden contact with the stone street. The child stood crying, and the rest of us stared in horror for long minutes until someone had the presence of mind to fetch a slave to remove the mess. Only then did I think to say a prayer for the soul who had once inhabited the remains.

When we reached the forum atop the higher of Hippo's two hills, we had a view of the Vandals, swarming over the blackened fields that Boniface had burned, hammering on their siege engines.

The forum was busy too, ringing with the sound of heavy mallets on marble. By the time we found Rufus, dust coated our skin and clogged our throats.

Rufus set down his mallet and wiped sweat from his forehead with one sleeve. "The general wants all the pagan statues turned to rubble," he told us, taking the lunch from our hands and sharing with his boys. "He's using it to reinforce the city walls. They say we'll start tearing down buildings next. Sure will be easier than breaking up this marble. Although we keep hearing rumors that we'll soon surrender."

I shook my head. "Don't believe it. The general and the bishop are determined to hold out through any length of a siege."

He glanced around and lowered his voice. "There's a lot of complaining that maybe the general and the bishop don't always hear."

I waited for him to go on.

"A lot of people aren't happy about the general taking control of the all the warehouses and livestock. They think that he just wants to make a profit for himself on it."

"The guilds were already doing that," I replied. "The general and the bishop seized the food supply to put a stop to it and make sure that there would be enough for everyone."

Rufus wiped sweat from his face with a dusty hand. "I'm just telling you what people are saying. And I can tell you too, that lots of the common folk listen when they hear talk that we'd be better off to just hand the city over to Genseric."

"You can be sure that Bishop Augustine will never allow the city to be handed over to heretics. And, remember, Rufus, Genseric surely sent spies into the city ahead of his army. The whisperings about surrender could be coming from them."

"I know, I know. I'm just telling you what I hear—since you have the bishop's ear."

"If we all keep our heads and ration food and water, we can outlast a siege," I said. "Pass that around, if you would."

"I surely will, Mother." He popped a last bite of cheese into his mouth. "Well, back to the work of destroying the old gods."

"Is it true?" Lucy asked me as we left Rufus to his work. "Will the food and water really last?"

"The water should last until the next fall rains, if we're careful, and as for food . . . General Boniface is hoping for resupply by sea by then."

"Someone should organize the food distribution to make sure it's fair," she pointed out.

"Yes, someone should, and I already have someone in mind to suggest to the bishop."

"Who?"

"Us."

---

Augustine, Boniface and their inner council were to meet that afternoon to discuss the food situation. Boniface already had a soldier at the door of each warehouse. Every baker in the city would get the same ration of flour daily, and prices, set by Boniface, would be posted in all of the shops and public squares.

The penalty would be death for selling anyone more than their daily ration or charging more than the mandated price. The bishop and the general also agreed that the Church would receive a ration of bread for free distribution to the refugees and other destitute people who could not afford to buy it at any price, and Augustine put forth my proposal that Lucy and I should manage the distribution.

"I'm not at ease with leaving the management of food distribution in the hands of women," General Boniface complained, refusing to look at me as always.

"Sister Leona presented me with an excellent plan to keep the distribution fair and to verify that no one received more than their daily ration," Bishop Augustine replied. "But I think you are right that they will need the help of a good man. Eraclius, I ask you to help the sisters manage this important task. And now I would like to move on to a matter that is of grave concern to me: the spiritual well-being of the citizens."

"The people need hope," Quintus said. His voice wavered, his back was bent, and his hands constantly shook, but he was as vehement and certain as ever, and for once he was right.

"They need food and water and strong walls," Boniface argued. "Then they will have reason to hope." He could never be still in these meetings. He rose and paced to the window as he always did, as if he could repel the Vandals with his eyes.

I reported what Rufus had told me. "Some people are whispering that we should just give up, that maybe the Vandals will show some mercy if we don't resist."

Bishop Augustine shook his head. "These barbarians must be resisted at all costs. They will show no mercy, and what's more they are heretics. Better that the whole city should starve or be put to the sword than surrender to heresy. The immortal soul of every citizen of Hippo is in our hands." He looked around the room, pinning each of us in turn with his eyes, as if scanning for disagreement.

"Then we've got to do something to strengthen their resolve," Marius said. "Already I hear rumors of the old rituals coming back."

"Tell me what you mean," Augustine urged gravely.

"Reading of entrails in the old Roman way, sacrifices to the old Roman gods, and worse."

"Worse? Meaning what?"

Marius smiled slightly, as if the bishop had fallen into some sort of trap. "The old Berber religions, Bishop. We might have thought that those had died with the Roman conquest, but it seems that they had only gone underground. We hear murmurings that the gods may require human sacrifice if the city is to be saved."

"Surely not," Eraclius argued.

Marius shrugged. "People are afraid. Terrified people do terrible things. And, then, of course, our sister Leona is also correct, that many would be willing to compromise with heresy if it would save their lives."

Nobody argued.

"We need a rallying point," Marius said.

"Yes," Eraclius said. "But what?"

"The Saint Perpetua relic."

*That old thing again*, I thought. Would they never give up? "We left that behind in Thagaste," I pointed out. "Remember?"

"No, we were mistaken, Sister," Marius announced. "We had it all along." He produced a small flask from the pocket of his robe.

I stared at it, hardly believing that Marius would even attempt to perpetrate such a hoax. "Marius, stop wasting our time. That isn't even the same flask."

"You're mistaken, Sister. It is." He smirked. "You can surely be forgiven for your mistake, given your advanced age."

I clenched my fists in my lap. "I've seen that flask every single year since the bishop got his hands on it. He brings it out every feast day of Saint Perpetua. I know what it looks like, and that's not it. This fraud it not going to save this city."

"It saved Thagaste from the Aitheopes and the Donatist heresy," Quintus argued, "and it will save us now."

I narrowed my eyes at my bishop. "You know that is not the same vial."

He looked away. "I know nothing of the kind. You're mistaken, Sister, and, I would add, in violation of your vow of obedience—as usual." He shot a pointed look at his old friend Augustine.

We all followed his gaze and looked at the Bishop of Hippo.

"This could be both a source of hope and defense against heresy," Marius said. "And if we are faithful, it may even produce a miracle again."

I scanned the room for a possible ally against this nonsense and settled against my will on the gruff, practical Boniface. "What does General Boniface think?" I asked.

The general refused to look at me, as usual. "On spiritual matters, I defer to the bishop."

Augustine closed his eyes for a moment. "These relics of the saints may sometimes work miracles," he conceded, "But, they must be carefully verified. Let us make a study of it. But leave me now. It's time for my afternoon prayers."

As we filed out of the bishop's office, Marius caught up with me. "This is another fight that you won't win, Sister," he whispered.

"Another?"

"Well, you've lost the fight about the tithe, of course. The milled flour you brought to town is forfeit to the grain seizure and therefore you won't be able to pay your tithe."

"The Church seized my grain and that counts as my tithe," I snapped, but my blood stopped for a second. I wasn't sure that my statement was strictly true.

"General Boniface seized your flour," Marius corrected me, "and therefore when we get back to Thagaste, your bishop will be pleased to accept some or all of your acres in payment of your annual tithe. Excuse me, now." He shouldered past me to catch up with Boniface and whisper something in his ear.

————•••————

I was back in Aurelius's office later that day to transcribe his arguments against Julian of Eclanum. I had marveled at how easily, after so many years apart, we had settled into our old routine of my taking his dictation, but this was not the first thing on my mind that day.

"Your old friend Quintus is still trying to get hold of your mother's land." I exploded the minute I walked in the door.

Aurelius looked puzzled for a moment and then his eyes lit. "Oh, yes," he said, turning back to the text he had been studying.

"We owe the bishopric a tithe each year," I went on.

"Yes, of course. That's only right."

"Well how can we pay it this year with the Vandals amok and the only little bit of wheat we could mill seized by your friend Boniface?" I eased my old bones into a chair next to him.

"Make it up next year."

"That's my point. Quintus and his little *catamitus* Marius won't wait until next year. They insist that I forfeit some of our acres in place of the wheat tithe. You have to stop them."

"Quintus is your bishop, Leona."

"He will listen to you. This was your son's last wish." I took one of his hands in both of mine, feeling how thin and dry his skin was.

"I remember." Aurelius withdrew his hand, but his watery old eyes softened on me. "All right, Leona, I'll exert my influence on Quintus one more time. I'll see if I can persuade him."

"Don't see if you can persuade him. Persuade him. Force him if you have to."

He smiled. "You're still a passionate young girl at heart."

"No, I'm a very old woman who doesn't want to see people starve. And another thing," I added, "That vial isn't the same one that Quintus has been trotting out every year on Saint Perpetua's day," I said.

"And you are sure of this?"

I drew my knife from my waist bag, and began to sharpen the quill that lay on the table. "Yes, I'm sure. Don't tell me you don't see what's happening here. Marius forgot to bring it, and now he's cooked up a replacement because he thinks it will keep the simple people firm in the Church. He wants to make a name for himself, to guarantee that he will be Quintus's successor as bishop of Thagaste."

"Your own bishop certifies it as the true relic."

I swallowed several possible responses before settling on one. "He's wrong."

Aurelius nodded, staring into space again.

I tried another angle. "You used to heap scorn on signs and miracles. When did you change your mind?"

"That was back when I relied on my own will and discernment."

"But what use are these supposedly miraculous objects? Shouldn't the Word and the example of our Lord be enough to convince us? "

Aurelius bent his head and rubbed at his forehead. "Yes, of course, Leona, certainly they are enough to convince *us*, but we are educated people. How can the ignorant peasant or dock worker possibly be kept in the fold by mere words? I've tried over the years. I've simplified the message, put it into poetry and song and crude little slogans that they'd find easy to remember. And still they will have their signs and miracles and pageants. You know this. You came from the simple class yourself, and you've made them your life's work."

"I took a different approach. I made sure that they were fed, comforted when they were distressed, and cared for when they were sick. Isn't that what Jesus told us to do? Didn't he say that even as we do to the least, we do to him?"

"Of course you did. Of course, and God will bless you for all the souls that you brought to him in your way." He patted my hand.

"Jesus said the first would be last, Aure—Bishop. When we trick them with false relics, I think we are just putting them under a new kind of sandal. Marius and Quintus are interested in power." There, I'd said it.

"You've always misjudged Quintus," he said. "You've never forgiven him for that first night in Carthage. Remember?"

*Of course I remember*, I thought, *and he's seldom given me any reason since then to change my mind about him.* But I could see that this argument was lost, and the name of Carthage brought a tenderness to my heart for our lost son and for the young man Aurelius and the girl that I had been, and so I just said, "I remember."

Aurelius bowed his head and rubbed at his temples again.

"Are you all right?" I asked. He looked pale, and the creases in his face seemed deeper just since this morning.

"Dizzy for a moment," he admitted. "Perhaps we should be done for today."

I poured him a cup of water from an earthen jug on his table. "Drink."

As he took the cup from me, my hand touched his. His big hands were splashed with dark freckles now, swollen and knotted at the joints, and I noticed a tremor as he took the cup. I remembered a time when the touch of his firm young hands sent currents of delight through me.

His eyes softened. "Leave me now. Your intentions are right, and our Lord sees that. You can copy my argument for me tomorrow when I'm feeling better." He made the sign of the cross before me with his free hand, and I left him.

# CHAPTER THIRTY-SIX

SWEAT TRICKLED down my torso beneath the empty bags of my breasts, and I flapped my tunic against my chest with one hand as I wiped sweat from my forehead with the other.

Even in the shade of the portico, I felt like I was standing in an oven. I could only imagine the suffering of the line of destitute people waiting for their daily ration, snaking through the forum and down the hill toward the cathedral: squirming children, sagging mothers, and impatient young men, all gray and stinking now that the baths had been closed for more than a month.

After the first three weeks, we realized that we would quickly run out of grain if we gave bread daily, so we had started dishing out porridge for the daily ration. Two weeks after that, we saw that even the porridge must be thinned if our supplies were to last. The port was still open, but Boniface had no word from Rome or Carthage about possible resupply.

Lucy dipped her ladle into a pot and slopped a ration into a filthy young man's bowl.

"Why so thin?" he asked. "It was nice and thick yesterday. And there was more."

He wasn't the first to ask. "Order of the bishop," Lucy explained for the hundredth time. "We've got to make our grain last until the siege is lifted."

"Or until the Second Coming," he spat back. "That army's not going anywhere unless the Lord himself comes back and sends them. We ought to just give up and save ourselves. A man can't live on this slop."

"You want to give it back?" Lucy said. "Plenty of people behind you will be glad to have your share."

The man spat on the ground and grabbed Lucy's arm. "Listen, Sister, no man can live on this slop. I'm not leaving until I get some of whatever you holy-holy women get to eat."

"You'll be leaving right now." The voice came from behind him, and a pair of hands pulled him away from Lucy and shoved him to the side of the line. His wooden bowl clattered on the stone floor, spilling thin, grayish porridge.

I hadn't seen Eraclius approach. He gave the man another shove. "You'll go hungry today, and come back tomorrow with a better attitude. Go on. Leave these women alone." He stood with his hands on his hips until the man scuttled out of the forum, spitting on the ground several times as he went.

Lucy continued ladling porridge for the next person in line. "Are you all right?" I asked.

She nodded, ladling her next bowlful. "He wasn't the first and he won't be the last. People are hungry. It makes them crazy. He didn't hurt me."

"Thank you," I said to Eraclius. Then I indicated Lucy's cauldron. "We're almost empty here. I was just going into the temple to see where our refill got to."

"We've already run out at the basilica," Eraclius reported. "I'll come with you to check on how your supplies here are holding up. It looks like you didn't plan for enough, and we'll have to start delivering more grain to each station."

In the weeks that we'd worked together, I had come to respect Eraclius's intelligence and hard work, and his defense of Lucy was not the first time that his masculine strength had rescued us, but he still resented my replacing him as Bishop Augustine's favored scribe and never missed an opportunity to point out to me any mistake that I made.

I swallowed a sharp retort. "Can you send someone for more grain?"

"I'll stop at the warehouse on my way back to the bishop's office and let them know to send you more. I need to get back and copy Bishop Quintus's sermon for Sunday."

"Oh, he'll be preaching in place of Bishop Augustine?"

"Bishop Augustine isn't well," Eraclius explained, and I almost smiled at his smug pride at having news about the bishop that he thought I didn't know. In fact, I had been increasingly worried about Aurelius. Every day he seemed to grow thinner, the creases in his face deeper, the shadows around his eyes darker.

"We're preaching on the relic," he went on. "Bishop Quintus will preach at the cathedral, and others of us are to deliver the same sermon at smaller churches throughout the city."

"The relic?"

"The vial of Saint Perpetua's milk," Eraclius replied, avoiding my eyes. "I remember you expressed doubt, but trust me, Bishop Augustine carefully verifies all miraculous claims. He insists on signed statements from witnesses in every case."

"And got them from Bishop Quintus and Brother Marius in this case, of course."

"Of course."

I nodded. As the weeks had passed without any further discussion, I had come to hope that I would never again hear of the false relic. I understood now that the question had only been discussed in my absence. And I had to admit that the city was near despair.

"We have to do something," Eraclius went on, as if reading my thoughts. "Boniface had to arrest a group of apostates just last week. They stole a chicken to sacrifice to Ammon."

I had heard of this, as well as of the baker who had been executed for selling extra loaves of bread to those who could pay a premium. The whispers that we should surrender were growing, and because Boniface and Augustine would never agree to this, violence was always just under the surface in the city.

The midden piles in backyards grew as no one could venture outside the city walls to dispose of garbage at the more distant dumps, and the city began to reek of rotting food scraps and human waste and to buzz with heavy, malevolent flies.

At least the Vandals had run out of body parts to catapult over the city walls. Now they used their war machines to hurl stones over the walls, so that each week several people were crushed from above and the whole city had taken to glancing up at the sky every few minutes.

I sighed. "Eraclius, that vial is not going to solve anything."

He shifted his shoulders and looked away from me. "We need a miracle of some kind."

I looked at the long, ragged line of hungry people waiting for their only meal of the day. My brother and sister had come to this city many years ago. Numa and Tito must both be dead by now, but I often thought I could be unknowingly serving porridge to a child or grandchild of theirs. As long as we could save lives for one more day and then another and another, as long as our food and water lasted, we had hope.

"Maybe we have a miracle already," I said. "The aqueduct hasn't been cut yet, and the water in the cisterns is holding up. If we can hold on for just a few more weeks, we can keep feeding even the poorest long enough to keep them alive until help comes from Carthage or Rome. Already, we've been able to feed more people than I'd have dreamed was possible."

Now Eraclius looked at me and smiled. "Just as our Lord did with the loaves and the fishes."

I laughed. "I hadn't thought of that, but yes. But seriously, Brother, I've never seen that vial of Bishop Quintus's work a single miracle, and I don't ever expect to see one."

"Well, Bishop Augustine accepts it as miraculous and that's good enough for me. We're presenting it Sunday. Pray that you're wrong and it produces a miracle—or at least that it gives people enough hope that they stop fighting in porridge lines and sacrificing chickens."

"I'll pray," I promised, "but I'm not expecting any miracles."

———•••———

Aurelius's door was open, and I found him sitting at the window.

"Hello, Leona. I don't think I feel up to dictating anything today, but you are welcome to sit with me for a while. How many did you feed today?"

"More than three thousand at the forum alone, in addition to whoever Eraclius and his crew fed at Saint Stephen's. Eraclius had to rescue Lucy from a roughneck today."

He shook his head and said almost exactly what Lucy had said. "Hunger and fear make men susceptible to the devil."

"Eraclius is a good man," I said.

"Yes."

"He's hurt that I've supplanted him as your scribe.'"

"Eraclius will be my successor as bishop of Hippo. But nobody can transcribe my words as you can, and I confess that I enjoy your company again after all these years." He rubbed his temples.

"Bishop? Are you all right?" I asked.

He turned to me. "I have pains in my head these days," he admitted.

"Let me rub your neck for you," I offered without thinking, and then felt myself flush, embarrassed at how easy it was to forget the years and fall into old habits.

He gave me a sharp sideways look for a second, but then his eyes went vague and he said, "That might help."

"My hands are as strong as they ever were," I bragged, rising and standing behind his chair. "I've spent many years hard at work and I think I've reached old age stronger than I was as a girl."

Aurelius nodded and submitted to my massage. His neck was red and creased from a lifetime in the African sun, and tufted with white hairs. The skin was loose as I kneaded and squeezed the muscles beneath.

"Remember the baths in Carthage?" I said.

He sighed. "I do. A hot bath would feel good now. But soon we'll be out of wood even for cooking fire. None of us should even think of heating water for bathing."

"I know. I see so much hardship every day. I worry about some of the parents. I see them give their share of the porridge to their children. Yet, if the parents die, who will care for the children who live?"

"God gives us all that we need, if not in this life then in the next."

"That's no answer for children who are starving or parentless here," I argued. It was the same old argument we had always had: the theoretical versus the practical, on opposite sides once again as if the years apart had never happened.

He reached back and patted my kneading hand. "You'd be surprised at how little it takes to sustain life."

My hands stopped moving. It suddenly made sense to me: the weakness and the headaches. "When did you last eat?" I asked him.

"I have what I need," was his reply.

"That isn't what I asked."

"Leona, I ate little to start with, only what I thought I needed to stay alive and save more souls. And I find now that I need even less than I thought. Love of food is yet another sensual pleasure that only distracts from love of the Lord."

"You're making yourself ill, and causing me work."

"You can stop when you like."

He grunted as I pressed hard on a knot of shoulder muscle. "I'm sorry," I said.

He held up a hand. "All right. But, we'll have to be done for now. Boniface will be here shortly to discuss the defense of the city if Genseric decides to attempt an attack over the walls."

"Do you think he'll do it?"

"No. Why should he? He only has to wait us out a few more months to starve us out, unless the Lord grants us a miracle."

"That flask of Quintus's isn't going to bring about any miracles."

"God can do anything, by any means."

I believed with all my heart that that was true, and yet I felt a sense of foreboding about the introduction of the relic.

# CHAPTER THIRTY-SEVEN

ON THE HOTTEST DAY of August, the day before the Saint Perpetua sermon, all the fountains in Hippo ran dry.

Lucy warned me early in the morning, while I was still at prayer. Even this early in the day, the heat in my little cell in the bishop's guest house was heavy as iron, and sweat trickled down my back and felt slick behind my knees and elbows. Lucy stood in the doorway and waited for me to finish my prayers, but I sensed a human presence and my feeling of the Lord's presence deserted me, so I turned, and creaked into a stand.

Lucy wasted no time. "Genseric has cut the aqueduct," she announced, and then rushed into more explanations, wringing her hands. "I sent one of the novices to the fountain to fetch water for our breakfast porridge, and she was gone so long I thought she had lain down somewhere and gone back to sleep. 'The fountain was running slow,' she said, and Leona, my heart about stopped. I knew what it must mean. I hoped it wasn't true, so I ran to see for myself. You know that fountain in the courtyard behind the cathedral gushes like a young man's stream. Oh, Leona, it was a trickle when I saw it."

My own heart sank like lead into my stomach. We had to expect that the Vandals would eventually cut the aqueduct. In the three months since the start of the siege, Boniface had had work teams laboring around the clock to divert water from the baths into cisterns, where it could be stored against the day when the city's supply of water from the distant mountains would be cut off. Now we would have to pray that the stored water would last until the fall rains started in November.

"What will the people do when we run out of water?" Lucy fretted. "How will we keep them alive?"

*What will they do indeed?* I wondered. Every fountain in the city must be as slow as our own, or soon would be, and within hours they would be as dry as a crone's teat. How long would it be before panic and violence took hold?

———••———

Boniface and Augustine had been prepared all along for the disaster of the severed aqueduct, and immediately issued emergency instructions, directing all residents of the city to cistern stations in their own quarter to fetch water, one quart per person per day.

The instructions were posted on notice boards throughout the city for the literate, and would be repeated in the churches on Sunday for the rest.

Boniface's soldiers guarded every cistern station and no exceptions were made for those too young or too ill to stand in line for their quart. Each person had a small cut placed on the back of their left hand as they were issued their precious quart, to prevent anyone from getting into line a second time in the same day.

"What about the ill?" Lucy worried, when I explained the system to her. "They need the water more than any. Isn't there some way they could get a ration?"

"Their family members will have to share with them," I said, and it hurt me too, to think of the awful choices that people would be forced to make, between saving themselves and trying to save a loved one who was ill and might die anyway. "Both the bishop and the general are adamant that the system must seem fair. There can be no room left for anyone to cheat, or they fear violence."

The forum had its own cistern, and so Lucy and I and our helpers were outside serving porridge just as usual after Mass on the Sunday of the Saint Perpetua sermon.

My dauntless Lucy stood at a cauldron, stirring with a wooden paddle, while a younger sister dipped and redipped the ladle, serving one after another of the gaunt, stinking citizens of Hippo. Lucy used her shoulder to nudge a drop of sweat off the tip of her nose, never pausing in her stirring, and I felt a renewed surge of love for this plain and courageous old daughter of my first friend.

I moved among the various cauldrons, directing more water or more grain or more salt to one or another as they began to empty. The sun was so bright that my eyes stung, and I had to squint to recognize Eraclius as he approached me.

"A private word with you, please, Sister," he said.

I glanced around the courtyard, and then nodded and followed him.

We sat under a tree in a corner of the courtyard, the shade a welcome relief to my eyes.

"How did you think the sermon went today?" Eraclius asked.

"Well, I suppose. Why do you ask me? You know I'm opposed to this whole notion of presenting this relic and placing so much hope in it."

"That's why I ask you."

I frowned and cocked my head, not understanding him.

"I overheard something on the way back from the cathedral that worried me." He hesitated and then went on. "I passed a knot of people listening to a man who looked agitated. When he noticed my approach, he suddenly stopped speaking, but I know I heard him say, 'I've seen it every year, and that's not even the same flask.' That was what you said about the milk when Marius produced it."

"I told the truth."

"I believe you," Eraclius said. "And now I'm sorry that I didn't argue in defense of your position." He compressed his lips, looking away from me for a moment, and then said, "The man I overhead must have been one of the peasants that came with Bishop Quintus from Thagaste. And there are others who have seen this relic every year. If many people listen to them, then the authenticity of the milk will come under question."

"Yes, it will," I agreed.

He chewed his lip. "We should pray that they don't talk to very many, or that nobody believes them. Even if the man speaks the truth . . . you must see how dangerous it would be if people believe him. We've already preached the sermon and promised a viewing of the relic in the forum this evening. Thousands of people will be here, maybe the whole city. Genseric has spies all over the city, spreading the lie that mercy will be shown if only the city will surrender, and people are already tense over the water situation. This couldn't have happened at a worse time."

I said nothing.

Eraclius slumped and ran his hand through his hair. "When Bishop Augustine accepted the relic, I believed with all my heart that it must truly be the milk of Saint Perpetua. You have to understand how strict he has been in the past over these claims. Always he demanded proof, and what more proof could you have than the word of two men of God, one of them a bishop and one of his oldest friends?"

"And now you have to share this with him."

Eraclius's squared his shoulders and took a deep breath. "I know. I wanted to talk to you first, and be sure of the truth I was beginning to suspect. I don't know what we can do, though, expect go through with the viewing and pray for the best."

"I think prayer is our only hope right now," I agreed.

———•••———

The presentation of the relic was scheduled for Sunday evening, and Bishop Augustine's inner circle met in his office on Sunday afternoon to decide what was to be done in light of Eraclius's news.

"One rumor being spread by one person—probably one of Genseric's spies," Marius scoffed. "With all due respect, Eraclius, you've blown this out of proportion."

"Except for the fact that the man he overheard was telling the truth," I argued.

Marius ignored me. "One man spreading rumors, out of a population of many thousands. It's ridiculous to think that there's any significance to it."

General Boniface, restless as always, prowled the perimeter of the room. He looked even more exhausted than when I had first seen him, after his defeated army streamed through the gates of Hippo. His face was grayish and deeply creased, and dark circles ringed his eyes. He rubbed at his face wearily as he spoke. "This city is like dry tinder in the fall, just waiting for a spark like this. It's true that Genseric has spies everywhere. The second they get wind of this they'll all be spreading it, and we could have full rebellion on our hands."

"But we've already said that the relic will be presented this evening! We can't change our minds now!" Marius insisted.

"The fact is most of these people want to give up," Eraclius said.

"Then it's up to us to save their souls for them," Bishop Augustine said. "They must not surrender to the heretics."

Boniface flushed and looked away for a minute. I knew that his wife and children, safe in Carthage, were baptized Arians, and therefore heretics themselves. He composed himself and looked at Augustine again. "You and I both know that, heresy aside, we'll all be put to the sword the minute the Vandals pass through the gates. Surrender is not an option. But, if we attempt to pass this thing off as miraculous and it comes under question, our authority is undermined."

"You're afraid of a few whispers?" Marius scoffed.

Boniface slammed his fist on the table. "I'm afraid of anarchy! I don't know how much longer my soldiers can keep this city from wholesale rebellion!"

"Then what's your better idea?" Marius shouted.

Boniface turned red and paced back to his usual place at the window without answering.

Nobody else had an answer. Quintus opened his mouth and lifted his trembling hand as if he wanted to say something, but then looked away.

"It may be," Augustine conceded, "that I was hasty in my approval and that we have made a mistake. But we have to think now of the spirit of the city. They've already taken a blow with the severing of the aqueduct. If we now withdraw this hope from them, they may grow violent or surrender to heresy. Our hearts are pure in this, and I am convinced that if what we present is not entirely truthful, God will forgive us."

"Some already know that this is no more the milk of Saint Perpetua than it is my own." I lifted a hand to my own shriveled breasts.

"We must pray that hope triumphs over rumor," he replied. "And I must ask you to be of help to us in that."

"I don't want any part of this," I said.

He continued as if I hadn't spoken. "I ask that you stand with Marius and Bishop Quintus when the relic is presented. You are known and loved by many of the poor of this city already, and you are known as a long-time resident of Thagaste who would have seen the relic many times over the years. If you lend your support, more people may be persuaded."

"But I know it's a lie!" I looked to Boniface for support, but he was gazing out the window with his back to us. I turned then to Eraclius, whom I had begun to count as a friend.

"The bishop is right," Eraclius pleaded. "Your presence may be persuasive to some. It could make the difference, and it seems we have no better choice. You don't need to speak. Just join us, this is all we ask."

I thought of the terrified eyes that I had seen that morning in the cathedral courtyard, and knew that Hippo was on the precipice of despair and anarchy.

I had no illusion at all that God would work a miracle through Marius's worthless vial, but held to the hope that perhaps he would still work a miracle through our own efforts, and I saw an opportunity to win something that I wanted personally as well, and so I said, "You can have my support under one condition. I want a receipt for the grain that I delivered as my tithe to Bishop Quintus."

"General Boniface seized that grain," Marius snapped.

I fixed my gaze on Bishop Augustine, who had promised to persuade Quintus and Marius.

"The Church and the military governor jointly made the decision to take charge of all the grain in the city," Augustine said. "Sister Leona delivered the tithe to you as promised, and then you and your bishop generously handed it over to us to be used to feed the city. We thank you for that. Are we agreed, my old friend?" He ignored Marius and looked at Quintus instead.

Quintus blinked and looked from Augustine to Marius and then closed his eyes and folded his hands for a moment. When he raised his head, he said, "Yes, it's as my old friend the bishop says. We must be concerned for the welfare of the souls under our care, and not distract ourselves with these worldly matters."

Marius flushed.

"I want a written receipt," I said.

"Fine," Marius spat.

"Then I agree."

———••———

Heat still covered Hippo like a heavy cloak that evening, when the city began to gather in the forum for the viewing of Saint Perpetua's milk.

The old temple to Mithra had a second-story portico, and Quintus and Augustine had decided that this was the best place to present the relic, so that everyone gathered in the forum would get a glimpse of it. Quintus would present it, Marius would speak, and the prominent clergy of Hippo would stand behind them in the portico. Boniface had provided a small contingent of legionnaires in the forum to keep order.

I sat sweating in the portico with Marius's receipt in my waist bag and Lucy at my side, waiting for Quintus to stand and present the vial. I felt light-headed from thirst and sticky with sweat under my wool tunic. The forum stood on the highest hill in Hippo and caught a breeze from the sea, but even the sea breeze was hot and sticky with salt on this sultry evening.

Marius stood and spoke first. "Christians of Hippo," he shouted. "The Lord sees how you have been steadfast against the barbarian heretics, and has thus far preserved you from their fire and sword. There are those in the city who would persuade you that the barbarian Genseric will show mercy to the city if only we will surrender." He paused, so that his words could be repeated in the forum for those standing too far back to hear him. The space was packed, and the earthy stench of several thousand unwashed bodies clogged my nostrils.

"Don't believe them," he went on. "Those words are spoken by spies sent to the city by Genseric before the start of the siege. Look around you, and see how many refugees arrived in the weeks before the siege. Any of them could be spies and heretics, sent to spread lies."

Alarm stabbed at my gut. I knew, of course, why Marius wanted to place suspicion on refugees to the city, but I wondered what unintended violence he might encourage with his words.

"This is Genseric's mercy." Marius brought forward a man I hadn't seen before, a hideous sight with knots of scar tissue where his ears had been and sunken red holes in place of his eyes. I could see from the drool on his chin that his tongue had also been cut out. The people nearest the front of church gasped, and a murmur began to spread from the front of the crowd to the back.

"This is what Genseric does to any who try to surrender—if he lets them live," Marius shouted. "Don't listen to the lies of Genseric's spies— and remember, anyone you don't know could be a spy sent by the heretics. Surrender won't save us, brothers and sisters. Only a miracle can save us." He paused. "In church today you were promised the sight of a relic of a miracle: the milk of the martyred mother, Saint Perpetua."

Eraclius helped Quintus to stand. I saw him grasp Quintus's elbow when my old adversary momentarily lost his balance and seemed ready to topple backward. Once he was steady, Quintus slowly lifted the vial over his head. The old bishop's face looked ecstatic and lit from within, and I realized that, against the evidence of his own eyes, he truly believed that he held the vial of the saint's milk.

"In this vial," Marius proclaimed, "drops of the saint's milk have been miraculously preserved for almost two hundred years, drops of a liquid even more precious than water. If God could lend Perpetua the strength to be martyred for her faith, if God could then preserve her milk for two centuries, how much more can he do for us in our time of dire need? We need only demonstrate our faith, brothers and sisters!"

Marius paused again, to let his words filter through to the crowd in the back, then resumed his oration. "Let us all kneel and pray that we will be as faithful and courageous as the martyred Saint Perpetua!"

The crowd stirred and began to kneel, but something flew through my line of sight, and suddenly Quintus fell to the ground. Another missile landed at my feet. We were being pelted with rocks. Lucy wrapped herself around me and pushed me to the floor.

I could hear sharp voices among the panicked murmuring of the crowd in the forum. "Lies!" "The relic is a fake!" "Surrender before we die of thirst!"

"Brothers! Sisters!" Marius cried. "These are the spies that I warned you about! Don't listen!"

The noise from the forum below us grew into a confused roar. Marius dodged a rock and then ducked to the floor.

As if it were happening in a dream, I saw Bishop Augustine rise to his feet, first supporting himself by leaning on the arms on his chair, and then raising his bishop's staff over his head.

"Get him down!" I called to Eraclius.

"Bishop, please," Eraclius urged, "get down before you're hurt." Rocks were still flying toward us, most of them missing the portico altogether, others whizzing past our ears.

Augustine turned on Eraclius a gaze so fierce that I admit it would have daunted me also, and Eraclius backed away, glancing helplessly at me. A well-aimed stone grazed Eraclius's temple, and he staggered and raised a hand to the side of his head. I tried to rise to go to him, but Lucy held me down in a crouch.

Augustine stood silently for a full minute, staff raised. The minute seemed long, and the rain of rocks abated. Finally, he roared, "Be at peace and go home! Trust in God to care for the city of Hippo in accordance with his will!"

The rain of rocks had ceased, but I could still hear the crowd buzzing and barking. I wrenched free of Lucy and rose to see one of Boniface's legionnaires knocked down and trampled by a small mob.

Another mob of roughnecks in the middle of the crowd raised their fists and began a chant of "Surrender! Surrender! Surrender!" The chant fanned through the crowd, and now the rough men who had started it spread out and attacked the rest of the legionnaires.

Horrified, I saw Augustine head down the narrow stairway that led to the street level of the forum. I started after him, but found myself held fast again by Lucy. "You just stay here!" she hissed, wrapping me in her work-hardened arms.

"Stop him!" I screamed at Eraclius.

Augustine was already halfway down the stairs. Bent double with his hand to his bleeding head, Eraclius followed him.

The legionnaires were fighting back against the mob, and one sliced a woman's head from her body as he frantically swiped with his sword while stepping backward to escape. He lost his footing, and the mob attacked, one man stabbing him over and over with his own sword.

Although he himself had predicted the violence, Boniface had failed to provide enough legionnaires to control the crowd. The small, well-disciplined contingent began to coalesce into three knots, one on each open side of the forum. Flailing their short swords, they slowly backed toward the forum exits. From my vantage point, it was clear that they were retreating to save their own lives, and had no intention of attempting to put a stop to the violence that was boiling in the crowd.

At the back of the forum, the more timid citizens escaped toward their homes, some at a run, but the crowd in the front heaved like a stormy ocean, between the bullies spoiling for a fight and other frantic people trying to follow the sensible souls to safety.

Augustine reached the level of the forum and slid into the crowd like a knife. Every second I was sure that he would be knocked to the ground and trampled to death, but with every second that passed, he penetrated deeper into the mob, staff raised, Eraclius at his side.

The cocooning heat, the incoherent roar of the mob, and the sheer improbability of what I was seeing made the scene seem like a dream. Across the open space of the forum, I could see that one small crowd had already broken into the shops at the back of the complex, and were running off with what little loot was left in the besieged city: an alabaster jar of scent, a few pairs of sandals, a tin pot. Some of the young roughnecks had lit torches and were already marching down the hill chanting, "Surrender! Surrender!" gathering more marchers as they went.

But as Augustine moved through the crowd, he left a wake of stillness behind him. One ancient arm held up the staff, and with the other he made the sign of the cross on one forehead after another, and as he did this, the crowd behind him began to melt away, first leaking and then flooding, out the side exits of the forum. I thought this must be what it must have looked like when Moses parted the seas. Lucy and I watched in stillness and silence.

I'd forgotten about Marius until he yanked open the door behind us and cried, "Someone help me get the bishop inside!"

As if waking from a dream, I looked down at Quintus, unconscious and bleeding on the floor of the portico. Marius had forgotten the hideously blinded man that he'd shown to the crowd. The man had squeezed himself into a corner and crouched with his hands over his head. I took him by the elbow and guided him into the church. Lucy bent to help Marius drag Quintus.

Quintus had shrunken to almost nothing in his old age, but, unconscious, he was a dead weight, and Marius was also a small man. Lucy lifted the old bishop's shoulders and Marius took his feet and they staggered into the stuffy darkness of the old temple. I slammed the door behind us and we stood for a few seconds, dazed and panting. Just as my eyes adjusted to the darkness and I was able to make out her face, I saw Lucy's eyes widen. She grimaced, clutched at her chest, and collapsed into a heap at my feet.

# CHAPTER THIRTY-EIGHT

MY BELOVED FRIEND and my oldest enemy died within a few hours of each other, as we waited out the night inside the temple of Mithra, until we felt assured that it would be safe to travel through the city. Augustine's walk had calmed the crowd in the forum, but none of us knew what might be happening elsewhere in the city and Eraclius thought it wise to wait until morning to venture out.

Lucy died instantly, her heart stopped, I supposed, by the effort of dragging Quintus into the church. Quintus himself faded slowly as the night passed.

The stone that felled him had been well-aimed, hitting him in the center of his forehead. Even in the dim light of the church, the bloody depression was clearly visible.

Augustine spent the night prostrate before the altar, and none of us dared disturb him. Eraclius kept glancing over at his bishop, and finally whispered to me once, "He should rest. This surely can't be good for him."

I agreed, but I also knew the bishop's personality from his youth. He was stubborn and extreme and passionately loyal to his friends. If he thought that prostrating his ancient body in prayer through a long night was going to save the life of his oldest friend, nothing would persuade him to do other than exactly that.

"Leave him alone," I advised.

The blood from Eraclius's wound had flattened the black curls on that side of his head to a tangled mat.

"You should clean your head," I said.

He lifted a hand to the side of his head and patted at it, as if he hadn't even realized he'd been hurt. He winced. "It would be a sin to waste the water," he replied. He looked at me. "I'm so very sorry about Lucy. I know how dear she was to you, and I had come to admire her in our short acquaintance."

"Thank you," I replied. I was too weary to say more. I hurt all over from the exertions of the weeks of siege and the night spent trying to sleep in the church. The physical pain was welcome, in a way, because it kept my mind from the sorrow of losing Lucy.

"May I ask you something?" Eraclius said.

I nodded but felt wary, wondering what he would ask.

"Is it true that you were once the wife of Bishop Augustine?"

"No, I wasn't his wife. We lived together in a state of sin for many years." I paused, searching my heart to know if I wanted to say more, and finding the answer. "We had a child together who died as a young man."

Eraclius nodded, holding my eyes. "Pardon me for asking, but there have been whispers of it among all the clergy since soon after you arrived. You know that he wrote in his *Confessiones* about a woman and a son who died, and it became rumored that you were the woman. I'm very sorry about your child."

"I still think of him every day. You resemble him. This may be one reason why your bishop loves you so."

"I love him."

I smiled and nodded. "I see that you do."

"I was jealous of you when you came. He seemed to reject me in favor of you."

"He doesn't love you any less. He was used to me from when we were young. The habits that we form in our youth are the ones that stay with us, and I think I've been a comfort to him in this crisis."

"I'm glad now that you came. I'm glad to know you."

"And I you. When things are darkest, God always sends us the comfort of each other if we can only see it. When I lost my son, Lucy and my old friend Miriam were restored to me. Now, I have lost Lucy and gained you as a friend."

A few candles that Eraclius and Marius had found flickered in the musty darkness of the temple.

Eraclius was quiet for a moment. "In a way, we got our miracle."

"I guess we did."

"It was amazing how he silenced the mob and how they parted before him." Eraclius smiled slightly and gazed into the distance, as if he were seeing a vision.

I thought of how the young Aurelius had longed to be a leader of men, and how he had struggled even to control a small classroom of unruly boys. "The power was God's, not his," I said.

By the time the morning's blinding sun scorched through the narrow windows of the church and Boniface sent soldiers to escort us back to the bishop's quarters, Quintus had taken his last breath.

# CHAPTER THIRTY-NINE

AUGUSTINE TOOK to his bed when we got back to the basilica complex, and Eraclius came to me the next morning to report to me that he was no better. "He can't move one side of his body and he has difficulty speaking," he fretted. "The physician thinks it's a brain fever of some kind. Can you come? He might respond to you."

I knelt by his bed and spoke close to his ear. "Aurelius, can you hear me?"

He turned his face to me and fixed his eyes on mine. I saw in them fear and helplessness, as if he would speak but had forgotten all the words he ever knew. He nodded slowly.

"Can you speak?" I asked.

"Psalm Fifty-One," he whispered.

Eraclius and I frowned at each other in puzzlement. "Can anything be done for him?" I asked.

"The physician says he knows of nothing," Eraclius said. "He doesn't seem to be in pain."

"He hasn't been eating," I reported. "Did you know that? He should eat."

Eraclius shook his head, and covered his face with his hands.

"I'll get him to eat," I announced.

Aurelius shook his head. "Psalm Fifty-One," he rasped. "On the wall." He lifted one trembling finger and pointed to the wall in front of him.

Eraclius raised his face. "I think I understand," he said.

———••———

I copied the psalm as Aurelius had requested and Eraclius had a boy nail it to the wall in the Bishop's line of sight.

"Read it to me," he whispered.

"If I read to you, will you eat?" I had brought with me a bowl of thin porridge. He turned his fading brown eyes to me and nodded. "Read."

I read it to him. The psalm is King David's tortured self-confession after Nathan confronts him with his sinfulness with Bathsheba.

*Have mercy on me, O God,*
*according to your steadfast love;*
*according to your abundant mercy*
*blot out my transgressions.*
*Wash me thoroughly from my iniquity,*
*and cleanse me from my sin.*

*For I know my transgressions,*
*and my sin is ever before me.*
*Against you, you alone, have I sinned,*
*and done what is evil in your sight.*
*So that you are justified in your sentence*
*and blameless when you pass judgment.*
*Indeed, I was born guilty,*
*a sinner when my mother conceived me.*

*You desire truth in the inward being;*
        *therefore teach me wisdom in my secret heart.*
*Purge me with hyssop, and I shall be clean;*
        *wash me, and I shall be whiter than snow.*
*Let me hear joy and gladness;*
        *let the bones that you have crushed rejoice.*
*Hide your face from my sins,*
        *and blot out my iniquities.*
*Create in me a clean heart, O God,*
        *and put a new and right spirit within me.*
*Do not cast me away from your presence,*
        *and do not take your holy spirit from me.*
*Restore to me the joy of your salvation,*
        *and sustain in me a willing spirit.*

*Then will I teach transgressors your ways,*
        *and sinners will return to you.*
*Deliver me from bloodshed, O God,*
        *O God of my salvation,*
        *and my tongue will sing aloud of your deliverance.*

*O Lord, open my lips,*
        *and my mouth will declare your praise.*
*For you have no delight in sacrifice;*
        *if I were to give a burnt offering, you would not be pleased.*
*The sacrifice acceptable to God is a broken spirit;*
        *a broken and contrite heart, O God, you will not despise.*

I managed then to slip a few spoonfuls of porridge between his white, cracked lips.

I sat with him through the rest of the morning, reading to him from the Bible when he seemed to wake. Dust motes spun suspended in the yellow light that streamed in the window like a river of honey. One could almost think the world was still in order.

After checking on his sleeping form, I took myself to the kitchen, determined to search out some morsel of food that I could offer to him besides porridge. I rummaged on the shelves of the larder, tipping wooden boxes to search them for any contents, standing tiptoe on empty boxes to examine the higher shelves, and came up with nothing but mouse droppings and dust. I sighed and looked around the room, and noticed a short door. Opening it, I saw that it led to a cellar, so I lit a candle and descended the steep stone stairs.

The dirt walls and floor were cool and dry, but the cellar had a musty odor of past dampness. Scattered about were more wooden boxes and these I searched methodically.

At last I found a box that I could feel contained a few rounded shapes, and I drew one out and saw that it was a pear: small and mottled with brown, but nevertheless an overlooked piece of fruit in this starving town.

Reaching back into the box, I found two more. One was so brown and rotted that it turned to pulp in my hand, but the other was no worse than the first. Two pears in a whole city of hungry people. I set my candle on the cellar floor and sat on the bottom step for a moment, my bones creaking against each other painfully.

A small corner of my conscience admonished me that some mother of small children should receive this little bounty, but how would we ever choose among the starving throngs that filled the forum and the church courtyard every day?

The two small pears were cool in my hands. I placed them in my pocket, picked up my candle, and ascended the stone stairs.

———••———

Aurelius's eyes were closed when I entered his room, his chin slack and receding. I could hear his shallow breath passing between his cracked lips.

I set down the plate of diced pear that I had brought with me, and dipped a clean napkin in precious water and brought it to his lips, squeezing gently to drip the water into his mouth. His lips were so dry that when he brought them together they stuck and he was too weak to open his mouth again, so I gently rubbed his lips with the damp napkin and then repeated the process.

His eyes fluttered open and he turned them to me gratefully. The irises were a pale, milky brown and the whites were yellow and delicately veined with red. How pale his skin was, I thought, so that every brown spot and web of broken veins stood out against the chalky flesh.

"I brought you some fruit," I whispered.

The fresh, pale morning sunlight shone on the pieces of pear, so that their white flesh glistened and each little grain in the softer flesh shone like a tiny teardrop. I picked up a piece between my fingers and a thin, cool trail of juice ran down my hand.

Outside, the thin song of a single sparrow broke the silence.

"Try this," I said, and moved the bit of pear toward his lips.

His lips clamped shut.

"Aurelius, open your mouth," I said. "Taste this. I brought you some pear."

His fading eyes went fierce and pierced mine, then moved toward the window.

"What?" I insisted. "You need to eat. Please open your mouth."

Once again, he turned his eyes toward the window and this time I thought I saw a small gesture of his head in the same direction.

"Oh, Aurelius," I argued. "Who would I give it to? How can one piece of fruit save all those multitudes? When it might save your life. Please."

His lips remained closed and his eyes met mine again, in an unspoken command.

I lowered my hand and felt my shoulders sag.

———•••———

I sat in his chamber through the long afternoon that followed, while the square of yellow sunlight crept across the floor and grew longer again, and the softening bits of pear released their sweetness and drew hovering bees.

Aurelius's eyes flickered open more seldom as the sun advanced across the stone floor. His breathing slowed, and I began to periodically lean my face toward his to make sure he was still breathing at all. Late in the afternoon, Eraclius and the physician, Timothy, joined me in my vigil. Timothy knelt beside the bed and measured his pulse with his fingertips.

"He's fading," the physician told us. "He won't last the night."

Eraclius put his face in his hands and I saw his shoulders trembling.

"Send for me if his condition changes or when . . ." Timothy didn't need to finish his sentence. I nodded, and, with a pitying look at Eraclius, the physician left the room.

I put my arms around Eraclius and eased him into a chair. He raised his wet face to me, eyes hollow with grief. "If only we hadn't attempted to show the relic. It was the strain of that evening and the grief of losing Bishop Quintus that's killing him."

"He's more than seventy years old," I reminded Eraclius. "He's a very old man and would die soon regardless."

Eraclius's tears stopped, but his shoulders sagged, and he turned his sorrowing eyes to his bishop. "He's a great man. He'll be sainted. We all thought so when he stamped out the Manichean and Donatist heresies and after last night . . . that really was a miracle." He turned to me. "What was he like as a young man? Did you know that he would be great?" His voice held a hushed reverence, as if he expected that the bishop had emerged great from the womb.

I thought for a moment before I answered. "What do you think he would say he was like when he was young?"

"Oh, he always claims to be all too human and to have been a terrible sinner, but that's part of his greatness, isn't it? His lack of pride."

"He was truthful if he said that," I said. "He was very human and a sinner, though I think not a terrible one."

Eraclius shook his head. "I find that hard to believe."

"It disappoints you."

"Well—yes."

I put my hand on his shoulder. "It shouldn't. It should give you hope. It shows that God can make glorious use of any of us in building his kingdom, even if we are flawed material."

"Well, maybe you're right," Eraclius said, and I saw that he had no intention of giving up his notion of Aurelius as a saint, and who was I to deny a saint to a darkening world so deeply in need of one?

We sat together in silent prayer into the evening, until pink sunset blazed into the room, the birds' lullabies built to a crescendo, and Aurelius gasped a tortured inhale. Eraclius and I leapt to our feet and bent over him, to hear his last breath leave him in a weak shudder. Eraclius lifted his Aurelius's gaunt, ashen arm to feel for a pulse, looking at me and finally shaking his head and dropping the bishop's arm. "He's gone," he whispered.

Eraclius made the sign of the cross over Aurelius's body. Outside, the humid curtain of darkness fell on starving Hippo, and Genseric's army sharpened their swords and raised their siege towers.

ISTORICAL NOTES

AURELIUS AUGUSTINUS, known to history as Saint Augustine, was born on November 13, 354 CE, in Thagaste, a small city in the Roman province of Numidia, about 60 miles south of Hippo Regius. His mother, Monnica, was a devout Christian and is herself sainted for having "prayed him into the church." His father, Paticius, was a magistrate and tax collector of the Roman Empire, and a pagan until shortly before his death. Patricius and Monnica had two other children, Navigus and Perpetua (not the Perpetua whose relic plays a role in this story).

As the novel portrays, young Aurelius was educated in Thagaste, Madaura and Carthage. He taught in Thagaste and Carthage before taking teaching positions at universities in Rome and then Milan. In his youth, he was a follower of the Manichean sect. Not until the year 386, when he was 32 years old, did he accept Christianity. He lived a monastic life for a short time and then returned to North Africa, where he served for many years as bishop of Hippo Regius. He died in 430, during the Vandal siege of Hippo.

He mentions his mistress of many years only very briefly in his *Confessions*. He never names her, but he laments that he led her into sin and mourns the death of their child.

The Roman Empire in Augustine's time was a cosmopolitan place. The population of the city of Rome alone was over one million in the second century, and the total population of the empire may have been as many as 70 million. People moved freely from one city to another, and in a large city like Rome or Carthage, Aurelius and Leona would have come across people from all over the empire.

But the empire was crumbling around the edges by the fourth century. In the fifth century, under pressure from almost every direction, the Romans progressively withdrew from the outer regions of their empire. Rome was sacked by the Visigoths in 410 and the Vandals in 455. By 476, the last Roman emperor vacated his throne, and the Dark Ages descended on Europe.

# FOR FURTHER DISCUSSION

1. How does Leona change as she matures and ages? In what ways does she stay the same?

2. How does Aurelius change as he matures and ages? In what ways does he stay the same?

3. Do you think people fundamentally stay the same as they grow older, or do most of us change a lot as we age?

4. How do the class differences between Leona and Augustine impact their relationship and their later lives?

5. What are Leona's greatest strengths? What are her weaknesses?

6. Aurelius is torn between different people's expectations of him. How does he resolve these conflicts?

7. Do you think Aurelius treated Leona well? Why or why not?

8. Urbanus was Aurelius's patron and had a lot of power over his life. How did his influence aid or hinder Aurelius and Leona?

9. What is the significance of the name that Leona gives to her son versus the name that Monnica requested that she give him?

10. Pears appear in both the first and the last chapters of the book. What do you think the pears symbolize?

11. In what ways was life in the late period of the Roman Empire similar to our modern lives? In what ways was it different? Were you surprised by any similarities?

12. In what ways is the accident at the circus a turning point in the story?

13. The Saint's Mistress takes place shortly after Emperor Constantine made Christianity the official religion of the Roman Empire. Most of the characters in the book were not Christians at the start of the story. What were their different reasons for converting to Christianity? How were they changed by their faith?

14. Saint Augustine's mother, Monnica, was also sainted, because her devotion "prayed her son into the church." Do you think that was justified? What were Monnica's strengths and weaknesses? Did you sympathize with her?

15. How do Leona's feelings toward Monnica change over the course of the story? How do Monnica's feelings towards Leona change?

16. What drives Leona to the convent? Do you think she made the right decision?

17. How does the reappearance of Miriam and Lucy help Leona deal with her grief over Adeo's death?

18. In his *Confessions*, Augustine mentions his long-time mistress only briefly, and never names her. Why do you think he did that?

19. Did you identify with any of the characters? Which one, and why?

20. Is the Roman Empire itself a character in this novel? How?

# ABOUT THE AUTHOR

AS A SMALL CHILD, Kathryn Bashaar earned the nickname Suitcase Simpson, for the little suitcase of books that she carried with her everywhere. She developed her own writing by keeping a journal starting at age 11. All 53 years of those journals still live in a closet in her home.

The idea for *The Saint's Mistress* came to her while browsing in a library. She picked up a short biography of Saint Augustine and was surprised to learn that he had a mistress and a child. She developed an obsession with finding out more about the mistress, but found that history has been mostly silent about her. Even Leona's real name has been lost. *The Saint's Mistress* is Kathryn's attempt to bring Leona back into the narrative, based on the known facts of Augustine's life and early Christianity. Kathryn and her husband traveled to Rome and Milan to complete research for the book.

Kathryn blogs about Pittsburgh history at www.kathrynbashaar.com. She lives in the South Hills of Pittsburgh with her husband Allen and a very cranky cat, within just a few miles of her mother, children, grandson, brother, sister and nephews. Kathryn and Allen have travelled extensively in Europe and North America, but are always glad to come home to their beloved hometown.

Kathryn's fiction and non-fiction have been published in *The Pittsburgh Post-Gazette, Civil War Times,* and the literary journals *Metamorphosis* and *PIF.* Her short story, "Infamy," won an Honorable Mention in *Glimmer Train's* 2014 short-short fiction contest.